# QUICK SILVER

# DEAN KOONTZ

# QUICKSILVER

**THOMAS & MERCER**

Published by Thomas & Mercer, Seattle

www.apub.com

Amazon, the Amazon logo, and Thomas & Mercer are trademarks of Amazon.com, Inc., or its affiliates.

ISBN-13: 9781542019880 (hardcover)
ISBN-10: 1542019885 (hardcover)

ISBN-13: 9781542019903 (paperback)
ISBN-10: 1542019907 (paperback)

Cover design by Damon Freeman

Interior illustrations by Edward Bettison

Printed in the United States of America

First edition

*This book is dedicated to the memory of four writers who pumped up my imagination in wildly different ways during the years I suffered through grades seven through twelve:*

*Ray Bradbury*
*Robert Heinlein*
*Theodore Sturgeon*
*Jack Douglas*

*Draw your chair up close
to the edge of the precipice,
and I'll tell you a story.*

—*F. Scott Fitzgerald*

**PART 1**
**GETTING TO KNOW ME**

## 1

My name is Quinn Quicksilver—or "Cue-Cue" to the mean kids when I was growing up—but I can't blame my parents because I don't know who they are. Soon after birth, I was abandoned on a lonely highway, seven miles outside of Peptoe, Arizona, where 906 people pretended that the place where they lived was actually a town. Swaddled in a blue blanket, nestled in a white bassinet made of plastic thatching, I had been placed on the centermost of three lanes of blacktop, where I was found shortly after dawn.

Although you might think that this was about as bad a start in life as one could have, I assure you it could have been worse. For one thing, this was coyote country. Had one of those creatures found me, it wouldn't have suckled me as did the wolf that saved abandoned Romulus, the founder of Rome, but instead would have regarded me as a Grubhub delivery. I could also have been run over by an eighteen-wheeler and turned into pâté for vultures.

Fortunately, I was found by three men on their way to work. The first, Hakeem Kaspar, was a lineman for the county, as in that Glen Campbell song I've always found lovely but weird, though at the time I was discovered on the highway, I hadn't yet heard it. The second, Bailie Belshazzer, worked as head mechanic at one of the country's first wind farms. The third, Caesar Melchizadek, was a blackjack pit boss in an Indian casino.

According to a newspaper story at the time, Hakeem tucked me snugly in the passenger-side footwell of his electric-company truck and drove me to the county sheriff's office, with Bailie and Caesar following in their vehicles. Why they felt it necessary that all three should turn me in to the law, the newspaper didn't say. This was all I knew of those men until, years later and running for my life, I visited one of them with the hope of learning some small detail that might be a clue as to who and what I am.

With a safety pin, a small envelope was fixed to the blanket in which I was wrapped. Neither Hakeem nor Bailie nor Caesar had dared to open it, evidently because they had watched too many years of *CSI* shows and feared that they would smear the kidnapper's fingerprints. Either they thought I had been snatched by some fiend who lost his nerve and left me to the mercy of fate on that hot morning, or they figured someone had nabbed my parents and were demanding a ransom from me. When the sheriff tore open the envelope, he found only a card on which was printed QUINN QUICKSILVER and my date of birth.

In those days, no one in the state of Arizona had the surname Quicksilver. Nevertheless, everyone at once assumed that was my name. I have been saddled with it ever since. Of course, *quicksilver* is another name for the liquid metal mercury, which was named after the Roman god Mercury. He was the messenger of other gods, valued for his tremendous speed; the guy could accelerate like crazy. And though Quinn is a variant of Quentin, it also derives from the Latin *quintus*, which means "fifth" or in certain contexts "five times." So perhaps it wasn't my name, but a cryptic message meaning "accelerate five times," though you will not find this advice in any book about caring for a newborn any more than you will find the instruction "marinate in olive oil with basil leaves."

I then became a ward of the county, the youngest ever dropped on that childcare agency. No foster family was willing to take in a three-day-old whose only possession was a soiled swaddling blanket and who had, in the words of Sheriff Garvey Monkton, "strange blue eyes and an eerily direct stare for such a tiny little cocker." Consequently, I was sent out of county to Mater Misericordiæ, an orphanage run by Catholic nuns in Phoenix.

By the time I was six, it became clear that I was not adoptable. Among adoptees, infants are the most desirable age-group, and they are usually placed in stable homes faster than you can say *coochy coochy coo*. This is because babies are generally cuter than older kids, with the possible exception of Rosemary's famous baby, but also because not enough time has passed for them to be screwed up by their birth parents; each grinning infant is a personality waiting to happen and therefore amenable to being sculpted into a reflection of those who adopt him. Although I was cute enough and willing to be shaped like clay, there were no takers for Quinn Quicksilver.

My failure to find a forever home was not for a lack of trying on the part of the good sisters of Mater Misericordiæ. They are as indefatigable and cunning as any order of nuns on the planet. They designed a marketing plan for me, prepared a fabulous PowerPoint presentation, and sold me to prospective parents as aggressively as Disney sells animated films about princesses or adorable animals, all to no avail. Years after the fact, I learned what explanation some would-be adopters had given for taking a pass on me; but perhaps I'll share their comments later.

The orphanage was also a school, because kids six and up often had to live there until they were eighteen. The sisters who served as teachers were superb imparters of knowledge, and the kids knew better than to resist being educated. If you didn't live up to your potential, you would spend a lot of time washing dishes, peeling potatoes, and doing laundry, none of which was a task assigned to you if you were a diligent learner.

The students of Mater Misericordiæ School always won city and state spelling bees, debate club matches, and science fair prizes. As a consequence, many of us were beaten up by some of the state's most accomplished young intellectuals.

Generous supporters of the sisters provided college and trade school scholarships to those who wanted them, of which I wasn't one. I aspired to be a writer. Profound intuition told me that the wrong university creative-writing program might hammer out of me anything original about my style and convert me into a litbot.

Sister Agnes Mary managed the placement office for those who weren't submitting to higher education. When I turned seventeen and a half, she used samples of my writing to snare a job for me with the publisher of *Arizona!*, a magazine about the wonders of the state and its people. I wasn't yet trusted to write about contemporary citizens, who were far more easily offended than were dead folks. Instead, I was assigned to research and write about interesting figures and places from the state's storied past, as long as I avoided brothels and bandits.

On my eighteenth birthday, after just six months of successful employment, I was able to afford a studio apartment and move out of the orphanage. After eighteen months at the magazine, I made a fateful mistake and have been in flight from dark forces ever since.

I find it eerie that, within a day of making that mistake, a full week before the consequences of it became clear, I had my first episode of what, for a while, I came to call "strange magnetism," as if someone was writing my life—not the story of my life, but my life itself—someone who knew the time was coming when I would need a substantial amount of cash in order to escape capture.

This was a Friday in early May. Having completed my assignments for the week, I took the day off, intending to avoid exercise, load up on wicked carbs, and stream old *Alien* and *Terminator* movies until my eyes began to bleed. Instead, I grew restless before I'd eaten a single chocolate-covered doughnut, and I felt strangely compelled to get in my vintage Toyota and test the bald tires by driving out of the city, into the desert. I distinctly remember saying to myself, "What am I doing? Where am I going?" Then I stopped asking because I realized that if I spoke in a slightly different voice and answered with a destination, I might be a case of multiple personality, something to which I never aspired.

Where I was going turned out to be not a ghost town, but a sort of ghost crossroads, not from the days of cowboys and prospectors in the nineteenth century, but from the 1950s. A section of a state highway had been made superfluous by an interstate. A Texaco service station, a restaurant, and a large Quonset hut of indeterminable purpose were left to be worried into ruins by merciless desert sun, wind, insects, and time. I'd been there once before, six months earlier, getting the flavor of the place to write a little mood piece about it for *Arizona!* magazine.

The big sign mounted on the roof of the restaurant had been faded by decades of fierce solar rays and had been shot full of holes by good old boys who thought that mixing strong drink and firearms was an entertaining way to pass an evening on little-traveled back roads. Generally speaking, they had no wives to object and no girlfriends to offer more appealing distractions. Research had taught me that the restaurant had been called Santinello's Roadside Grill.

I parked on the fissured, sun-paled blacktop, took a flashlight from the glove box, got out of my car, and approached Santinello's. The windows had been broken out long ago, and the front door had rotted off its hinges.

Inside, lances of sunlight slashed through east-facing windows, forcing the shadows to retreat to the west side of the dining room, where they gathered as if conspiring. The booths, tables, and chairs had been sold off in 1956, along with the kitchen equipment. Wind had blown debris and decades of dust inside.

No herpetologist I queried had been able to explain to me why a couple of dozen snakes had slithered here to die, mostly rattlers. When I had come exploring on the previous occasion, I'd freaked out until I realized they were air-dried, fossilized, lifeless.

Nevertheless, on this return visit, I stepped carefully among them and went into what had been the kitchen. Although everything of value had long been stripped away, splintered wooden crates that had once held oranges and other produce were heaped against one wall, along with all manner of empty food tins.

On my first visit, I had stirred through that flotsam, hoping that something in it would give me a hook for a poignant paragraph about how the Santinello's ship had run aground on the jagged rocks of progress, their lifelong work and dreams for a better future having been pirated from them. In those early days of my magazine career, I was as enthusiastic as a puppy, capable of a rare but embarrassing mixed metaphor in my earnest efforts to shake readers into an emotional response. That was long ago, and I am much more mature now that, as I write this, I've spent a year struggling to stay alive while gradually uncovering and adjusting to the true nature of the world.

Anyway, on that initial exploration, as I'd stirred the flotsam in the kitchen, something bright had reflected my flashlight beam and caught my eye. When I reached to pluck a scrap of yellowing paper off the object to fully reveal it, a disturbed tarantula erupted out of the debris and scampered up my arm. I knew the creature wasn't poisonous, that it wouldn't bite, that its kind were said to be gentle, that it was supposed to be the Mohandas Gandhi of arachnids. But when a hairy spider the size of a soccer ball—or so it seemed—is coming for your face, the fight-or-flight response kicks in big-time. I staggered backward, managed to knock the beast off my arm, and lost all interest in whatever bauble had glittered in the trash.

Now, inexplicably, I was back, searching with my flashlight not for the tarantula, to which I didn't feel the need to apologize, but for the item from which the spider had frightened me away. I found it: a very old coin—judging by its sheen, pure gold.

As I turned the heavy coin between my fingers, I marveled that my subconscious must have recognized what it was on the day of the tarantula and must have held that knowledge for months. However, why I would suddenly be impelled to return here after all this time was even more of a mystery than how such a coin had come to be in an abandoned restaurant in a once-busy crossroads that now led nowhere in four directions.

I left the lifeless snakes to rest in creepy peace and returned to the city, where I visited a shop that bought and sold everything from French antique furniture to Meiji-period Japanese bronzes.

The owner, Julius Shimski, knew everything anyone could know about all things old—coins, stamps, paintings—not least of all because he was eighty-nine and had spent his life learning. Julius had a monk's ring of white hair, eyebrows as lush as albino caterpillars, blue eyes as clear as the water in Eden, and a face that had not lined with age but had smoothed into a semblance of what he must have looked like just before his bris. In a profile of him in *Arizona!*, he had explained his pink-cheeked appearance by saying, "When you fill yourself with knowledge about any subject, it plumps you." I didn't write the profile, because Julius wasn't dead, but after I read it, I began stopping by his shop now and then to chat.

The place is more than a shop, really. It's a two-story brick-clad concrete-and-steel building, designed to be so fireproof that even the Devil couldn't get it to take a destructive spark from his finger. The shop's stock is worth millions, so to be admitted, you have to have an appointment or be known to Julius. In either case, entry is through a bulletproof-glass vestibule, where you're scanned for a weapon before being buzzed through the inner door. When Julius was just forty-one, working out of another location, he was robbed at gunpoint and pistol-whipped, whereupon he built a fortress of a shop because, as he said in the profile, "Paranoia I can live with, but not a bullet in the head."

On that Friday, his granddaughter, Sharona, was staffing the front room, which made me feel doubly lucky when I saw her from the glass vestibule. With her jet-black hair and dark eyes and exquisite arrangement of features, she is one of those women at whom you can't look for long without losing the ability to speak coherently, or at least I can't. She's thirty, eleven years older than me, so from her perspective I'm hardly out of adolescence, while from my perspective she's my dream girl. Among other things, she's a philatelist, which isn't as sexy as it sounds; she knows everything there is to know about collectible postage stamps. Like her grandfather, she is a knowledge sponge. I can't imagine why she's not married. Although she treated me with the affection that an aunt might show for a favored nephew, I fantasized that one day I would do something—maybe save a family from a burning house or take a gun away from a crazed terrorist—that would cause her to look at me in a much different way and see me as the romantic figure of *her* dreams.

She waved and then buzzed me through. I passed by the cluster of Tiffany lamps and the Japanese gold-lacquer boxes that dated from the Taishō through the Heisei eras, and went to the sales counter, where she stood. A display of highly collectible wristwatches lay between us. If I had been more attuned to the menacing melody that destiny had chosen as background music for what was coming, I might have seen those watches as an omen that time was running out for me.

Instead, I regarded Sharona with a smile that was probably more like a boyish grin, and declared, "You look so Friday," when what I meant to say was that she looked lovely today.

She smiled that aunt-to-nephew smile. "No one has ever said that to me before, Quinn. What does Friday look like?"

"Well, just like you." Elaboration seemed essential, so I kept going. "Friday is the best of days, don't you think? The workweek is done, and Monday is still in the distant future, so for a while we're free. Of course, I've got the day off, and you don't, so maybe you see the whole situation in a different light. But to me, right now, this week anyway, Friday is great. Friday is beautiful."

There. I'd actually said it. I had told her she was beautiful, even though she might need a translator to have my meaning properly conveyed.

She cocked her head at me. "You're really wired, Quinn. How much coffee have you had this morning, dear? My Uncle Meyer was an eight-cups-a-day man and ended up with a bleeding ulcer when he was just thirty-four. Three days in the ICU."

"Oh, not to worry. I'm a two-cup man. That's all it takes to charge me up. A good Jamaican blend." In fact, I didn't often drink coffee. I favored caffeine-free Pepsi or Coke, but I worried that she would think I was still a boy if I preferred a soft drink to a good cup of joe. I was ashamed of myself for lying, even if about something as inconsequential as coffee. To avoid plunging deeper into the swamp of deceit, I produced the gold coin from a pocket. "Why I stopped by is I found this. I think it might be worth something."

"I'm mainly a philatelist, though I know a lot about Tiffany, Art Nouveau, and Art Deco. Grandfather is the ace numismatist."

I so much liked the way "philatelist" sounded when she said it that I wanted to ask her to say it again, but I restrained myself.

"You know where Grandfather's office is. I'll intercom him and let him know you'll be stopping in to see him."

Julius's office was at the back of the building, on the first floor. I passed through a storeroom of treasures and found him at his Art Deco desk, which I knew was by Ruhlmann, because he had once told me its history when I asked if I could buy one like it at Ikea. He was examining a cockroach with a jeweler's loupe.

"What's that?"

"A brooch," he said.

"Why would anyone wear a cockroach brooch?"

He looked up from the loupe and raised his bushy eyebrows. "It's not a cockroach. It's a very different species of beetle, a scarab. It's made of silver, tarnished at the moment, and adorned with some of the finest sapphires, rubies, and emeralds it has ever been my pleasure to see."

"Cockroach, scarab—beetles are beetles. I don't like bugs."

"Scarabs were sacred to the pharaohs of ancient Egypt."

"That's probably why their civilization didn't last. Look what I found."

He put aside the jeweled scarab and the loupe to examine my coin. "Where did you get this?"

I told him a version of the truth without lying, leaving out the tarantula because I didn't want him to tell Sharona how I'd been scared off by a mere spider. "Is it worth something?"

"At retail, from a collector, it would bring forty thousand dollars, maybe a few thousand less."

I was gobsmacked. I'd been hoping for maybe a hundred bucks. "Holy moly, puddin' and pie!" I declared, which was something we said at the orphanage to avoid a cruder exclamation in the presence of the nuns. "I guess I better find out who it belongs to."

Julius frowned. "Belongs to? From what you told me, I'd say it belongs to you. It's not as if anyone who ever owned that restaurant is still alive. Anyway, if I remember the article you wrote for the magazine, all that property was eventually condemned and taken under the public domain laws."

"Then the county owns it. Or Washington. There'll probably be a finder's reward."

I'd been standing by the desk all this time. Now Julius pointed to a chair and said, "Sit down. You're light-headed."

When I said I felt fine, he told me to sit down again, this time more sternly than I'd ever heard him speak.

He said, "What might the government do with forty thousand dollars? Buy a hand-soap dispenser for one of the Senate restrooms? Add two feet of new track for a train to nowhere? Listen, son, if you were anyone else, I'd offer twenty-six thousand, maybe a smidgen more. But I'm pretty sure in a month I can sell this to a collector for near that price I mentioned, so I'll take some more risk and come up to thirty thousand. Young as you are and poor as you are, this is a blessing you should just thank God for and get on with your life."

Maybe I was too innocent for my own good, or maybe I didn't want him to think I was all *that* young, meaning too young for Sharona, if she suddenly became enamored of me. Whatever my absurd reasoning, I said, "I'm not so young, really, I mean I've got a nice job, my own apartment. I've got prospects."

"Son, if you're not young, then I'm older than dead." He leaned forward in his chair, balancing the coin between his thumb and his forefinger. "Say you'll take the money, or I'll flip it. If I flip it, then if it's heads, I'll flush the coin down the john, and if it's tails, I'll also flush it down the john."

"You're joking."

"Try me."

"But what kind of choice is that?"

He got up from his chair. "It's the only one I'm offering you. I won't participate in your reckless confusion. And if you think I'm too old to keep you from taking this away from me before I can flush it, you'd better be wearing a metal cup and be prepared for other injuries."

In retrospect, I think that the idea of suddenly having thirty thousand dollars scared me. I'd come into the world with nothing and had lived on the orphanage's dime for eighteen years. Even with my job at *Arizona!*, I'd never had enough money to worry about losing it. I didn't want to prove to be a fool by misspending thirty thousand, because then not only Sharona would write me off as a loser, but so would any other woman with a brain.

So I took the thirty thousand. Julius paid twenty-nine thousand with a check and gave me a thousand in cash, so that I could replace the bald tires on my rust-bucket Toyota right away and even have a small celebration. I went directly to the bank and made a deposit.

Because my bank and Julius's were the same, they phoned him for verification and made the funds available the next day, Saturday—which had by then become my choice for best day of the week.

The following morning, after I'd showered and had a bowl of Cap'n Crunch, I was seized once more by the strange magnetism that had drawn me to that ghost crossroads. This time, I was impelled to return to the bank and withdraw four thousand dollars in hundreds and twenties. I didn't spend a dollar of it. I took it back to my apartment, secured it in a small ziplock bag, and tucked the bag under a cushion of my only armchair.

I recalled having read an article that recounted a time when banks had failed, and I supposed I was just being paranoid about losing my newfound wealth.

On Monday, during my lunch break, I returned to the bank and withdrew two thousand more and put it in the ziplock bag. After I withdrew three thousand more on Tuesday and another three thousand on Wednesday, I had begun to scare myself. No, I didn't feel that I was out of control. Rather, I sensed that I was preparing myself for something more than the collapse of the bank, that somehow I *knew* trouble was coming, as I had known where I would find a valuable coin.

Thursday, I alarmed myself further by being unable to resist the urge to buy a small suitcase and pack it full of two changes of clothes and toiletries. I put the suitcase in the trunk of my car and left the vehicle in the long-term parking section of a downtown garage, paying a week in advance with cash.

I also withdrew another four thousand from the bank, where they must have begun to think that either I'd become a compulsive gambler or was in thrall to a gold digger.

When I reported to work Friday morning, two ziplock bags, each containing eight thousand dollars, were fixed to my bare chest with adhesive tape. I wore a loose shirt so it wouldn't appear that I had begun to develop breasts.

By this time, I was no longer certain of my sanity. A week had passed since I'd come into all that money and since I'd begun to prepare to be a fugitive. Being compelled by intuition to make such preparations didn't mean my intuition must be reliable. Most people under a compulsion to do unusual things were in fact as screwy as a squirrel on methamphetamine. I had to wonder if my fear might be irrational and might have arisen from guilt related to selling a coin that didn't belong to me. Having been raised by nuns, I'd had all the shall-nots drummed into me in the kindest but most insistent way for eighteen years. It was reasonable to assume a surfeit of moral suasion had sensitized me to transgression to such a degree that I would feel guilty for keeping a dime found in the street. So the threat was surely imaginary, a pinball of anxiety ricocheting around in my disordered head. Or at least that was a theory I entertained until the thugs showed up at lunch.

Two fry cooks who might one day be as famous as Andy Warhol saved me from a pair of well-dressed men with bad intentions.

I ate lunch five days a week at a place across the street from the magazine's offices because I was a creature of habit, because the joint was clean and the food was good and it was cheap. The Beane family owned the operation. Hazel Beane was a fifty-year-old divorcée whose husband, an attorney, had run off with a client for whom he had won a ten-million-dollar judgment in the death of her husband, Darnell Ickens. The jury had unanimously agreed that a police officer had responded with excessive force when he shot Darnell six times after Darnell attacked him with a pneumatic nail gun and skewered him four times. Hazel would still accept a lawyer as a customer, but she would never greet one with a smile. Her children—Phil and Jill, twenty-six-year-old fraternal twins—were excellent fry cooks, working the griddle and grill with style, even though it was not their destiny. They were born to be artists. Phil dyed his spiky hair purple and shaved off his eyebrows, while Jill dyed her spiky hair green and at all times wore black pajamas with red shoes. They had not yet been able to sell a significant number of paintings because, as they explained, the art establishment valued the marketability of the artist's image as much as or more than his or her paintings, so the big breakthrough depended on finding the right look. Lately, Phil and Jill had been giving a lot of thought to shaving their heads and having themselves dyed blue from top to bottom.

Anyway, I usually crossed the street to Beane's Diner toward the end of the lunch rush, so I could sit at the counter without being crowded into a conversation with another customer who might want to talk about something as absurd as politics or something as evil as, well, politics. I was more interested in hearing about art and the art world, of which Phil and Jill had such extensive and enthralling knowledge. That Friday, the diner's booths were still full of those upper-echelon employees who could linger at lunch without having their fingers smacked with a ruler by the boss, but most of the counter stools were unoccupied.

After Jill recounted a fascinating anecdote about the weird surreal images incorporated subliminally in the paintings of Andrew Wyeth, Phil served up a three-cheese hamburger with lettuce, tomato, and mayonnaise. The French fries were extra crispy, as I like them. I was washing down the second bite of the hamburger with a cherry Coke when two men appeared on the stools flanking mine as if they had materialized at the summons of a sorcerer. I got an immediate bad vibe from both of them, and although I took a third bite of my sandwich, I had some difficulty swallowing it.

The new arrivals were dressed in black suits and white shirts and black ties. They wore sunglasses, which they took off and folded and inserted in their shirt pockets in a most impressive display of synchronization.

I looked to my left, and the guy there smiled at me. He was as handsome as any male model, with brown eyes that were almost gold, like those of a cat. Something about his smile said it came too easy to him, that he smiled all night while sleeping, that it didn't mean he liked you or was in a good mood or even that he knew what a smile was meant to signify.

To my right, the other guy was a hulk with a hard, flat face and looked as if he had run at top speed into a wall more than once, just for the fun of it. He smiled, too, but in his case, I could see that such an expression required concentration.

The one with golden eyes said, "Kind of hot out there today."

I said, "Well, it's May in Phoenix."

"You've lived in Phoenix all your life, have you?"

"Mostly, yeah."

The hard case on my right said, "You like Phoenix better than where you came from?"

"Sure, I like it pretty much. I don't remember anything about where I came from."

Looking past me at Leftie, Rightie said, "This young man has amnesia."

Leftie traded his easy smile for a look of faux sadness. "I'm sorry to hear that. Must be tough, no memory."

"I don't have amnesia," I assured them. "I come from Peptoe, Arizona, but I only spent a few days there after I was born."

I looked back and forth as the men engaged in synchronized, solemn nodding.

Hazel Beane appeared, slapped menus on the counter, and said, "Get you guys something to drink?"

"Give us a minute here, why don't you?" the handsome one said.

She squinted at him, then at his partner, and said, "Are you attorneys?"

"No, but we've arrested a few."

This didn't please Hazel as it ought to have done. She said to me, "Honey, are you all right?"

I took a deep breath of diner air scented with fried onions and the sizzling beef on the griddle. "I don't know yet."

"This here is a good boy," Hazel told my dining companions.

"If you say so," Leftie said.

Rightie added, "We have his best interests at heart."

A waitress, Pinkie Krankauer, leaned past Rightie to tell Phil she needed two draft beers for booth four. After giving me a worried look, Phil went to draw the brews, leaving the griddle work to his sister.

When Hazel retreated reluctantly, the man with golden eyes said, "So you don't remember what happened in Peptoe?"

"I was sent to a Catholic orphanage here when I was three days old. Anyway, not much happens in a town of nine hundred and six."

"They've had a growth spurt since then," Leftie said. "There's now nine hundred and twelve."

"Though it's become a metropolis," Rightie said, "a little baby abandoned in the middle of a highway would be a big deal even in the new and improved Peptoe."

"Well, I guess it would be. Listen, what agency are you with? I have a right to know who I'm talking to."

The handsome one on my left produced an ID wallet. He was with the Internal Security Agency. I'd heard of it, but I didn't know how it was different from the FBI, NSA, DSA, ATF, Homeland Security, or any other law-enforcement agency. These days, America is a lot more policed at the federal level than it was only a decade earlier.

Putting away the ID wallet, Leftie spoke softly, as if everyone in the diner was trying to eavesdrop, and maybe they were. "See, we could've been waiting for you in your apartment when you came home, but we didn't know what surprises you might have up your sleeve."

"Surprises?" I said, puzzled.

Rightie whispered, "If you try anything tricky here—"

"Tricky?" I said.

"Try anything unique, with all these witnesses, it'll be a big story. We don't think you want a big story."

"Unique?" I said, having been reduced to one-word responses.

Neither of them said anything for half a minute, merely stared at me in a way that at first I thought was meant to be intimidating. But as I turned my head from side to side, I realized that the hard-ass manner they'd affected was not just who they were as agents but was also intended to mask their fear. They were afraid of me.

In my nineteen years, no one in the world had been afraid of me, not even once. I had been beaten up by angry spelling-bee losers, for heaven's sake.

The brute with the mashed-in face swallowed hard, as if for a moment something had been stuck in his throat. He said softly, "The first one we knew like you, this guy named Ollie, we tried to sit him down for a talk in a nice private place."

The one on my left, who had slipped a hand under his suit coat, murmured, "Two of our people are in the booth behind us. They've drawn their guns and are holding them under the table."

Rightie said, "With Ollie, we quietly explained our intentions, laid out why it was in his best interest to cooperate—"

"—but it was downhill from there," said Leftie.

Rightie said, "He did some really mean shit to some of our people."

Their back-and-forth patter seemed as well rehearsed as an Abbott and Costello routine, though not as funny.

"I'm not mean," I said lamely.

"What we want you to do," the brutish one said, "is let us cuff your hands behind your back and take you outside to our van. We just need to have a talk, need to understand. We don't want to hurt you."

"But we will," said Leftie, "if you go unique on us. So don't get tricky."

Rightie grunted agreement. He was so hushed that I could hardly hear the voce in his sotto voce. "We'll shoot you in the head. All four of us. That's what worked well before."

The *GQ* model with golden eyes hissed, "Yes, yes, very well."

As you might imagine, I was by now so terrified that I worried about the retentive strength of my bladder. "Listen, guys, you're making a big mistake. Whoever you think I am, I'm not."

No one watching our little lunch-counter drama could have been sure who these men were and might well have thought they were mob thugs to whom I owed money. Later I learned the ISA is widely despised, so it might not have mattered if anyone had heard Leftie identify his agency.

My attention was so focused on Twiddledum and Twiddledee that the diner seemed to fade away into a fog. I suppose they were likewise so focused on me that they never noticed that the diner staff had overheard enough to be alarmed. Being the kind of food-service patriots who would stand up for a friend, Hazel Beane's crew had wordlessly coordinated an intervention on my behalf.

Having drawn a basket of crisp potatoes out of the deep-well fryer, Jill pivoted and threw the hot contents of the basket in Rightie's face.

Having drawn two sixteen-ounce beers from the draft spigot, ostensibly to put them on the counter for the waitress who requested them, Phil instead splashed the contents of one mug and then the other into the golden eyes of the man on my left, just as the guy on my right got an order of fries that he hadn't requested. Behind me, I heard Pinkie Krankauer say, "Don't even think about it," as she dumped a tray heaped with dirty dishes into the laps of the agents in the booth.

If a week earlier we had been playing a game of What Would You Do, and you had described the Beane's Diner scenario to me, I would have said that I would most likely spin off my stool, slip and fall on the way to the front door, and be captured by highly agitated ISA agents. Instead, I surprised myself by knocking aside my lunch and scrambling across the counter, availing myself of the cover that it provided. As I stayed low and scuttled past Jill, heading toward the kitchen, she slipped a spatula under a half-done beef patty, scooped it off the griddle, and sailed it into the face of the guy who was still wiping French fries out of his eyes.

In the kitchen were refrigerators and ovens and worktables, as well as Pepe Chavez and Tau Hua. He said, "Quinn, my man," and she said, "What's up?"

I said, "Gotta run," and sprinted past them. At the back door, I snatched a fire extinguisher off its wall mount and threw open the door, expecting machine-gun fire.

The guy in the alley was wearing jeans and a Hawaiian shirt, but he was big and alert. He said, "Hey there, boy-o."

No normal person calls a stranger "boy-o," so I figured he was ISA, and I foamed him relentlessly with the fire extinguisher. As he staggered around like Frosty the Snowman dissolving in the Phoenix sunshine, I ran west, carrying the extinguisher just in case I might encounter another overheated federal employee.

## 3

On the north side of the alley, behind Dirty Harry Clean Now, the dry cleaner's van was being loaded with freshened clothes to be returned to customers' homes. The driver—Juan Santos, who often had lunch at Beane's Diner—slammed shut the back doors of the van and saw me coming. With the perspicacity of a first-rate deliveryman, he recognized that I was fleeing from a threat, and he waved me toward the passenger side of the vehicle. "Get in, let's scoot."

"He's the law. You'll get in trouble."

"I eat trouble for breakfast," Juan said. "Anyway, he won't see us."

I glanced back and discovered that the boy-o in the Hawaiian shirt was staggering away from me, disoriented, temporarily blind, with gobs of fire-suppressant foam cascading from him as if he were a hellhound with rabies. None of the other ISA agents had yet made it out of the diner, where perhaps they continued to be obstructed by barrages of food.

With reluctance, I dropped the fire extinguisher. Defenseless, I clambered into the passenger seat, pulled the door shut, and slid low as Juan started the engine. The air was crisp with the faint but lingering scent of the solvents used to process the racks of clothes in the back of the van, and I sneezed so hard that the cartilage between my nostrils vibrated for a few seconds afterward.

"Gesundheit," said Juan.

"Thank you."

*"De nada."*

At the west end of the alley, Juan glanced at his side mirror to scope the scene behind us. "Foam guy just fell into a cluster of trash cans." He turned right into the street. "You can sit up now."

"I think not. The ISA is after me. They have eyes everywhere."

"The secret police?"

"Semisecret," I said. "Everyone knows they exist, but nobody knows what they do."

"Why're they after you, Quinn?"

"I have no idea. They said I'm unique."

Juan snorted with contempt. I've never known anyone else who has such a variety of snorts, each of which is easily interpreted. "Everyone is unique, amigo. If unique is a crime, they'd have to arrest all of us."

"Maybe they will eventually. Right now, it's me."

"You want me to take you across the border?"

"To Mexico? No, no, no. You have clothes to deliver."

"So I'm a day late. Mr. Dai will understand. He's a nice man."

Gi Minh Dai had escaped Vietnam as a teenager in the seventies and, when he was just twenty, had founded what became a highly successful dry-cleaning service.

"I know good people in Mexico who'll take you in."

"That's sweet of you, Juan. But I'd be eternally grateful if you'd just drop me off at the parking garage where I stowed my car."

I gave him the address, and he said, "That crap Toyota of yours might not make it to Scottsdale."

"I bought new tires and this terrific air freshener I hung from the rearview mirror."

"I hate that pine smell. Always reminds me of urinal cakes."

"It's shaped like a pine tree," I said, "but it smells like oranges."

"Why wouldn't they shape it like an orange?" His snort conveyed frustration with the outsourcing of American manufacturing, and he answered his own question. "Made in China—that's why. Well, one good thing about your crap Toyota is it's so old it doesn't have GPS. They can't track you by satellite." He braked to a stop at an intersection and looked down at me as I huddled below window level. His expression was kind and, so it seemed to me, informed more by sympathy than pity. "What's your plan, Quinn?"

"Plan? Well, just to stay free long enough to figure out why they're after me. It has to be some kind of mistake, a screwup. I just have to get it straightened out."

"I said I eat trouble for breakfast, and it's true. My sister, Maria, she got out of prison, lives with me now until she can get back on her feet. She's a great lady but can't cook worth a damn. She insists on sending me to work with a hearty breakfast, so I have bowel trouble all day." He paused. As he stared down at me, I swear I saw the moment when his sympathy turned to pity. "Maria, before she did what she did, she didn't have a plan, either."

The light changed, and we cruised through the intersection.

I said, "What'd she do?"

"To get sent to prison? She mocked a congresswoman by posting several funny memes about her. They said the memes were threats."

"Were they threats?"

"Yeah—if you think portraying someone as a drunken chipmunk is a threat. Maria did it, but she didn't have a plan for what might come after. Sentenced to a year, served nine months."

"Who'd think you'd need a plan for that?"

"Things have changed, Quinn. Before I do or say *anything*, I have a plan, sometimes two or three plans."

"How could I know the ISA would decide I was unique? Who has a plan for being accused of uniqueness?"

"All I'm saying is, you better have a plan. You can't just run forever."

For maybe two minutes, neither of us spoke. His silence was the silence of pity, and mine was the silence of fear and confusion. My inability to imagine how even to *start* making a plan so distressed me, I sought to relieve my stress by changing the subject. Pushing up in my seat, I said, "I've always wondered why it's called Dirty Harry Clean Now."

Juan's snort was of amused affection for his employer. "First two years that Gi Minh Dai was in the States, he worked three jobs and lived cheap, saving his money to start a dry-cleaning shop. When he finally took time to see a movie, it was the Eastwood film. He loved it. Saw it eight times. Harry wore some cool suits in the movie, and in spite of all the action, he always looked clean and sharply pressed. Gi wondered where Harry took his dry cleaning, and he thought everyone else must wonder, too. At first, he meant to call his shop Gi Minh Dai Dry or Wet, but he went with the other name so the millions of people wondering who was Harry's dry cleaner might come to Dirty Harry Clean Now. His English wasn't as good then as it is these days, so he thought the meaning was clear. The funny thing is, it worked. He has three shops and does more dry cleaning and laundry than anyone in Arizona. You understand why it worked?"

I said, "Gi Minh Dai had a plan."

"Exactly." Juan pulled to the curb and stopped in front of the six-story parking garage where I'd left my car. "Get a plan, amigo."

"I will," I promised. "Somehow, one way or another, I'll get a plan. Thank you for giving me a lift. I realize now it was a big risk, aiding and abetting a fugitive."

Juan smiled. He had a warm smile. If it had been any warmer, he could have toasted bread with it. "*De nada*. Anyway, I had a plan. If some ISA types pulled us over, I'd have taken a pistol from under my seat, shot you dead, then claimed you kidnapped me and I took the weapon away from you."

I did not know what to say to that, so I said, "Huh."

Juan's smile became a wide grin. His grin was so wide that it made me think of a jack-o'-lantern. "I'm joking, Quinn. I like you too much to ever shoot you. But I wish you weren't so clueless."

Dismayed, I said, "'Clueless' is kind of harsh."

"Not really. I like you too much to sugarcoat it. Get your shit together, amigo. But keep your sense of humor or you'll go insane, like so many seem to have done these days."

Opening the door, I said, "I will. I'll get my shit together."

"Another thing. You have a smartphone?"

I withdrew it from a jacket pocket. "Apple. You want me to stay in touch?"

"Not really. I want you to stomp hard on that phone and drop it in the nearest storm drain. It's got GPS. They can track you as long as you carry it."

"But I've got all these apps. I've got weather and maps and podcasts."

"You want to survive, you've got to be totally street from here on, Quinn." He held out his cell phone. "It's a burner, disposable. Nothing fancy. I didn't use my name when I activated it."

"I can't take your phone," I said.

He threw it at me, and I caught it. "And one more thing, amigo. You know about three-hundred-sixty-degree license-plate scanners?"

"Should I get one?"

He snorted in a prayerful sort of way and rolled his eyes. "Jesus, Mary, and Joseph, protect this boy. Quinn, every police car and a lot of other government vehicles are equipped with scanners that record license plates all around them and transmit in real time to the National Security Agency's million-square-foot data center in Utah. You'll be scanned half a dozen times before you're out of this city. If they want you as bad as you say they want you, they'll be alerted every time you're scanned, and they'll track you down sooner than later."

"How do you know that?"

"How could I not? It's the kind of thing everyone needs to know in the new America."

"So I should take the plate off my car?"

"That would be a start."

As traffic whooshed past, sunshine flaring off the windshields, I got out of the van and looked in at him. "What if a cop stops me because I don't have a plate?"

"Then you're a burnt burrito. Still sure you don't want to take a trip to Mexico?"

"No, I've got to stay here and clear my name. This is all some terrible mistake."

After a snort of exasperation, Juan said, *"Vaya con Dios."*

"You too," I said, and closed the door.

As he drove off, I stood there in the searing sun, feeling small and alone. My shadow seemed to be straining to get away, as though it didn't want to end up in a coffin with the rest of me.

A Ford F-150 crew cab cruised toward me, bulging tarps full of landscape clippings swelling like bulbous mushrooms in its open bed. Rather than draw attention to myself by stomping on my smartphone in a fit of Rumpelstiltskin rage, I tossed it among those tarps so that the ISA might chase it around Phoenix for a while.

| 4 |

The cavernous garage offered an elevator and enclosed stairs, but both felt like traps. The vehicle ramps were two lanes wide, two per floor. I walked up to the long-term parking on the sixth level.

In those days, I never felt safe in a huge public parking structure. I wasn't concerned about motorists who drove too fast, though some seemed to think they were on a slot-racing track. The massive supporting columns would prevent the ceiling from collapsing on me, so I didn't worry about being crushed in rubble. Muggers rarely worked these buildings, for there weren't enough routes by which to make a quick exit. However, such garages always struck me as eerie, especially when I got to the less busy higher floors. Maybe vent fans produced the faint whispery sounds that suggested gremlins conspiring under the vehicles as they watched my feet move past. Maybe the lack of natural light and the granite-gray concrete and the silent cars lined up like rows of coffins inspired thoughts of death. Sometimes I felt that I was on the brink of an encounter with something otherworldly, perhaps a tribe of pale, feral children with smoky eyes and sharp teeth, the big-city twenty-first-century equivalent of the boys from that island in *Lord of the Flies*.

Later, of course, I'd come to understand that these feelings arose from a subconscious awareness that sinister presences live among us, passing for human. And they aren't restricted to parking garages; the world is their playground.

Anyway, when I reached the sixth and highest level, I warily surveyed the rows of vehicles, expecting to see among them a brace of men in dark suits and sunglasses, like the pair who'd flanked me at the lunch counter in the diner. Considering that I had escaped the first crew sent to arrest me, maybe I shouldn't have regarded the ISA as omniscient and omnipresent. However, even though the government is so deep in debt that it's technically bankrupt, and even though a dollar today will buy only what a dime would buy in the 1950s, the feds can still print money almost as fast as trees can be felled to make paper, which means that when they field an agency like the ISA, its name is Legion. I felt watched where no watchers waited, heard where no listeners lurked, and I approached my Toyota with caution, wishing I had a fresh fire extinguisher and a cloak of invisibility.

In addition to my suitcase and a spare tire, the car trunk contained a simple tool kit. I was able to remove the license plate quickly.

At that point, I began to act with what some might insist was criminal cunning, though I preferred to think of it as the street smarts of a wrongly accused fugitive. A Porsche stood next to my rust bucket. I removed the plate from it, put it on the Toyota, and then attached the Toyota plate to the fancier vehicle. The owner of the Porsche would incur the cost of ordering a new plate, and until he realized what had happened, he was at risk of having his car stormed by ISA agents hot for vengeance.

The chance was small, however, that Mr. Porsche looked enough like me to be gunned down in a case of mistaken identity. Anyway, the ISA didn't want to kill me. They wanted to interrogate me, and depending on what they meant by "unique," they might want to put me through a lot of annoying tests, maybe a few exploratory surgeries, but surely nothing worse.

Nevertheless, as I drove down through the garage, I knew the good sisters of Mater Misericordiæ would not approve of the cost and inconvenience to which I had subjected the owner of the Porsche. Were I still living at the orphanage, they would have me peeling potatoes for a week.

If I was slightly embarrassed by what I'd done to Mr. Porsche, and if I was afraid for my future and my life, which I was, then I was also pleased with myself because I had devised a plan while swapping the license plates.

If I'd had a list of the dry-cleaning deliveries Juan Santos was making, I would have tried to find him and thank him for having mentored me regarding the need for having a plan. I was so pleased to have one that I wanted not merely to express my gratitude but also share my delight.

My plan was to drive to Peptoe, Arizona, and track down the three men who found me in a bassinet in the middle of that highway nineteen years earlier. During most of my life, I'd been as ordinary as mud. However, the strange magnetism that recently compelled me hither and yon seemed to suggest something might indeed be unique about me. Back in the day, perhaps Hakeem, Bailie, and Caesar had concealed an important fact, or they might have seen something that seemed inconsequential at the time but that would be a key piece of the puzzle that was me.

They had not been old men at the time, but after two decades, perhaps one or more of them had died. Or they might have moved away from Peptoe to a more exciting town, like Gila Bend or Tombstone.

I have always been an optimist, because pessimists seldom have any fun and usually fret their way into one of the horrible fates they spend their lives worrying about. Of course, being an optimist doesn't guarantee you an unrelievedly happy life. You can still lose your job on the same day that your house burns down and your spouse informs you that he or she has shot the sheriff. But the optimist, unlike the pessimist, believes that life has meaning, that there is something to learn from every adversity, and even that the absurdity of such an excess of misfortune will likely seem at least somewhat amusing after enough time has passed. That is why, years after they have lost everything, optimists are frequently richer and happier than ever, while pessimists often had nothing to lose in the first place.

As I piloted the Toyota out of the garage and into streaming traffic in the street, I assured myself that I would find Hakeem, Bailie, and Caesar thriving in Peptoe. I could be there in three hours and perhaps would be able to speak with the first of them as early as that evening.

For all that Juan Santos knew about the need for having a plan, he didn't know everything on the subject. In 1785, in a work titled "To a Mouse," the poet Robert Burns warned "the best laid schemes of mice and men gang aft a-gley." You don't have to understand Scottish dialect to know he wasn't assuring the mouse that its plans were certain to win it a life of comfort and fine cheeses.

I felt rather like a frightened mouse when, instead of taking Interstate 10 south out of Phoenix, as was my intention, I suddenly began switching from street to street. I whigged along on a zigzag course that seemed to have no purpose other than to elude a tail, though my mirrors didn't reveal any vehicle whipping this way and that in my erratic wake. That inexplicable compulsion had overtaken me again, a kind of psychic magnetism drawing me toward I knew not what. This time it was alarmingly more powerful than it had been previously. I felt almost as though the car was driving itself, the steering wheel pulling my hands where the possessed Toyota wanted to go. I ran two yellow lights, treating the speed limit as if it were a mere helpful suggestion.

If a policeman pulled me over and ran the tags on the car, he would not be so slow-witted as to think that Porsche had designed a down-market version to break into the destitute-motorist market. The ISA might even have distributed a photograph of me to the computer in every patrol car in Phoenix. I would be extracted from the Toyota and encouraged to kiss the pavement. Some serious backup would be on the way faster than I could say *I can explain*, which would be a foolish thing to say because I had no idea what the hell was going on with me.

Then I was on federal highway 60, headed northwest toward an outlying suburb aptly named Surprise. Glittering Phoenix dwindled in the rearview mirror, a megaplex of high-rise buildings that looked as improbable as the Emerald City of Oz in the great flatness of the desert.

The compulsion that gripped me grew rapidly less intense. I felt that I could pull to the shoulder of the road, take slow deep breaths, and settle my nerves. However, I didn't *want* to stop. A strange magnetism still drew me northwest, but I was also motivated by curiosity, by a need to know where I was going, why I was going there, and what all this craziness meant.

As it turned out, my journey's end wasn't the town of Surprise. I blew by that whistle-stop and somehow knew that my destination was in the vicinity of Wickenburg, a little more than an hour from Phoenix.

If you prefer your weather dry and hot, if you favor landscapes with a minimum of annoying shade trees, if you find pea gravel no less attractive than grass, if tall buildings oppress you and beige stucco soothes, Wickenburg is the place for you, a pleasant town of wide streets, little traffic, cheap land, and friendly people.

In the general vicinity are world-famous three- and four-star dude ranches, where you can learn to fall off a horse, develop the useful skill of roping a faux calf, take line-dancing lessons, play golf, or dress up like a cowboy and drink yourself into a stupor every evening.

I didn't know it yet, but as it turned out, I was headed for one of those dude ranches beyond the town limits of Wickenburg. The operation—Sweetwater Flying F Ranch—would prove to be a desolate and desperate place. Eventually, I would learn that it had declared bankruptcy twelve years earlier and been reimagined by the owners as a secret marijuana farm, its barns and stables filled with thriving hemp plants. In those days, everyone thought that marijuana was a narcotic instead of just a lifestyle. When the Drug Enforcement Agency raided the place, the owners proved obstreperous. Guns were produced, shots were fired, blood was drawn, and everyone at the ranch ended up in prison for a long time, with the exception of those who were dead. The IRS seized the property to satisfy a tax lien.

As a young man who had been raised by nuns and who preferred city life to the rigors of suburbia, a place as far out there as

Sweetwater Flying F Ranch would never have been on my just-have-to-see-it list if I had been in control of myself.

Considering the events of the day, I expected trouble when I reached wherever I was going, and that expectation was fulfilled. What I didn't foresee was that my destiny would be found in that place. An adventure-filled life bathed in as much darkness as light, a life shaken by frequent terror but pierced by greater joy, a life of mysteries and revelations waited for me there, and also a recipe for cinnamon-pecan rolls that was to die for.

# 5

The federal highway led to a state route, and the state route led to a county lane that brought me to the long approach road to Sweetwater Flying F Ranch. Two stone columns supported a beam that overhung the entrance. To the beam was fixed a sun-faded sign featuring the name of the ranch and a silhouette of a cowboy riding a bucking bronco. In the distance, the drab gray buildings appeared to have swaybacked roofs and canted walls. The blacktop driveway was fissured, crumbling at the edges. Beside one of the entrance columns lay two long-dead coyotes, now nothing but skeletons and dust-matted fur; maybe they had been shot by some idiot or succumbed to disease, or maybe they had died of boredom.

Sweetwater Flying F Ranch creeped me out. It looked like a place where a bargain-basement nut-cult leader like Charles Manson would hole up with a raggedy band of followers who practiced their stabbing techniques on kittens while waiting for some poor fool to knock on the door.

A little less than an hour remained before sunset. I didn't want to be here in the dark.

Although I didn't have a clue why I was here in daylight, I was nonetheless pulled toward the ranch by a power as irresistible as the sun and moon that attract the tides of the seas. I drove between the stone columns and under the decaying sign.

Time and a lack of maintenance had done to this place what a force-five hurricane might have done to a four-mast galleon in the days of sailing ships. The stone-and-stucco main building, which once no doubt housed a restaurant and bar and various public rooms, must have been a handsome single-story structure in its time, but it was battered and breached; sand had drifted against its walls so that one end of it was partly buried in the manner of a shipwreck that had washed up on a beach. The wind had stacked tumbleweed against one wall, where it clung like enormous barnacles. The bungalows, where guests evidently stayed, and the stables were in worse condition than the primary building.

At the extreme point of the second loop of the figure-eight service road stood an immense barn that most likely had once been traditional red but was now a rusty pink. The previously convex roof had assumed the concave form of a saddle, and the substrate had shed perhaps half the shingles that had been fixed to it.

Nothing about the barn suggested that it contained anything of interest. I cruised past, heading back to the other buildings. As I approached the end of the secondary loop, instead of continuing into the primary loop, I found myself turning left, into the lane I had just traveled. With the barn ahead of me once more, I pressed the accelerator.

Magnetism.

This was not like the pull I had felt that led me to the gold coin, not akin to the gentle but insistent force the moon exerts on tides. I felt as if the barn was the world's largest electromagnet and I was but a helpless scrap of iron. The attraction wasn't only physical, but also powerfully emotional. I wanted more than anything to be *in that barn*, desired it as a maniacal gambler might desire a seat at a gaming table, as a starving glutton might desperately fling himself at a buffet table. Being in that barn was essential, an urgent necessity, the reason I had been born, so if I didn't get into that barn *right now*, if I didn't penetrate those walls, I would have no reason to exist. Maybe this sounds like passion, a thrilling libidinous desire, but just keep in mind that the object of my lust was a *barn*. As I pressed the accelerator to the floorboard, terror rather than testosterone flooded through me.

I aimed for the big rolling door, through which once must have passed horse-drawn wagons bearing dudes and dudettes headed out on many a quaint hayride. I won't say that the engine of my Toyota was screaming; that sad heap was too old and tired to scream, but it squealed like a pig on the slaughterhouse ramp, as if it knew what was about to happen to it. You can probably figure out that I didn't die from the impact, but I certainly expected to, and yet my foot would not relent from the gas pedal. If I'd had a longer stretch of pavement, I might have passed a hundred miles per hour by the time of impact, but I was going only fifty-eight.

There's an old movie about a guy's severed hand that is imbued with supernatural life and crawls around with evil intentions. Although it's not an Oscar-worthy production, I was reminded of it in that moment because my stupid foot, though still attached to my leg, seemed to possess a mind of its own. In spite of the fact it had committed me to a headlong collision with the barn, at the last second it jumped from the accelerator to the brake.

Evidently, the big plank door had suffered from years of dry rot or some such, for it exploded into dust and spongy chunks and thousands of prickly splinters. Because my traitorous foot jammed the brake down hard, the Toyota fishtailed as it plowed into the barn. A guy in there heard me coming and drew his gun and squeezed off a round that blew out the back window on the passenger side just before the rear fender clipped him so hard that he tumbled off his feet. As the Toyota completed a full turn in place, as if it were a carousel, another guy came into view, a pistol in a two-handed grip. The car swung to a stop. He put two rounds through the windshield. The safety glass dissolved. This time I was the master of my foot when I stomped on the accelerator.

As you must know by now, I am not an angry person, and neither am I given to violence when I am in full control of my extremities. However, there is only so much abuse a person can endure in one day before he goes John Wick on his tormentors. I didn't build up a lot of speed in the fifteen feet that separated me from this second shooter, but I hit him hard enough to lift him off his feet and carry him across the barn and slam him into a wall that was not eaten with the same dry rot as the door.

Pinned between the car and the wall, the disarmed gunman opened his mouth as though to protest, but spewed a mortal gout of blood instead of words.

I threw open the driver's door and clambered out of the car and doubled over, seized by the urge to vomit. John Wick could kill ten guys in two minutes and not even grimace with regret. Of course, he was a professional assassin, and I was a staff writer for a magazine about which the most exciting thing was the exclamation point in its name.

Never before had I killed anyone. Although I'd acted in self-defense, I felt cold to the bone, as if some essential spark in me had been snuffed.

After all, I didn't throw up, in part because I remembered the first guy I'd hit when the car fishtailed, the one who shot out a passenger-side window. He was down, but that didn't mean he was no longer a threat. Shaking, vision pulsing with the hammer blows of my heart, bewildered and alarmed by what happened, I went looking for him and found him lying facedown, head turned to one side, bloodied but maybe alive. His gun was nearby. I confiscated it just in case he regained consciousness and felt he had a score to settle. Then I knelt and felt for his pulse. Wasn't one. On closer inspection, I saw that his neck was broken.

I had trouble getting to my feet, and I wasn't steady when I got there. I stood over the corpse, wondering at the compulsion that had brought me here. Was strange magnetism a power I possessed—or was I a puppet on a string?

Only then did it register with me that both these men were wearing black suits, white shirts, and black ties. They seemed to have the same tailor as the men who braced me in Beane's Diner.

I was about to search the guy's pockets for ID when a clink and rattle drew my attention. I took the pistol in both hands, the way I had seen these well-dressed thugs do, and I surveyed the barn.

Late-afternoon eastern light ventured tentatively through the place where the door had been, and bolder shafts of direct sunshine dazzled through holes in the roof, but most of the barn lay in shadows. I needed a few seconds to find the source of the rattling. She was sitting on the barn floor, her back to the metal ladder that led to the hayloft, both arms raised above her head and zip tied to a rung. The ladder was rickety, and when she mumbled and moved in her sleep, the loose rung worked noisily in the side rails.

In the gloom, I couldn't see the woman clearly. Considering the Toyota's explosive entrance and the subsequent gunfire, I assumed that she wasn't merely taking a nap before dinner but must have been drugged.

I hurried to the Toyota, opened the trunk, discarded the gun, opened my suitcase, and retrieved the small pair of scissors from my shaving kit. When I returned to the woman, her head hung low, chin on her chest, as over and over she muttered, "Gotta get, gotta go, gotta be there," as if she was late for the same appointment as the White Rabbit.

I cut one zip tie, and her left arm dropped into her lap. As I cut the second tie, her head snapped up, and her eyes opened wide. She seized my face with her right hand, digging her fingernails into my left cheek. "What've you done? *What've you done with him?*"

With her hand clamped tightly over my chin and mouth, I wasn't able to answer her with more than a muffled "Done with whom?" Even I couldn't understand what I said.

Her eyes shone in the shadows as she demanded more fiercely, *"Tell me what you've done with him, you freakin' Nazi zombie!"*

She let go of me and thrust to her feet and staggered and almost fell but kept her footing. She looked at the gap where the barn door used to be, at the Toyota, at the guy dead on the floor. Then she looked at me again, her face wrenched with emotion. "What have you done with him? Where is Sparky?"

If she was distressed and a little crazy, I was no less so. "I didn't see a dog."

"Dog? Dog? *Dog?*" She regarded me as if I'd just claimed that I myself was a dog. "What're you talking about? What dog?"

"Sparky. The noise, things crashing, all the gunfire—he must have been scared and ran away."

This woman wasn't merely angry. She wasn't just enraged. She was *infuriated.* She stepped closer and punched me hard in the chest. "Don't jerk my chain, you worthless piece of garbage. Dog? Dog? You know he's not a dog."

"All I know is they shot at me, both of them, and I'd never been shot at before. Nuns don't prepare you for being shot at, even though you were beaten up after a spelling bee. So I had to do what I had to do, which is I ran them down."

Given my talk of gunfire and considering her situation, she ought to have been afraid, but instead my babble seemed to further incense the lady. Her fury became so hot that I thought maybe I was about to witness one of those cases of spontaneous human combustion that you read about in those stranger-than-fiction books that detail weird but true occurrences. She punched me in the chest again. "Sparky Rainking, my grandfather. *What've you done with Sparky Rainking?*"

"I didn't do anything to him. I never met Sparky Rainking. I don't *want* to meet him. Seems like it's dangerous to know Sparky."

In silence, she seethed at me for a moment. She scanned the barn again, and then she looked me up and down. "Where's your suit?"

"I don't own a suit."

"Then you're not one of *them?*"

"They're all about the suit. How could I be one of them if I don't have a suit? You do know who they are, don't you?"

"Oh, yeah. Yeah, I know who they are. Internal Security Agency Nazi zombies." Suddenly alarmed, she said, "Oh, shit. I remember now. More of them are coming."

She turned away from me and ran toward where the barn door had once been.

Hurrying after her, I said, "Where are you going?"

"I think I know what they did with Grandpa Sparky."

# 6

Half an hour before sunset, oblique orange sunlight gilded the prairie grass, painted long shadows across the land, and transformed the former dude ranch from mere rack and ruin into a sinister assemblage of shapes, like half-toppled megaliths erected thousands of years earlier to serve as a place at which to worship cruel gods.

Behind the barn stood two vehicles: a new black Suburban with government plates and a midnight-blue Buick older than my Toyota.

"They came on foot, snuck up on us, then brought the Suburban here afterward. We were too sure we couldn't be found."

The granddaughter of Sparky Rainking popped the trunk lid of the Buick. A sixty-something guy was in that cramped space, wrists and ankles bound with plastic straps, hands connected to feet with a trammel.

"Bridget!" he declared. "All that noise and gunfire, I thought you were dead. I'm so glad you're not dead."

"Me too," she said.

I used my scissors to cut his bonds, as I had cut hers. His muscles had stiffened. He needed help to get out of the trunk.

"And what's your name, young man?" he asked.

"Quinn Quicksilver."

"That's a mouthful, isn't it—especially for Porky Pig. Pleased to meet you, Quinn."

"Likewise, Mr. Rainking."

"Call me Sparky. It's from the Old English *spearca*, meaning 'to provoke and set in motion.' I try to live up to it. Who got shot?"

"No one," I said. "Those ISA guys shot at me, but they missed."

Bridget said, "He ran them down with his Toyota. A coupe, if you can believe it."

Walking back and forth, flexing and stretching, Sparky Rainking said, "Quinn, if you're going to be running people down on a regular basis, you'd be wise to invest in a larger, sturdier vehicle."

Never having experienced a grandfather of my own, I hadn't spent any time studying the species, but it seemed that Sparky was not a standard-issue grandpa. Yes, he had the wizened face that you might expect, crinkles at the corners of his eyes, white hair, and a thick white walrus-style mustache. But one small detail suggested his outlier status: Each of his largish earlobes featured a tattoo of a tiny, grinning skull.

Squinting his steel-gray eyes, he scanned the ranch as the place darkled in the fading light. "We're grateful for your Bruce Willis heroics, Quinn. But how did you come to be here?"

"I came from Phoenix. I'm a staff writer at *Arizona!* magazine."

With one eye still squinted and the other eyebrow raised, his expression made it clear that he knew I had avoided answering his question. "Seriously? You're writing about this dump?"

"No, sir. I came here because."

"Because?"

I shrugged. "Just because."

"Just because what?" he persisted.

"You wouldn't believe me if I told you."

"I'm a simple, trusting, gullible old man. Try me."

"Magnetism," I said.

Sparky looked at Bridget.

I, too, looked at Bridget. Now that no one was shooting at me and I wasn't busy running them down, it was as if I saw her for the first time. She was beautiful, but even better than that, she was cute. Always before, when I saw something so cute that it made me go all gooey inside, it had fur. Bridget didn't have fur, but I felt as if I was a marshmallow on a stick held over a campfire.

After she and her grandfather exchanged meaningful looks and said, "Magnetism," in unison, Bridget glanced at me. Judging by the way she rolled her eyes and sighed with exasperation, she understood that at the moment I was two ingredients short of being a s'more.

I turned my attention to her grandfather. "Magnetism makes sense to you?"

"Perfect sense."

"It doesn't make sense to me."

"It will," he said.

"What were you doing here? Why would you be in a place like this, the middle of nowhere?"

"We came here to hide for a few days," Sparky said. "Till we could figure things out. But they found us."

"Figure out what things?"

"Later, Quinn. Now we better scoot. When the backup they called for gets here, I suspect there'll be so damn many, you couldn't run them all down even if they lined up like tenpins for you."

Bridget said, "Your Toyota is maybe totaled."

"Yeah. And there's a dead guy squashed in the grille."

Sparky said, "You'll come with us. You can drive. We have a lot to discuss."

"I'll get my suitcase." I started to go around to the front of the barn, then stopped and turned back to them. "Hey, if you have a phone, that's how they found you."

"We're wise to that," Bridget said. "We only have an anonymous disposable cell. And the Buick's too old to have GPS."

"License plates," I said. "Nearly every police car and a lot of other government vehicles are fitted with three-hundred-sixty-degree plate scanners. They transmit to the National Security Agency's Utah Data Center in real time. Where were you coming from?"

"Flagstaff," she said.

"Oh, sure, you'd have been scanned a few times along the way. Then maybe they tapped archived satellite video and found where you went from the last time you were captured by a scan."

They regarded me with something like awe, impressed with my street smarts, as if I'd been raised by gangbangers instead of nuns.

"I'll strip the plate off my car, which I took from a Porsche in a parking garage, and we'll swap it for yours. It's not a long-term solution, but it'll buy us some time."

They returned to the barn with me, to retrieve their luggage, supplies, and blankets from the hayloft, where they had intended to hide for a few days while they figured things out.

The Toyota had no windshield, one flat tire, and the tired look of machinery that no longer understands its purpose. It was leaking radiator fluid. When I got behind the wheel, the dead agent pinned between the car and the wall appeared to be shouting accusations.

The urge to vomit did not return. I didn't know what these men had intended to do to Bridget, but I was not so naive as to believe that their every action would have been according to the provisions in a neatly typed warrant. Furthermore, I'd seen enough movies about the Mafia to know that guys who were tied up and stuffed into car trunks, like Grandpa Sparky, were either going to be crushed and compacted along with the vehicle in a scrap-metal salvage yard or driven to a construction site, shot, dumped in a deep hole, and buried under many yards of concrete, becoming part of an office building foundation. I hadn't already become desensitized to violence, but for sure I was coming to terms with the true dark nature of this world much faster than I would have while writing about our state's colorful past for *Arizona!* magazine.

The car didn't start. Then it did—coughing, shuddering. I reversed, and the dead guy slid to the barn floor, out of sight. I needed just a few minutes to unscrew the Porsche's plate.

When I carried my luggage behind the barn, Bridget was closing an open suitcase that lay in the trunk of the Buick.

Sparky stood near her, inserting a pistol into a holster on his right hip.

I heard myself say, "You've got a gun," as if this would be news to him.

"I should've been wearing it when those bastards took us by surprise. I thought we were safe here." He pulled on a sport coat.

"I've had things too soft for too long. I should've remembered—no one is ever safe anywhere."

With the Porsche plate on the Buick, as I drove away from the Sweetwater Flying F Ranch with Bridget riding shotgun and Sparky in the back seat, the sun broke like a bloody yolk on the sharp horizon and the purple of twilight was preceded by the red sky at night that is supposedly every sailor's delight.

In less than six hours, I'd gone from being just another hungry customer of Beane's Diner to a fugitive hunted by the closest thing the US has to a secret police. Most likely I would soon be charged with two murders that were actually acts of self-defense committed while in the grip of a strange magnetism that compelled me to rescue a young woman and her grandfather, whom I hadn't known existed until I drove more than seventy miles and crashed through a barn door to free them. When I brought that story before a court, at trial, I'd probably be the first person burned at the stake in centuries.

## 7

Rumor had it that the ISA employed more agents and support staff than the FBI, although that could have been wild social media speculation. Regardless of the truth, they suffered no shortage of manpower, and the nearest large city where they maintained an office was surely Phoenix. The called-for backup was probably on its way to the Flying F Ranch both by ground transport and helicopter.

Because the elderly Buick was conspicuous, south of Wickenburg we departed federal highway US 60—which the ISA would follow coming out of Phoenix—and we headed east on State Route 74. Eventually, to get around the city, we would weave through a few suburbs—Scottsdale, Tempe—on a series of surface streets and connect with Interstate 10 heading southbound to Tucson.

I told them I had been abandoned at birth, raised by nuns, and had a plan that involved driving to Peptoe to research my origins.

Before I could explain further, Sparky said, "We're short of a plan ourselves, and we seem to be in this together, so your plan is now our plan, if you don't mind."

I considered Bridget long enough that the Buick drifted onto the shoulder of the highway, requiring me to recover with a sudden hard pull of the wheel. "Yeah. That's good. That's great. We're in this together, whatever the heck 'this' is."

Bridget and Sparky wanted to know when the ISA came after me and how I escaped, so I told them about my day, beginning with the unfinished three-cheese hamburger and ending with the barn door that proved to be a mere curtain of dry rot.

Then I said, "When did you end up in their sights?"

"The day before yesterday," Sparky said from the back seat. "We had a nice little house on five acres of pine forest in Flagstaff."

Bridget said, "Deer used to come look in our windows. They were so sweet."

Sparky said, "They came so often, nearly every day. We gave them names. Comet and Cupid."

She said, "Donner and Blitzen."

He said, "We had squirrels that would eat out of your hand."

She said, "Samson and Delilah."

He said, "There was a fox so tame it would curl up in its own rocking chair on the porch, while we were rocking away in ours."

She said, "Cary Grant. That's what we called the fox, because he was so elegant. Movie stars aren't elegant like that anymore."

He said, "The cougar was a little scary at first."

She disagreed. "Oh, she never was, Sparky. She was always just a big pussycat." Bridget sighed. "The property outside Flagstaff was our little paradise."

"Then the day before yesterday," Sparky said, "Bridget and I were having breakfast when two black Suburbans pulled into our driveway, and eight men in black suits got out."

Bridget said, "It was like a chorus line from some musical about funeral directors."

"They knocked," Sparky said, "and I told them to go away. They said they were ISA agents, needed to talk to us, and I told them to go away again."

I glanced at the rearview mirror, in which Sparky was briefly revealed by the headlamps of a truck sweeping past in the westbound lane. The fleeting light seemed like a mask of a face that peeled up and away, revealing a half-formed shadowy countenance beneath.

I said, "Those people aren't used to being told to go away. Things must have gotten ugly."

"Not immediately," Sparky said. "We just put down the automated window shades, so they couldn't see into the house. They called our landline and told me they had a warrant. I said I wasn't impressed with warrants when their kind have so many corrupt judges in their pocket. They were a little miffed at that, so I said maybe I'd open up for them if I knew what this was about, and the guy on the phone said they had some questions related to what Bridget ordered on the internet, which was when I knew we were in the soup."

To Bridget, I said, "What did you order?"

"That's the payoff. First, tell him how it went, Grandpa."

As we cruised through a pass in the Hieroglyphic Mountains, the moon rose like a dot waiting for the stroke that would make it an exclamation point.

Sparky was silent for a long moment, and then he revealed that the Rainkings were not your typical family next door. "When I didn't let those bad boys in, they started shouting through a bullhorn. They were rude. They threatened to break down the door if we didn't disarm and come out. It would have been fun to watch them try. The front and back doors had a quarter-inch plate of steel sandwiched between layers of wood, and they were set in a steel frame with high and low deadbolts two inches long. So unless those fancy-dressed fascists could get a motorized battering ram, they were going to be a long time knocking it down. They might have been able to shoot out a window, but that would've taken a while, because the bulletproof glass would withstand everything but high-caliber armor-piercing rounds, not the kind of ammo in their sidearms. While they were jabbering their threats, Bridget and I went to the cellar, into the walk-in wine cooler, cycled open the secret door, and vamoosed into the escape tunnel."

I thought my amazement gland had been previously squeezed dry for at least a week, but I was wrong. "Wow. If the Dirty Harry Clean Now delivery van hadn't been in the alley behind the diner, I'd be locked up in a prison for the criminally unique. I got through on luck. But *you* had bulletproof glass, a secret door, and an escape tunnel. Are you survivalists or something?"

"No, no, no. Nothing silly like that," Bridget said. "We stay as real as a stick in the eye. But Grandpa has something of a past. Don't you, Grandpa?"

"Something of," he acknowledged. "Here and there, this and that. You know how it is."

"He was something, then something else, then another something that we don't talk about. Then when he was thirty-six, twenty-three years ago—I wouldn't be born for another five years—he became a contractor."

"I built things," Sparky clarified, perhaps so that I wouldn't think he was a contract killer.

"By the time I was four," Bridget said, "Grandpa realized we might need an escape tunnel. He had a construction company at the time, and he called on only his most trusted employees to work with him on our house without getting permits from the county."

"When we finished," Sparky said, "I gave the guys the company, so they had an incentive to keep their mouths shut."

"That's when he became Daphne Larkrise," Bridget said. "So he could work from home and always be with me in case something wicked happened, which now it has."

As I tried to track the history of Sparky Rainking, I became almost too dizzy to drive. "Daphne Larkrise. I've heard that name somewhere."

"Of course you have," Bridget said. "Everyone has. Daphne Larkrise is the most successful romance novelist of his time."

"Her time," Sparky corrected.

"Oops. Grandpa's old friend, Daphne Larkrise, is the face of Daphne Larkrise and does all the interviews and publicity stuff for twenty-five percent of the action, but Grandpa writes the books. He is a brilliant writer."

"I'm no John Grisham or Thomas Pynchon," Sparky said, "but I've always been an incurable romantic, even though it could have gotten me killed back in the day when I was something and then something else and then another something that we don't talk about."

I glanced at the rearview mirror. At the moment, there were no headlights from westbound traffic to flense the mask of shadow from his face. "Where does this escape tunnel of yours lead?"

"Under the backyard and two hundred feet into the woods," said Bridget, "to this fake boulder that's like a lid. Hydraulics flip it open, so we can exit."

"From there," Sparky said, "we went on foot about a half mile, down through the woods to the county road, another property I own under the name Aurora Teagarden."

"Ever since I was five," Bridget explained, "we've kept one nondescript car or another there, packed with everything we'd need if we had to go on the run."

I had maybe a hundred questions, maybe three hundred, but two big ones pried at me harder than the others. "So ever since Bridget was four and five, you've had a plan to escape. From whom?"

"We didn't know," Sparky said. "It was just obvious someone was going to come looking for her sooner or later. Turned out to be the ISA, but we've reason to believe there's others more dangerous than they are and a whole lot stranger."

"Why was it obvious?"

"Because she's special."

"Oh, I can see she's special, but *how* is she special?" I asked, thereby both revealing my enchantment and making a fool of myself.

"You'll see soon enough," Sparky said. "It's better you see it happen instead of me trying to describe it."

By now, I understood them well enough to know that if they were determined to be enigmatic, I would suffer a hernia trying to throw off their veil of mystery.

I proceeded to my second big question, which I addressed to Bridget. In the glow of the instrument-panel light, she was so radiant that I thought of the Roman deity Diana, goddess of the moon and hunting. I'd never met the goddess Diana, of course. I had only seen her depicted in art, sometimes running with a pack of wolves. If I were a wolf and Bridget were Diana, I would without question run with her under the moon. This time I managed to avoid steering the Buick off the pavement onto the graveled shoulder of the road as I said, "What did you do to get the ISA on your tail?"

"I suspect the same thing you did," she said.

"But I didn't do anything. They just walked into Beane's and interrupted my lunch. I think it's still legal to have a three-cheese hamburger, even one with mayonnaise."

From the back seat, Sparky said, "She spit in a cup."

Because she didn't seem like that kind of woman, I said with some skepticism, "You spit in a cup? Whose cup?"

"My cup. It had a little screw top. It came with the kit after I signed up on the internet."

She was right. I had spit in one, too. "I spit in one, too," I said, feeling connected to her by that ritual, hoping she would feel closer to me, feel a bond, even if it had to do with spit.

"You *spat* in one," she said. "My cup was from Getting to Know Me dot com."

"Mine, too!"

Getting to Know Me was a competitor of Ancestry.com and of 23andMe. They read your genome and told you all about yourself: where you came from, who was a relative and who wasn't, whether you had a tendency to develop a horrible disease, all kinds of useful stuff.

Bridget said, "I wanted to learn who my father might've been."

"I was abandoned as an infant," I reminded them. "I have no idea who *either* of my parents are. I was raised by nuns in an orphanage. But why should the ISA come down hard on us for wanting to know our ancestry? We have a right to know. What business is it of the government if we want to know?"

"Did you get your genome report?" Sparky asked.

"No. Not yet."

"Neither did I," Bridget said. "But the company sent it to the ISA. Those two suits you killed at the ranch—they explained the situation to us. I'm sure you were targeted for the same reason."

"What reason?"

When she turned those sea-green eyes on me, the instrument-panel light tinted them a color that I couldn't name. She said, "Several sequences in my genome are not human."

She looked like the best example of a human I had ever seen. Confused, potentially more disappointed than frightened, I said, "You're not human?"

"I'm human, yeah, but I'm something else, too, something more."

"More what?"

"That's what the ISA wants to know about me *and* about you. You're like me."

"I'm pretty sure I'm human."

From the deep shadows of the back seat, Sparky said, "You're human, son, but like Bridget you're also something more. And maybe just a little slow on the uptake."

Bridget said, "In your own way, you're as different as I am, Quinn Quicksilver. You have your magnetism. I have . . . what I have."

"Keep your speed up," Sparky advised. "We don't want to be tail-ended."

I had allowed the Buick to slow to under thirty miles an hour. I accelerated, even though I felt that I was speeding toward a cliff with a void beyond.

A creepy possibility occurred to me. "Are we like in that movie, *Village of the Damned*? Were we fathered by aliens, something from another world?"

"Maybe," she said. "Or maybe something else. Turns you inside out a little, doesn't it?"

Leaning forward, gripping the backrest of the front seat to steady himself, thrusting his head between me and his granddaughter, Sparky Rainking said, "How do you propose to research your origins in Peptoe?"

"There are these three men. Nineteen years ago, they found me in a bassinet in the middle of a lonely highway. My name and date of birth were written on a card. I was three days old. When this magnetism thing started, I thought just maybe those guys might have seen something—might know something, suspect something—that they never told the county sheriff when they took me to him."

"Do you feel pulled to Peptoe, or is it just a place to go?"

"I don't feel drawn, no. But what else do I have?"

"Then let's do it," Sparky said.

"Let's do it," Bridget agreed.

We drove to the town of Carefree, then south toward Scottsdale, and the moon that had been ahead of us now kept pace on our port side. If the night harbored wolves that raced in time with our car, they were likely to be the human rather than the lupine kind, not in the thrall of my passenger goddess, but in pursuit of her.

# 8

Whether part alien or part something else, I was suddenly all appetite. My lunch had been interrupted by an attempted abduction, and thereafter I had been too busy escaping, succumbing to strange magnetism, and running people down with my Toyota to have time for even a small snack. In spite of all the weirdness associated with Sparky and Bridget, they were good company, even when they were silent, as they were for a while as we followed a serpentine route through Scottsdale and then through Tempe, where the unfortunately named Hohokam people ruled so long ago that not even the wisest and most farsighted among those ancestors had foreseen the rainbow's end that would be Indian casinos. Like me, my companions were probably wondering if our lives would ever be normal again. We already knew the answer—which was *no*—so we might as well stop our pointless brooding and eat. As it turned out, they hadn't been yearning for normality, but for dinner, so we were simpatico.

If we drove straight through to Peptoe, we wouldn't get there until about ten o'clock in the evening, too late to seek out Hakeem Kaspar, Bailie Belshazzer, and Caesar Melchizadek. Instead, we swung onto Interstate 10 and followed it only a short way, past Chandler, to an exit for one of those truck stops that is a town unto itself, offering showers, haircuts, massages, an on-call minister, a crew of superb mechanics, and other services in addition to an archipelago of fueling islands where eighteen-wheelers schooled like whales, simple but clean motel rooms, a gift shop, and a restaurant.

The restaurant was large but as cozy as a diner, with booth banquettes and chairs upholstered in red vinyl. Lots of chrome. A long counter with swiveling stools. Large four-page menus in plastic binders. Country music piped in neither too loud nor too soft. The waitresses could balance an array of plates along an arm from hand to shoulder, navigate a crowded room without dropping an order, and almost seemed to be part of a floor show.

After the hostess seated us in a booth—Bridget and Sparky on one banquette, me on the other—Bridget went to the ladies' room, and I was alone with her grandfather.

Putting down the tabloid-size menu, he said, "Nuns, huh?"

"Yes, sir. An order of Poor Clares."

"Why weren't you adopted out?"

"They couldn't find anyone who wanted me."

"Were you an ugly, fussy baby?"

"I'm told I was cute and happy."

"Maybe the nuns didn't try hard enough."

"I came with twelve years of free tuition at the Catholic school of your choice, free diapers, and a plenary indulgence."

"Maybe if they'd thrown in a new car."

"One of their most generous supporters owned a Ford dealership, but after he took a look at me, he said a car wouldn't be enough."

"Did all this rejection traumatize you?"

"Not at all. I was an infant. I didn't know it was happening. I was busy learning how to suck my thumb."

He leaned over the table, drilling me with that sharp gray stare. "Are you well balanced, Quinn? Are you psychologically and emotionally stable?"

"I like to think I am, sir. Except for this recent magnetism business."

He studied me in silence for maybe ten seconds. "It's damn important to me that you're psychologically and emotionally stable."

"I understand," I assured him. "This strange situation we're in, the ISA on our tails, you need to know you can rely on me in a crisis."

He dismissed that idea with a wave of his hand. "No, that's not it. I need to know you're fit to marry Bridget."

I gaped at him. Some country singer was crooning about killing the man who killed his hound dog, which almost seemed more romantic than how Sparky had broached the subject of marriage.

When I couldn't think of a reply, he said, "What's wrong?"

I swallowed twice and then said, "I'm nonplussed."

"That's a word I'd never use in a romance novel. Too fancy. You shouldn't use it in a magazine article, either. Just say perplexed or bewildered, even confused, but never nonplussed. Do you already have a girlfriend?"

"No. I don't."

"Do you like girls?"

"Well, of course. Everyone I dated was a girl. It's just that most girls these days—most guys, too—they're about social media and what they saw on YouTube and what the influencers say about everything. I just don't have much in common with most of them."

"You and Bridget have a lot in common. Wanted by government thugs, on the run, maybe alien DNA. Don't you like her?"

"Of course I like her. What's not to like? I love her attitude. And she's funny, witty."

"That's it? Funny, witty, attitude?"

"I'm talking to her *grandfather*."

"You're blushing," he said. "That's sweet."

"Okay, all right, she's a goddess. She's so dazzling that I could maybe go blind looking at her."

He smiled broadly. "That's better. That's more like it."

"But we've hardly just met, and I don't think she likes me."

"Of course she likes you. She's been waiting two years for you to show up."

"What're you talking about?"

"She knew you'd have blue eyes and that you'd save her life with a car somehow, although she thought you'd be a lot taller and driving a Porsche rather than a Toyota."

"I'm not short," I said. "I'm five eleven."

"Don't fret about it," Sparky said. "She's five six, so you're plenty tall enough."

Bridget returned from the ladies' room, and a waitress arrived to take our drink order—coffee, coffee, cherry Coke—and Sparky went off to the men's room.

"You're blushing," Bridget said.

"No," I lied, "it's just warm in here."

The monsters wouldn't show up for twenty minutes—I didn't even know there would *be* monsters—so I had plenty of time to be further nonplussed before my confusion gave way to terror.

She said, "I should have apologized to you back at the Flying F Ranch. I'm sorry I called you a freakin' Nazi zombie."

"I've been called much worse," I assured her, which was true. Those public-school kids who lost the spelling bees had been a foul-mouthed bunch.

"I was still coming out of the chloroform they used on me, confused and sick with worry about Grandpa. I shouldn't have called you a worthless piece of garbage, either, and I'm sorry I punched you in the chest."

"You have a solid punch."

"Did I hurt you?"

"No, no," I lied. "But you have a very solid punch."

"Grandpa hung a punching bag from the cellar ceiling and taught me how to go for a guy's ribs. He sparred with me, too. When I was fourteen, he stopped pulling his punches. He's a great teacher."

I was afraid that at any moment she would mention marriage and that I would again be rendered speechless. So I said, "Why did you hide out in a place like that ranch? You're from Flagstaff. How did you even know about the Sweetwater Flying F?"

"It was once a beautiful resort and also a working ranch, not just a dude ranch, so you could have any level of experience you wanted. That's where Sparky and Jeanette spent their honeymoon, roping and branding calves, breaking wild mustangs. It was also a rattlesnake farm. Grandpa and Grandma milked venom from the snakes so it could be sent away to make antivenin. Isn't that a marvelous, *different* kind of honeymoon?"

"Romantic enough for a Daphne Larkrise novel," I said.

"Grandma Jeanette must have been something. I never knew her. She died a year before I was born. Grandpa has been a wonderful substitute father, but it would have been nice to have a substitute mother as well. My real mother, Corrine, didn't want me."

I couldn't have stopped looking at her even if something in the kitchen had exploded and a fire alarm had gone off. "Who wouldn't want you? Anybody would want you." I heard myself and hurried to clarify. "I mean, why on earth wouldn't she want you?"

"Sparky and Jeanette couldn't have children, so they adopted Corrine when she was four. Apparently Corrine's mother either drank a lot or did drugs during her pregnancy, so Corrine was never right. She was a problem as a child, more of a problem as an adult. Very pretty. I have photos of her. But a week after I was born, she gave me to Sparky, and she split. He never saw her again. He reported her missing, but the authorities couldn't find a trace of her. Neither could any of the three private detectives that Grandpa hired to chase her down during the first two years after she left. It was like she walked out of this world into another."

When you were raised in an orphanage, the other kids weren't all abandoned on a highway when they were three days old. Some ended up at Mater Misericordiæ after they were old enough to have known the parents they lost—or the parents who abused them or otherwise failed them. Some hid their pain. Others could not. We were an extended family, and largely a happy one because the Poor Clares loved us and because we cared about one another, but we were aware that our happiness was a ship sailing on waters dark with sorrow.

I said, "To know your mother's name, to have seen her face even if just in photographs—that makes it a lot worse than if she'd been unknown, a total mystery. I'm sorry, Bridget. That's a terrible burden to bear."

She shrugged. "Well, it's not like I loved her and lost her. I never knew her."

I had often used a similar line. It was a defense against the resurrection of sharp emotions.

Unfolding her napkin and smoothing it on her lap, Bridget said, "But I think Grandpa was torn up by it. In spite of all the trouble Corrine had been, he loved her. And he'd lost Jeanette to cancer not long before all this."

"He was so lucky to have you," I said. "Having you would have made all the difference, such a blessing." I heard myself again and said, "I mean, a widower with a thankless daughter—he needed someone to give him a sense of purpose."

At that point, Sparky returned from the men's room, and the waitress, Darlene, brought our drinks. She was a zaftig, fortyish brunette with maybe three pounds of hair swirled up in a fabulous creation and pinned atop her head. Darlene had the silken, smoky voice of a chanteuse, the physical presence of an opera diva, and the confidence of a matador. She called Sparky "Mr. Man," called me "Choirboy"—I don't know why—and renamed Bridget "Angel," which I entirely understood. Darlene warned us away from the chicken soup. She recommended the pulled-pork sliders with coleslaw and fried onions, which came with French fries, and she took our orders.

After Darlene departed with the promise to be back in ten, Sparky said, "So have you kids been hitting it off?"

I said, "I'm sorry about Jeanette and Corrine."

"Well," he said, "you can either do the wrong thing and let a loss like that destroy you, or you can do the right thing and be properly grateful for all that came before the loss. Grief should drive you to your knees, but if you stay there forever, you're saying you know better than God how the world should work. And you don't." He looked at Bridget. "So he's five feet eleven. Is that okay with you?"

She put a hand on his shoulder and squeezed affectionately. "He's just right, Grandpa. Actually, I worried that he might be as tall as a basketball star, and people would stare at us everywhere we went." She smiled at me. "I take it that Grandpa told you I've been expecting you for two years."

Her eyes were the warm green of Caribbean waters, and I felt myself floating away on her gaze. "Uh, so then, you know, um, what if the guy in this vision of yours, what if he wasn't me?"

"It wasn't a vision. A presentiment. And he's you. I'm sure. How could he not be you, considering how we met and what we are?"

"But we don't know what we are."

"Precisely." She frowned. "I'm certain you're him and this is meant to be, but maybe you're not sure."

Sparky didn't give me a chance to fumble the moment. "Quinn is sure. It's just that he hasn't had much luck with girls, so he lacks confidence when it comes to romance. Daphne Larkrise knows his type. He's rather like Kenny Talbot in *Love Insurance*."

"I adored that character," Bridget said.

"He's shy like Kenny," Sparky said, "unsure of himself, perhaps too humble for his own good, but he's got great potential."

I said, "You know, I'm *right here*."

"Oh, yes, absolutely," Bridget said. "That's what I like so much about you. You're always *right here*, in the moment, never lost in yourself and off somewhere. That's a rare quality these days. We just met this morning, but I feel like I met you two years ago."

Sparky recognized the moment when I began to adapt to the high weirdness of our situation, when my perplexity began to mellow into a kind of delightful amazement. He shifted from being a cheerleader for romance to being a substitute father with the usual concerns. His brow corrugated. His gray gaze grew flinty. "You realize, Quinn, that there can be no marriage until we understand this wild river we're in, run whatever rapids must be run, and reach calm water."

I shaped my face into that of a responsible suitor with only chivalrous intentions, which in fact was the truth. "Of course."

"And until there is a wedding, there will be no hanky-panky."

Bridget appeared to be amused. But she also sounded as sincere as a stick in the eye when she said, "None. As Daphne Larkrise has written, 'Delayed gratification leads to greater satisfaction.'"

"Quinn?" Sparky said.

"Yeah. Yes. I feel the same." When he continued to skewer me with his stare, I said, "Remember, I was raised by nuns."

"Oh, I remember. Just so you don't forget."

I said, "It's not a thing you forget if you don't want to spend a week peeling potatoes."

That was when the monsters arrived.

| 9 |

I didn't immediately realize they were monsters. They appeared to be about twenty years old, clean-cut Ivy League college boys, the kind who had gone to the best private schools since they were two and learned to read by paging through *GQ* magazine. The blond wore Converse sneakers, black jeans, a black polo shirt, and a pale-gray summer-weight knee-length topcoat. His companion wore bright-yellow sneakers, a gray suit, a white-and-yellow T-shirt; he carried a red-and-black-checkered tote bag.

The hostess tried to seat them near us, but they wanted a booth at the very back of the room, though that meant sitting near the two swinging doors to the kitchen. They didn't appear to be accustomed to sitting near the kitchen, but they insisted on it.

Bridget said softly, "Screamer alert, Grandpa."

"Quinn," Sparky whispered, "don't stare at them. They're major bad news."

As the two glided through the restaurant, they surveyed the customers with what seemed to be amused contempt. I had sometimes wondered what it must be like to be their type, to be so self-assured in all circumstances, so certain of being superior. My imagination was not up to the task.

"We never know what their kind are looking for. We're afraid it might be Bridget."

I looked away from the duo as they followed the hostess in our direction.

Bridget reached across the table. "Give me your hand."

Holding her hand was preferable to taking a punch from her.

She raised her voice and put a little gush in it. "Darling, the Arizona Biltmore is the perfect place for the reception. Yes, it's expensive, but if Grandfather insists on paying for it—"

"I do," Sparky said. "I insist. My only grandchild is marrying the son of my best friend on my own wedding anniversary. What could be more romantic? It makes me feel young and in love again. There's no price too high for that feeling."

From the corner of my eye, I saw the college boys slow as they passed our booth, perhaps giving us a close inspection. "Sweetums, I want whatever you want," I declared. I turned my smile on Sparky. "Sir, I'm knocked out by your generosity. Really knocked out. Just totally knocked out."

The stylish pair moved away from us. I dared to look up— and saw the right hand of the one carrying the tote. His hand was no longer a human hand. The six fingers lacked knuckles and resembled tentacles, gray and sinuous. Wickedly sharp talons gleamed for an instant, but then were gone, retracted as if they did not exist. The hand appeared to be highly articulated and yet amorphous, as if by an act of will the creature could remake that instrument from a tool into a lethal weapon.

As I squeezed Bridget's hand, she gripped mine tighter and said, "You see?"

"Yes." I looked after the retreating pair.

These beasts were like menacing presences from those disturbing dreams that have their origins in generations long before our own, those dreams that boil up from the primordiality of our creation. They moved through the restaurant and settled into the booth near the entrance to the kitchen. They lacked anything that could be called a face. *Screamer alert,* Bridget had told her grandfather. I understood why she would call them Screamers. These things seemed to be perpetually straining to scream, although no sound escaped them. Where a face should have been, there were no apparent eyes or ears or nose, but only a pale-lipped mouth fixed open wide, as circular as a drain, like the mouth of a hookworm. At a distance, I couldn't be sure, but I thought that a repulsive organ slithered continuously within those disgusting orifices, as though they were greedy for sustenance.

As the well-dressed pair perused their menus, their double identities faded back and forth from human to fiend to human, as if in sympathy with the slow pulse of an alien heart. The expressions that occupied their human faces now conveyed the arrogance of those who considered humanity to be the dispossessed, who sneered at our corrupted nature, though our wickedness was a risible and pathetic reflection of their own much darker desires and impulses. The longer I watched these beasts, the more palpable their evil became. For all their strangeness, the Screamers grew more familiar by the minute, as if I'd known their kind all my life, in fact had known them even before I was born. This eerie familiarity chilled me to the marrow.

My understanding of the true nature of the world was undergoing a seismic shift. Or was I merely shedding adult illusions for the fantastic truth that every child knows? In spite of one bizarre turn of events after another, in spite of all my rushing around and my reckless surrender to the pull of mysterious forces, I sensed that I wasn't falling away into a new reality. Instead, I felt as though I might be coming home to the world I knew a long time ago, where the monsters lurking in the closet weren't always imaginary, where a desperate but secret war was being waged by two armies in disguise, where victory had nothing to do with conquering territory, where the battlefield was the human heart, the spoils of war the human soul.

When Bridget withdrew her hand from mine, I thought I would see the college boys only as they had first appeared to me, but instead the monstrous faceless "faces" continued to come and go. I don't know if Bridget, by her touch, passed to me the power to see through their masquerade or whether my gift had evolved without her aid.

In any case, when I looked at Sparky, he said, "Whatever you two are, I'm not. I can't see them as they really are, but I always believed her when she told me about them."

A thin sweat greased the nape of my neck. "What in God's name are those things?"

Bridget said, "I don't know. I didn't see the first one until two years ago. I've seen quite a few since. There was a really hairy incident with one of them a few months ago."

"What incident?"

Instead of explaining, she said, "Maybe they're from another world, another dimension, another time. Whatever they are, my sense is they're nothing new, that they've been among us for a long time."

If the events of the day had been profoundly disturbing, they had also inspired in me a pleasing sense of adventure, a tentative longing for a life flavored with more excitement than that enjoyed by a magazine writer who'd spent most of his years in an orphanage. Suddenly, excitement struck me as being the pursuit of fools, and *adventure* seemed to have become a synonym for *suicide*.

Darlene arrived with our plates balanced on her left arm, from hand to shoulder. With her right hand, she dealt the three orders of pork sliders onto the table, spilling not one drop of sauce or a single French fry. "Enjoy yourselves, children. I'll be right back to refill your drinks."

I thought the repellent pair of masqueraders must have killed my appetite. But even condemned men on death row eat a hearty dinner before the lethal injection, in denial of their mortality. It is human nature to know we die and still to disbelieve it; otherwise, we might not carry on. When the aroma rising from the sliders made my mouth water, I picked up the first of the two small sandwiches and finished it by the time Darlene returned with a Pyrex coffeepot in one hand and a fresh cherry Coke in the other. I ordered a second plate of sliders, and so did my companions.

Darlene beamed at us. "I like folks who know what eatin' is all about. Some come in here, they don't want dressin' on their salad, don't want butter on their baked potato. They want a plant-burger. They should just save themselves some money, go on out in a field, and graze."

"We haven't eaten here in a while," Bridget said. "Is José still the head chef? I think it was José or Juan or maybe just Joe."

"There was a José back when. He was good. But now it's one of us—Paloma—and she's even better than he was. Don't you think?"

"A woman cooking at a truck stop!" Bridget clapped her hands with delight.

Darlene said, "There was a time I never thought I'd see it, what with the good-old-boy management you get in this business."

I couldn't understand why Bridget cared a whit who the chef was when *there were monsters in the room.*

When Darlene left us to our meal, I said, "Screamers, huh?"

"It isn't just the open maw," Bridget said. "First time I saw one, I thought of that painting, *The Scream.* These creatures terrify me, but I also think there's something despairing about them. If a scream ever came out of one, it would be a howl of hatred but also of blackest insanity, like an entire asylum full of mad voices all shrieking at once."

In the spirit of a man slated for execution immediately after dessert, I found myself licking the sauce off my fingers, craving every iota of pleasure available to me, assuming that pleasure can be measured in iotas. "What do they want? What're they doing?"

"We don't know," Sparky said. "Maybe we'd rather not know, but we think it's inevitable that we'll find out. Unless one of them realizes Bridget and you can see the truth of them."

I stopped licking my fingers. "Is that possible?"

"Why couldn't it be?"

"And then?"

"Nothing good. Which is why we have to play ignorant."

I thought about that. I didn't like thinking about it. I almost lost my appetite, after all.

"By the way," I said, "you two were great with all that wedding reception patter. I wish I could be that smooth. I'm sorry I said 'knocked out' three times. Once would have been better."

Bridget said, "You did fine, Quinn. But just never again call me 'sweetums.'"

"I couldn't believe I heard myself say it." We ate in silence for a minute or two, and then I remembered. "You said there was an incident with one of them. What incident?"

Bridget put down what remained of her second slider and wiped her fingers on her napkin, like an adult. Evidently, she'd seen enough Screamers that the sight of two more didn't reduce her to the morbid conviction that she'd soon be torn apart and swallowed by a large walking worm with wicked hands. I expected her to reveal the details of the aforementioned incident. Instead, the napkin fell out of her hands, and she went as still as if she'd been flash frozen, and her gaze fixed on something as distant as a moon of Saturn.

Although Sparky didn't put down his slider, he lowered it from his mouth without taking another bite. He said, "Uh-oh."

I didn't ask, *Uh-oh what?* My brain had already downloaded too many weird and scary events for one day. Yeah, I had more storage capacity, but I wasn't going to *solicit* additional freaky data.

After maybe twenty seconds, Bridget unfroze. Her expression remained grim, but her stare shifted several million miles to her grandfather. "They're going to kill a lot of people."

I didn't ask, but Sparky seemed to think I had, so he said, "She means the Screamers."

"They're heavily armed," she said. "They're waiting. As the dinner hour peaks and the restaurant gets full, they're going to open fire. It'll be a massacre."

We lived in a strange, dark time. Massacres were growing more common, and not all of them involved guns. Sometimes the weapon of choice was a bomb, sometimes Molotov cocktails thrown into a crowded church or synagogue. Now and then an airplane was flown into a building or a train of tanker cars was intentionally derailed and several square blocks of a town were set afire by the spilled petroleum. More often than not the perpetrators claimed a just and noble cause. Throughout history, whole societies that seemed stable have imploded when self-righteous narcissists, enflamed by insane ideologies, so threatened the larger population of the sane that soon everyone feared to stand against the violence, whereupon madness accelerated. No one seemed to remember the lessons of history—or cared to learn them. Perhaps we would persevere through this current darkness. But the very fact of it argued for a second order of pulled-pork sliders—which Darlene now brought to table—and, if time permitted, the richest dessert on the menu, just in case it would be our last.

Bridget picked up her second slider, which she had left half-finished, and she polished it off.

I said, "What—you had a vision?"

"I don't have visions. It was a presentiment. A feeling, an impression. But pretty specific." She pushed the empty plate aside and slid one of the fresh orders in front of herself. "We've got time to enjoy these, but we'll have to split before we can tackle the banana cream pie."

As Sparky tucked into his food again, I said, "But."

"Yes, dear?" Bridget said.

"But shouldn't we call the police?"

"That won't do any good," she said. "They'll think it's a crank call. And the minute they show up, the Screamers will open fire."

"Then shouldn't we warn these people?"

Sparky said, "Same situation, son. We'd only be precipitating the massacre. The moment we shout a warning, the Screamers will start blasting away."

"But."

"What is it, dear?" Bridget asked, though her mouth was full.

"We can't just walk out and let people die."

"Of course we can't," said Sparky.

"Then what are we going to do?" I asked.

"Kill the Screamers," Bridget said.

"They can be killed?"

"Of course they can," she said. "We've done it before."

"The incident," I surmised.

"There you go," Sparky said.

# 10

There is a famous story of demons being cast out of men and into a herd of swine that thereupon ran into the sea and drowned. Bridget, Sparky, and I had neither the power nor the pigs, nor a nearby sea, that would allow us to deal in that fashion with the demons that came to dine in the truck stop. Envisioning the combat to come, I foresaw myself bullet-riddled, slipping across a floor littered with a variety of fried foods, taking a pratfall into several spilled orders of banana cream pie.

I do not find any death to be a laughing matter. However, I expect that in the aftermath of my own demise, I'll probably find the circumstances of my murder—I am convinced it will be a grisly homicide—to one degree or another absurd and probably amusing. After all, the human pageant is both tragic and comic. Those who are unable to perceive the humor of it also do not grasp the true horror of it; therefore, they fail to understand life or where it's taking them. Maybe that's a blessing, but I don't think so. They say that ignorance is bliss. I think ignorance is the mother of extreme behavior, ensuring either a colorless and tedious life or one of passionate commitment to foolishness of one kind or another.

So each of us ate two more small pulled-pork sliders, wishing they were larger. With two mass-murdering Screamers waiting for the restaurant to get busy enough to provide a large number of victims, we ate in silence. We didn't have time to finish our dinner *and* discuss the state of modern interpretive dance, or whatever we might have discussed in less fraught circumstances.

Bridget wiped her hands on her napkin, neatly folded it, put it beside her plate, and said, "Logically, we'd leave the restaurant by heading away from the kitchen. When we start toward the back, those two wormheads might be suspicious."

"Then you *do* think they know some like us can see them?"

"Maybe," Sparky said. "But if so, it seems like they aren't able to detect who those seers are."

"However," Bridget said, "they're highly suspicious by nature. Look at one of them with revulsion, and you're liable to trigger a violent reaction quicker than if you started to sing the national anthem at a college faculty luncheon. So we have to put on a little performance. You know what I have in mind, Grandpa?"

"Paloma," Sparky said.

"Since we won't be stopping at the cashier, leave plenty of money for the full check plus tip. We don't want to stiff Darlene. We're already going to screw up her evening."

"What performance?" I asked. "What am I supposed to do?"

"You just trail close behind us," Sparky said, as he counted bills out of his wallet. "And don't say anything, especially not 'sweetums.'"

"We'll wait till a hostess escorts customers to a table toward the back. Get ready to move quickly, so the timing will work," Bridget said.

Bridget and Sparky seemed eerily calm, while I was hoping to get out of this with clean shorts. "The place is filling up. There aren't many empty tables left."

Picking up her large purse and zippering it open, Bridget said, "We've still got a little time."

"You're sure?"

"If I wasn't sure, I'd be shrieking like a little girl and running for the exit."

I warned her: "I'm maybe a minute from doing that."

A minute passed, and I didn't make a spectacle of myself.

When a hostess appeared, moving among the tables in the center of the room rather than along the booths, trailed by a young couple, Bridget slung the straps of her purse over her right shoulder and moved to the edge of the banquette. "Wait . . . wait . . . *now.*"

She slid out of the booth. Sparky followed her, and I followed him. I told myself that if I wasn't eaten by coyotes while lying in a bassinet, I was meant to survive for a purpose more important than having a meal of pulled-pork sliders in an Arizona truck stop before being shot down by wormheads.

Calculating a trajectory with exquisite precision, Bridget angled off among the tables, as if she had no intent other than intercepting the hostess. Only the most suspicious Screamers would notice that at the same time she was drawing closer to them, with her right hand in her open purse.

"Excuse me, please," she said, waving her left hand, speaking a little louder than necessary. "Is Paloma in the kitchen tonight?" The hostess meant to come to a stop to respond, but Bridget took her by the arm and moved her along with such aplomb that it seemed quite natural. "No, no. I don't mean to delay you. I'm Paloma's friend. May I pop in the kitchen for a sec, tell her what a *fabulous* job she's doing?" Although the hostess said the kitchen wasn't open to the public, Bridget pretended to misunderstand, responding loud enough for her targets to hear. "Oh, that's *so sweet*. Paloma is a *treasure*. I'll only be half a sec."

As they reached the empty table toward which they had been headed, Bridget let go of the hostess and covered the last few steps to the booth beside the kitchen entrance. Sparky had been following her, but as she closed in on the Screamers, he quickly moved up to her side, drawing the pistol from under his coat as she drew hers from her handbag. One of the college boys slash monsters reached into the checkered tote on the banquette beside him and withdrew a pistol with an extended magazine that held maybe twenty rounds, and the other began to pull aside a panel of his topcoat to draw a weapon, but they were too late.

The point-blank fusillade that Bridget and Sparky unloaded on the pair caused a sensation in the restaurant. Dishes and flatware rang off the floor, toppled chairs clattered, shrill cries erupted as people dived for cover or fled toward the nearest exit. Such is the temper of our strange times that the reaction was instantaneous and universal, as though everyone present had been anticipating such a moment for years.

Leaving two dead something-or-others in the booth, Bridget and her grandfather moved directly to the adjacent swinging doors and disappeared into the kitchen.

As I passed the bloody booth, those bizarre creatures no longer fluctuated between being college boys and wormheads. Somehow, in death, their bodies locked into the human mode, which would be most inconvenient if we were ever required to stand trial for executing them. I might have doubted that I'd ever seen those monsters, but the guns they possessed and the ten or twelve spare magazines that had spilled out of the overturned tote established their intentions and thereby also seemed to confirm that the horrific creatures that Bridget and I had seen were no illusion.

I hurried through the swinging doors and saw my companions rushing toward the back of the enormous kitchen. The staff regarded us wide-eyed, less fearful than perplexed. The culinary cacophony in the kitchen had partly masked the gunfire. The busy workers appeared in fact to be in a state of such utter perplexity at our frantic intrusion that you might say they were nonplussed, even if you could expect to be criticized for using that word.

We found our way into the night and sprinted along the back of the enormous building, which covered a few acres. I suppose Bridget must have been as radiant as ever, no less so than the Roman goddess Diana. She was certainly lithe and swift, considering the volume of pulled pork that she'd eaten. But running with her under the moon in the aftermath of a hunt was far less romantic than I had imagined and not at all mystical.

I thought we'd never make it around the building to the parking lot without pursuit, would never make it to the Buick without being apprehended by truck-stop security. I was wrong. Sparky took the keys from me and said he would drive, and Bridget meant to ride up front. I plunged into the back seat and pulled the door shut and lay gasping for breath, at first staying below the windows lest more Screamers were in the vicinity and would open fire on us.

# BACK IN THE DAY

## THE BOY, THE FATHER, THE ANTS

My best friend at the orphanage was Litton Ormond, though only the nuns and I knew that was his real name, and even I didn't know it until he had been my roommate for almost a year. He lived with us under the name Peter Claver, which the sisters selected for reasons more clear to them than to me; Peter Claver was the saint who fed—and pressed hard for the freedom of—the African slaves in Colombia in the early 1600s. Litton, a.k.a. Peter, was nine when he came to Mater Misericordiæ, a year older than me, and for the next three years, he looked out for me as if he were my older brother. He wasn't strong or tough, but he was steadfast and brave.

When he finally shared his story with me, late one night when neither of us could sleep, I was in awe of him because of how he had coped with a horror that I could not imagine being able to endure. And I knew it was all true, because it had been a media sensation the previous year.

Corbett Ormond, Litton's father, was a wife beater. In May of the year that Litton turned eight, his mother, Roxanne, left his father, filed for divorce, and moved in with her parents, Mark and Laura Rollins.

Although Corbett never contested the divorce, made no threats against his wife, even granted her sole custody of their son as if the issue meant nothing to him, he was furious. Hot-tempered and vengeful, he was also patient and cunning. For six months he had no contact with his ex-wife or his son, so that they came to feel safe. On Thanksgiving Day, when Roxanne and her brother and her sister and their children gathered at the Rollins' home for the annual feast, Corbett came calling. He shot and killed seven adults and four children, sparing only Litton.

Instead of taking the boy with him, he forced him to stand at the center of the slaughter and said, "This happened because of you, Litton. When you chose her over me, you killed them all. Now live with it, boy." We know this because Corbett left a video—an angry, rambling statement so chilling that the news media reached a new level of depravity in the exploitation of what they insisted on referring to as his "manifesto," which wasn't a manifesto by any definition, but only an insane rant.

Litton called the police.

Because Corbett remained a fugitive and inspired fear, Child Welfare found it impossible to place Litton in any foster family longer than a few weeks. For months he was cycled from home to home, until he came to the orphanage, hidden under a new name.

He told me his story just that one time. By mutual unspoken agreement, we never returned to the subject. I remember how he sounded in the telling: his voice colored neither by fear nor by grief, neither by anger nor bitterness, but hushed and reverent, much like the subdued and chastened tone the sisters took when speaking of the mysteries of the Passion or the rosary.

I often puzzled over why he trusted only me of all the kids at the orphanage. Considering where my life has taken me since then, I wonder if he intuited that I was destined to deal violently with those violent souls who would bear away all our peace and hope.

Some nights he cried in his sleep. When awake, he never wept over his losses or about what he had seen. However, his dreams wrung tears from him, as well as pitiable sounds of fear and grief.

Before he became my roommate, I had a night-light, for I used to think that something sought me as I slept, but that it could harm me only in the dark. By that dim glow, I often moved a chair beside Litton's bed when he suffered his worst dreams and watched over him. I found that if I spoke to him in the softest of whispers, I could reach him without waking him, and gentle him out of a nightmare into peaceful sleep.

Meanwhile, Corbett Ormond had shaved his head and grown a beard and gone off the grid, living under another name, dealing drugs. He made a new life *for* himself but couldn't make a new man *of* himself. He didn't use the drugs he sold, for the only drugs that got him high were anger and resentment. The police never learned how Corbett discovered where his son had been given refuge.

Mater Misericordiæ stood at one end of the block, Bellini's Italian Specialties at the other end. We children received modest allowances and were permitted to buy candy, cookies, or other treats at Bellini's, as long as one of the sisters accompanied us.

On the day that it happened, Sister Margaret took four kids to Bellini's. I am grateful I wasn't one of them, but Litton was among the four. Later we assumed Corbett had been running surveillance of the orphanage, because he followed them into the store.

As the kids were at the checkout counter with small bags of their favorite cookies, Corbett approached and asked, "Who did the bitch, your mother, sleep with behind my back?" As twelve-year-old Litton turned toward his father, Corbett said, "You don't look anything like me," and shot the boy dead.

Corbett turned the gun on Sister Margaret, a freckled redhead as sweet as she was shy, young and devout and quiet, as helpless in those circumstances as a lame kitten in the path of a high-speed train. Michael Bellini, son of the owner, was behind the counter, where they kept a gun to defend against robbery. He was quicker with his first shot than Corbett was with his second; he put an end to the murderer before Sister Margaret could become yet another victim.

A profound spiritual darkness settled on Mater Misericordiæ, and everyone within its walls was traumatized. Hearts and minds heal with time, which is a grace of the human condition. Mine healed more slowly than others, and in fact for the first time I, the happiest of children, slipped into depression. I could not understand why such evil could befall a gentle boy like Litton, why the world was shapen to allow it. I was despondent, beyond the present exercise of hope, sad and distressed.

Sister Theresa, who'd earned a doctorate in psychology and who counseled many children and adults through times of crisis, was not able to reach me with the tools of psychology or the tenets of her theology. Although unfailingly patient, she was often frustrated with me. Her beautiful mahogany skin, so in contrast with her white habit, mostly hid a flush of annoyance, but I still saw it.

After a few weeks, when I came to her office at the appointed time, I found that she had acquired an ant colony: a two-foot-tall, four-foot-long box with glass walls through which we could watch the tiny residents conduct their affairs. She also had a DVD documentary about ants as well as several books about them.

"We're going to study ants for the next week, nothing but ants, hours and hours every day. You and me together, but also you alone."

"Why?" I asked.

"That is for you to figure out, Quinn. You're a smart boy, more learned than most eleven-year-old boys. I'm confident that you'll have an aha moment sooner than later."

"They're just ants," I said with a note of indifference.

"And to an ant, you're just a foot."

I frowned. "A foot?"

"That's all they see of you, if they see even that when you step on them. But there's more to you than a foot, isn't there?"

We studied several varieties of the family Formicidae: the architecture and organization of their colonies, the classes into which they are divided, the tasks each class is given. The winged queen. The wingless female workers. The male drones that exist only to breed and die. Those that cultivate food sources. The warriors.

Perhaps beginning with ants, I came to realize that everything in the world, regardless of how humble it might seem to be, is more complex and fascinating than it at first appears.

Yet nothing I had learned about ants could cure my depression. When I wasn't studying bugs, I was doing little else than sleeping the sleep of despondency, twelve and more hours each day.

When Sister Theresa deemed that we'd studied ants to the point of diminishing returns, she asked me if I would want to be an ant.

"No," I said.

"Why not?"

"They don't do anything but work."

"That's the sum of it?" she asked. "You don't want to be an ant because they work too much?"

"Yeah. And I'd always be scared some kid would step on me."

Sister Theresa sighed. "All right, then. You're a hard nut, Quinn Quicksilver, but we'll crack you. Next we'll study birds."

**PART 2**
**DIRTY MONEY, ATTACK DOGS AND SPURTLES**

## 11

Remaining strictly under the speed limit, we were southbound on I-10 when I sat up in the back seat and stared at traffic speeding past us and at the traffic racing north, at the scattering of lights in the darkness of the Gila River Bapchule Indian Reservation, at a sign announcing the distance to Casa Grande and Eloy and Tucson. As both a proud resident of the Grand Canyon State and a former writer for *Arizona!* magazine, I would once have found all that as familiar as my own face in a mirror. On this occasion, however, nature's realm and that of humankind were laced with mystery. Once, I might have idly wondered who occupied all those passing vehicles. Now I brooded instead about what infernal creatures might be traveling the night, what destinations they had in mind, and what outrages they intended to commit.

Bridget retrieved a box of ammunition from under her seat. She began reloading her pistol and the one her grandfather had used.

We cruised in silence for a while. I guess she and Sparky were thinking about how the scene in the restaurant could have played out less advantageously, with the three of us lying dead among scores of other victims. That was for damn sure a consideration that plagued *me* mile after mile.

Eventually I said, "They must have security cameras. There'll be video of us."

"If the quality's any good," Sparky said, "we'll have the ISA on our tail again in a few hours."

"What about the car?" I asked. "Maybe they've got video of us making for the Buick."

"We'll have to ditch the car," Bridget said. "Grandpa, I think I better load two spare magazines."

"Four," he said. "We can't abandon the Buick until we have new wheels, and we're not likely to find those until we're in livelier territory. Tucson's maybe an hour and a half. Once we get in the vicinity, you or Quinn can get behind the wheel, and we'll see what psychic attraction can do for us." He glanced at me in the rearview mirror. "We say 'psychic attraction,' and you say 'strange magnetism.' Po-tay-toes, po-tah-toes; to-may-toes, to-mah-toes."

"You've got it, too?" I asked Bridget.

"It's useful," she said, "although it can also be dangerous. Sometimes it takes me to what I need, whether I'm consciously aware that I need it or only subconsciously. But other times it can lead me into big trouble."

"Like the tiger," said Sparky.

"No, the tiger was cool. I was thinking of the bomb factory," Bridget said as she inserted cartridges into a spare magazine.

"Psychic magnetism led you to a tiger?"

"Hey," Sparky said, "I like that—'psychic magnetism.' Says it better than either of the others."

Again I asked, "Psychic magnetism led you to a tiger?"

She said, "We were taking a little vacation in Georgia—"

"It was peach season. I love their peaches," Sparky said.

"—and some idiot had illegally bought a tiger cub for a pet. It quickly got big—"

"Peach pie, peach cobbler, peach jam—"

"—and it got away. Scary news story. And, well, I've—"

"Peach custard, peach tarts, anything peach."

"—always been fascinated with tigers—"

"My Jeanette was from Georgia, and she was a real peach."

"—but I didn't know the tiger was what I was being drawn to."

Having exhausted the subject of peaches, Sparky said, "We're driving along with woods on both sides, and Bridget insists that I pull over. I thought she was car sick."

Bridget said, "I've never been car sick."

"There's always a first time. So I pull over, and she springs out of the car and takes off into the woods."

"It was an extremely powerful attraction. I couldn't resist."

"So I ran after her, and when I found her, she had her back to a tree, and the tiger was growling at her, and the only weapon I had was a four-inch rip blade."

"No melodrama now. Alphonse wasn't growling, he was purring."

"He gave me the evil eye," Sparky said.

"Maybe you deserved it, waving that knife around."

"I still say it could have turned out worse."

"But it didn't."

"Could have."

"Didn't."

"I'd have fought him if I had to."

"I know you would have, Sparky. You're a valiant warrior."

They fell silent, and I waited, but finally I asked her, "So then what happened?"

"You mean with Alphonse?"

"What else would I mean?"

"Well, we walked him out of the woods, coaxed him into the back seat of the car, and drove him to the nearest animal shelter."

I said, "Okay, come on—what're you leaving out?"

"Leaving out? Nothing. Alphonse was domesticated."

"Semi-domesticated," Sparky said. "No tiger is ever totally cured of its wildness."

Bridget made a dismissive noise. "Alphonse was about as wild as that tiger who sells breakfast cereal. What's his name?"

"Tony," I said.

"I was big into Frosted Flakes in those days," she said.

"Those days? When did this Alphonse thing happen?"

"About ten years ago. I was nine."

Sparky said, "Actually, we did leave out one detail about Alphonse. The frozen custard."

"Oh, that's right," Bridget said. "On the way to the animal shelter we passed a Dairy Queen, and I just knew Alphonse would enjoy that, so we stopped."

"He enjoyed three big cones," Sparky said. "I was sure he was going to throw it all up."

"Grandpa has this fear of having to clean up after someone gets car sick."

"I'd rather just trash the car and get a new one."

She reached out to pat his shoulder. "But it's an unnatural fear, since it's nothing that ever happened to you, dear."

I managed to rewind the conversation. "You already had psychic magnetism at nine?"

To her grandfather, she said, "When did it start with me?"

"The magnetism when you were seven, almost eight. The thing with animals, I first noticed when you were about four."

I remembered what they'd said about the deer looking in their windows, the squirrels that ate from their hands, and the fox named Cary Grant that kept them company by curling up on a rocking chair on their back porch.

Troubled by a sense of inadequacy, I said, "You're seven when you get magnetism, and I'm nineteen. You start seeing the Screamers two years ago, and I see them for the first time tonight. You're Doctor Dolittle at four, and I've not once yet talked with an animal."

Turning her head to look back at me, Bridget said, "I'm sure you're not developmentally disabled, Quinn. Whatever you and I might be, apparently our gifts come to us only as we need them. Living snug and protected by a lovely bunch of nuns, you just didn't need your gifts as early as I needed mine. Anyway, some-times animals tell me things, but they don't talk. It's more of a mind meld—images and feelings."

"Oh. Just a mind meld. No big deal. What other gifts do you have?"

"That's it, I'm afraid. Don't have X-ray vision. Can't fly."

"You handle a pistol as if it's an extension of your hand."

"That's not a gift. That's training. Grandpa knows everything about weapons. Every girl should have a Sparky."

To the back of her grandfather's head, I said, "Did you learn everything about weapons when you were something or when you were something else, or when you were another something that you don't talk about?"

"Exactly," he said, as I'd known he would.

| 12 |

Built in the days when cars were steel rather than fiberglass and light alloys and glue, the heavy Buick rolled through the night with the certainty of a train on tracks, with a reassuring rumble. It seemed we would be safe within it even if the world beyond its windows metamorphosed into a kingdom of eternal night and infinite terrors.

Having been, by age and custom and law, gently exiled from the orphanage and the only family I had ever known, I had the incipient sense that a new family was forming around me. Our kinship wasn't defined by bloodline—or by being parentless—but by affinity and the need to meet a threat common to the three of us. The sisters of Mater Misericordiæ had provided a loving but firmly ordered matriarchy offering stability and encouragement, an environment in which I had thrived. This new little family was far stranger than that provided by the nuns but warm in its own way, its history a ball of twine that, in its every loop, concealed a mystery.

I was comfortable with mysteries. I'd been raised on them; and I was one myself. Life without mysteries was incomprehensible—like a sandwich made of nothing but two slices of bread—and too tedious to contemplate.

When we passed the town of Picacho, chasing our future south through the Sonoran Desert toward Red Rock and Rillito, I broached a sensitive subject. "You said that your mother, Corrine, was 'never right,' because *her* mother drank during pregnancy."

"FAS—fetal alcohol syndrome," Bridget said.

At first Sparky spoke dispassionately, as though reciting a doctor's diagnosis that he had memorized. "Not a severe case. You wouldn't know it to look at her. No physical deformities. No organ damage. Just attention deficit disorder, spells of hyperactivity, mood swings. She was often argumentative for no good reason." He hesitated. When he continued, his voice was softer, and a thread of sorrow raveled through it. "But there was a goodness in her, too, a sweetness that I think was the true Corrine, that would have been the only Corrine if she hadn't been warped by FAS."

I said, "Bridget hoped that Getting to Know Me might take her cup of spit and find her father. But, Sparky, didn't Corrine give even a hint of who the father might have been when she left her baby with you and split?"

"Two important things," he said. "First, she didn't look pregnant until the last two months of her third trimester, and then only slightly. She was one of those rarities who gain maybe ten or twelve pounds max. When she told me she was pregnant, she said she hadn't realized it for the first seven months. I don't see how that could be, but she was quite adamant. Although Corrine didn't drink alcohol, there was concern that the baby would be underweight and have birth defects. No need to worry. Bridget popped out at seven pounds, fourteen ounces, as lovely a baby as you've ever seen."

She had grown lovelier over the years. I didn't say as much, because I thought that might sound as dopey as "sweetums."

Instead, I reminded Sparky that he'd said he had *two* important things to reveal.

"Well, you have to consider how Corrine was. When she was in a hyperactive state, which could last hours or weeks, she could become obsessed with odd ideas. Like that there's a city on the dark side of the moon. Or that the *Titanic* never sank and the whole story was invented to cover up a conspiracy of some kind, though she couldn't figure out what that conspiracy might be. So when she brought the baby to me a week after the birth, said she was going away for a while, and then insisted that she'd not had relations with any man for fourteen months, that she'd become pregnant without coitus, I figured this was another fantasy. She wasn't a virgin. She didn't claim that an angel appeared before her to announce the birth of a savior. She was more inclined to believe that this had something to do with those who lived on the dark side of the moon or with a new protein drink that she had tried. She was always half-lost, the poor girl. But one thing I'll swear to at the cost of my soul—Corrine didn't lie. She had fantasies, or call them delusions if you will, but she did not lie. The day she left her baby with me, she wasn't hyperactive, only bewildered and fearful. She believed what she said, though I knew it couldn't be right. Then as the years went by and Bridget proved to be so gifted . . . Well, like I said, Corrine didn't lie. And maybe in this case, somehow, she wasn't delusional, either."

For several miles, that stunning revelation crowded everything else out of my mind. Yet in spite of all the undivided consideration that I gave to the idea, I could make no sense of it.

As we passed the town of Cortaro, on the outskirts of Tucson, Bridget broke our mutual silence when she said, "Well, if my father came down out of the stars, I hope he was Luke Skywalker rather than Jabba the Hutt."

## 13

Surrounded by four mountain ranges, the city of Tucson occupied a high desert valley that was once the floor of an ancient sea. The first people settled there along the Santa Cruz River about twelve thousand years before the night that I arrived riding shotgun, with Sparky in the back seat once more and Bridget Rainking at the wheel. We were relying on her mojo to draw us to a vehicle that could replace the soon-to-be-hunted Buick.

Just as the sea became a desert, so in a few millennia, the city would become something other than a city, perhaps a sea again, or a jungle, because all things pass. Earth convulses violently when its magnetic poles shift, continental plates thrusting over or under one another, lowlands abruptly surging up, mountains crumbling, three-thousand-foot-high walls of seawater racing several hundred miles inland and scrubbing away everything in their path. Then there's also the fact that to remain livable, the planet depends entirely on solar activity, which can decline and induce ice ages that last thousands of years, or which might one day flare violently enough to boil oceans and incinerate an entire hemisphere. Yet we humans have the hubris to think we can build eternal cities, stop the aging process, control the climate, and create utopia at the point of a gun. I used to believe our subconscious recognition of our true helplessness in the face of cosmic forces was what explained the insane lust for power that makes so many into murderers, rapists, thieves, and raving-mad ideologues. For their kind, such mean control allows the illusion of greatness, inspires even the foolish hope of immortality on Earth.

However, now that I was aware that there were monsters in the world with diabolical intentions, I wondered what percentage of human misery might be a product of our own actions and how much was the work of the silent Screamers. Since time immemorial, the world's legends and faiths had included demons and other malevolent spirits, so perhaps in our postmodern rejection of the past, we cast aside more wisdom than ignorance. If envious humanity sought godlike power and fell from grace, it might be true that some race before us did the same, that we share this broken world with predators who were once beings of light and promise, but transformed themselves into creatures that worship the outer dark and wish the world to be one vast graveyard.

Those were the Big Important Thoughts that occupied me as I repressed belches inspired by pork, which escaped as hisses through my clenched teeth.

Meanwhile, we were drawn through Tucson on such a circuitous route that I began to wonder if the benefactor who granted us psychic magnetism was using it to mock us.

In a commercial district, when we stopped at a traffic light, six men, ranging in age from perhaps thirty to fifty, stood under a lamppost on the corner. Dressed in off-the-rack suits and ties, they looked too solemn to be bankers, too lacking in style to be high corporate executives. Judging by their stiff posture and pinch-faced displeasure, they might have been a firm of lawyers anticipating yet another catastrophic accident—and a brace of new clients—at this notoriously unsafe intersection or maybe college presidents in town to attend a conference on the urgent necessity of book banning.

As the light changed and they entered the crosswalk, two by two, I suddenly saw their otherness. Like those at the truck stop, their faces—such as they were—and hands fluctuated between human and not, the truth of them invisible to the other pedestrians whom they encountered in this neighborhood busy with nightlife. My first glimpse of them in the restaurant had shocked and repulsed me. But this second sighting strummed a deeper chord of horror. They were parasites made large, and yet they went about their work with as much secrecy as those roundworms that can invade a human being and attach to the walls of the intestines, there to slowly destroy the host without his knowledge.

"Six Screamers," Bridget warned Sparky.

Watching them pass in the flux of fully human pedestrians who crossed the street from the far corner, I wondered if the entirety of human history had been infested with these creatures, swimming through civilization like blood flukes navigating arteries and veins, feeding on our pain rather than on our flesh. Or perhaps on both. The shivers that passed through me seemed to originate not in the muscles of the skin, but in my bones.

"Where are they going? What are they up to?" I wondered.

"If we follow them, we draw attention to ourselves," Sparky said. "No element of surprise. Six wormheads, just three of us. You can bet their briefcases contain something nastier than paperwork."

Passing in front of our Buick, three of the Screamers turned their heads toward us, those gaping maws working as if they might be lined with olfactory receptors, in which case the same organ gave them the sense of smell and the sense of taste. The apparent absence of eyes reminded me of what I'd once read about scallops, which are covered with scores of eyes so tiny that we don't recognize them as such. Perhaps these creatures were equipped in the same manner; the flesh around the always-open always-questing mouth might be prickled with numerous eyes as small as pencil points, presenting them with a strange view of the world that conceivably conveyed more data than our eyes brought us. Or maybe the human form in which the parasite concealed itself wasn't merely a disguise but also a functioning avatar with which it perceived the world through the same five senses that we do.

Of the three whose attention we'd drawn, two glanced at us and then moved on. However, the third came to a stop in front of our car and stared at us through the windshield. Lacking features, the face of its hidden nature produced no expressions that could be read. However, the face of its human disguise, which I saw alternately come into focus and fade, expressed puzzlement verging on suspicion, as if the creature sensed something wrong with us, a wrongness to which it was unable to apply a name.

Although the light had not yet changed, I said, "Blow the horn, get him to move."

"Not rude enough," Sparky said. "Show it that you're number one, Bridget."

She put a hand to the windshield and favored the beast with her middle finger.

The Screamer remained inscrutable, but the puzzlement on its human face dissolved into a sneer. It turned from us and hurried to catch up with the others in its group.

"Why did that work?" I asked.

From behind me, Sparky said. "Misdirection. If they're the essence of evil and suspect that guardians like you and Bridget are in the world . . . then they won't expect you to be crude, obscene."

"Guardians?" I said. The word unsettled me no less than had being scrutinized by the Screamer. "Guardians of what?"

The traffic light changed to green, and Bridget motored on.

When neither she nor Sparky answered my question, I repeated it. "Guardians of what?"

"Maybe of everything," she said.

"'Everything' as in . . . ?"

"Everything as in everything," she said. "Now isn't the time to discuss our theory of all this, Quinn."

"When will it be time?"

"It'll be time when it's time, sweetheart."

"When will I know it's time?"

"When I tell you."

"That's what I thought you'd say."

She smiled at me. "Maybe you're becoming psychic yourself."

After we traveled awhile in silence, I said, "'Guardians' sounds like a full-time lifetime job. Maybe we're not guardians. Maybe instead we're just being sent on a quest."

"We're guardians," Bridget said.

I didn't want to give up on the idea of a limited commitment. "I mean like a great and noble quest, the kind knights in medieval romances set out upon. They traveled far, into strange lands, until they found the Holy Grail or the Ark of the Covenant or whatever, and then they went home and spent a few years drinking mead, eating roast haunch of wild boar, competing in lance-throwing contests."

"We're guardians," Sparky said.

"Well, maybe," I said, "or maybe not. I guess we'll see."

At last we arrived in an eclectic neighborhood of bland stucco houses standing next door to charming craftsman-style bungalows and across the street from mid-century-modern travesties. Bridget slowed almost to a stop. She peered beyond me, out of the passenger-side window, as we coasted past a dark residence that looked as if it should have been on the hill above the Bates Motel.

"It's a Nottingham," she said cryptically.

"Doesn't look much like one," Sparky said.

"The pull is strong."

"What's a Nottingham?" I asked.

"You'll see," she said as she pulled to the curb and parked two doors away from the house that intrigued her. "You and I will go in together. Grandpa will be our getaway driver if we need one. He's a maniac behind the wheel when he needs to be."

"That's comforting to know. Who might we have to get away from?"

"The kind of people who, if they catch you trespassing, cut your feet off with a reciprocating saw and urinate on you while you bleed to death."

"I have no experience of such people," I said. "I don't think I'll be of much use to you."

"Nonsense, Quinn. You've got everything it takes, which I knew you would all the while I waited two years for you finally to show up. You're the right stuff. Anyway, my sense is that no one's at home right now."

"Is your sense of a thing like that as reliable as your presentiments?"

"Oh, heck no. It's more like a hunch."

The Buick was so old that it had a bench-style front seat. Her handbag stood between us. She withdrew from it the pistol she loaded earlier, while we'd talked about tigers, peaches, and car sickness.

"Should I have a gun?" I asked.

"Do you know how to use one?"

"Not really."

"Then we won't give you a gun until Grandpa can teach you."

"Better be soon," Sparky said. "I'd hate to see his head blown off, which is sure to happen if we don't get him geared up."

"I don't like knives," I said. "They're too personal. What will I have if I don't have a gun?"

"Your wits," she said. "That's all you'll need when you've also got me." She took a roll of blue painter's tape from her purse.

"What's that for?"

She smiled and pinched my cheek. "You're a question monkey, aren't you, dear? Come on, let's go." She got out from behind the wheel, and her grandfather took her place as she walked around the back of the Buick.

Reasonably certain that we weren't going to do anything as mundane as paint a room in the target house, I got out of the car and closed my door and met her on the sidewalk.

The evening was quiet except for music issuing from a residence across the street. Instead of one grim variety or another of the stultifying noise with which narcissists tortured their neighbors these days, the night was graced by Mozart's K. 488. I knew the concerto because Sister Theresa was a Mozarthead, and this was her favorite piece by the composer, which she had often played while we studied ants and whatnot. With bats kiting soundlessly overhead and eating unsuspecting insects in midair, with the black moonlight-dusted mountains thrusting at the stars, this music seemed to seep into the desert dark as if from another, better world.

As Bridget and I walked back to the house that interested her, where perhaps foot fetishists waited with a reciprocating saw, a soft breeze sprang up. Overhead, the fronds of palm trees whispered as we approached the front door.

"If I'm wrong and someone's home after all," she said as she rang the bell, "then we'll just say we thought that Bill and Mary Torgenwald lived here. We've been given the wrong address."

"Why Torgenwald?"

"It sounds more real than Smith."

"Eric and Inga would seem to go with Torgenwald better than Bill and Mary."

"*My* imaginary friends," she said, "are the children of the children of Swedish immigrants, so they're third generation and thoroughly Americanized."

After she'd rung the bell three times without a response, she led me to the back of the residence. Stucco property walls and tall cypresses screened the yard. In the moonlight, the grass appeared to be dead and matted flat.

The back door was hinged on the left and featured four panes of glass. Bridget peeled strips of blue tape from the roll and began to cover the lower pane on the right.

"You're going to break the glass," I said softly.

"With as little noise as possible," she whispered. "Bill and Mary won't mind."

"What if there's an alarm?"

"Won't be. An alarm system would suggest there's something here worth stealing. That's the last thing these people want anyone to think. The house is in poor repair, a dump. Your average burglar sees no reason to bother with it."

"We're not your average burglars."

"We decidedly are not."

When the pane was fully taped, she hammered with the butt of the pistol, producing quiet thumps. The cracking of glass was hardly audible. When she pushed on the tape, the fractured pane fell out of its frame and into the room beyond with a soft clatter rather than a sound you'd associate with breaking glass if you were a neighbor.

She reached through the gap, felt for the deadbolt thumb turn, and found it. I followed her inside, continuing a crime spree unprecedented for a Mater Misericordiæ boy.

With a penlight taken from a jacket pocket, hooding the lens, she swept the kitchen with the beam. Judging by the dirty vinyl-tile floor, the overflowing garbage can, the crusted dishes, and the open pizza box that contained two moldy slices, whoever lived here had no interest in housekeeping and no fear of disease.

"What's that sour smell?" I asked.

"Stale pot smoke. Somebody does a lot of weed."

The refrigerator was stocked with a variety of cheeses and lunch meats and at least forty bottles of Corona. A small bowl contained four eyeballs.

We stared at the eyeballs in silence, and then I said, "I don't think they're real eyeballs. I think what they are—they're one of those gross candies that kids like. If they were real eyeballs, they would've been pried out of someone, so they wouldn't look as perfect and neat as these."

"You're right," she said, whether she thought I was or not, and she closed the refrigerator door. She stood listening, turning her head left and right. "The best thing with an attack dog is to move slowly, don't challenge it. For sure don't turn your back on it."

Because I was still convincing myself that the eyeballs were the equivalent of candy that looked like green snot and candy that looked like worms, and all the other grotesque candies with which children proved their courage, I needed a moment to absorb what Bridget had said. "Attack dog? There's an attack dog?"

"Maybe. I'm not sure. We'll see."

She walked out of the kitchen, debris of some kind crunching under her feet.

Following her into the hallway, where the hardwood flooring was as dirty as the vinyl in the kitchen, I said, "What'll you do—shoot it if it attacks?"

"I would never shoot a dog."

"But a really bad dog—"

"There are no bad dogs, Quinn, only dogs that people have taught to do bad things."

"That's sweet, probably even true. But maybe it's been trained to kill."

"I think if I was going to be killed by a dog, I'd have a presentiment of it," she said. "And I haven't."

"Yeah, but what about me?"

"We'll see."

# 14

In the hallway, Bridget opened a door, revealing plank stairs descending to a cellar. In Arizona as in Nevada and California and other places in the American West, most homes do not have basements but are built on concrete slabs, a sensible practice in earthquake country and in states where land is plentiful. Exceptions include multimillion-dollar estates that feature large home theaters and wine cellars and enormous garages for automobile collections, where windows aren't wanted. The home we'd broken into wasn't one in which a billionaire oligarch would stash Ferraris in twelve different colors.

She flicked a light switch, revealing drywall with water stains and fractal patterns of mold riotous enough to command a million dollars from a collector of abstract expressionist paintings. On the second step, three cockroaches were engaged in what might have been a ménage à trois. Startled by the light and embarrassed to be caught in their depraved conjugation, they scattered down the stairs, seeking dark crevices where they could hide in shame.

"It's down there," Bridget said.

"What is?"

"What we need."

"It's been a hard day. What I need is sleep. I'm not going to sleep down there."

Descending the stairs, she said, "The night is young, Quinn. It's not even nine o'clock yet."

She left me in the wedge of pale light from the cellar, with a length of dark hallway to my left and another to my right, with the possibility of an attack dog not disproven. Fear of being thought cowardly by a beautiful woman is a major reason why men go to war, get in cage fights, wrestle alligators, and subject themselves to ballroom dancing lessons. I followed her down the stairs. *Half a league, half a league / Half a league onward / All in the valley of Death / Rode the six hundred.*

The stench in the cellar was unlike anything I had encountered before, a mélange of rotting flesh and sewage and spoiled milk and baby puke and maybe half a dozen toxic chemicals. My gorge rose four or five times, as if something that lived in my throat wanted out, and I successfully swallowed it. My eyes watered, and my nose burned as it would have if I'd inhaled rubbing alcohol, and the thick air had a flavor so vile that I regretted having taste buds.

Gagging like a cat trying to expel a hair ball, I said, "What the *hell?*"

Trash was stacked everywhere—old wooden crates, splintered chairs, broken lamps, a couple of buckets with sprung handles, a bicycle without tires, cardboard boxes containing disordered heaps of beer bottles, several baby dolls with limbs missing—but I couldn't see anything organic that might be rotting.

"It's not a natural stink," Bridget said. "They concoct it and saturate the space with it. I've encountered it before."

"Why would they do that?"

Scanning the room, she said, "Well, so that no one will think there's anything of value here, so no one can bear to linger."

"Who? Who concocts it?"

"This particular house, I don't know. Maybe MS-13. Whatever Central America gang uses this place."

"Those guys *behead* people for the fun of it!"

"No, not mainly for enjoyment. It's to intimidate the public."

She went to the largest stack of trash, which was against the back wall, and she began to move item after item aside.

"This is crazy," I said.

"They pile the trash highest in front of the thing they need to conceal."

"We gotta get out of here. I didn't expect anything like this."

"Now, Quinn, I prepared you. I told you about the reciprocating saw, how they'd urinate on you while you bled to death."

"I thought you were exaggerating."

"I don't exaggerate. We can't leave till we have what we came here for. The stink isn't so bad if you breathe through your mouth."

"If I breathe through my mouth, I'll vomit."

"Then don't breathe through your mouth. Help me shift all this stuff out of the way."

I was listening for the clicking claws of a running attack dog. I was listening for MS-13 thugs returning, like the three bears, to discover that Goldilocks had violated their home. Therefore, I moved the trash with less noise than Bridget did, as she seemed convinced that no one would return anytime soon.

We uncovered a manhole-like cover, the bolted-down lid of a sump-pump pit. I viewed this as a disappointment, but Bridget was pleased.

"It appears to be bolted in place, but it isn't. They always want to get at a stash quickly if need be."

From among the items we'd moved out of the way, she retrieved a crowbar that had seemed like just more junk but that had in fact been left among the trash for exactly the purpose to which she put it.

As she inserted the pry blade under the rim of the cast-iron cover, I said, "I can do that."

"So can I," she said cheerily, and quickly levered the heavy lid out of the hole and to one side.

In the pit was a thick mass of white fabric, which she pulled out and put to one side. "Fireproofing."

The sump pump had been removed and the pit expanded. The walls were of mortared firebrick.

She directed the beam of the flashlight into the depository, revealing three duffel bags.

After getting on my knees, I reached into the hole and withdrew one of the large canvas sacks. It was very heavy.

Bridget zippered open the duffel and withdrew tight rolls of currency. "Hundreds and twenties. At least three hundred thousand."

"Drug money," I said. "Dirty money."

"So we steal it and do good with it. Your nuns would approve."

"I'm not so sure. Why is it here, so much money, three bags?"

"These gangs make hundreds of millions a year. Maybe they can use some banks in the third world, but they don't really trust any institution that would deal with them. Anyway, it's a cash business, and they need to stash a lot of it here, there, and everywhere."

"You know this how?"

"Grandpa. One of the things he used to do was go after these creeps. That was back when men like him were allowed to enforce the law without interference from politicians on the dark side."

"You called this place 'a Nottingham.' Why?"

"Robin Hood operated out of Sherwood Forest, which was in the county of Nottingham."

"Stole from the rich to give to the poor."

"That's the modern version. He stole from corrupt government authorities in Nottingham. In the twelfth century, there weren't banks as we know them. The county's rulers kept their spoils in secret rooms, hidden potato cellars, and the like."

"So a stash is a Nottingham. When you need money, psychic magnetism brings you to it."

She grinned. "Cool, huh? Now we can buy a car."

"Do you give some to the poor?"

"You'll see."

I thought of the coin I'd found in the kitchen of the long-abandoned restaurant. It was worth forty thousand. Chump change.

She returned the rolls of currency to the bag and closed it. "Carry this for me?"

"You're leaving the other two?"

"The creeps will return soon. We're running out of time."

Alarmed, I said, "Why didn't you say so?"

"I just did."

She hurried up the stairs, and I followed close behind, out of the stench that lay like a heavy fog below. When we stepped into the ground-floor hallway, the German shepherd attack dog growled and bared teeth that a vampire would have envied.

# 15

Muscles tensed, tail held low, head raised and thrust forward, ears laid back, eyes flaring yellow in the flashlight beam, the shepherd was not in the same business as Lassie. If Timmy fell down a well, this guy wouldn't give a damn, and if rescuers showed up to retrieve the boy, they had better be wearing Kevlar butt protectors.

When the shepherd growled louder, Bridget said to him, "Who got up on the wrong side of the dog bed today, hmmm? We don't have time for your silliness, Mr. Tough Guy."

She reached out a hand, and the dog snapped at it, its teeth an inch from taking off a few fingertips, but she did not pull back.

"Smell my hand, pooch. Come on. Get over yourself and smell who I am. If I don't smell friendlier than the idiots who trained you, then you can do your werewolf impression and go for my throat. Come on, smell, smell."

The dog took two steps backward and cocked its head.

"He doesn't like it here," Bridget said.

The shepherd worked the air with the many muscles in his nose. Depending on the breed, a canine's sense of smell is between ten thousand times and a hundred thousand times greater than ours. A dog receives far more data through its nose than a human being receives through all five senses combined.

"He's left alone too much," Bridget said, "and he's bored, even depressed sometimes."

At the orphanage, we'd had a golden retriever named Rafael. We used to hide a frankfurter in some remote corner of the second floor of that large building, start Rafael at the ground floor, and say, "Find the weenie." He would always locate the prize in less than three minutes, with a pack of kids chasing after him. His best time ever was one minute and twelve seconds.

Bridget dropped to one knee and made a come-to-me gesture, which elicited another, even more fierce growl from the dog. "Oh, booga-booga-booga right back at you, such a big scary fella."

I told myself that when the German shepherd tore her up, I would stand by her through the long hospitalization and numerous surgeries, would always be at her bedside to reassure her that she would be put back together as good as new, and would never once reveal by word or expression how much she resembled the phantom of the opera.

"He never gets any play or cuddles," she said. "He's lonely. I'm not sure, but I think they call him Hitler."

When she spoke the name, the dog's ears pricked up, and he stopped growling.

"That is so wrong," she told Hitler. "You shouldn't have to live with such a horrible name. These are very stupid, mean people."

"And they're coming back soon," I reminded her. "Stupid, mean, and violent."

"Yes, but we have a job to do here."

"What job?"

"Rehabilitating Hitler." She reached out to the dog with both hands, making it easier for him to bite off all her fingers rather than just five of them. "I'm going to call you Winston, after the magnificent Mr. Churchill, quite the opposite of nasty old Adolf." She repeated the come-to-me gesture with both hands this time. "Do you like your new name, Winston?"

The dog relaxed, lying on the floor, head up, focused on her but with a different attitude. He issued a soft, mewling sound that seemed to signify submission.

She moved closer to him, still offering her hands.

Winston licked her fingers. His tail swished back and forth, dusting the hardwood floor.

Remembering what Sparky had told me, I said, "You've had this ability since childhood?"

Scratching under the dog's chin and then behind his ears, she said, "At first I wasn't as confident about it as I became, as I am now. Better turn off the basement light and close the door."

I did as she suggested, and we were left with only the thin beam of the penlight. The tableau of kneeling woman and prone dog appeared to be rendered rather than real, a painterly scene of soft light and softer shadow, a fragment of an unseen and much larger allegorical canvas, every color and stroke and texture possessing profound meaning beyond my understanding. The radiant woman and the adoring dog were of one world, while in the darkness behind them, I was of another. Bridget was transcendental, as was the shepherd that she rescued from wickedness and restored to innocence, but I knew that, whatever I might be, I was less than she. There was no envy in the recognition of this truth, no frustration, no sorrow. I was happy to be with her on this mysterious journey, happier than I'd ever been before, because I sensed that, although in her shadow, I was moving toward the light for which I'd been yearning all my life.

As Bridget got to her feet, Winston rose with her. Referring to her relationship with animals, she said, "The confidence came with the tiger, and then with the bear."

"What bear?" I asked.

A burst of loud male laughter suggested at least two inebriated companions approaching the front of the house.

"Back door," Bridget said, and Winston led the way.

Carrying the duffel bag full of money, I hurried after them.

In the kitchen, Bridget snatched up the square of blue tape that held together the broken pieces of glass. She switched off the penlight as she followed the dog onto the porch.

The drunken laughter grew louder as the men entered the front of the house. I pulled the back door shut behind me, hoping they wouldn't notice the empty pane immediately on entering the kitchen.

Light bloomed in windows as the three of us hurried alongside the house, with jubilant Winston in the lead. I brought up the rear, a position so familiar to me that I could never believably claim to have a hawk-eyed American Indian scout among my ancestors.

Less than a minute after leaving the house, we were rolling. Sparky behind the wheel of the Buick. Bridget up front. Winston in the back seat with me. The dog grinned and panted, tongue lolling. The duffel bag full of cash was on the floor, under my feet.

"Are they Screamers?" I asked.

"Who?" Bridget wondered.

"MS-13, other drug gangs like them."

"Could be, but probably not," she said.

Sparky said, "There are plenty of real people who're eager to make a buck corrupting others with drugs. The wormheads don't bother with stuff like that. They seem to have a unique agenda."

"What agenda?"

"We haven't quite figured it out yet," Bridget said.

Sparky said, "Who's the new member of the team?"

"They called him Hitler, but I call him Winston."

As if to confirm his awareness of the name change, Winston let out a howl that rose from bass to soprano.

"He's an attack dog," I said.

Winston leaned against me and licked my neck.

I said, "He could kill with his breath."

"Those creeps haven't taken care of him," Bridget said. "We'll take him to a veterinarian as soon as we can, get him a bath, a teeth cleaning, make sure he has all his shots."

"We're on the run for our lives," I reminded her.

"That doesn't mean we won't bathe and brush our teeth, Quinn."

"So you're keeping him?"

She looked back at me and smiled. "I'm keeping you, aren't I?"

## 16

The motel rated only one star, but the rooms were as clean as they were threadbare. Three side-by-side units were available. It was the kind of place where you didn't need to present ID if you paid cash up front. In fact, the clerk at the front desk was so incurious that he would probably take your cash and give you a room key even if you showed up with bloody hands, holding a dagger in your teeth.

We gathered in the middle unit, where Bridget would bunk. We emptied the duffel on the bed. The three of us sat there to count the money, while the newest fugitive among us consumed two cans of gourmet dog food that we had bought at a supermarket en route.

Winston didn't seem to mind that he was eating out of a soft plastic bowl that was a cheap version of Tupperware, also purchased at the market. He kept looking up from his meal with what seemed to be an expression of astonishment, as if to say, *If there's stuff this good, why the hell were they feeding me cheap kibble with eyeballs?*

When I'd counted thirty-five thousand and Bridget had forty thousand, she combined our piles of cash and placed them in another plastic container with a lid. "Grandpa can finish the count. Let's you and me go find a car."

"It's ten past ten," I said. "Who's selling a car at this time of night?"

"We'll find out, dear."

"Can't it wait till morning?"

"No. The Buick is already hot. We've got to dump it."

"You kids have fun," Sparky said.

Winston leaped onto the bed, perhaps to assist with the tabulation.

I said, "You seem to have reformed Winston, but somewhere down inside he's still the attack dog that was. Should you really leave your grandfather alone with him?"

Leading me out to the Buick, she said, "Grandpa would never hurt him."

Because the motel was fully booked, its sign had been turned off. In the infinite sea of darkness overhead, uncountable stars glowed like channel lights. With its dry climate, Tucson has limited cloud cover, enjoying more hours of sunshine than almost any other city in the country, and its night skies offer the spectacle of eternity.

Bridget drove because her psychic magnetism was more developed than mine and because she was far more confident than I was that we could find someone who would sell us a car at that hour.

"Confidence," she said, "improves the efficiency and accuracy of the magnetism."

"What were you confident of finding when you found the bomb factory instead?"

"Don't be snarky, Quinn."

"No, I'm really curious."

We cruised along a boulevard, turned onto a lesser street, segued into an alley while she said, "Last year, we took a road trip to Austin. Grandpa had a friend from the old days he'd fallen out of touch with. Harry Peacemaker. Rumor was Harry moved to the Austin area, but we couldn't find a phone listing. So while Grandpa told me colorful stories about this Peacemaker guy, we let magnetism take over. It pulled us to this small industrial building with a sign that said PEACEMAKER UNITED. We went in through the main door. No one was in the public area. There was a call button, but it didn't work. Grandpa being Grandpa, he opened the gate in the counter and went looking for someone, and I followed him. We found this big room with maybe a hundred assault rifles and shotguns racked along one wall. In the center of the room were these tables where three guys were building bombs with bricks of C-4 plastic explosives and cell phones for triggers. You'd think terrorists would have at least *some* sense of security, but no. Of course, the kind of people who're into such things are usually eight cards short of a full deck."

"So the peacemakers were bomb makers."

"A lot of people these days are the opposite of what they say they are, and a lot of them probably don't even realize it. They're opposed to racism even as they act like racists. They're opposed to fascism, even as they act like fascists. The world's gone weird."

"On the other hand, if you blow someone up, they rest in peace thereafter, so then you would be sort of a peacemaker. What happened in the bomb factory?"

"We had an altercation."

"Which evidently you didn't lose."

"We're always prepared for trouble. It's why we don't fly, we do road trips instead."

"You always go everywhere with guns?"

"Well, only since I was fifteen and Mr. Scuttler followed us home on parent-teacher night, clubbed Grandpa, and tried to rape me prior to killing us both."

I felt increasingly that I, an orphan abandoned at birth, had been so sheltered that I needed to apologize for having had such a cushy life to date. "Who was Mr. Scuttler?"

"My English teacher. After that, I was homeschooled."

"Good idea. What happened to Mr. Scuttler?"

"I held him off with a battery-powered carving knife until Grandpa pounded him silly with the debate-club gavel."

"Gavel?"

"You know, a wooden mallet like a judge needs in a court-room. Mr. Scuttler was adviser to the student debate club. He'd brought the gavel as a weapon."

"You said Sparky had been clubbed."

"Yes, with the gavel. This may sound odd, but it's extremely difficult to knock Grandpa out. And even if he's unconscious, he refuses to stay that way for long."

"I don't find that at all odd," I assured her.

"Here we are," she declared as she pulled to the curb and parked.

The neighborhood was either zoned for mixed use or, having once been residential, was later rezoned for commercial enterprises. The result was a hodgepodge of older single-story homes scattered among fast-food outlets, used-car lots, and small strip malls with six or eight stores each.

Bridget had parked in front of a property consisting of two structures: an unusually sizable two-story bungalow featuring a widely bracketed gable roof with multi-windowed dormers and a deep front porch supported by stone columns; and next to it, a massive Quonset hut with a large roll-up door above which a sign announced BUTCH HAMMER'S AMERICAN AUTO REPAIR. Between the buildings stood a tall flagpole with an up light that shone on an American flag that stirred with silent sinuosity in the soft breeze.

On the blacktop in front of the repair garage stood an older model Ford Explorer. In the front window was a FOR SALE sign.

It was 10:33, twenty-three minutes after we had set out on our quest.

"I have a good feeling about this," Bridget said.

"Well," I had to admit, "so far it doesn't appear to be a bomb factory."

We got out of the Buick. Carrying the plastic container that was packed full of cash, Bridget headed not toward the repair garage but toward the residence with such brisk intention that she was obviously guided by psychic magnetism. I began to feel it as well.

Thin draperies were closed over the downstairs windows. Soft light passed through them and shone brighter along the edges. The porch light revealed that the house was painted a pale blue with white trim; it appeared to be meticulously maintained. Above the door, a transom window of red, gold, and blue stained glass invoked divine protection with the words "God bless our home."

By now, it was clear that the Rainkings had little patience for negative thinking. Because I devotedly wished to accept and see to fulfillment the proposal of marriage to Bridget that I received from her grandfather, I refrained from expressing the thought that the residents of this house were unlikely to cooperate in the kind of shady deal she had in mind. With a budget of seventy-five thousand to purchase a vehicle worth a fraction of that, she clearly wanted an off-market sale for which no papers would be filed with either the tax authorities or the department of motor vehicles. People who sought God's protection of their home might expect that, in return for granting it, the Big Guy would be aware if criminal activity occurred within those walls, whereupon He would be rightly expected to revoke what they had invoked, and set upon them plagues of frogs and locusts, the divine equivalent of an eviction notice. However, with the hope of wedded bliss and a life of sanctified hanky-panky, I kept my mouth shut.

"Leave the talking to me," Bridget said as she pressed the doorbell button.

"Absolutely," I agreed.

The guy who answered the bell filled the open doorway from jamb to jamb and threshold to lintel. He must have been six feet five, at least two hundred sixty or seventy pounds, with the broad chest of a grizzly bear, the shoulders of an ox, and a neck thicker than the neck of any creature that Nature had otherwise ever produced. He was about fifty, with a shaved head, eyes as fiercely blue as a natural-gas explosion, and a thick salt-and-pepper mustache. His arms were so powerful that they would have made a young Arnold Schwarzenegger tremble with respect, his hands so big that he might have been able to strangle me with just a thumb and forefinger. He wore black engineer boots, blue jeans, and a black T-shirt emblazoned with a single word in white block letters—DON'T.

Bridget said, "Mr. Butch Hammer, I presume?"

His teeth were as white and even as piano keys when he smiled and said, "Yes, ma'am. And to whom might I be speaking on this fine May evening?"

I expected her to invent new identities for us, but she said, "I'm Bridget Rainking. This is Quinn Quicksilver, an orphan who never knew the parents who saddled him with that name. Quinn is my fiancé, although there isn't a ring yet. We're interested in the Ford Explorer you want to sell, but we have an unconventional offer to make."

He regarded her, smiling and nodding. Then he looked at me and seemed to decide that, if it became necessary, he could tear my head off without straining himself. "Come on in, and let's bargain."

## 17

The living room was anchored by a contemporary Persian carpet with an intricate pattern in jewel tones. The simple but elegant craftsman-style furniture of dark wood was like what would have graced a house designed by Greene and Greene a century earlier, the upholstery in frosted-blue and dark-gold fabrics. Three stained-glass lamps were aglow, two in a wisteria motif, the third depicting roses and ribbons. Reprints of Maxfield Parrish paintings added the artist's magic to the room, and on the wall behind the sofa hung a gallery of photographs, twelve in all, two portraits each of three young men and three young women.

I had expected La-Z-Boys, posters of heavy metal bands, and a Harley-Davidson presented like a work of art. I realized now that Butch Hammer's arms weren't sleeved with tattoos, which should have prepared me for something else entirely.

As he led us from the foyer into the living room, he called out, "Mother, we have guests!"

The woman who appeared through a hallway door was an attractive brunette too young to be his mother, perhaps just old enough to be his wife. She wore white sneakers, pale-green jeans, and a white blouse with the tail out and the sleeves rolled up. At about five feet eight, she was statuesque, but beside her husband, she looked petite. Butch introduced her as Cressida, and she told us to call her Cressie. She asked if we wanted coffee or anything, and Bridget said that wasn't necessary, and Cressie said it was no trouble at all, and Butch said negotiations were always more pleasant when there was good coffee, so he went to the kitchen with his wife to help her provide refreshments.

Bridget and I sat on the sofa. She put the container of cash between us.

I said, "I always wondered what Thor's home might look like."

"Now you know."

"Why did you use our real names?"

"He would have known if I didn't, and he wouldn't have bothered further with us."

"How would he have known you were lying?"

"Because of who he is, what he is."

"What do you mean? What is he?"

"I don't know. He's not one of us, and he's not a Screamer, but he's something."

"Something?"

"Yes. There's a secret war they never cover on the news. You and I and Grandpa and probably a lot of other people are on one side of it, and the wormheads are on the other side. And then there are people you meet, like Butch and Cressie, who seem to suspect the truth of the world but have no proof of it. They're . . . righteous. They're persuadable, and they'll help you when you need help, if you respect them, if they know you're telling the truth."

"Okay, but how do they know when you're telling the truth?"

"They just do. They probably don't know how they know. It's their gift."

I thought about that for a few seconds. Then I said, "That T-shirt he's wearing—what do you think it means?"

"Just what it says."

I was silent a few seconds longer. Then I said, "What's the likelihood they'll put knockout drops in our coffee, and we'll wake up in chains and be sold on the black market and have our organs harvested for illegal transplants?"

She said, "Almost zero."

"How can you be sure?"

"Because of who I am."

"That was all very circuitous."

She said nothing, smiled, and patted my knee reassuringly.

"I wish you'd said *zero* instead of 'almost zero.'"

"It's a fallen world, dear. No one's perfect."

Quicker than seemed humanly possible, bringing with them the delicious aroma of a fresh-brewed Jamaican blend, Butch and Cressie Hammer returned with a wheeled cart holding a coffee service. There were also a few liquors to enhance the brew, if any was wanted, and an assortment of tiny homemade two-bite cakes and a variety of little cookies.

Bridget and I took some Bailey's Irish Cream in our coffee, which was delicious, as were the miniature cakes and cookies.

When our host and hostess were in armchairs, facing the sofa, Cressie said, "Butch tells me you're engaged."

"Just today," Bridget said. "We sort of fell into it in the loveliest way."

"I haven't bought a ring yet," I said. "There hasn't been time. We've been so busy. But I know how to do it. I mean, I know where to buy one. A ring."

Butch and Cressie stared at me with something like pity.

She said, "Relax and just give yourself to it, child. No need to be tense. A good marriage is like a sound ship that will carry you through all the storms of this world."

"You're a lucky young man," Butch said. "I was a lucky young man once." He smiled at his wife. "And my luck has grown into a great fortune."

Cressie blew a kiss to her husband. "You're still a young man, Mr. Hammer." To me, she said, "What line of work are you in?"

"I'm a staff writer for *Arizona!* magazine."

"We've thought of subscribing," she said.

Butch said, "Frankly, we're put off by the exclamation point."

"I understand," I said. "It gives the impression that we're some kind of chamber-of-commerce hard sell. But we're not."

Before she could be asked about her career, Bridget said, "Cressie, however do you get so much flavor into such tiny cakes?"

We talked a little about baking, about the beautiful stained-glass lamps that Butch and Cressie crafted together as a second business, and about the photos behind the sofa, which were high-school and college graduation portraits of their six children, among whom were a doctor, a dentist, an Air Force fighter pilot, a Navy SEAL, and an investment analyst with a hedge fund. One daughter was currently earning an advanced degree in molecular biology.

Even though I had psychic magnetism and could see monsters and was not yet twenty, I felt like the king of the slackers.

Finally, Butch said, "So, the Explorer. I completely rebuilt that baby. She's in tip-top condition. You'll want to inspect her."

Bridget eased forward on the sofa. "Having gotten to know you, we'll take your word for it. We have an unconventional offer."

"So you said earlier. I'm intrigued."

"We have an old Buick to trade. We don't want anything for it."

"I like the deal so far," Butch said.

"We want you to dismantle it for parts or take it to a salvage yard and have it squashed into a cube, so no one will ever find it."

"So whoever's looking for it," Cressie said, "will continue to look for it."

"Yes, ma'am."

"Now I'm worried for you, child."

"No need to be, Cressie. We've got our act together."

"Famous last words," Butch said. "But go on."

Placing the plastic container on the coffee table, Bridget said, "Seventy-five thousand dollars."

Butch's bland expression suggested that he was accustomed to people insisting on greatly overpaying for things. He put aside his coffee, the mug like a demitasse cup in his big hands. "The Explorer's worth a small fraction of seventy-five thousand."

"We're paying extra because we don't want you to report the profits to the IRS or register the sale with the DMV."

To her husband, Cressie said, "They don't want their names and the vehicle linked."

"I've got the picture, love," he assured her.

Bridget said, "The money isn't hot, the serial numbers aren't sequential, nothing like that." She opened the container and dumped the rubber-banded wads of bills on the coffee table.

Butch Hammer slid forward, propped his right elbow on the arm of his chair, rested his chin on his fist, and made eye contact with Bridget for at least a minute, as if her irises were disks of data that he could read. At last he said, "Where did you get the money?"

She continued to meet his stare. "We stole it. But not from anyone who rightly earned it. We stole it from a drug gang. They don't yet know it was taken, and when they find it missing, they won't know who took it."

"So you say."

"Yes, I do."

Neither of them looked away from the other. "So are you and Quinn drug dealers?"

"No," Bridget said. "We hate their kind. If you think I could be one, take a good look at Quinn. Him—not in a million years."

"I already have his number. You're harder to figure."

"I'm telling you the truth."

"Oh, I know that. But you're still hard to figure."

"She's a bit like me," Cressie told her husband. She winked at Bridget. "I was something of a firecracker, too, when I was your age."

Butch Hammer got up from his chair and stood for a moment to look at the photos of his children. Then he went to a window and pulled aside a panel of the draperies and studied the night as if perhaps the place was being surveilled.

"Is there a GPS in the Explorer?" Bridget asked.

Butch let the drapery fall into place and turned and shook his head. "No. And I bought her from a salvage yard after she was in an accident. She was delisted by the DMV. I haven't re-registered her yet."

"Perfect. Then you can carry it on your books as if you never restored it, only used it for parts."

Butch paced the room for a minute, pausing to gaze forlornly at one object or another, as if he might be leaving and never coming back. He seemed too big for his own house.

He returned to his armchair but no longer looked comfortable in it. "Who are you running from, Bridget?"

"The ISA. You know who that is?"

His expression of disgust was answer enough.

Cressie said, "The Gestapo Lite. Whoever thought anything like them would take root in America?"

Her husband's gas-flame-blue eyes seemed like windows to a fire in his head. "Why are they after you?" He focused on me. "Something you wrote in that exclamation-point magazine?"

Bridget looked at me, and I shrugged.

She said, "No, sir, nothing Quinn wrote. He and I sent away to Getting to Know Me Dot Com, hoping to learn about our ancestry. The company alerted the ISA to something unusual in our DNA."

Butch Hammer thumped a giant fist three times against his massive thigh. "People used to take that Orwell book, *1984*, to be a warning. Now they see it as an inspiration. Your ancestry is your business, not the ISA's."

After a silence, Bridget said, "Do we have a deal?"

Getting up from her chair to take a cookie from the tray on the coffee table, Cressie said, "What about license plates, sweetie?"

"We'll use the one on the Buick. It's from a Porsche. Tomorrow we'll swap plates with some other vehicle. We can keep doing that every few days, before any set we're using is reported stolen."

"Even considering the risk factor, seventy-five thousand is too much," Butch said. "On the run like you are, you need all the money you can get. Let's split it at thirty-seven five."

Indicating the photographs of the Hammer kids, Bridget said, "All that education must have cost a fortune."

"They all got scholarships," Cressie said. "But there were a slew of other bills."

"And one of them still in school," Bridget said. "We can get money any time we need it, dirty money that we'll make clean. Hard times might be coming for this country. Very hard. Take the seventy-five. It's our final offer."

Reluctantly, the Hammers accepted it.

When we said goodbye to Cressie and stepped outside with Butch Hammer, he said, "Time was that Tucson seemed far away from all the capitals of crazy in this world, but maybe nowhere's far away anymore."

He drove the Explorer into the Quonset hut, and we brought the Buick in after him. Out of sight of the street, we transferred the license plate to the Ford.

The enormous garage had a hydraulic lift and a full array of other equipment. It appeared to be almost as ordered and clean as the house next door.

When we were ready to roll, the big man said, "One more thing. When I rebuilt this girl, I filed the numbers off her engine block and then torched away the ghost of them. She can never be traced back to me, so don't worry about that."

Bridget said, "We're not the first like us who've found their way to you, are we?"

"Been a few," he acknowledged. "Do you see things, strange things, that other folks can't?"

"We do," I said.

Bridget asked him, "Do you?"

"No. I think I'm glad I don't. How did you find me?"

"We're drawn to what we need," she said.

I added, "We call it psychic magnetism."

"Question for question," Bridget suggested.

Butch nodded.

She said, "People can't lie to you, can they?"

"A lot of them try, but I always see the truth behind the lie. Cressida, too. It's scary how much lying there is. What's all this about that you're caught up in?"

"We're *all* caught up in it," she said. "You as much as we are."

"We're on a quest," I said.

"We're not on anything as easy as a quest," Bridget disagreed.

"That's an issue we're still debating," I told Butch.

Bridget said, "We're trying to figure it out. We'll let you know if we ever do."

Butch said, "Others before you—they were trying to figure it out, too. All anyone agrees about is that something bad is coming."

"Something always is," she said.

He frowned. "This time it's going to be a bigger bad than maybe we've ever seen before. Be careful out there. Godspeed."

When Butch and I shook hands, mine disappeared up to the wrist.

Bridget stood on tiptoe to kiss his cheek.

Just then Cressie arrived with a colorful Christmas-themed tin full of tiny cakes and cookies. "It's always Christmas here," she said, and it occurred to me that, with a full beard, Butch Hammer would make an impressive Santa Claus, though he might scare the pee out of some little kids. "Share them with whoever," Cressie said. "There's nothing so bad in life that a good little cake can't make it better."

## 18

When we returned to the motel shortly before midnight, Sparky Rainking was waiting for us in his granddaughter's room, watching a cable program on TV. "They seem to be reporting news from another planet, 'cause they sure aren't talking about the earth I know."

Neither the cable channel nor a local station had carried any mention of the shooting at the truck stop. These days, any incident involving a mere two killings failed to be violent enough to qualify as news.

Sparky had finished counting the money. In addition to the seventy-five thousand that we'd left with Butch Hammer, the duffel bag had contained another hundred and ninety thousand, mostly in hundreds, but some in twenties.

"After I counted the last, I washed my hands for ten minutes. Still don't feel entirely clean, considering the moral degenerates who handled those bills. Then I got in the shower with Winston and used some shampoo on him. He smells like lemons. We don't need to have him groomed in the morning, though we should get his teeth cleaned before too long."

We told him about the Ford Explorer as he sampled the baked goods in the Christmas tin. After he interrupted us twice to say that he would marry the woman who made those treats if she ever became available, we finished our account of the events at Butch Hammer's American Auto Repair. Then we agreed to hit the road by eight o'clock in the morning and said goodnight.

Sparky retired to his room and I to mine, and Winston wisely remained with Bridget. I don't know what condition Sparky was in, but after a long day on the run, I felt as though my muscles were sliding off my bones and my joints were coming unhinged.

I took a shower as hot as I could tolerate, toweled off, slipped into pajamas, got into bed—and could not sleep. The quiet abraded my nerves. I knew that no monster stalked me in the dark, and yet the very silence seemed to be evidence of its stealthiness. Minute by minute, I grew increasingly, irrationally convinced that something nearby, coiled to strike, was listening to me as I listened for it.

I turned on a cable channel and lay watching infomercials for spurtles and copper-infused underwear and diarrhea remedies.

This will sound weird, but I suppose no more so than everything that I have written to this point: I didn't know myself anymore, and I found the new me a little scary. During the course of the day, I'd become a stranger to myself, a different person from the guy who had gotten out of bed to go to work at *Arizona!* magazine the previous morning. The path to the future that I long envisioned had withered away in the wild woods of recent experience, and I was unable to imagine where this new path might lead. I had killed two federal agents with a car, albeit in self-defense. I was on the run. I was engaged to be married. Sort of. I could see monsters. The world had not changed; however, my understanding of it had undergone a most radical revision, which in turn revised *me*. I was unsettled by the thought that I was destined to become a warrior. I didn't see myself as a warrior. I didn't want to be a warrior. I just wanted to avoid diarrhea, enjoy the health benefits of copper-infused underwear, and have my own little kitchen with a collection of spurtles. However, the mysterious forces at work in my life might give me no choice in the matter. I might have to become a warrior or die. Of course, if I became a warrior, I would almost surely die, because the role did not suit me.

On the other hand, whatever enigmatical power had first taken control of me on the day I'd found the coin seemed to be benign. It manipulated me, yes, but first to prepare me to escape web-spinning spiders from the ISA, and then to send me literally crashing into the life of my stunning and amusing future bride. If I had changed, maybe I *needed* to change to adapt to the truth of the world in order to survive. And if I was in some strange power's employ, maybe that employment would be more satisfying than writing about rotting buildings at a ghost crossroads of abandoned highways, even as thrilling as that might be. Maybe I needed to live by the old saying popular with Californians—"Go with the flow"—though that's exactly what happens to a dead goldfish when you flush it down a toilet.

I left the TV on as a night-light, the volume low, and at last fell asleep during an infomercial for a law firm that was eager to get me the financial settlement I deserved if only I would fall down a long flight of stairs in a commercial enterprise or be so lucky as to find my car rear-ended and simultaneously T-boned by a pair of eighteen-wheelers driven by the reckless employees of a heartless trucking company.

I don't remember dreaming, and I had no nightmares. In the morning, however, there would be a moment of terror.

At 7:12 a.m., I woke to an infomercial about copper-infused face masks for those who either wanted to be prepared for the next pandemic or had taken a fancy to this stylish head accessory that had been made popular in the previous crisis. This was not yet the aforementioned terror.

Having showered before going to bed, I had only unmentionable bathroom tasks to attend to. As was my habit, I took a book with me. In Phoenix days earlier, when I had been compelled to pack a suitcase to flee I knew not what, I included a memoir by a famous actor. The word "love" was in the title, but judging by the first chapter, the book seemed to be about all the many people whom he hated and why he hated them with such seething passion. Welcome to utopia.

After setting the book on the vanity beside the sink, I washed my hands and shaved with my cordless razor. As I studied my face, vigilantly seeking any missed stubble, my peripheral vision alerted me to the fact that the actor's memoir did not appear in the mirror. It remained on the counter, but in the reflection, the counter was without a book. My disquiet was related more to perplexity than to fear. I put a hand on the tome, not because I doubted its existence, but as if to rectify the curious difference between reality and the image in the looking glass. With my hand on that memoir, I regarded the mirror again and found that the book I could feel was still absent from the image.

As I stared in disbelief, both I and the motel bathroom around me faded out of the reflection. The mirror became a window into a shadowy subterranean passage only partly revealed by eerie light pulsing from rooms along either side.

What followed seemed like a blend of the real and metaphorical, as if I was drawn into some revelation so complex and profound that the truth of it could not be conveyed by ordinary images and not by words at all, only by resort to visual symbolism of the most extreme and urgent kind, which would speak to my subconscious and provide it with answers that it might understand not now but in the weeks and months to come.

The mirror that had become a window now morphed into a door. I was drawn across that threshold without taking a step, as if I were weightless. I doubt that I went anywhere physically; the sensation of movement was illusory. My viewpoint became that of a video camera mounted on a drone as I plunged through a labyrinth of tunnels wide and narrow, through the warren of chambers they served, through vast caverns and across dark lakes that I knew to be pools of time. The structure changed continuously, a surreal architecture in which every horror ever imagined might lurk in anticipation of being fed what it most relished. Walls of raw earth molded themselves into mortared stone; stone became steel; the steel became organic, a fleshy construct pulsing with menace; flesh became magma, molten and fluid; magma hardened into walls of bones compacted with shattered skulls, acrawl with pale glistening forms that I'd never seen before, which might have been worms or insects or something else unthinkable. There were rooms in which men and women, evidently dead, hung from the walls or else reposed on catafalques, spectral light emanating from their open mouths and breathless nostrils and sunken eyes. In half-lit chambers, people writhed in the grip of grotesque men and women with large misshapen heads, ghouls that were devouring them much as was depicted in the painting by Goya, *Saturn Devouring His Children*. In bleak passageways, crowds of naked people surged in terror, panicked by some menace behind them or called by something far ahead; sometimes they hurried alongside racing trains of cattle cars, from the slatted sides of which the people within reached out in desperation. In tunnels as smooth as polished wine-dark glass, people flowed by the hundreds, tumbling slowly, as if they were beyond the gravity of Earth. All this occurred in silence, but for the tympanic thunder of my heart, as if I must be in an airless void incapable of conducting sound.

A last tunnel abruptly turned upward. I soared at a terrible velocity, as though ascending a long missile silo, in the grip of existential dread. When I erupted out of the earth, I was in a city afire from its center outward to every borough, under a low sky that reflected the flames as if even Heaven were ablaze. Sudden sound burst through streets iced with broken glass: screams of terror, howls of wordless rage, curses, pleas, lunatic laughter, rattling gunfire, explosions, sirens, horns blaring, vehicles racing from nowhere to nowhere—a celebration of nihilism in the name of justice that is really vengeance. Everywhere, outrages were committed without fear of consequences: savage gang rapes, beatings with clubs and tire irons and chains, vicious murders in a war of all against all, the crowds driven by lust and bloodlust, by lust for power and lust for money, and by the lust that is known as envy. A shrieking horse galloped past me, pulling a burning carriage. A sobbing woman ran with a bloody baby in her arms. A boy of five or six wandered shell-shocked toward one mortal fate or another, as civilization collapsed in a sea of fire. And throughout the chaos moved those creatures that Bridget called the Screamers, scanning the carnage with what eyes they might have. Their slithery tentacular fingers writhed as if they could feel the misery in the cries of their enemies. Their maws worked as if they were greedily drinking the pain of the dying, themselves without a wound, as though they operated under some royal imprimatur that made them untouchable.

Barefoot, in pajamas, I staggered backward, into the bathroom wall, the actor's memoir in my left hand. The mirror became only a mirror again, and the cacophony of madness and anguish gave way to the quiet of the morning in Tucson.

In the bedroom, I sat in the armchair and bent forward with my head in my hands. I breathed deeply, waiting for my heart to quiet.

Whatever else the vision might have been, it was an orientation film aimed at the new recruit—me—as well as a call to duty and an urgent warning that the secret war could soon erupt into conflict on a greater scale, perhaps evolving into Armageddon.

My sense was that if I didn't answer the call to battle, the war would come to me anyway. This was a matter of destiny. If I gave destiny the finger and walked away, that wouldn't be the end of it. What would have happened would *still* happen. The malevolent beings that I'd had a chance to stand up against would crush me without resistance. That was how fate worked. It wasn't pretty. I had no desire to pull the sword Excalibur from the stone, but if I didn't, the stone and the sword would roll downhill and flatten me.

To prepare for what might lie ahead, I needed to learn more about how I had ended up in a bassinet on a lonely highway.

I got up from the chair and dropped the actor's memoir in the trash can.

As I shed my pajamas and dressed for the drive to Peptoe, an infomercial on TV offered a revolutionary nonstick frying pan. The ad guy proved the pan's effectiveness by making a cheese omelet in it, then by melting caramel and chocolate in it, and then by cooking a mixture of glue and shredded plastic. All three delicious treats slipped out of the pan without leaving the tiniest bit of sticky residue, though no advice was provided as to whether red or white wine was the best complement to a glue-and-plastic entrée.

I love this country. This is the greatest country in the world, as long as it will be allowed to last.

When I stepped outside, Sparky and Bridget were waiting by the Ford Explorer. Winston was in the back seat, his head out the side window, looking nothing whatsoever like a drug-gang attack dog, having been reformed by my moon goddess.

Sparky and I asked each other how we'd slept—like a stone in my case, like a baby in his case, both of us lying.

Bridget said nothing at first, watching me intently as I loaded my suitcase along with their luggage and closed the tailgate.

Then, as her grandfather went around to the driver's door, she said quietly, "Bad dream?"

"No. I just didn't like what I saw in the mirror this morning."

"You too, huh?"

Surprised, assuming that she had the same experience, I said, "What *was* that?"

"Orientation. To let us know what our enemies want. The world as the Screamers and their acolytes will make it if given a chance."

"Acolytes?"

"We have people like Butch and Cressida Hammer, and Grandpa. On the other side are fools who think a world of pure materialism will be a utopia. The Screamers will give them the world they want, a world of absolute indulgence—and rule it. Too late, they'll realize their utopia is in fact an empire of suffering and death."

Sparky started the Explorer.

"What you saw—you're hiding it from your grandfather?"

"Sparing him from it," she corrected.

"Why? He's not a delicate flower."

She put her arms around me and held me very tight, and I held her, and she was silent for a moment before she said, "As I endured that . . . whatever that was this morning, I had a presentiment, a strong one. Not all of us are going to survive what lies ahead."

I had read novels in which the author wrote that a character's heart had sunk at the receipt of one bit of bad news or another, and I had often paused to ask, with snark, where the heart had ended its descent. In the stomach? In the colon? Now I felt my heart sink into a slough of foreboding, and the sensation was so disturbing that I was beyond snark. We all arrive in this world with a ticket out of it, but somehow, in spite of all evidence to the contrary, we remain convinced that those we care about will be with us for a long ride.

"You mean . . . Sparky won't make it?"

"I don't know. Maybe him or me or you. Maybe all of us won't make it. All I know is . . . at least one of us won't. If he knows, he'll take even greater risks for my sake. I don't want him doing that. What happens will happen." She let go of me, stepped back. "That's the only way it can be. Understand?"

"Yes. Unless . . . unless we don't play the game."

Her eyes were clover green and Celtic fierce. "That's not you. You're better than that."

I hesitated and then said, "If you say so."

"I say so, and you know so." She got in the front of the Explorer with her grandfather and pulled the door shut.

Winston politely made room for me in the back seat. He licked my cheek. I didn't return the lick. I just wasn't in the mood.

# BACK IN THE DAY

## THE BOY, THE FATHER, THE BIRDS

So Corbett Ormond frequently beats his wife, murders her and ten others, and a few years later shoots and kills his own twelve-year-old son, Litton, my roommate and best friend. How can a just world be shapen to allow such outrages? Why aren't we designed to be unable to harm one another? Why aren't our brains wired so that we can't kill or rape or steal or lie or deceive? Why are we formed with the capacity to hate and envy? They say that this world and life in it are a gift, but how can it be a gift when it so often subjects us to fear or even terror, and to unbearable sadness?

At eleven, rocked by grief, having lost the ability to find happiness, I dwelt obsessively on those questions, arriving at no answers, eating too little, sleeping more of the day than not.

Sister Theresa, psychologist and counselor, sought to relieve my unrelenting depression by teaching me about ants. Although it was odd to have a therapist who was a dead ringer for Aretha Franklin, I learned a lot about several varieties of the family Formicidae, but nothing I learned cured my despair, for I was a stubborn patient.

Having brought a large glass-walled ant colony into her office for our study, Sister Theresa said, "If ants didn't enlighten you, then bees probably won't."

I stood at her office window, staring out at the heavy rain that fell in gray plumb-bob lines through the windless day, foaming like corrosive acid on the black street and gray concrete sidewalks.

"Anyway," Sister Theresa continued, "I'm certainly not going to bring a hive into my office."

"Why do bees have to sting?" I asked.

"To defend themselves and protect their colonies. But we're not going to spend any time on bees."

"Why do animals bite? Why does everything kill everything?"

"Not every animal kills. Rabbits don't kill, unless you think that grass and flowers and carrots and berries can be murdered. If you do, then we should at once start putting rabbits on trial and sending them to bunny prisons."

"Don't be silly."

"I will if I wish to be," she said, leaning back in her creaky office chair. "I rather like being silly on occasion. However, in the interest of accuracy, I should report that even rabbits can be violent with one another. They use their powerful hind legs to kick when they're contesting for mates, and they'll even bite one another now and then if they disagree."

As I watched the rain, I thought of the flood that was said to have scrubbed the sinful world clean of everything except Noah's family and the animals on his ark. When the flood receded, however, they all got off the ark and started killing again.

"I don't want to hurt anyone. I don't want to kill anything."

"Then don't," Sister Theresa said.

I didn't care to believe it was so easy. She always had a quick answer I couldn't dispute, which began to irritate me. "Yeah, well, I could get mad, lose control. Lots of people are always angry."

"Quinn, dear, you'll have moments when you're mean and you hurt people's feelings, just as they'll hurt yours. You'll do stupid things, maybe even something cruel now and then. But you'll never murder anyone."

"What if there's a war and I get sent?"

"Defending your family or your country in a war, you might have to kill, but killing in defense of your own life or the lives of innocent people isn't murder."

I wished that the rain would fall harder, harder than it had ever fallen before, until the streets were rivers and the cars were swept away. I wanted to see the people on the sidewalks, in their raincoats and carrying umbrellas, trying to get into the safety of the buildings but finding the doors all locked, so they would know that they, too, would be swept away, so they could feel what Litton must have felt when he looked in the muzzle of his hateful father's pistol. None of that made sense in my despair, but I was eleven, an age often short of reason. I said to Sister Theresa, "I could go to war with you right now, come over there and punch you in the nose."

"You could choose to do that," she agreed. "And I could choose to punch you back. It wouldn't be a wise move on your part, since I am much bigger than you."

"You're a nun. You aren't allowed to punch anyone."

"I'm a nun, but I'm also human. We humans make mistakes. Am I likely to punch back? Probably not. No guarantee. So, Quinn, you make your choice and you take your chances. Take a swing at me if you really think it'll make you feel better."

The rain fell harder, as if granting my wish, and the world beyond the window appeared to begin flooding, melting. Suddenly I was crying. I had wept alone in my room, but now it was happening right out in the open. I kept my back to her, tried not to make a sound, just let the tears flow until there were no more. If she came to me and tried to console me, I would punch her as hard as I could because I didn't want to be comforted, not with Litton dead.

After a silence broken only by the susurration of the rain and the creaking of her chair as she shifted in it, she said, "Nature is a place of constant competition between individuals in a species, and between one species and another. In this broken world, animals aren't able to rise above violence. But people have the ability to forsake it. People should. People must. But that is our work, Quinn. Not nature's and not God's."

"But why?" I said when I could at last speak.

"Perhaps the birds will teach you what the ants couldn't. We will study birds together."

So the subject became birds. Sister Theresa provided DVD documentaries and books. We sat in the park and watched the crows, the doves, the sparrows. She took me to a university to spend two hours with an ornithologist in his research aviary, where there were more birds of different kinds than I had ever seen before, although only a tiny fraction of the more than a thousand species that exist worldwide.

We studied their feathers. A simple sparrow has thirty-four different kinds of feathers. Every member of a species is feathered exactly the same as every other member.

We studied different ways that species build their nests. Every individual within a single species builds in the very same manner.

They raise their offspring by precisely the same rules, and with entirely predictable results.

We studied species that fly in formation. We studied species that don't fly in formation but that, in a flock of hundreds, will change direction in the same instant.

We studied what they feed on and how they find food. Every member of a species sustains itself with the same food and seeks it in the same manner as the others of its kind.

I was repulsed by the fact that owls sometimes eat smaller birds, as do some raptors like hawks and falcons. I called them "cannibals."

Nothing I learned seemed to explain what any of these things had to do with human violence or with why it was allowed in a world that had supposedly started out as a paradise named Eden.

As with the ants, Sister Theresa would not tell me what lesson I was supposed to learn. "You have to realize the truth on your own, believe it, accept it—or otherwise it is just something you've been told that you don't trust to be true. Next, we'll study fish."

# PART 3
# WHAT THE SEER SAW

# 19

I had not returned to Peptoe since being sent to Phoenix in the first week of my life, because I'd been too busy being an orphan and then earning a living in the cutthroat world of regional magazines. Months before I met the Rainkings, however, I'd researched Peptoe without going there, preparing a file to justify eventually visiting the town for a few days on the dime of *Arizona!* magazine. I hoped to write a story about being abandoned on my third day of life and perhaps learn something, however little, about my origins.

From Tucson, the way to Peptoe was via I-10 east, then by an undivided federal highway, then along another undivided highway, across saguaro flats, across playas dry and cracked at that time of year, between mountains as stark as rough-forged iron, through lands where blood had been spilled in tribal wars of which history made little note, where through at least a thousand years many slaves were kept and suffered, their grim ordeal and existence now long forgotten or at least left unremarked in the interest of addressing more recent outrages. The only way to Peptoe was through human history in all its striving and conniving, mercy and meanness, nobility and ignobility, despair and hope.

The town was not a town, not officially, but one of those odd settlements that form like rust on iron, less by intention than by some process of nature that no one has yet been granted government funds to study. Those who made it their home were for the most part people who found crowded cities unnatural and any large government Orwellian, but were likewise averse to the intimacy of small towns and the officious nature of village councils. The citizens of Peptoe and places like it wanted to have neighbors, though at a respectful distance, which meant cheap land. They wanted a sense of community, but mostly they wanted to live their lives with as few annoyances as possible, beyond the easy reach of thought police and sanctioned con men of all kinds.

To simplify their lives, they needed a one-stop business that sold them everything from gasoline to groceries to basic tools. In Peptoe, that retailer was Ching Station, a U-shaped single-story structure at the crossroads of a two-lane federal highway and an unpaved gravel road, with small windows and thick slump-stone walls to ward off summer heat, no landscaping but cacti, and a windmill to pump water. Ching Station served not only Peptoe but also other similar communities in the area.

After arriving at 11:05 a.m., we cruised at random while Sparky waited for Bridget and me to employ psychic magnetism to locate one of the three men who long ago saved me from being bitten by a series of rattlesnakes and squashed by a huge truck while being devoured by a coyote: Hakeem Kaspar, Bailie Belshazzer, and Caesar Melchizedek. However, the gift wasn't ours to use at will. Maybe the mysterious benefactor who chose us for service in this cause believed that an element of unreliability was essential to temper any tendency in us to become besotted with our power and as arrogant as the fascist superheroes that have long populated Hollywood blockbusters. By 11:15, when we failed to feel any compulsion other than a slow-building need for a public lavatory, we returned to Ching Station, which we had passed three times in our fruitless seeking.

"Now and then," Bridget revealed, "I think my ability to see through the Screamers' masquerades also isn't one hundred percent reliable. I have the disturbing feeling some of them are better shielded, better disguised, and I'm unaware of them."

"Good to know," I said. "I've been concerned that I'm not half as paranoid as I ought to be, but you just solved that problem."

Among the numerous products and services advertised on the extravagant signage mounted on the roof of Ching Station was the promise of CLEAN RESTROOMS.

Only one other vehicle stood in front of the enterprise, a faded-blue pickup truck with a rifle in a rack and a bumper sticker that announced I SHOOT TAILGATERS. The station was open eighteen hours a day, and the lifestyle in this hot territory was laid-back; there was no such thing as a rush hour with lines for anything.

While Sparky stretched his legs and Bridget poured bottled water into a bowl for Winston, I went inside to request lavatory keys and to learn how to obtain gasoline from the antique pumps.

A fifty-seven-year-old man, five feet nine, with brown hair and brown eyes, born on Christmas Day, was replenishing a depleted rack of candy bars near the first of two checkout stations. He had one of those friendly faces into which was also built evidence of a keen sense of humor and irony, the kind of face that would be a treasure to any standup comic who was graced with one. I recognized him from the photograph in the official state files of retailers who had been granted licenses to sell alcoholic beverages, which I'd perused in my aforementioned researches.

"John Kennedy Ching," I said. Although I'd had no intention of speaking his name out loud, seeing him in the flesh after learning about him and his family was, for me at least, a little like coming face-to-face with a celebrity.

Holding a PayDay bar in each hand, he smiled. "I have been known to answer to that name. And you?"

"Me? Oh, I'm nobody. Bart. Bart Simpson."

He raised one eyebrow. "Your name must be even harder to live up to than my John Kennedy."

I don't know why I'd chosen that name or why I was surprised that he had watched *The Simpsons* on TV. I wasn't yet accomplished at the level of deceit necessary for my new cloak-and-dagger life.

Now I felt obliged to explain how I, a stranger to him, knew his name and recognized him on sight. "My friends and I have been looking for property over in Winkelville."

He nodded. "A very competitive real estate market. Everyone in the world wants to live in Winkelville."

"Anyway," I said, digging myself in deeper, "since they don't have anything like this place, like a general store, I wondered where they, you know, go to shop. Everyone spoke very highly of Ching Station, John Kennedy Ching, and in fact the whole Ching family from your grandparents to your children."

His voice and expression were deadpan. "They lay it on thick over in Winkelville."

My difficulty in negotiating this encounter arose because, as a result of my research, I knew his family's history and admired what they achieved. His grandparents and their two sons—one five years old, the other seven; the latter John's father—escaped from China in 1948, after the Communists opened reeducation camps and mass murders began. They made their way to Taiwan, which was then called Formosa, and soon immigrated to the United States. For a while, they settled in San Francisco with its flourishing Chinese American community. However, having fled a large city that was besieged by a violent ideology, they no longer felt safe in a metropolitan area, not even in America. I didn't know—couldn't begin to imagine—how John's grandparents found Peptoe or how they were able to envision building Ching Station and making it into the mercantile center of the county. For seven decades, four generations of Chings had been serving the people of Peptoe and Winkelville (population 802) and Sunnyslope (population 746) and Sulphur Flats (population 635) and several much smaller sunbaked settlements. The industrious Chings occupied five houses in the vicinity of the crossroads where their enterprise was located, and all five flew the Stars and Stripes from flagpoles.

Deciding that I had best stick strictly to business, I said, "Your gas pumps are older than I am. How do they work? I mean, how do I pay and everything? I want to pay cash."

"It's a mystery," he said, "but we can solve it together. I'll switch on pump number one from behind the counter. You go out there and turn the crank until the meter shows only zeros. Then fill up with however much you need and come back here to pay me what the meter says you owe."

"It's just that in Phoenix, you put your credit card or debit card right in the pump."

"Phoenix," he said, "is a place of great wonders."

"Don't some people pump the gas and then drive away without coming back in here to pay?"

"One such scofflaw did exactly that in 1996," John Kennedy Ching said, "but we tracked him down to Cleveland, Ohio, and burned his house to the ground."

I laughed and nodded. "All right, you're pulling my leg."

Stepping behind the counter to activate pump number one, he said, "You pulled mine first, Bart Simpson. But unless you have excellent insurance on your residence, you better return to pay me."

"I know it sounds unlikely, but my name really is Bart Simpson. My cross to bear. Oh, and could I have the keys to the men's and women's lavatories?"

"You do not seem to be a young man who is in doubt about his gender," Ching said as he passed the keys to me. "I hope I may meet the lady traveling with you. She must be very interesting."

By that point, I should have known that it was going to be a day of Ching with more twists than the woven chains of dried red peppers that were for sale in his store.

Outside, where Winston had drunk a bowl of water and was busy peeing in the dead grass beyond the parking lot, I gave one key to Bridget and one to Sparky. "All right. I told Mr. Ching that my name is Bart Simpson, so be careful not to call me Quinn or anything."

"Bart Simpson?" Sparky said, favoring me with a look of pained incredulity.

"It was the first thing that came to my mind."

"There's actually a Mr. Ching?" Bridget asked. "I assumed that must be some Native American word meaning the end of nowhere."

"Mr. Ching thinks you must be very interesting."

"Why would he think that?"

"I made quite an impression on him."

Sparky snorted and gave me the key to the Explorer and headed toward the men's room.

"One more thing," I said. They turned to me. "He thinks we've been over in Winkelville looking at property to purchase."

"There's actually a Winkelville?" Bridget asked.

"It's about four miles from here, two miles east of Sulphur Flats and three miles south of Vulture's Roost."

"If they ever want to build an Arizona Disneyland," she said, "it won't be in this part of the state."

After telling Winston to sit and stay, I drove the Explorer to pump number one. I cranked the numbers from the previous sale off the meter, filled the tank, and parked again in front of the store.

In the men's room, Sparky had finished his business and was studying his face in the mirror.

I said, "Handsome fella, huh?"

"How'd I ever get to be so old?"

"You didn't die."

"I'm working on it," he said, stepping outside.

I at once regretted being flippant when I remembered Bridget's prediction that not all of us would survive what might lie ahead.

A few minutes later, refreshed, I found my three companions waiting for me in the shade of the scalloped green awning near the entrance to the store. Snakes of heat were writhing up from the blacktop highway.

"We're starving," Sparky said, "and the sign on the roof says fresh sandwiches."

"It also says that well-behaved dogs are welcome," Bridget said. "I'm thinking they might sell dog stuff. We need a leash."

Just then a grizzled character exited the store with a purchase in each hand—a box of shotgun shells and a fifth of bourbon.

Wild tangles of white hair flared out from under his cowboy hat, and the length of his beard suggested that he might once have been a member of that old rock group, ZZ Top. He looked as if he'd had a part in every Western movie ever made. As he passed us, he glanced at me and said, "Tell Homer and Marge they done a nice job with you," and proceeded to the faded-blue pickup truck with the I Shoot Tailgaters bumper sticker.

Inside, Mr. Ching had concluded resupplying the candy rack and was engaged with small bags of salty snacks. I introduced Bridget as Vanessa and Sparky as her uncle Vernon, and I sounded pretty slick if I do say so myself. For a long moment, Mr. Ching stared at her with astonishment, and then regarded me for two seconds, and then looked at her again as he said, "Only in America. Excuse my saying so, Vanessa, but you do not look like Winkelville."

"Maybe not," she said, "but I much prefer it to Vulture's Roost."

Ching Station did indeed cater to dog owners no less than to grumpy, grizzled old coots who needed ammo and liquor. We selected a nice red collar and leash, a can of tennis balls, and a white lamb squeaky toy for Winston, as well as a packet of teeth-cleaning chews and a case of gourmet dog food.

A pretty teenage girl worked the small deli section that offered three homemade soups, potato salad, macaroni salad, cakes, cookies, and sandwiches. She said her name was Taylor Ching, that the sandwiches were made fresh every morning and stored in a cooler, that they sold out every day by two o'clock, and that she thought my sister, Lisa, deserved better treatment than she got from me.

If I'd just used a name from *The Family Guy*, no one would have known, and the Chings wouldn't have had so much fun at my expense.

Sparky paid for everything with drug-gang money, and Mr. Ching said he hoped to see us again, once we'd moved to Winkelville and took up life along the Little Snake River.

We sat in the Explorer, with the air conditioner blasting, to eat our submarine sandwiches—Italian cold cuts for Bridget and me, chicken for Sparky—and wash them down with cold bottles of flavored water.

As we ate, we brainstormed ways to find one of the three men who had rescued me back in the day. We could drive thirty miles to the Indian casino where Caesar Melchizadek had been a blackjack pit boss and see if he still worked there. We could check out the wind farm where Bailie Belshazzer had repaired the expensive equipment that suffered regular, grievous damage from the thousands of birds that threw themselves so recklessly into the giant, chopping blades. We could go to the county office of the power company to learn if Hakeem Kaspar was still living out the Glen Campbell song.

"Or," Bridget said, "we could save a lot of time and just ask Mr. Ching about one of them. After all, he must know everyone from Sulphur Flats to Vulture's Roost to Tarantulaburg."

"There's no town named Tarantulaburg."

She said, "I find that hard to believe. So we don't want word getting out that you're poking around here, and suddenly the ISA gets wise to us. We can't ask Ching about all three men, because he surely remembers the baby being found on the highway, and he seems like a guy who can read the stitching on a fastball with his eyes shut."

From the back seat, Sparky said, "Our story could be that I'm an old friend of Hakeem's, I lost track of him years ago, and I'm hopeful of getting in touch while we're here, see if he has any advice about Winkelville."

I said, "That sounds simultaneously ridiculous and workable. Go ahead and give it a try."

"Not a good idea," Sparky demurred. "Ching is an intuitive guy. He kept giving me suspicious looks, like he knows my kind."

"You mean he suspects you were once something, then something else, and then another something that you don't talk about."

"Precisely."

"That's amazingly intuitive," I said. "As if he has a nose on him more sensitive than Winston's."

"Grandpa has incredible intuition of his own. I'd trust him on this, Quinn. Bart."

"Anyway," Sparky said, "son, you're the only one who has any kind of established relationship with Ching."

"Relationship? We aren't going steady, for heaven's sake."

"But he likes you," Sparky insisted. "You amuse him. Go in there and amuse him and get an address for Hakeem Kaspar."

When I went inside once more, John Kennedy Ching was moving large bags of water-softener salt from a cart onto a display near the front door.

I said, "We wanted to tell you that those sandwiches were absolutely delicious."

He cocked his head like a bird looking at something curious. "You seem surprised. I would have thought, considering all that the good people of Winkelville had to say about Ching Station, they would have especially praised our sandwiches."

I was no match for this guy, so I stopped trying to be clever. "The thing is, my future father-in-law, Vernon, fell out of touch with an old friend of his who lives in this area. He's hoping to find him while we're here, pick up where they left off, share some stories about the old days. We thought you might know him, where he lives now."

"Who is this old friend?"

"Hakeem Kaspar."

"Yes," said Ching, "he is a lineman for the county."

"That's him!"

Ching said, "He rides the main road."

"Vernon will be so happy."

"Like most days, he's been searchin' in the sun for another overload," Ching said.

"Do you have an address for him?"

"His place is on the old Apache Trail. It's a dirt road with no signs. I'll draw you a little map. You'll be there in ten minutes at this time of day. At night, in May, with the spring insects at their peak, spattering your windshield, and the bats swarming, you'd need twenty minutes, maybe more. Go while it's light."

He went behind the checkout counter and took a small tablet from a drawer. He wrote directions on the front of a page and then drew a map on the back of it.

When he handed the paper to me, I said, "Swarming bats?"

"From mid-May through mid-June, when the flying insects are most plentiful, the bats come to feed on them in flight. Thousands of bats, clouds of wings that hide the moon."

"Wow. That must be quite a sight."

"Yes," Ching said, "but not one that a sane man should want to see."

"We'll scoot right out there. I hope he's not on the job."

"Well, the lineman is still on the line. He starts before dawn," Ching said, "but he finishes with that stretch down south about now. You'll probably catch him just as he's getting home."

## 20

John Kennedy Ching had not only written directions and drawn a map, but he also had sketched a perfect image of the mobile home in which Hakeem Kaspar lived. It was a handsome fifty-footer raised on concrete blocks. At one end was a covered patio where you could sit during an afternoon and watch the desert vegetation wither in the heat as small animals and lizards dragged themselves across scorching sands. At the other end was a carport in which stood a Ford F-150 pickup with oversized tires. An array of three satellite dishes on the roof evidently provided him with TV and internet access, though I couldn't imagine why anyone would seek refuge from the madding crowd in this wasteland and then subject himself to Twitter.

Hakeem's front yard was dirt and gravel stone and a few sprigs of gray grass. I didn't feel that it was rude to park on it.

When we got out of the Explorer, we heard a generator most likely fueled by propane. Hakeem was beyond the reach of the public power supply, so he had to provide his own electricity in order to enjoy the amenities of civilization, as well as to pump water from his well. He evidently had added a muffler to the generator, because it labored softly, like a family of bears snoring in hibernation.

I powered the windows of the SUV down an inch and left the engine running to ensure that Winston continued to have fresh and cooled air.

Bridget gave him the lamb squeaky toy for company. Maybe it was the first toy he'd ever had. He just stared at it as it lay there on the back seat, until she picked it up and encouraged him to take it in his mouth. With what seemed to be a bewildered expression, the lambkin hanging from his jaws by one leg, he watched us walk toward the trailer.

Considering that Hakeem Kaspar's residence was the only one in sight and that, past his place, the dirt road seemed to lead into either a prehuman past or a posthuman future, it was no surprise that he heard us arrive and opened the door as we approached and carried a pistol in a holster on his right hip.

He appeared to be in his late forties, with decades of sunshine stored in his deeply tanned face. Judging by his name, I assumed his ancestors came from the Middle East, though he looked like a twin to the Cuban bandleader who was married to Lucille Ball in that old TV series *I Love Lucy*. His large eyes were open wide, as if something about us alarmed him.

Instead of asking us who we were, he said, "Stop right there and come forward one at a time to be scanned. I don't know you. I can't trust anyone I don't know, and I don't trust half those I do know."

In his left hand, Hakeem held an object the size of a slim hardcover book, something rather like a Kindle, to which was wired an instrument resembling an infrared digital thermometer that he gripped in his right hand.

Assuming the thing wasn't a weapon, I stepped forward. He needed perhaps half a minute to scan me, consulting a screen on the book-sized device. Bridget complied next, and then Sparky.

Hakeem said, "Okay, all right, you seem to be what you appear to be, if that means anything. Now *who* are you? ID please."

I saw no point in pretending to be Bart Simpson or, for that matter, Bugs Bunny. I'd come there to ask him about the morning he'd found me in a bassinet.

When I held out my driver's license, his wide-eyed gaze widened further. The suspicion that had iced his every word now melted into astonishment. "Q-Q-Quinn Q-Quicksilver? Not the one and same?"

"The one and same," I assured him.

"From the bassinet?"

"I outgrew it."

"They sent you away."

"I came back."

"My life was never the same."

"The same as what?" I asked.

"Never the same—after you."

"I've come to thank you for *my* life," I said. "And to ask you about that morning. This is Bridget, who tells me she's my fiancée, and this is her grandfather, Sparky. Do you want to see their ID?"

"No. That's all right. They passed the scan. I've got to trust the scanner. If I can't trust the scanner, then what can I trust?"

"So very true," Bridget said.

"Is that a dog in your SUV?"

"Yes," I said.

"You must be all right if a dog will associate with you. Dogs can always be trusted."

He regarded us in silence, scanning our faces without using the scanner this time.

Then he said, "The only people I let in here are my best friend and my girlfriend. Everyone else I know, I either visit them at their homes or on neutral ground. You can understand that."

We all agreed that we could understand, and I said we would be happy just to sit in the shade of the covered patio and ask a few questions.

His voice now hushed with awe, he said, "But you're the baby in the bassinet."

"Yeah, that's me."

"I often dream of you as a baby. They're good dreams. In them I'm famous and honored for finding you on the highway. You're always three days old no matter how much time passes, and I never grow old as long as I'm with you, and all kinds of animals look after you, including a bear that feeds you honey with a golden spoon."

I didn't know what to say to that, so uncharacteristically, I said nothing.

Finally, Hakeem said, "Well, I guess if you were going to spin me up in a cocoon or plant an egg in my brain or kill me, you'd have done it already. Come on in. Can I get you coffee or anything?"

I followed Bridget and Sparky up the three metal steps and into the habitat of a man consumed by an obsession.

## 21

Taped to the ceiling, walls, cabinet doors, and permanently lowered window shades were photographs torn from fringe magazines and downloaded from the internet, images of classic flying saucers as well as UFOs of other configurations. Some blurry or captured in half light. Others crisp and intriguing. Many of them sure to be hoaxes. Crowding every surface, they were a claustrophobia-inducing collection of extraterrestrial mystery.

The place smelled of clove buds that were piled in small dishes and placed strategically throughout the trailer. The essence was so thick in the air that I could taste it as well as smell it.

In the living room, forward of the galley, I had settled on the sofa with Bridget, while Sparky occupied an armchair. Hakeem sat in a second armchair but repeatedly got up to pace restlessly, now and then patting the grip of the holstered pistol, as though to reassure himself that he was still armed in case one of us attempted to plant an egg in his brain, after all.

"What I'm going to tell you is between us. If you speak a word of it to anyone, I'll deny I ever said what I said. We didn't tell any of this to the sheriff when we brought you to him. We didn't want everyone in the county thinking we were either doing magic mushrooms together or cooking up a story to maybe get a movie deal. Anyway, the sheriff is a good man, but he has no more imagination than a rock. He'd have thought we were liars or lunatics, and he might have sent us to County General for psychiatric evaluation."

From under his pleated and beetling brow, he glared at us until we solemnly agreed never to quote him.

"I had no interest in UFOs before that day," said the lineman. "Zero, zip, nada. They were a joke to me. Not anymore. I usually hit the road an hour before dawn, but I set out late that morning. I was heading north out of Peptoe on the federal, as the land took shape in the first light. I've got my punch sheet of inspections to make, and I'm always studying the lines, so I don't speed. I was poking along like usual when I noticed some white thing in the center of the three lanes. When I slowed almost to a stop, I saw a young girl, maybe in her late teens, out there on the flats, running away from the road toward one of those three-wheel all-terrain vehicles with big fat tires, like a tricycle for grown-ups. This young thing slips astride it and speeds away among the sage and mesquite, dust spewing up behind her. I suppose she was your mother."

No mention of such a person had appeared in the news story about the baby on the highway. For so long, I had accepted being an orphan and being never able to discover who had abandoned me, so I was surprised to be overcome by a sentimental yearning to know more about that young woman—if nothing other than the color of her hair, her eyes. But Hakeem had seen her only at a distance and not clearly enough in the early light to report any details about her with confidence.

Bridget took one of my hands and held it in both of hers. Her hands felt unusually warm, so mine must have gone cold.

Hakeem erupted from his armchair and paced back into the dining area, into the galley, and then came toward us again. "I parked on the pavement with the truck's emergency lights flashing and went to see what the girl had left in the basket. I didn't realize it was a bassinet. When I saw a baby, I felt sick that someone would be so desperate to throw away such a precious thing."

Stopping at a set of bookshelves that contained volumes about UFOs and ancient astronauts, he plucked one of the many clove buds from a small dish on a shelf and brought it to his nose. He breathed deeply a few times and returned the bud to the dish.

"Just then," he continued, "I heard engines approaching fast from both the north and south. The first was Caesar Melchizadek on his way to work at the casino, and the other was Bailie Belshazzer in his Chevy pickup, headed for the wind farm. With my power-company truck blocking one lane, something bad could have happened. I should have grabbed the bassinet and taken you off the highway, but I was kind of—I don't know—emotionally paralyzed by what I'd found. I wasn't thinking straight. I waved down both Caesar and Bailie. They pulled off on the shoulder of the road and got out of their vehicles to see what the trouble was."

He sat once more, back stiff, arms on the arms of the chair, hands clutching the upholstery, feet pressed flat on the floor, as though bracing himself for an earthquake. He remained wide-eyed, and gradually it became clear that neither our unannounced visit nor my identity accounted for his expression of surprise, which seemed perpetual, as though every smallest thing he looked upon astonished him.

"We gathered around the bassinet," he said. "I was on my knees. Caesar was on one knee, and Bailie was crouched down. They were facing me, so they didn't at first see what I saw behind them. Forty feet past them, right there on the highway . . . it was as if this large door opened, maybe fifteen feet wide and twice as high. An invisible door. *A door in the day.* It opened inward, and beyond it there wasn't the highway or desert. Cobblestones, like an ancient road, dwindled away into darkness, not just into night, but . . . into a star-filled nothingness. As if the cobblestones were floating in space, with stars under and above and to all sides."

Even one day earlier, I might have sided with Sheriff Monkton in the prescription of a psychiatric evaluation for Hakeem, but not after the Screamers at the truck stop.

He flung himself up from the chair and began to pace again, combing his hair back from his forehead with the fingers of his right hand, his left hand shaking like that of a man with a benign tremor. As if the weight of his revelations made him heavier, each footfall sent a soft, hollow thump through the crawl space under the floor, as had not been the case before.

"Weirder still, I get the feeling that someone or something is coming toward us along that cobblestone road, coming out of the stars. No, wait. That's not right. It's not just some feeling. I *know* for sure that something's approaching along the cobblestones. Because, I can feel it coming, something powerful, the way you feel the air taking on weight when a thunderstorm is coming. And then I can almost see what it is. It's invisible but I can see the space where it is, just inside the door in the day. It's like how heat rising off a highway distorts the air, so the air ripples and quivers. The air is quivering in the shape of a man, a very tall man or something like a man, but I can't see him, only this suggestion of him. I think I must be losing it, having a breakdown. But then somehow I know he's real and that he's there because of the baby, worried that the baby has been abandoned on a highway, and wants to be sure it's safe. I don't know what I said then, but I must have said something, because Caesar and Bailie turned to look. I expected maybe they wouldn't see anything, but they did. They did."

He went into the kitchen, opened the refrigerator, and withdrew a beer. He popped the cap off the bottle and returned to his chair and took several long swallows. He didn't offer us a drink. Reliving the supernatural event on the highway probably so unnerved him that he expected to need every bottle he had before the day was done.

After a silence, Sparky said, "And?"

Hakeem stared at him for maybe half a minute. He looked at the bottle of beer that he'd half finished. He took another swallow. "So then we all shoot to our feet. We're like, *this can't be happening.* I mean, *it's a door in the day!* Then a hissing sound and a gust of wind make us look up. Overhead there's now a hole in the sky. *A hole in the sky!* Do I sound crazy to you? I'm not mental. Do you think I'm mental?"

As earnestly as we were able, the three of us assured him that we did not think he was mental.

Hakeem said, "So it's like somebody just opened a big lid on the day. Through that opening, maybe twelve feet in diameter, we see a night sky, darkness and stars going on forever, just like beyond the magic door. I think we're about to be sucked up into that night sky. Instead, these concentric circles of blue light come out of the hole, out of the stars, and wash over us. We feel them as well as see them, a tingling sensation in our bones—and something funny happens to time."

I was pretty sure he meant funny scary, not funny ha-ha.

He finished the beer. "None of us has any memory of getting in our vehicles. The next thing we know, it seems like an instant later, we're in Peptoe, me with the baby—that's you—in the power-company truck, Bailie and Caesar following. We all had this terrible feeling that the baby was in great danger, that someone could come for him—for you—at any moment. Hell, not someone. Some*thing*. Something that would kill us to get at you. I swear, we were flat-out terrified. It makes no sense how crazy frightened we were. We'd been *made* terrified. I think that weird blue light, those concentric circles . . . somehow they programmed us to guard you and get you quickly away from that lonely stretch of highway, into the hands of the authorities, eventually to someone who would care about you as if you were their own child. I kept thinking that your vital thread had been broken, that the ends of your vital thread couldn't be tied together again until you were in loving hands."

"What does that mean, 'vital thread'?" I asked.

"I don't *know* what the hell it means. But I was in a panic about it."

He raised the bottle to his lips and seemed surprised that he had drained it.

Bridget's turn had come to say, "And?"

"No, I'm done. I'm empty. I have no more for you. Bailie and Caesar didn't see quite the same thing I did. You need to hear their side to get the whole picture."

"Where are they?" Sparky asked. "How do we contact them?"

"Two months after what happened, Caesar quit his job as pit boss and split from the casino scene. Maybe he didn't get religion, but he got something. He went to Florida to work in a hospice his sister founded, taking care of people who're dying. Bailie still lives in the heart of Peptoe. Wife passed away. He'll tell you his side and Caesar's. He up and quit the wind farm back when, started making a living with music."

He put the empty bottle on the table beside his chair. He stared at it as if it were a mystical object filled with recondite meaning, and then he looked at me the way you might stare at a two-headed goat.

He said, "What is it with you, Quinn Quicksilver?"

"What do you mean?"

"What are you?"

"Confused," I admitted.

"Why are space aliens so interested in you?"

"I'm not aware of any space aliens," I assured him. "We just came here because I was hoping, you know, I might get a lead on who my parents are."

"Maybe the best way to find out," Hakeem said with apparent sincerity and no quality of menace in his voice, "is to send your spit to one of those places like Getting to Know Me Dot Com."

"There's an idea," I said. "I'll definitely look into that."

While Bridget took a pen and paper from her purse and wrote down the directions to Bailie Belshazzer's place that Hakeem gave her, Sparky went to the bookshelves to have a look at the titles on the spines of the volumes. He took a clove bud from the little dish and brought it close to his nose and said, "Hakeem, why the cloves?"

"I read somewhere that the smell repels the Grays. It's like garlic with vampires."

"Grays?" Sparky asked.

Just then we heard a sudden bass throbbing that quickly became louder, the air-chopping clatter of a helicopter, not a small two-man police helo, but something larger. Through the window behind Hakeem's chair, I saw it coming, flying low and fast: black, twin engines, high-set main and tail rotors. The big craft roared over us and away. As the sound of it diminished and the mobile home stopped vibrating, I didn't give the helo further thought. Military bases are a common feature of the Southwest; I assumed that some pilot was engaged in flight training.

"Grays," Hakeem said, "are the most common type of ETs reported by people who were abducted and taken up to the mother ship. Their skin is gray. You must've seen drawings of them. They're kind of short, sexless, hairless, with big oval heads and huge dark eyes with no whites. The Grays are up to something, and it's not good. They want something from us that we can't begin to imagine. I hope to God I never find out what it is. I hope they don't get what they want from *me*."

This was a haunted man, a troubled man, his life forever sent off the rails because he had been in the wrong place at the wrong time and had seen something that he could neither understand nor forget. If I had found him amusing, it was because I tend to find most people amusing. Not least of all myself. After all, each of us is an eccentric in one way or another, to one degree or another. However, I was beginning to feel that Hakeem was a tragic figure, a victim of post-traumatic stress disorder who was trapped in a spiral staircase of dread with no exit at the top or bottom, ceaselessly racing up and down and up.

I indicated the scanning device that he had left on the coffee table. "Is that a Gray detector?"

"No, no. Grays aren't shape changers. I got this from a techie flying-saucer guru in Arkansas. He builds and programs them himself. It's based on a Chinese facial-recognition system, LLVision, but without the usual glasses. And it's not about facial recognition, but about scanning for structural anomalies, anything that might indicate the human form is merely a costume. I'm not mental."

"Of course you're not," I said. "Have you ever scanned anyone who's set off an alarm?"

"Not yet. But with UFO activity increasing, it's bound to happen one day. Thank God for Miles Bennell. He's a genius."

"Miles Bennell?"

"He's the guru techie in Arkansas who sells these things."

Bridget said, "Is UFO activity really increasing?"

Springing up from his chair with the kinetic energy of a jack-in-the-box, Hakeem Kaspar said, "It always has been, ever since the 1940s. It's always accelerating—the activity, number of sightings— toward some end. Who knows what end? Many nights, I sit out in the yard, in a lawn chair, and I watch the sky. Many nights. If you do that, you'll be surprised at what you'll see. You'll see things that never took off from an earthly airport and will never land at one, immense craft without running lights, dark forms that blot out the stars as they pass. I've seen them. I watch, and I see them, and I'm not mental." His feverish gaze slid from Bridget to me to Sparky. He took a deep breath. "Don't tell anyone what I said. My job at the power company depends on this being secret. My interest in . . . in these things is something they wouldn't understand."

After we promised to keep his secret, we departed.

I was the last to leave. At the door, I put a hand on Hakeem's shoulder and said, "I'm sorry." I looked around at the hundreds of UFO photos papering nearly everything. "I didn't leave myself in the middle of that highway, but I feel responsible for what you've been through, for what you're going through."

His eyes at last narrowed. He squinted at me, as if scanning for structural anomalies. Then he startled me by throwing his arms around me and saying, "No, no, no. No, no, no." He released me. His eyes were owlish again and now glimmering with unshed tears. "Before you, before baby you, before that door in the day and that hole in the sky, I was just marking time, just existing. There was no wonder in my life, no magic, nothing to believe in except a paycheck and a six-pack. That day, what happened on that stretch of highway—after that, I understood the world wasn't just a movie screen, wasn't just flat, there was depth to it, strangeness and meaning. I don't know *what* meaning, but it's something big, and I'm a part of it. If there are evil Grays—and there are!—then there must be other ETs, good Blues or some other color. Whatever's out there, it's anything you could imagine, *everything* you could imagine, because the universe is *that big*. I owe you, Quinn Quicksilver. I owe you for my happiness."

Well. Even I, for all my limitations, discerned two lessons from Hakeem's heartfelt response. First, it is a mistake to presume to know anyone's internal emotional landscape based on what external emotional signals they seem to be sending. Second, you can apologize for something you have done, but only a fool apologizes for things that other people have done, for he has no authority to do that. And so I felt like a fool as I left the trailer, though like a fool with the best intentions. I took solace in the fact that, although I had inspired Hakeem to pursue profound meaning where he would never find it—UFOs, Grays, Blues, mother ships, abductees given rectal exams by freaky aliens—at least I had inspired wonder in the poor guy. In time, wonder might lead to that more elevated feeling that is awe, the yielding of the mind to the reverence of what is supremely grand and true.

When I joined Sparky and Bridget in front of the Explorer, she said, "Winston is going to be so excited. We smell like hams baking in an oven. What was that all about, the huggy thing?"

"He says he owes his happiness to me. Baby me, to be specific."

Sparky frowned. "Happiness?"

"It's contagious, isn't it?" I said. "I went in there glum, and I came out so carefree I want to dance. Now we better go see Bailie Belshazzer. There's still plenty of daylight left, but I want to be sure to be out of Peptoe before the curtain opens on the bugs-and-bats show."

Looking past us toward the trailer, Sparky said, "What's this?"

"This" was Hakeem, hurrying toward us, holding his smartphone high overhead, as if carrying the Olympic torch. He enjoyed phone service out here. His connectivity must have had something to do with one of the satellite dishes on his roof.

"John Ching just called. You can't go to Bailie's place," Hakeem warned. "Not now. Not ever. That helicopter was carrying ISA agents. Eight or nine of the bastards. They're already at Bailie's house. They've commandeered his SUV and two of the sheriff's patrol cars. No doubt they'll be here as soon as they can get anyone to tell them how to find my place, which won't be right away because the people of Peptoe don't traffic with their kind. You've got to go straight to Panthea. Bailie would have sent you to her after you'd visited with him. Panthea has been expecting you for weeks."

"Weeks?" Bridget said. "We didn't know we were coming here until yesterday."

"Yes, but Panthea sees."

"Sees what?"

"What a seer sees when a seer dreams."

"Well, of course. Silly of me not to understand."

"You must go to Panthea. She's waiting for you. You'll be safe with her. No one will think to look for you there."

I was sure that was true, because even *I* would never have thought to look for me there, wherever "there" might be. "Yeah, okay, but I don't know anyone named Panthea. Panthea who?"

Hakeem regarded me with frustration and amazement, unable to comprehend how the miracle baby from the stars could be so clueless. "Panthea who? *Panthea who?* Panthea Ching, of course!"

## 22

Winston had arrived at an understanding of the purpose of a toy.
During our trip from Hakeem's outpost to Panthea's home, to
which the UFOlogist had directed us with extravagant gestures,
the pooch lay on the back seat, beside Sparky, incessantly squeak-
ing the white lamb, all the while happily slapping the seat with
his tail.

"I knew a guy," Sparky said, "wanted to protect his children,
he had an attack dog that lived up to its name. If you'd tried to
give it a toy, it would've taken off your hand and eaten it."

"Seems dangerous, a dog like that around little kids," I said.

"Not these kids. They were tough little bastards. The dog had
profound respect for them."

With afternoon light slanting across the still and colorless
land, short shadows of low cacti and mesquite prickled the earth;
but the usually reliable sameness of a desert day would not sustain
until nightfall. A tide of dark-gray thunderheads stacked on squall
clouds was surging in from the southwest, soon to drown the sun.
In advance of the storm, the hot air began to cool, and its faint
alkaline scent faded.

Panthea, the daughter of John Kennedy Ching, didn't occupy
one of the family's five houses in the vicinity of Ching Station. She

lived beyond the vaguely defined limits of Peptoe, in that other-wise unpopulated suburb that, I knew from my research, locals referred to as Dead Dan's Wasteland, though Dan was so lost in the dust storms of history that no one remembered who he'd been, when he'd lived, or how he'd died. Panthea's place was at the end of a gravel road, in a large, insulated Quonset hut that she'd con-verted into a residence. The structure dated to early World War II, when the government had conducted secret experiments here that no one dared speak about, resulting in thirteen deaths and the toxic contamination of the soil that took over half a century to resolve. Rumor had it that an unintended consequence of the experimentation had been the mutation of six-legged Jerusalem crickets into terrors as big as dachshunds, with teeth that would shred bone as easily as flesh, creatures that had to be exterminated with flamethrowers and submachine guns in a desperate three-day bug war. Eighty years had passed since then, and no one had seen such a fearsome beast. So whatever else had happened here, the cricket business must have been an apocryphal story with no more substance than the rumor that, in the same decade, an atomic bomb had been developed elsewhere in a program called the Manhattan Project.

Three satellite dishes were fixed to the curved roof. Like Hakeem, the resident considered connectivity a high priority.

Now thirty, Panthea had moved at a distance from her family when she was eighteen because she had foreseen that eventually she would be murdered in the night by unhuman assassins, and she didn't want her relatives to be collateral damage. As he'd fin-ished giving us directions, Hakeem Kaspar, who'd seen a door in the day and a hole in the sky, who had shaped the previous twenty years of his life according to the belief that the territory hereabouts served as a hub of extraterrestrial activity, had winked when he told us about the unhuman assassins and said, "Panthea is a bit of an eccentric, but this territory produces more than a few. All in all, in spite of the unhuman assassin silliness, she's a great lady and true seer."

Having heard the Explorer approaching, Panthea was waiting for us in the open door of the Quonset hut. She was five feet one and weighed maybe ninety-five pounds, prettier than any desert flower, of which there are many that dazzle. If her ears had been slightly pointed, I would have been convinced that she had elf DNA, for her blue eyes were quite large and so limpid that you could see the radiant pleats of the layered muscles in her irises.

Although she had the physique of an adolescent and the innocent face of a child, she was an undeniably powerful presence, standing spread-legged, wearing a blood-red tunic and gray jeans tucked into black combat boots. Her black hair was chopped in a short shag, her hands fisted on her hips, as if she was confident of being able to Jackie Chan us all if we proved to be a threat.

As we got out of the Explorer, she told us to bring Winston. When he was freed from the SUV, he raced across the hardpan, past Panthea, and into the Quonset hut, as if he had once lived here and was excited to return home.

Panthea looked each of us in the eyes, nodding as if confirming our identity by some sixth sense. "Quinn, Bridget, Silas who calls himself Sparky. I knew you would come. The squad is now complete."

"Squad?" I said.

"One squad of many but no less important than the others. Each of us is an *aluf shel halakha*, with a great responsibility."

"We're on a quest," I said.

"It's nothing as simple as a quest," Bridget said.

"Isn't it a quest?" I asked Panthea the seer.

"Perhaps a quest, but not only a quest."

I was having none of that. "We find the equivalent of the Holy Grail, the Ark of the Covenant, the elephants' graveyard, and then it's done."

Sparky said, "What does that mean—*aluf* whatever?"

"When you know *why* you are," Panthea Ching said, "you will know what those words mean."

"Why I am? My mom and dad wanted a baby. That's why I am. Now, please, Ms. Ching, what does *aluf* shell halibut mean?"

"It means nothing to you now. In time it will."

Frustrated to be on the receiving end of the kind of enigmatic statements that he and Bridget had often dished out to me, Sparky said, "It was a simple question."

"There are no simple questions," the seer replied, "only simple answers, some of which it's best you discern for yourself. Anyway, some squads prefer to say *aluf shel teevee chok*. Still others say *Legis naturalis propugnator*. The sentiment is the same."

"And what is the sentiment?" Bridget asked.

"Resist," said Panthea.

"Resist what?"

"You need not ask what you already know. Come in, come in. The ISA will be saturating the county with agents, but we have a few hours yet before they'll be breaking down my door. You must see what I paint in my sleep. You will recognize it."

I began to realize that this was not going to be the date on my calendar when I would learn the identity of my parents or even the least thing about them. The theme of the day was instead about the strange, cognizant Destiny that links human lives in unexpected ways. The Ching-Rainking-Quicksilver squad had been drawn together by something more than psychic magnetism; however, any attempt that I might make to define "something more" would lead me nowhere except to the insolvable mystery of human existence or into the cold waters of Hakeem Kaspar's obsession.

As to the latter, when we followed Panthea into the Quonset hut, she seemed to have heard my thoughts, though she was merely acting in her role as the squad's seer, disabusing us of whatever credibility we might have given to the possibility of mother ships and off-worlders who were gray or any other color. "This isn't about extraterrestrials from other galaxies, or from a farther arm of our own, or from a moon of Saturn. That stuff is for the movies. If only our adversaries were evil ETs, I'd rejoice. But the war into which we've been drafted is older than Earth itself and older than the stars, and we have no choice but to give ourselves to the current battle. The war predates the universe, as do our enemies."

How like madness that sounded at the time Panthea said it.

As I wrote earlier, I see every human being as an eccentric to one degree or another. This can be true only if our assumption that there is a standard for normality is wrong. And I believe it is wrong. The human race is at the apex of all life-forms because, no matter how strenuously sociologists and politicians and others of their persuasion insist on defining our species into interest groups and factions and classes and tribes, the better to control us, in truth our greatest strength is in the uniqueness of each of us. Einstein, in his genius, can reveal to us much about the workings of the universe, and a child with Down syndrome can teach us, by his or her profound gentleness and humility, how urgently this troubled world needs kindness. Everyone has something to contribute.

Everyone but sociopaths. Those empty souls possess no genuine human feelings—other than a lust for power—but are excellent at faking them. Some say that as many as 10 percent of human beings are sociopaths. Some are street thugs who will kill you for the contents of your wallet or merely for the thrill of it. Others are among the most elite and privileged groups in society.

Although Panthea's claim that our adversaries were older than the universe sounded like lunacy, I knew she wasn't a sociopath. I found it nearly impossible to think of John Kennedy Ching producing one. However, madness is a different thing from sociopathy, and the potential lies in every heart. Auschwitz and Dachau and Belsen. The killing fields of Cambodia. The tens of millions murdered by Stalin, by Mao. When feverish politics and demented ideology entwine, those who are not well anchored to the beliefs that allow a civil society can be swept away, becoming part of the storm of madness that lays waste to everything. When she spoke of a war that had raged before stars ever formed, she seemed to have bought into a cultish creed that might lead to fanaticism and madness.

In Panthea's home, however, Bridget and I found our experience of the morning—what we had seen when drawn into mirrors as if into another world—replicated on the walls of the front room. If these murals were part of Panthea's madness, then we were mad as well.

As we would learn, the Quonset hut, which faced directly east at its entrance and west at its back door, was laid out like a shotgun house, without hallways: first, a large living room; then beyond a doorway, a smaller dining room; thereafter, another door into a kitchen; beyond the kitchen, a bathroom; beyond the bath, a garage in which a vintage Range Rover stood in wait.

The initial space, a living room with a circle of six armchairs and small tables to serve them, also included a large adjustable drawing table with a tall swiveling chair, a cabinet in which she stored brushes and paints, and a pair of easels to each of which was fixed a painting in progress.

Judging by just those two incomplete works, I thought Panthea Ching was immensely talented. Sadly, the paintings by the fry cooks Phil and Jill Beane—he with spiky purple hair and shaved eyebrows; she with spiky green hair, black pajamas, and red shoes—were by comparison much less affecting. If my friends, the twins, shaved their heads and dyed their skin blue, and if the art establishment decided they were marketable, perhaps the two paintings of theirs that I'd bought, which currently hung in the employee bathrooms at *Arizona!* magazine, would soar in value and provide me with the funds for a comfortable retirement. However, I had to admit that such a bonanza now seemed even less likely than a monster hunter's living long enough to retire.

The Quonset hut was big, and the front room, by far the largest of its spaces, measured perhaps sixty feet square. On the long north and south walls were the halves of the mural she purported to have painted in her sleep.

"Each wall was completed over a period of weeks," Panthea said. "I would often wake at night and be working on these. At times during the day, I'd be overcome with weariness, lie down, fall into sleep, only to wake hours later and find myself with the trolley, brushes and tubes of acrylics arranged on top, painting feverishly."

We moved to the left of the front door, to the long south wall, where the eight-foot-tall mural began, portraying in vivid detail what I had seen in the motel-bathroom mirror that morning. Then it had been a three-dimensional underworld with its denizens in motion. Here it was a two-dimensional static image, although the artist's passion and technique gave it unsettling power. The labyrinth of tunnels, the surreal architecture. Dead people hanging from the walls or lying on catafalques, spectral light emanating from their open mouths and sunken eyes. Ghouls devouring.

There were other terrors that I had only half registered when falling through the world of the mirror, a scene with the intricacy of a canvas by Hieronymus Bosch, but more horrific than anything Bosch could have conceived.

Panthea had painted this weeks before Bridget and I had been briefly plunged into a vision of this wretched, perilous future—if that's what it was.

The mural continued on the north wall. Swarms of terrified, naked people panicked through a dark train tunnel in which cattle cars packed with the condemned rollicked along. The burning city, violent crime rampant in every corner. The shrieking horse pulling the blazing carriage. The sobbing woman with a bloody baby held in her arms. In this end-times metropolis, the Screamers moved among the rapists and murderers, as though more than observing, as though mentoring, encouraging. Yet we came to something that unsettled us more than anything we'd seen elsewhere in the mural. Floating above the dying city in a smoky sky orange with reflected fire, rendered as a pair of pale moons, were my face and Bridget's, gazing down on the destruction and brutal murders, our expressions as they almost certainly had been when we'd looked into the motel mirrors and found ourselves plunging into the abyss.

"You painted us before we'd ever had this vision," Bridget marveled. "You knew we'd have it."

"I knew nothing," Panthea said. "I really did paint it all as a sleepwalker, or in a fugue state if you prefer. When I woke, I was always chilled by the images I'd created. But when I finished it—*then* I knew you'd be coming and that together we would do our small part to resist the world becoming as it is here on these walls."

Hearing this, Sparky turned to his granddaughter, his scowl so fierce that it confirmed he could have been, in his younger years, capable of merciless retribution against the enemies of his country. "Vision? You saw all this in a vision, not a mere presentiment? Why didn't you tell me?"

"It was only this morning, Grandpa. Quinn and I experienced it separately. I've been processing it ever since. So has he. I didn't want to talk about it until I understood it."

"You evidently talked about it to Quinn."

"Not really, not much," I said. "We only confirmed with each other that we'd seen something terrible in our mirrors."

Bridget put a hand on my shoulder to silence me.

Sparky said, "Girl, we've never hidden a thing from each other. We've been in this together."

"And we still are, Grandpa. I wasn't hiding it from you. I only needed time to think it through and then to understand what Quinn made of it." She went to him and put one hand to his cheek. "You know, Sparky, it's not just two of us anymore. It's three of us—"

"Four," said Panthea.

"Four of us," Bridget corrected.

Winston grumbled.

"Five," Bridget said. "You and me, Sparky—we've been through a lot together, and we've been great. But we need help now, and it's being given to us. How many were in a SEAL team? Just two? I don't think it was just two."

Face-to-face with her, he could not hold his scowl. He shook his head and sighed. "Suddenly, I feel old."

"You're not old," she said. "You're seasoned. The squad needs someone seasoned. It doesn't work without you."

Sparky looked at me and said he was sorry, and I said he didn't need to be, and he told Panthea Ching that he still wasn't sure about her, and she said, "Likewise," which made him smile.

Bridget withheld from him her presentiment that not all of us would survive. I wondered if she had withheld anything from me.

| 23 |

Although the desert lives with less water than seashores and for-
ested mountains and fruited plains, the rare storms sometimes
pound the earth in torrents that turn dry arroyos into raging rivers and inundate low-lying areas with flash floods. The rain that
broke upon us that day didn't gently rataplan upon the Quonset
hut, but rattled against it in violent barrages, as if Nature misun-
derstood our purpose and, siding with the Screamers, had gone
to war with us.

Panthea said that we would be called to service soon, would
be leaving Peptoe this evening, and needed to have dinner to
fortify us for what we might endure between now and dawn.
She spoke with quiet confidence and authority. Her pellucid blue
eyes seemed like windows to a serene mind incapable of deceit.
Bridget, Sparky, and I didn't doubt she was a seer and our ally; if
we were anxious about what came next, we were also relieved that
we'd found the person able to lead us to a full understanding of
the Screamers and our purpose.

Given her petiteness and seeming inclination toward mysticism, Panthea might have been expected to put before us a meal
of organic greens and tofu, but happily her tastes ran counter to
those of the kale-and-carrots crowd. She had prepared for our

visit, and the spread that she produced included sliced roast beef, sliced ham, sliced chicken breast, a variety of cheeses, three artisanal breads that she baked herself, potato salad, three-bean salad with bacon, and numerous condiments. She intended that we accompany dinner with icy bottles of beer kept in a refrigerated drawer at thirty-six degrees, and she was met with no objections.

The Dionysian nature of the buffet suggested the indulgent last meal of those condemned to death, but if Panthea foresaw that this feast would be followed by multiple fatalities, she had the grace to keep that knowledge to herself.

Her dining room, an industrial-chic space, featured two big round tables of polished pine with seating for eight at each, to accommodate gatherings of her family. We sat at one table with an open chair between each of us, and yet the moment felt intimate. The room was illuminated by maybe sixteen flames wimpling on wicks in red cut-glass cups and by pulses of fierce lightning that flared through the small windows and made shadows leap as if they were agitated spirits. The effect was like a séance with refreshments.

Noble Winston sat on what would otherwise have been the empty captain's chair between Bridget and me. He accepted pieces of beef from her—refusing them from me—but never begged, behaving with the decorum of a prime minister.

"What you call Screamers," Panthea said, "were once beautiful beings, not monsters in appearance, though in their minds and hearts they became monsters. I've dreamed of them for fifteen years. My dreams aren't just dreams, but lessons in the reality of the cosmos. I'm being instructed in dreams. The Screamers are from the *first* universe, which preceded ours. The envious among them corrupted all of their kind, seeding suspicion and resentment that became hatred, which they called a virtue, bitter hatred so destructive that they brought Earth to ruin. That devastated world was the legacy they made for themselves. The physical appearance of those who survived the destruction then changed to reflect the condition of their souls. They became immortal monsters in the prison of that first universe. When they were beautiful and radiant, they were called *Rishon*. When they became monsters, they were called *Nihilim*."

The softness of her voice and the ease with which she spoke reminded me of a girl, Annie Piper, at the orphanage. Annie was eight years older than me, and for a few years when my age was in the single digits, she read stories to us, tales written by others but also by her. They were stories of things that had never happened and could never happen, but she told them with such quiet verve and conviction that we believed them and wanted to continue believing even after time robbed us of our sense of wonder. Encouraged by Sister Margaret, who took a special interest in her writing, Annie went to college on a scholarship, and we all expected great things of her, at least that she'd become a well-known writer one day. Instead, she dropped out of college after a year and drifted into some other life she evidently preferred, and we never heard from her again.

Sad as that was, I could nevertheless understand it. Writing novels seems like a glamorous and exciting occupation, although in reality I suspect that it's a lot less glamorous than professional wrestling and only marginally more exciting than being a librarian.

To create good fiction, you have to like people enough to want to write about the human condition—but close yourself alone in a room for a large part of your life to get the job done right. It's as if a wrestler forsook the ring in favor of getting his own head in an armlock and slamming himself into walls for a few hours every day.

"We are the Rishon of the second universe," Panthea continued, "though we're a species with fewer gifts than those that the Rishon of the first universe possessed. Think of it like this—the genome of those original Rishon was edited to make us humbler and give us a better chance of avoiding the arrogance that would destroy our world as they destroyed theirs. The Nihilim, those you call the Screamers, can never by their own choice cross from their universe into ours. But the worst among us, the most morally deranged, are able to open a door to them, invite them, which is what happened long ago."

Sparky said, "What dunce would invite those wormheads?"

Winston chuffed as if in agreement.

"A dunce," Panthea said, "who believes all the legends that are based on the Nihilim, who knows the Nihilim by other names that have been given them in myths that in fact are not merely myths, a dunce who admires them for their selfishness and ruthlessness, who wants them to make him powerful. There are rituals to open the door, but it's not rituals that draw the Nihilim. They're drawn by the passion of those who call them. Rituals aren't essential. The Nihilim can also be welcomed into our world by someone who's been consumed by such an intense desire for power that he or she will commit any crime, any atrocity, to gain dominance over others. That person becomes a doorway without even knowing it."

"Then we're doomed," I declared, and shoveled a heaping forkful of the delicious three-bean salad into my gob. I didn't mean we were without hope. Even as a one-ton chunk of limestone cornice falls from ten floors above and you stand directly under it, puzzling over the meaning of the swiftly growing shadow on the sidewalk, there is still hope. If I'd thought there was no hope, I would have put aside the bean salad and gone straight for the cinnamon-pecan rolls that waited as dessert. "Doomed," I repeated.

Bridget knew what I meant. While my mouth was full, she said, "Increasingly, everywhere in the world, people are not governed by those who wish to serve them, but *ruled* by those mad with power and determined to have total submission. They seem ever more fiercely inspired to greater ruthlessness. They call their hatred justice and see it as a virtue. How many Screamers, Nihilim, have they knowingly and unknowingly brought among us?"

Panthea said, "Could be legions. Or not. But when those who govern us achieve absolute power, it always and everywhere leads to insanity and mass murder. Regardless of the numbers arrayed against us, we must resist. If we fail, then the sane among us will die in holocaust after holocaust, along with the madmen and madwomen who hate us for not sharing their delusions."

Maybe it was time for the cinnamon-pecan rolls.

We ate in silence for a minute or two as drafts stirred candle flames, as salamanders of light wriggled up the walls and slithered across the food laid out before us. Thunder crashing, rolling. Wind-driven rain snapping hard off the corrugated metal roof and walls. In the movies, they call that "atmosphere." Mother Nature was being Hitchcock when what we needed was the Hallmark Channel. Each bite I took only seemed to leave me hungrier, and the beer did not affect my sobriety, as perhaps no volume of fine food and drink can satisfy a prisoner dining in the shadow of the electric chair.

Sparky had been considering all Panthea told us. "'Immortal,' you say. But we killed two of them at a truck stop just yesterday evening."

"They're immortal in the first universe. They've been condemned to immortality there. But they're mortal when they come here where they don't belong. And when they come here, they pass as Rishon."

To anyone who hadn't experienced what we'd been through, the conversation would have sounded like teatime exchanges at the Mad Hatter's table.

Sparky persisted. "Why would they surrender immortality to come here and risk dying?"

Although Panthea had an appetite of someone twice her size, and although in her soft-spoken way she was a powerful presence, in that shadowy room lighted by tongues of flame, she seemed at times as thin and transparent as the diaphanous films of light that passed through the red cut-glass cups to reveal her. "Why risk death? Because in their world, they live in the ruins they made, and they have no capacity to create anything new. They exist to destroy. Destruction is their only joy. That's the condition to which they willfully reduced themselves when they achieved the complete depravity of the Nihilim. Because in their world nothing remains to be torn down. There's only rubble and dust. They live in frustration and rage that can never be assuaged. What would it avail them to reduce the remaining rubble to dust, the dust to even finer dust? There's no pleasure in that. Being immortal, they lack the power to kill one another or themselves. And so they yearn for this second universe, where so much remains to be obliterated, where there are people on whom to impose great suffering, so many waiting to be corrupted and killed—and so many who are already on the path to becoming Nihilim themselves. Having once been favored godlings, the Nihilim know a new creation exists, and they yearn to rise from their universe to ours and be among us, even at the cost of losing their immortality."

A dire feeling overcame me then, and I took nothing more onto my plate. At first I thought that both forms of choking disquiet—anxiety and anguish—had spoiled my appetite. Anguish is in regard to the known, anxiety in regard to the unknown. The horror of what I now knew and the terror of what might yet be to come were enough to put even a starving man off his food. However, as I listened to the others talk, I realized that fear was not what made me put my fork down. The dire feeling was instead a sense of loss, a recognition that, beginning in Beane's Diner yesterday afternoon, when the ISA agents bracketed me at the lunch counter, and continuing since then, I'd been slowly robbed of my sense that I lived in a culture that still valued reason above unreason, civility above rote invective, which had once been the case. I wanted to be that naive nineteen-year-old kid crafting articles for *Arizona!* magazine and dreaming about writing a novel, but there was no way back to him.

I needed a good antacid. An invisibility cloak would also have been useful. And the bulletproof Popemobile that the Vatican has.

Bridget said, "We shot those two at the truck stop, prevented mass murder—but as far as we can tell, the incident doesn't seem to have made much news."

Panthea speared a crescent of cantaloupe from a platter and sliced it into bite-size pieces. "Media mostly do what authorities want them to do. In any case involving dead Nihilim, the authorities want to bury the story as much as possible, because they can't explain the deceased."

"You mean . . . what the autopsies show?"

"No. When the Nihilim die in this world, they die as Rishon like us. Only we, the *alufimshel halakha*, are able to see them for what they are. Autopsies won't reveal monsters. The true nature of Creation always remains hidden."

"Because the Nihilim aren't of this world," Sparky said, "they have no history here. No past. No identity."

"Exactly," Panthea confirmed. "Their fingerprints aren't on file anywhere. They hold no jobs, have no families. They steal the money they need, or kill for what they want. They live under false names, manufactured identities. A dead man or woman like that, utterly untraceable, is a mystery to the authorities—one that's plagued them for decades."

Panthea paused to eat the cantaloupe.

Deciding that no more beef would be coming his way, Winston curled up on his chair and went to sleep.

Darkness had come beyond the window. Lightning and thunder still tormented the heavens, and rain still fell, so there would be no bug-and-bat show.

"In the nineteenth century," Panthea continued, "even into the early twentieth, when there were no such things as drivers' licenses and social security cards and medical insurance, a stranger found dead and unidentifiable was considered just a rootless vagabond of one kind or another. No one thought much of it. Now, when the government tracks everyone from birth and Google knows you better than you know yourself, a body that can't be identified is deeply troubling to them. Especially when the cause of death was violence of one kind or another, and when the unidentifiable victims committed violence before they themselves were killed. Ironically, considering dear Hakeem's obsession, the authorities have increasingly come to believe that the dead Nihilim may be extraterrestrials."

In fact, they came from farther away than a distant galaxy. They came from another universe, from an Earth that came to an apocalyptic end before our Earth in *this* universe finished forming in the void. My brain wasn't elastic enough to stretch around that concept. I was a guy who liked hamburgers with three cheeses and chocolate-covered doughnuts, who contentedly watched old *Alien* and *Terminator* movies over and over again, who was still a virgin and who had half expected to die as one at the age of eighty, until I met the moon goddess who told me that I'd marry her. I mean, expecting me to absorb and adapt to all this while having dinner was like expecting Bart Simpson to produce an exquisitely nuanced translation of Proust's *Remembrance of Things Past*.

Bridget said, "How many of these creatures, these Nihilim, do squads like ours manage to exterminate?"

"I don't know. They're not easy to kill. You were lucky at the truck stop. I believe more of us die at their hands than the other way around." Panthea regarded me in solemn silence and then said, "If we don't get you gunned up, you'll be the first of us to die."

"Is that an opinion or something you've foreseen?" I asked, for it was of some concern to me.

"Without a pistol, you will be held down by two of the Nihilim. A third monster will slice off your tongue, pry your eyes out, cut open your chest with a circular saw, and eat your heart."

"That's convincingly specific," I said. "I'm sorry I asked for clarification. I won't do that again."

"Eating your heart is a symbolic act, though they take almost as much pleasure in eating human flesh as in corrupting human souls. Primarily they feed on your pain, like a vampire feeds on blood."

Maybe I was too sensitive, but having my heart eaten was more than a symbolic act to me. The Nihilim could buy a heart-shaped cake with my name on it and eat that, and I'd get the message. "So maybe I don't have what it takes to be a member of a squad like this."

Reaching across the sleeping dog curled between us, Bridget patted my shoulder. "You'll be fine, sweetheart."

A sound arose not of the storm, a low rhythmic groaning in the night above—*waaaah . . . waaaah . . . waaaah . . . waaaah*—as if we were in a pressurized habitat on the floor of an ocean and some leviathan were swimming toward us, calling out to others of its kind with whatever mysterious purpose. As it passed overhead, each bass groan thrummed through the corrugated walls of the Quonset hut.

We fell silent, looking at the ceiling, expecting something to breach our shelter. The groaning faded, and the thing passed, and Panthea said, "It's an ISA ghost drone as big as a Volkswagen van. A microfusion engine allows it to fly for a year without the need to land or refuel. Cutting-edge stealth technology makes it invisible to the naked eye, but they haven't been able to resolve the problem of the propulsion noise. Very top secret."

We all stared at her. Sparky said, "How do you know all that?"

Panthea's answer was to raise one eyebrow and cock her head, which was as good as asking if he didn't know the meaning of *seer*.

"Is it looking for us?" Bridget asked.

"Maybe. But if my perceptions can be trusted, it's more of a weapon than it is a search engine. Maybe the ISA is so freaked out about your alien genome and your ability to escape their every trap that they've decided it's safer just to kill you when they find you instead of trying to take you into custody."

"That's so not right," I said, as if I were still ten years old. "Okay, yeah, they're not about what's right. They're about control. No surer way to control someone than to kill him."

To finish dinner, I had taken a cinnamon-pecan roll with a brown icing. Ambrosia. It was so good I almost forgot the ghost drone. "I need this recipe," I said.

"If you live long enough to make a batch, I'll give you the recipe," Panthea said, and that seemed fair enough to me.

Returning to more immediate matters than ghost drones in the sky, Sparky said, "Quinn has never shot a gun. He'll need training."

"In fact, he won't," Panthea said. "He was born for this. You have no doubt read of prodigies, as young as five, who hear perhaps a Mozart concerto and then sit at a piano for the first time in their lives and play it perfectly. Quinn will be that way with any weapon put in his hands."

"I needed handgun training," Bridget said.

"You believed so," Panthea said, "because your grandfather thought you required it." She smiled at Sparky. "You must have been surprised at how quickly Bridget was able to put into practice all that you taught her."

Sparky looked thoughtful, although probably not as thoughtful as I must have appeared when I considered Panthea's words. Hoping that we might all consider that I had been drafted into this mission in error, I said, "Is it possible that I was maybe meant to be a piano prodigy, but I ended up here by mistake?"

Rising from her chair, our elfin hostess said, "I've got a small armory. Let's get a pistol for you. We need to hit the road soon. We've got somewhere we need to be by tomorrow."

As the rest of us rose to our feet, Winston woke and yawned, and Sparky asked, "Where? Where do we have to be?"

"Beats me," Panthea said. "I don't see everything. My gift has limits. I can be surprised, make mistakes. Which is as it should be. Otherwise, I'd be a puppet in a play. I'm not a puppet. You aren't puppets. But wherever we need to be, that place will find us."

## 24

Panthea gave me a single-action Glock 19 modified with a 3.5-pound connector and New York trigger module, which provided a 5.5-pound trigger pull and eliminated any danger that the manufacturer's standard trigger spring would break.

I had no idea what any of that meant. However, when I accepted the pistol from her, it felt as natural as if I'd been born with it in my hand. I sheathed it in a sharkskin-and-horsehide vertical belt scabbard, which she also provided. At her insistence, I practiced drawing it half a dozen times; it came out of the holster and into a two-handed grip so slick that I impressed Sparky and scared myself.

After we loaded Panthea's luggage and her locked ammunition case in the cargo hold of the Explorer, she sat in back with Sparky, Winston between them. Bridget drove, and I sat up front. The moon goddess said, "I'm feeling we should backtrack federal to federal to I-10 eastbound," and I agreed, and Panthea said, "Then do it."

"Stay sharp but guard against panic," Sparky warned. "The ISA might not know for sure we came to Peptoe, might be here on a hunch. Even those bastards aren't likely to use a ghost drone to incinerate every car that's out and about."

The fact that he felt compelled to credit the ISA with a capacity for restraint meant that he wasn't convinced they had any.

No one spoke for maybe ten miles, silenced by the increasing strangeness of our situation. I had been telling myself that we were forming a kind of family, bonded not by blood but by the shared mystery of our circumstances, by mutual respect and affection and necessity. Now it seemed that before we could be a family, we would be a posse, four spiritual heirs of Professor Van Helsing, chasing down Nihilim as the professor had chased down Dracula. A posse was not a bad thing to be if it was righteous and its quarry was evil. Peril and stress and a sense of purpose could inspire an affinity among the members of a posse. Maybe even an enduring sense of family would grow from that. Of course, a posse in pursuit of murderers was itself a collection of targets; and the dead don't tend to celebrate Thanksgiving with their kin.

The gravel road was a bit slushy but passable. The old federal highway flooded in the lower swales, the pools shallow enough that we could negotiate them, pale wings of water flaring on both sides of the Explorer. In the flashes of lightning, the lonely landscape appeared to be a ghastly vista of wet soot and ashes, and the windshield wipers thumped like the drums in a funeral cortege.

For Bridget, perhaps the storm and the silence were oppressive. Although she couldn't put an end to the former, she chose to break the latter. "Quinn having no knowledge of his origins, my background being mysterious in its own way—I thought that might be a pattern. But you, Panthea, have a family."

"Yes and no. I'm a Ching by adoption. My parents were told my birth mother, born and raised in Tucson, was fifteen when she had me, and she refused to identify the boy who was the father— perhaps because there was no boy."

"Do you think that all of us, the other squads wherever they might be, have been brought into the world in the same way, with as few blood connections as possible?"

"Yes. When I was twenty-one, I tried to find my birth mother and thank her for my life. The agency in Phoenix that handled the adoption was out of business, most of their records destroyed in a fire. The woman who had handled placements was willing to help. She turned up my mother's name in what files remained—Heather Ing-wen Han. But I never could find anyone by that name or any record that such a person had ever been born in Arizona."

Bridget had not been spared from the mood that had damped the spirits of the rest of us. "But why should we be denied the roots that give us a sense of belonging to a place, a time, a people?"

"Having asked the same question," Panthea said, "I arrived at two answers, though I don't know if either—or maybe each—is true. First, the work we've been chosen to perform will require us to have learned to be comfortable with being rootless, because we'll be nomadic, going wherever we need to go to confront the Nihilim."

I found it possible to come to terms with our extraordinary mission in part because the risks came with the reward not only of Bridget Rainking but also of her genuine affection. However, I was sobered, if not even discouraged, to consider that in order to serve humanity, we had to be to some extent separated from it. I like people, after all, and have always thought of myself as being as potentially noble as the best of them and certainly as foolish as all of them. I didn't want to feel . . . apart, estranged.

This concern was exacerbated when Bridget asked for the second of Panthea's reasons why our origins were such a mystery.

The seer said, "Could it be that Heather Ing-wen Han, Corrine Rainking, and the unknown young woman who left Quinn's bassinet on that highway weren't our mothers? Could it be that they were merely the vessels, surrogate mothers, by which we were brought into the world, and that we share no DNA with them? I suspect that we're fatherless and motherless in a basic biological sense, that we were created—engineered—by some mysterious maker and that the sequences in our DNA that alarm authorities aren't from an extraterrestrial race, but are from the Rishon of the first universe. If we have in us genetic material that provides us with a watered-down version of that race's special gifts before they grew arrogant and destroyed their world, if we have *no* biological roots in this world, maybe we don't exude the scent of prey, so to speak. We're not recognized by the Nihilim as potential targets. Because they aren't drawn to us either to kill us or make us suffer. They aren't concerned with us at all—and so we may therefore stalk them."

"That's an unsettling notion," said Sparky.

"I didn't mean it to be so," Panthea assured him. "I offer the thought only so that we might better understand ourselves."

"The thing is, I want a mother," Bridget said, not plaintively, but with a solemnity that left no doubt that this mattered to her. "Even if I never meet Corrine, even if I meet her and then don't much like her, which seems quite possible, I nonetheless want to believe that she'll return some day, that at least the chance exists I could touch her, hug her. Maybe ask her why she went away. Even though I suspect she might have no good reason why."

Panthea sympathized. "I've been fortunate to have adoptive parents who loved me. It's easier for me than for you to consider that we might be . . . outsiders in this fundamental way."

Most of my life, I'd fantasized about my parents, not always in a sensible fashion. For instance, in my mind, my mother sometimes had been a former supermodel whose face was horribly scarred in an accident. Destitute and unable to show herself in public without causing pregnant women to miscarry and children to be so traumatized that they had to be institutionalized for the rest of their lives, she did the selfless thing—leaving me to be found on the highway and retreating from civilization to live in a convent with a sack over her head. Sometimes I imagined my father was a famous actor or a mob boss, or a millionaire with amnesia who would come looking for me when he remembered I existed, or he was that guy who invented the world's best pillow and sold millions on cable TV commercials.

If what Panthea proposed was true, I would regret not being able to indulge in such fantasies anymore, but a second reason for dismay occurred to me. "Does this mean we're not human?"

"No," Panthea said. "Even if what I've seen as a seer is correct, we're human, of course. The difference is that we were engineered maybe in a laboratory or else someplace beyond our easy comprehension, then brought into the world by surrogate mothers who perhaps didn't have full knowledge of their role."

"That doesn't sound exactly human," I said.

"Surrogate mothers have been around for decades," Panthea said. "They have helped many couples when the wife was physically unable to carry her own fetus. Some of our DNA, our special abilities, may be from the Rishon of the first universe, but they, too, were human."

"Until they degenerated into Nihilim," Bridget said.

"Which does not mean you and Quinn and I will likewise become moral and then physical degenerates. Many Rishon of this second universe are well along that path. We have been seeded into this world to prevent their further slide into an apocalyptic disaster, at least as they are being encouraged and assisted by the Nihilim."

"I don't want to be one of the X-Men," I said. "There's way too much angst involved in being one of the X-Men. Being one of the X-Men only works if you're as handsome as Hugh Jackman, and then not much. Anyway, even the X-Men aren't big box office anymore."

Maybe Sparky was impatient with all of us or maybe just with me, but he was snappish when he said, "No matter how you got here, you're human, Quinn. And you're human, Bridget. Your special talents come with an obligation, a serious one. Both of you have a duty to use them for the purpose you were given, a duty to your country, the world, humanity. Duty isn't to be taken lightly. Get over yourselves and get your asses in gear."

I like to think I would have gotten over myself and shifted my ass into gear before much longer, but just then dire events began to cascade with such velocity that I had no choice but to embrace my otherworldly heritage and the duty that came with it.

"What's this?" Bridget asked in the tone of voice with which a curious but wary character in one of the *Alien* movies might express interest when about to examine the large purselike egg in which a face clutcher waited to seize her head.

We were on the federal highway, approaching its intersection with the interstate, which was at this point somewhat elevated above the lesser road. Heavy rain slashed the night, the skeins dividing it into diagonal slivers like a completed puzzle in which the narrow slices of the image did not quite align. Bridget let our speed fall. Leaning over the steering wheel to squint through the rain-blurred windshield, she said, "That cluster of lights on the interstate, to the west. There's been an accident—or it's a roadblock."

From the back seat, leaning forward, Panthea said, "Roadblock. The ISA is looking for us. And a blockade to the west means there's also one in the eastbound lanes we can't see from here."

Bridget pulled to the side of the road and stopped and switched off the headlights.

"We can't go back to Peptoe," Sparky said. "They know we were there. Otherwise, they wouldn't be setting up roadblocks to catch us leaving. But they can't be sure we've left, so they're still in Peptoe, behind us and ahead of us."

Bridget said, "So we'll go overland a few miles beyond the roadblock before we get on the interstate."

"Even if we use low beams, they'll see us in all the darkness," I worried. "They're not more than half a mile from here. They might already have noticed you pulling off the road."

"We don't need headlights. We have psychic magnetism."

The idea chilled me. "No moon, no stars, driving blind? Even the lightning has moved off to the east."

"Magnetism always takes us to what we're seeking, what we need. Right now we need safety. Magnetism won't lead us off a cliff."

"It led you to a tiger. It led you to a bomb factory."

"Alphonse was as sweet as a kitten," Bridget said.

Sparky said, "The bomb factory wasn't a problem."

"There was an altercation," I reminded him.

"Yes, but we weren't the ones who ended up . . . ended."

"There aren't cliffs in this territory anyway," Panthea said, apparently siding with Bridget and her grandfather. "Deep arroyos. Some of them have been briefly turned to rivers in this weather. Rough terrain. Some low brush. But no cliffs."

I felt the need to explain, sternly but patiently, that while we might be at no risk of driving off a cliff in this territory, we could as easily die by driving into a deep arroyo that had become a raging river. I said, "Being trapped in a sinking Ford Explorer, being swept along in violent currents, desperately sucking the last air trapped near the ceiling of a sunken vehicle, inhaling great quantities of dirty water full of drowned tarantulas makes dying in a sudden hard fall off a cliff seem, by comparison, a good death."

"All right, then," Bridget said, "so we're all agreed," and before I could protest her interpretation of my remarks, she drove off the shoulder of the highway, down a low embankment, to the floor of the desert.

Panthea said, "With lights off, if you parallel the interstate but stay at least half a mile from it, they won't see us, not in this downpour and the dark of the moon."

The weak light from the instrument panel provided no guidance, but instead ensured that our eyes did not become fully dark-adapted, thereby making the land ahead even more obscure than it otherwise might have been. Bridget hunched over the wheel, piloting us along at just five miles per hour, which seemed like a daredevil speed in those circumstances. The soil most likely had a high concentration of powdery fossil shells, which is the constituent of chalk, and the palest radiance issued from it. However, in spite of the rock and rattle of progress over rough ground, the visual impression was of motoring across a cloud or across a subterranean lake surfaced with a frothy mist, in a vast cavern where the walls and ceiling were as dark as the bowels of a whale.

Half a mile to our left, on the elevated interstate, the lights of the ISA vehicles at the roadblock and those of motorists lined up for inspection glimmered, dull and rutilant, through the screening rain, like the balefires of a cult that burned alive the sacrifices that its gods demanded. The distant glow did nothing to illuminate our course. The tense silence in the Explorer belied the apparent faith with which everyone but me had endorsed reliance on psychic magnetism to get us to safety.

In that regard, I felt nothing, was drawn neither to the left nor right, nor forward. Bridget murmured to herself—"Maybe, maybe, okay, to the right, a little, not too much"—and I remembered what she had said about confidence improving the efficiency and accuracy of psychic magnetism. Evidently, she was focused, as I was certainly not. She'd never before muttered to herself while behind the wheel and seeking something, but I attributed this to the stress of these unique circumstances.

Abruptly she cried out and pulled the wheel hard to the left, and Winston barked loud enough to cause me to startle forward in my restraining safety harness. A vehicle without running lights crossed in front of us, moving at a reckless speed. It was so close, no more than six feet away, that I could see some details of it: half again as large as our SUV, jacked up on tires with tread as deep as those on a farm tractor, an all-terrain transport with what might have been a rack of spotlights on the roof, above the windshield. I had the distinct impression that it was a military vehicle and knew it must be part of the ISA search party, lying in wait here in case we tried to avoid the roadblock by going overland.

I expected the transport's motorized spotlights to burst with light and swivel toward us, but that did not happen.

Bridget corrected course to parallel to the interstate, and tramped on the accelerator.

Out of the side window I could see hardly more than the faint suggestion of the transport executing a fishtail turn, like a shark in murky water that had passed its prey and was coming around to take a mortal bite.

As we shot across the chalky terrain, scattered clumps of sagebrush whisked the flanks of the Explorer, its bristling twigs screeching like fingernails punishing the paint.

"He's coming after us," Bridget said, her observation based on intuition rather than on anything she could see.

"Why doesn't he pin us with those spotlights?" I wondered as I braced myself for a collision with a thrusting formation of stone or a plunge into an arroyo.

From the back seat, Sparky and Panthea responded to my question with the same three words, one answer based on military experience, the other on what the seer saw—"Night-vision goggles"—and Winston agreed with a thin whimper of anxiety.

By now you must realize that it isn't my nature to have moments of satori, when in an instant I achieve understanding of something puzzling. I need to study ants and birds and fish, with the patient guidance of a teacher, to understand what ants alone should have taught me. And even after the fish, I need time to ponder. However, in that frantic desert-night pursuit, I leaped to enlightenment: The ISA knew about our psychic magnetism; they must have successfully captured, imprisoned, and interrogated others like us. In this instance, they preferred to pursue and corner us in the darkness rather than draw the attention of potential witnesses in the backup of cars on the interstate. They were confident that their night-vision gear would serve them far better than the gift we possessed by virtue of our Rishon DNA from the first universe.

The Explorer shuddered across what might have been an exposed stratum of washboard stone, and then through a field of loose gravel that clattered against the undercarriage. The speedometer needle pricked thirty, and I thought of an old news story about people in a helicopter, flying blind through fog—straight into a mountainside.

"Hang on," Bridget advised, as if we had any other option.

# BACK IN THE DAY

## THE BOY, THE FATHER, THE FISH

Litton Ormond was dead at twelve years of age. His father was dead at last, after murdering so many others.

Eleven years old, I slept the sleep of the near dead, which is the sleep of depression, and did not get out of bed of my volition.

The ants regimented themselves into classes and performed tasks according to their station, each day like every other day.

Each species of bird built a nest identical to the nests of all the others of its kind, ate what all the others of its kind ate, raised its young predictably.

And now Sister Theresa insisted that we study fish.

Some were bottom-feeders, thriving on what grew on the floor of a lake or pond. They were content with their bland diet, and in fact lacked the capacity to think of any food but that.

Others snared insects that alighted on the surface, rising to take them by surprise. They sought no other sustenance, nor did they need to. In nature, there never was a shortage of insects, which were hatched in battalions to work and die.

Particularly in the ocean, fish schooled in awesome numbers, executing sudden turns in unison, in the manner that hundreds of sparrows suddenly turn as one in flight.

"I'm done with fish," I told Sister Theresa on the third day of our studies. "If I was a fish, I'd die of boredom."

"No, you wouldn't. Fish are not ever bored," she said. "Do you know why?"

"Fish are stupid."

"Perhaps they are, by comparison. But that's not why they're never bored. To be bored, Quinn, you have to imagine yourself doing something else. But a fish can't imagine being anything but a fish, so it goes about being the best fish it can be."

I sighed laboriously. "I wish I could swim like a fish. I wish I could stay underwater for hours. If I could, then I'd swim deep down where you couldn't find me to teach me any more about fish."

"But of course you could swim underwater for hours. It's called scuba diving. Or you could learn to pilot a plane and join the birds and fly up where I couldn't take you by the ear and bring you here to my office."

"Yeah, well, they don't let kids fly planes."

"You won't be a kid forever," she said, "but a fish will always be a fish, and a bird a bird, and an ant an ant."

Even in retrospect, all these years later, I don't quite know how Sister Theresa did it, but that day, with that conversation, she brought me to one of the rare satoris of my life.

That night, I dreamed of ants and birds and fish, and in the morning, as I was brushing my teeth, I understood why Corbett Ormond could kill his wife's entire family and then his son, and still the world could be right in its design.

# PART 4
# 380 MILES TO MORDOR

# 25

Bridget was so absorbed in the challenge posed by driving blind and fast under the influence of psychic magnetism that she seemed to be in a trance.

Everything beyond the windshield and in the three mirrors was apparitional, an eerie phantasmal landscape: dimly visible, chalky soil in the foreground, seemingly as insubstantial as a low-lying toxic fog; lakes of darkness in the distance; bristling clumps of strange and insectile vegetation jittering past as if they, not the Explorer, were in motion; vertical forms, so pale and blurred by the downpour that they were less like thrusting formations of stone than like manifesting spirits cloaked in ectoplasm. Black rain inked the night, but in the backwash of the dashboard light, the drops were dull silver when they burst against the windshield.

The military transport raced close after us, driven by someone wearing night-vision goggles that no doubt provided him with a view to inspire confidence, for there is always light in the infrared spectrum that we can't see unassisted. In the starboard-side mirror, the rain-veiled grille of the truck suggested the snarl of a ghostly menace in a dream. The vehicle was so close that if Bridget jammed her foot on the brake pedal, we would be tail-ended with such force that our fuel tank would burst; when we tipped and rolled in a ball of fire, whatever power had chosen us to be *aluf shel halakha* would be terribly disappointed in us.

*"Oh, shit!"* Bridget exclaimed. Anticipating the threat before it appeared, she pulled the wheel hard to starboard as a second all-terrain transport swept in from the right and flashed past us as though the driver's intention had been to ram the Explorer. If that vehicle was as armored as it appeared to be, it might have been able to T-bone us with no cost to itself or to those riding in it.

Four things were obvious to me. First, the Internal Security Agency was as determined to get us as Wile E. Coyote was committed to snaring the Road Runner. Second, the ISA's budget was humongous, and its equipment far more formidable than any traps or weapons the coyote could purchase from Acme. Third, these transports were large enough to carry seven people in addition to the driver, which amounted to fourteen agents who would be heavily armed, who would be pissed off about how things had gone down at Beane's Diner, and even more pissed off about the two dead agents at the Sweetwater Flying F Ranch. Fourth, until now, I hadn't taken seriously enough Bridget's presentiment that at least one of us would die in the near future.

She swung west again so sharply that I felt as if we were in a carnival ride. Although not as focused as Bridget was, I began to feel the irresistible pull of psychic magnetism and sensed that our only hope lay straight ahead and that speed was of the essence. She accelerated to thirty-five, to forty, plowing through low brush that raked the undercarriage. We dropped a few feet into a barren swale, soared out of it, dropped into another and exited it as well, the tires stuttering across stony ground. The Explorer encountered soft terrain that clutched at the tires and slowed it, but at least one wheel found traction, pulling us out of that slough. We accelerated again.

On our port side, about twelve feet away, the second transport, the one that tried to T-bone us, pulled parallel with the Explorer. In the sheeting rain, the lightless vehicle appeared to shimmer like a mirage. Evidently, the windows were heavily tinted; I couldn't see the driver or any passenger in the cockpit.

A glance at the side mirror confirmed that the first transport had dropped back until the night and storm allowed only the merest suggestion of a pursuer. I assumed this meant the two ISA drivers, in communication, were agreed that the newcomer would take the lead in bringing us to heel.

"If he was crazy enough to try to T-bone us," I said, "then he'll side slam us." The military-style transport was heavier than the Explorer and had a lower center of gravity. SUVs like ours were prone to roll in extreme conditions, and being repeatedly bashed by a five-ton vehicle was the definition of *extreme*. "He's going to side slam us for sure."

Bridget had blanched zombie white, the instrument-panel glow painting morbid green highlights on her brow and cheeks, and her jaws were clenched, and her teeth were exposed in a fierce grimace, and a fine sweat sheathed her face from brow to chin, one fat salty bead depending from the tip of her nose. She looked fabulous.

The transport eased toward us, closing from twelve feet to ten, from ten to eight. The guy behind the wheel didn't care what damage might be done to the expensive piece of government machinery in his care. The cost wouldn't come out of his pocket. We would not have been in such a dire situation, pressed to take such reckless evasive action, if he'd been a person with a higher regard for taxpayers and a sense of responsibility for the community purse. But I supposed the country might not again enjoy the high-quality public employees who once served it, at least not in my lifetime, especially not if my lifetime ended in three minutes.

Under other circumstances, Bridget could have angled away from him, but she stayed on course, straight ahead, because she had no choice, which I now understood since my own psychic magnetism had drawn me as taut and target focused as a quarrel in the groove of a crossbow.

We raced westward at forty-five miles per hour, then fifty, fifty-five, over furrowed ground on which the tires drummed, testing the springs. The body of the Explorer rattled at every connection to the chassis, and we accelerated to sixty, sixty-five.

The transport closed to six feet, so near to us now that the previous illusion of immateriality could not sustain.

Simultaneously, Bridget and I issued an identical, prolonged exclamation—*"Ohhhhhhh"*—as though tuning our voices to sing a noble anthem in harmony. Then we were airborne, launching off a brink we couldn't see. No longer relieved by lightning, the night beyond the rain-blurred windshield gave no clue to our imminent fate. A quick glance out of the side window revealed some substance of a slightly lesser darkness, which I perceived to be in turbulent motion. As the Explorer reached the apex of a low arc and began to fall, I realized the surging mass below us was a temporary river, fed by flash flooding, racing through an arroyo that would probably end in a sinkhole that fed an aquifer. I turned my attention to the left in time to see the transport, also airborne, no more than two feet from our port-side flank. With a sudden respect for public property, that profligate driver might have dramatically cut his speed at the last moment, when he realized what lay ahead, or perhaps the greater weight of his vehicle proved less aerodynamic than that of Ford's finest, or maybe we met the arroyo at a slightly narrower point in its course than he did. Whatever the explanation, the transport fell faster than our SUV, and fell short. As I saw that armored vehicle drop out of sight into the arroyo, Bridget and I completed our harmonized response— *"Ohhhhhhh, shit!"*—as the Explorer's front tires met the riverbank an instant before the back of the SUV touched down with a jolt. The steering wheel whipped out of her hands, but she regained control a moment later. We rocked on, no less blind than before, as from the back seat came two voices, each expressing relief and incredulity, one with a vulgarity and the other with a reference to the deity, and Winston barked just once.

# 26

Having dropped back to let the driver of the doomed transport torment us, the remaining ISA pursuer would have had time to stop before plunging after his compatriot.

The tempestuous torrents were an effective barrier between him and us. However, unlike an ordinary river formed in the mountains and descending to a sea or lake, this one was not hundreds of miles long. It would end abruptly in a mile or two, five or six at most, when the arroyo terminated in an open fault in the underlying strata of rock. A vortex of water would swirl into the substructure of the desert, perhaps continuing for a while as an underground river, but eventually expiring in a subterranean reservoir, deep water for those who chose to drill for it.

Already, the driver of the remaining transport would be chasing the river south, seeking the end of it, so that he might come around its terminus and head north in search of us. Furthermore, it would be foolish to suppose that the posse was comprised of only two parties. Considering that the ISA's budget was, although highly secret, rumored to be as much as two hundred billion per year, they could afford to assign to us a dozen transports or, if they fancied, a fleet of spanking-new desert-adapted Rolls-Royce sedans, at least until runaway inflation resulted in two hundred billion being just enough to buy a McDonald's Happy Meal.

There was also the ghost drone to worry about. If it was, as Panthea thought, an instrument of attack, a mere weapon rather than also a search engine, spotters on the ground would have to provide a target's location before the drone could strike. The trick then was to get far away from this territory without being seen.

The night was long, the desert vast, the storm obscuring, and we were in a vehicle that could not be tracked by GPS. However, the driver of the remaining transport would have radioed those manning the interstate roadblocks, providing them with a description of the Explorer and the license plate number that belonged to a Porsche in Phoenix. The ISA was likely to have issued an all-points bulletin, making no mention of our bizarro DNA, but naming us as suspects in the murder of two agents at the Sweetwater Flying F Ranch. After this, if we dared return to the interstate or in fact to any major highway where we might encounter any federal, state, or local law enforcement, we would sooner than later be apprehended or abruptly terminated.

If taken into custody, we wouldn't have an opportunity to plead self-defense in the matter of the Flying F Ranch. We'd never even be charged with a crime. Perhaps we would spend the rest of our lives in the caring custody of the ISA, in some research facility where scientists of numerous disciplines would spend the next fifty years trying to reach a consensus about what galaxy we came from. If we were to forsake our duty and violate the secrecy surely required of our kind, if we told them about the first universe and the Nihilim among them and the *aluf shel halakha*, whatever that might be, they would consider everything we said to be disinformation. We would be subjected to a pharmacopoeia of drugs—if not eventually torture—to squeeze the truth from us, until our brains were no more capable of cognition than were bowls of tapioca.

For the immediate future, we were limited to off-road travel, to the likes of Winkelville and Sulphur Flats and Vulture's Roost and points between, until we could acquire a new set of wheels. We'd paid Butch Hammer seventy-five thousand dollars for the anonymous, untrackable Explorer. It was now worth about eighty-seven dollars to us, having depreciated almost twice as fast as a new Mercedes-Benz in the first twenty-four hours after purchase.

Bridget brought the Explorer to a full stop. She took deep calming breaths and wiped the incredibly attractive sweat from her face. "Panthea, what do you see?"

From the back seat, Ms. Ching said, "I saw my entire life flash before me."

"I should have said what do you *foresee?*"

"Nothing at the moment. I suspect that if and when I do foresee something coming, it will be nothing good at all."

I could have told Bridget as much, even though I had no talent whatsoever as a seer.

Sparky said, "What happened back there was a piece of cake. We're not in a fix. I've been in a lot worse situations than this, should've lost a limb or an eye on a hundred occasions, but I've still got all my pieces. As long as we're not soaked in blood and trying to stuff our intestines back into our bodies through a gut wound, we'll be okay."

"That's very inspirational," I said.

"Because it's the truth," Sparky said. "The unvarnished truth is always inspirational. Bridget, sweetheart, you better turn your mind to thoughts of getting a new vehicle, and let psychic magnetism take us to it."

"I'm already on it, Grandpa," she assured him as she let the Explorer coast forward once more into blinding darkness and rain, still not daring to switch on the headlights.

Panthea said, "I wonder if they have other drones, the small ones, capable of doing reconnaissance in weather this bad."

"Not yet, not for a few years anyway," Sparky said with what I hoped was conviction based on deep knowledge of the technology. "But if the rain stops, which it soon will, that's another thing we'll have to worry about."

Bridget motored forward, the speedometer needle quivering from a point just below the five to just above it. Even this return to a more moderate pace seemed suicidal, considering how abruptly we could find ourselves at the edge of a deep arroyo with steep walls, with or without a raging river.

My mind was formed in part by sensible, cool-headed nuns who couldn't work themselves into hysteria even if Godzilla suddenly erupted through the pavement of the street in front of the orphanage and ate a busload of commuters. Unfortunately, my mind was also in part formed by the apocalyptic, death-obsessed culture of the past several decades. Tens of millions were supposed to have died in an ice age back in the 1980s, just as predicted in 1969, and still more were said to be doomed by a bath of acid rain shortly thereafter, as well as in radiation that would fry the world when the ozone layer disappeared. Hadn't hundreds of millions more perished at the turn of the millennium—Y2K—when every damn computer went haywire and all the nuclear missiles in the world were launched, to say nothing of the lethal effects of canola oil in theater popcorn? Living in the End Times was exhausting.

When you were assured that billions of people were on the brink of imminent death at every minute of the day, it was hard to get the necessary eight hours of sleep, even harder to limit yourself to only one or two alcoholic drinks each day, when your stress level said, *I gotta get smashed.*

As a product of my culture, therefore, I trusted as best I could in Bridget's psychic magnetism, but there were times during the next fifty minutes when I closed my eyes and covered them with my hands in expectation of catastrophe. Inevitably, I thought of the door in the day that Hakeem, Bailie, and Caesar had seen. I wondered what would happen if a door in the night opened and we didn't see it and we drove through on an old cobblestone road that led away into the stars. Would our lungs implode in the vacuum of deep space?

For some reason, that made me think of the transport that had fallen into the arroyo and had either been swept away or had flooded and sunk. I said a little prayer for the men who went down with it, because maybe not all of them were evil. Maybe some of them truly thought it was righteous, even noble, to zip tie old men and lock them in car trunks, to brace innocent citizens at a lunch counter and attempt to spirit them away for the purpose of interrogating them and testing them to destruction in a laboratory, for the noble purpose of protecting the establishment from the possibility of a diminishment of its power.

All that and more occupied my feverish thoughts as we moved blindly through the night. I was as nervous as Samson might have been when, eyeless in Gaza, he felt for the pillars with which he would pull the roof down on the Philistines who had blinded and imprisoned him. That legend might have been inspiring if I hadn't remembered that, when all of Samson's tormentors were killed in the collapse, he died with them.

The rain began to relent, and thunder rolled no longer. In a drizzle, under a thinning cloud cover that revealed a veiled moon, we came out of the rough land onto a two-lane blacktop road that no doubt dated to the 1950s; it was in middling repair.

The interstate lay beyond view, and in spite of the county road under our wheels, we remained in a place so remote that not a light was visible in any direction.

Bridget started south, then hung a U-turn and cruised north.

I felt drawn that way as well.

"Do you see anything, Panthea?" Bridget asked.

"Yes, I was just struck with a quick vision, but I don't know what it means. I saw an old man sitting in a throne-like chair with carved-wood heads of dogs, German shepherds, at the top of the two stiles that supported the back rail. He was eating what appeared to be a brownie and drinking a beer."

Movies and novels have conditioned us to believe that when a clairvoyant is assaulted by a vision of something yet to happen, she or he always glimpses a moment of high drama—a bridge collapsing, an assassin with a rifle taking aim at a head of state. I wondered if sometimes Panthea foresaw John Kennedy Ching, of Ching Station, restocking the candy display the day after tomorrow or maybe a mail carrier delivering a new issue of *Arizona!* magazine next Tuesday. The idea of a seer glimpsing mundane moments of the future rather charmed me, although it would be regrettable if seeing the geezer with the brownie and beer distracted her from seeing, instead, that my head would be cut off by a guy with a chainsaw.

As if Panthea was embarrassed by the apparent uselessness of her vision and felt the need to make it seem a little more relevant, she said, "He was sort of a weird old man. He was wearing a white shirt with a string tie, khaki shorts, white kneesocks, and saddle shoes. Oh, and a Tyrolean hat."

In the unlikely event that this detail would eventually prove to be a matter of life or death, I said, "What's a Tyrolean hat?"

"It was slightly more boat shaped than round. A soft-brimmed green-felt number with a small red and green feather tucked in the band."

"Do you think he's evil?" I wondered. "He doesn't sound very menacing."

"I don't know. I didn't get much of a feel about him. Maybe something more will come. We must not wait for the equivalent of a Wikipedia entry on this old man. Our gifts assist us, but they don't control us. We distinguish ourselves by the efforts we make, by taking the initiative whatever the risks."

"We aren't puppets," I said, recalling her brief dissertation on that subject at the end of dinner in her Quonset hut.

"Indeed, we are not," Panthea said. "Nor would we want to be even if that assured our triumph. It's by our choices and actions that we succeed or fail. Without the freedom of choices, we would have no dignity."

"You've given all this a lot of thought," I said.

"When you live alone in the true desert, miles from Peptoe and even farther from Sulphur Flats, when you also work at home, making your living as an artist, you have a lot of time on your hands. You either think deeply about everything or you go mad. I have not gone mad, so far as I am aware. I credit my adoptive parents for that. There is a certain Ching attitude that nurtures sanity."

During the next mile, the sky went dry. Bridget switched off the windshield wipers.

As tattered clouds alternately unraveled from the face of the moon and raveled over it again, the pall of darkness fluctuated.

A signpost loomed on the left. Six feet high, the tallest object in sight, it was the first sign of any kind that we had seen on this lonely road. Bridget braked to a stop alongside it and put her window down, the better to read the black hand-painted notice on the white placard.

The first line declared in large letters, WALLACE EUGENE BEEBS AUTONOMOUS ZONE.

In smaller letters, the second and third lines informed the reader as to the meaning of "autonomous zone": THE LAWS OF THE UNITED STATES DO NOT APPLY HERE.

The fourth through sixth lines were more ambiguous than what came before them: LOVERS OF FREEDOM SEEKING THEIR UNIQUE BLISS ARE WELCOME TO INQUIRE AS TO AVAILABILITY.

The sign stood beside a rutted dirt lane that crossed a field and appeared to slope into the desert equivalent of a glen. If a residence lay at the end of that track, we could not see it from the highway.

Considering that we hadn't passed one structure or encountered a single other vehicle on this two-lane artery between the Twilight Zone and Transylvania, I wondered how long it had been since a lover of freedom had knocked on Wallace Eugene Beebs's door, seeking bliss.

"This looks like the place," Bridget said.

"What place?" I asked.

"The place where we might be able to trade this Explorer for another set of wheels."

"You think there's a used-car lot down there?"

"All we need from Beebs is one vehicle on which he's willing to make a deal. What do you think, Panthea?"

"I don't get any vibes, bad or good. But I don't much like the idea of autonomous zones."

"If it were anywhere else," Bridget said, "you could pretty much conclude there must be at least a few violent crazies down there. But intuition tells me . . . out here in the middle of nowhere, Mr. Beebs is just another Sonoran Desert eccentric, as harmless as Hakeem Kaspar. What do you think, Quinn?"

I didn't like the idea of autonomous zones, either. However, when I thought about needing another vehicle that the ISA didn't know about, I felt psychic magnetism pulling me toward that glen.

I said, "What's the worst that could happen—that maybe this Beebs dude turns out to be a cannibal, and a trapdoor on his front stoop drops us into a cellar, and in the cellar there's a stew pot and the sucked-clean bones of fifty freedom lovers who inquired about the availability of their unique bliss? I'm up for that."

Bridget pinched my cheek. "You're so totally my kind of guy."

"Well, in fact it could be something worse than a cannibal," Panthea said. "Not that I've foreseen anything bad. I'm just sayin'."

Sparky said, "So how much money might you need, sweetheart?"

Bridget thought for a moment. "Let's try to get it done for less than fifty thousand."

The duffel bag that contained the remaining hundred and ninety thousand dollars of drug-gang money was on the floor under Sparky's feet. At the motel in Tucson, when Bridget and I had been off to coffee and cakes with Butch and Cressida Hammer, Sparky had finished counting the loot and had packaged it in five-thousand-dollar rolls held together with rubber bands.

As he began to withdraw ten of those rolls from the bag, he said, "Okay, let's go."

"I'm not driving down there," Bridget said. "I don't think that would be wise. We need to do a little reconnaissance on foot, be sure just how autonomous this autonomous zone is, how many citizens of Beebs's America there might be."

"Makes sense," Sparky said.

"You should stay here to look after Panthea," Bridget said.

"No, no. I can look out for myself," the seer insisted.

Bridget shook her head. "Three of us going down there in the dead of night, we're liable to unnerve Mr. Beebs."

"First, it's not the dead of night," her grandfather said. "It's not even ten o'clock. Second, just the two of you going down there, you're more likely to end up in a stew pot."

Bridget was having none of it. "It's best for you to stay here behind the wheel, the engine running, just in case we have to make a quick exit. We can't risk having this vehicle taken from us until we have another."

At first answering her argument with silence, Sparky finally said, "What's this about? Why don't you want me going down there?"

He didn't know she'd had a presentiment that one of us would die or that she was afraid it would be him because he would become too protective of her.

"All right, Grandpa, it's just this. You look tough and ready to kick ass. You look like what you once were, full of righteous authority, a cop's cop, a soldier's soldier, and the very something that we don't talk about. You look like all of that, and sometimes, with someone fragile like Hakeem Kaspar, you scare them when scaring them isn't what we need to do."

Astonished, Sparky said, "I scared Hakeem?"

In fact, he hadn't scared Hakeem, but his granddaughter had alighted on an argument that Sparky found potentially convincing. She pressed it hard. "Oh, you scared him silly, Grandpa. Didn't he, Quinn?"

"Silly," I agreed.

"So if we go down there to see Mr. Beebs and he turns out to be a pitiful eccentric and a fragile soul like Hakeem, which I suspect he might be, judging by this sign of his, he'll take one look at you and freak out. He'll be certain you're FBI or something worse, that you're there to entrap him, and then we'll never make a deal. But if I go down there with just Quinn, it'll be a whole different story. My Quinn can handle himself—you know he can—but he looks like a big goof, a whiffet, about as threatening as Mary Poppins, which is just the kind of backup I need for this."

I thought Sparky might come to my defense and insist that I looked at least as threatening as Tinker Bell, but he said, "Okay, yeah, I get your point."

He passed rolls of hundred-dollar bills to us. I distributed five in my jacket pockets, and Bridget tucked five away in hers.

My moon goddess and I got out of the car, and I met her at Wallace Eugene Beebs's sign.

As Sparky came around to occupy the driver's seat, Panthea put down her window and said, "I'm pretty sure neither of you will die tonight."

Although I knew she was capable of jujitsuing me into a human pretzel, she looked like such a tiny person there in the back seat, heartbreakingly vulnerable, as is everyone ever born. "Stay alert," I urged. "Be careful."

"I'm not saying that one of you won't be grievously injured or seriously wounded," Panthea explained, "but it's most unlikely that you'll die here tonight."

"Thanks for the clarification," I said.

Sparky got into the Explorer and pulled the door shut, and Panthea put her window up.

Bridget and I turned and stepped off the highway, into the autonomous zone, where the laws of the United States did not apply.

## 27

Bridget and I stayed off the unpaved track, proceeding overland approximately fifteen yards parallel to it, in case there might be sensors or a guard to alert Wallace Beebs that we were approaching. The terrain gave us little to use as cover; but we were wearing dark clothes, and the moon was half wrapped in ragged clouds.

"Mary Poppins?" I whispered.

"You can be my governess any day," Bridget said, "and I'll do exactly what you tell me. Thanks for backing me up on that bit about scaring Hakeem."

After the downpour, I expected the ground to be muddy, but for the most part it wasn't. I supposed this territory was essentially a sandbox, and water quickly drained through.

Now that the night was clearing, I wondered if seething swarms of spring insects would erupt into the air, as advertised, followed by a pandemonium of bats feeding in flight. Having been delayed by bad weather, maybe they would just say to hell with it and wait until tomorrow night.

As anticipated, the flats led to a long slope and a glen that lay about a hundred feet below. The floor of the vale wasn't a realm of gravel stone and mesquite and sagebrush, as I had expected, but in part an oasis with palms and other trees, which must mean that an aquifer provided ample water effortlessly obtained.

Porch lamps and soft light spilling from windows suggested a prefab log house that looked no less out of place in this territory than would have an igloo. It wasn't a weekend-getaway cabin but a sizable residence, perhaps as much as three thousand square feet. Like Hakeem Kaspar, Wallace Beebs evidently produced electricity with a sound-shielded propane-powered generator.

Moonlight shaped another structure about fifty yards from the first, although that one didn't appear to be a house. As large as the residence, its lines simpler, at the moment without lights, it might have been a barn or a storage building, and it, too, was shaded by trees.

We descended the slope far enough to avoid being silhouetted against the sky, and then stood watching, listening. There seemed to be no jackbooted autonomous-zone police, no machine-gun emplacements protected by barbed wire, no slavering pack of attack dogs, not even a border checkpoint with an officious bureaucrat wanting to see a passport. As the trailing garments of the storm grew threadbare and the moon had greater influence on the glen, this unguarded compound—the quaint log house, the warm amber light in the windows, the grace of trees in an otherwise hard land—seemed to be nothing more than a retreat for an eccentric who sought refuge from the bustle and demands of our increasingly authoritarian society, a man who preferred seclusion and privacy, perhaps to meditate or to pursue some talent. He might be a painter, a sculptor, a sensitive poet. He might be a philosopher, seeking meaning in the quiet of nature, an Arizona Thoreau. Whatever he was, curmudgeon or gregarious bard of the Sonoran Desert, the sign at the entrance to his property made it clear that he had issues with authority, suggesting that he might be delighted to be overpaid for a vehicle and then fail to report it stolen for a week or two.

"Second thoughts?" Bridget asked.

"No. The sooner we have new wheels, the better. That other transport is still out there somewhere, and the weather's making drones more likely."

We walked down the rest of the slope and across the glen. The porch lamps seemed welcoming, as did a sign hanging above the top step—REMEMBER THE "KIND" IN HUMANKIND—and another sign above the front door—LOVE IS A FOUR-LETTER WORD—and an adage woven into the nubby material of the doormat—IMAGINE ALL THE PEOPLE LIVING LIFE IN PEACE.

I scrubbed my feet on the doormat. The doorbell push was aglow, easy to find even if the lamps had not been turned on, and I pushed it. A merriment of chimes arose in the house.

Although living in this lonely place and in a time when nowhere seemed entirely safe, Wallace Beebs came quickly in response to the bell and opened the door without giving us a lookover from one of the flanking windows.

Fiftysomething, tall and robust, stout but not excessively so, with long white hair and blue eyes and ruddy cheeks and Popeye forearms, he seemed to be the embodiment of hospitality when he spread his arms wide and smiled broadly and said, "Welcome to the Republic of Beebs!"

He wore a Tyrolean hat, a short-sleeve white shirt, a string tie, khaki shorts, white kneesocks, and saddle shoes.

"Mr. Beebs?" Bridget inquired.

"The one and only," he declared. "President, vice president, speaker of the house, majority leader of the senate, secretary of the treasury, housekeeper, and cook. Who are you two magnificent-looking people?"

Before I could claim that we were Homer and Marge Simpson, Bridget said, "Mr. President, I'm Mary Torgenwald. And this is my husband, Bill. We hope it's not too late for two heads of state to consult with you on a matter of great importance."

He appeared to be a guy who was always ready for a bit of fun. "And what sovereign state might you be representing?"

"The autonomous zone known as Torgenwaldistan," Bridget said. "It's not as large and impressive a sovereign state as the Republic of Beebs. In fact, its territory is limited to a six-foot radius around each of us. However, we love our little country and will defend it at any cost."

Whether Wallace Beebs merely chuckled or whether his chuckle became as gleeful as a chortle would be a matter of debate for a panel of linguists whose specialty was to interpret the nuanced meaning of such vocables, but I can say without doubt that Bridget thoroughly charmed him. He looked at me and said, "Bill, I hope you realize what a lucky man you are."

"Sir," I replied, "if I didn't realize that, I'd be the biggest fool in the world, but I've seen enough of humanity to know that I'm probably not even in the top ten."

His response to me was a mere chuckle, nothing as mirthful as a chortle. He stepped back and said, "Come in, come in. Join me in the library, and let's discuss what unique bliss you're seeking."

The library was most likely the largest room in the house, about forty by thirty feet, entirely lined with hardcover books. A large sofa provided space for a man the size of Wallace Beebs to lie down. Four commodious armchairs, each with side rails crowned with the exquisitely detailed carved-wood heads of dogs, formed a circle with side tables.

Beebs directed Bridget to a chair that featured a pair of Great Danes and motioned me to sit under the beneficent smiles of golden retrievers, while he settled into the chair topped with two German shepherds. Surmounting the fourth chair were Irish wolfhounds.

I noticed that the legs of the sofa were carved to resemble the feet of a dog. Canines are toe-walkers, and the sofa appeared to be poised for action in case anyone threw a tennis ball.

"I see you like dogs," Bridget said.

"I adore them, but I can't have them anymore. Haven't had one in years."

"Allergic?" she asked.

"No. But Uncle Erskine is. His eyes swell, he itches all over, and in about a minute flat he goes into anaphylactic shock. As much as I like dogs, I owe more to Uncle Erskine than to all the canines who have been my boon companions, so I now lead a dogless life. It was Erskine's idea to retreat here from the greed and narcissism that define our times." He swept one arm in a grand 180-degree arc to suggest the world beyond the Republic of Beebs. "Uncle and I make a difference by being indifferent. We fully engage by retreating. We defend the truth by living a lie." He made a fist of his right hand and raised it high. "We support social justice by being antisocial." He leaned forward in his chair, lowering his voice as if imparting a secret. "We protest poverty by living well. And we champion freedom by providing folks like you with whatever you think makes you free."

Because Wallace Beebs broke into a broad, sunny smile at the conclusion of that speech, Bridget and I smiled and nodded as if what he'd said was no different from the lessons in good citizen-ship that, while growing up, we had learned from the Muppets of *Sesame Street* and Mister Rogers of *Mister Rogers' Neighborhood.*

Sometimes it is difficult to identify the border between mere eccentricity and craziness. As I tried to determine on which side of the line this man lived, I surveyed the impressive library. "You're quite a philosopher. I guess that comes from being so well read."

"Half of these volumes," he said, "are in German, as I was on the ambassador's staff at the American embassy in Berlin for nine years, and the other half are in Íslenska, the language of Iceland, where I served three other ambassadors over eleven years."

Bridget said, "You must be the only person in Arizona who can read Íslenska."

Collapsing back into his chair with a hearty laugh, Beebs said, "Oh, no, no, dear lady. I can't read a word of either Íslenska or German. I don't buy books to *read* them. I'm too busy for that."

I was about to ask why anyone would purchase books if not to read them, when another man entered the library. He appeared to be in his sixties, as handsome as a movie star from the days when icons of the silver screen were often supernaturally good-looking. He had a full head of salt-and-pepper hair and blue eyes as clear as those of a newborn. With a face of symmetrical perfection and nobility, with the posture and grace of a trained dancer, he stepped into the room as though arriving onstage to perform in one of Shakespeare's histories. His smile was less extravagant but warmer than that of Mr. Beebs, and in fact he had considerable charisma.

Wallace Beebs said, "Uncle Erskine, these young people are Bill and Mary Turgenwald."

The uncle was such a presence that I found myself starting to get out of my chair to show due respect, but he said, "No, please, don't get up," and quickly settled into the remaining chair, under the carved heads of Irish wolfhounds.

He did not share his nephew's tendency toward costume, but instead was dressed in black snakeskin loafers, soft gray slacks, and a black silk shirt.

Wallace Beebs slid forward in his armchair, so that his bare knees dimpled as though they were smiling at us. He regarded his uncle as a puppy might regard its beloved master. "Mary and Bill have come in response to our sign declaring our autonomy. I don't know what they're seeking. So far, we've just been having a nice little chat."

"Although I didn't hear a car," said the uncle, "you aren't soaked from the recent storm. So if you walked out of that dismal wasteland and through a storm without getting wet, I hope perhaps you're mystical beings on a mission of great mystery. Things have been a bit dull here lately. We need some mystery."

Bridget said, "I'm sorry to disappoint, sir, but—"

"If I may call you Mary, please call me Erskine."

"Of course, Erskine."

Wallace Beebs said, "You can call me Wally."

"Erskine, Wally," said Bridget, "I'm sorry to tell you, we're no more mystical than two potatoes. We parked out on the road and walked in after the rain stopped." She hesitated. "We're taking a chance, risking a lot, by assuming that your autonomous-zone sign means what it says."

"It means all that and very much more," Erskine said. "Both as a reassurance and a warning, I must tell you that we are—shall I say—'sanctioned' by certain county authorities who understand the symbolic nature of our protest and the necessity of our mission."

I took that to be a fancy way of saying that they had paid off the right officials.

"You appear to be sincere young people," Erskine continued, "too young to be federal agents of any kind. I also do not believe you would want to cheat us in any transaction. I beg your pardon for suggesting even the possibility of such a motive." He smiled more warmly than ever. "However, if for a moment you think you're dealing with two vulnerable old men, you're woefully mistaken. Should you attempt to harm us in any way, you will die either where you sit or before you can leave our happy home. Sadly, others have met that very fate. Do we understand one another?"

"Perfectly," Bridget said.

The golden-retriever armchair had been wonderfully comfortable until I realized now that Beebs had specifically directed me to it. I wondered how it had been rigged to kill me.

"I hope you'll forgive me," Erskine said, "if it seemed that I threatened you, which was not my intention."

Bridget matched his smile better than I could when she said, "Not at all, Erskine. We understand the difference between a threat and a helpful explanation of the circumstances."

"Lovely," he said, and he seemed to cast a blessing on us by making something like the sign of the cross in our direction. "Now to business."

Bridget said, "We need a vehicle. We'll pay a lot more than it's worth. You wait two weeks and then report it stolen."

"Are the police after you?" Erskine asked.

"We're fugitives from a corrupt, oppressive system," she said, which I thought struck the right note. God knows what I might have said if I'd opened my mouth.

"What have you done?" Erskine asked.

"You don't want to know," Bridget said. "If you sell us a vehicle, you'll need to drive our Explorer miles from here and abandon it."

"You need guns?"

"No. We have a friend waiting in the Explorer with guns."

"You need drugs?"

"Thank you, no."

"It's perfectly safe to deal with us for anything, anything at all," said Wallace Beebs. "How about ID in new names?"

"We don't have time for that. So it's just the wheels."

Wallace regarded his uncle with the bright-faced excitement of a boy hoping to be taken on an adventure, and the older man regarded us with analytic intensity.

After a silence, Erskine said, "We believe that what little we love is defined by what all that we hate and how much we hate it. What do you think?"

"Hate makes the world go around," Bridget said, and it was clear the sentiment was well received in the Republic of Beebs.

I had a lot to learn about deception from this splendid woman.

Erskine's voice was as gentle as that of a truly caring grief counselor, his expression as kindly as that of a fairy godmother in a Disney cartoon. "Wallace and I believe that if you want to build something better, you must first burn down everything that exists."

My fiancée smiled with tender malice. "Just give me the matches."

Putting us through the perverse equivalent of an ethics exam, Erskine said, "History is the enemy of the future."

Bridget called him and raised him one: "The past is a cancer that kills all dreams of progress."

"Power is beauty, beauty power."

Lifting her chin and thrusting her chest forward as if she took overweening pride in her beauty, she said, "Keats was such an idiot, confusing truth for power."

We were all silent as Wallace turned his grin on his uncle, on Bridget, on me, and then on each of us again, clearly waiting for Erskine's decision.

No doubt about it—we were across the border from eccentricity, in the mad kingdom of the Red Queen.

When Erskine finally spoke, he said, "We have now and then assisted others like yourselves, who needed a vehicle to get them safely into Mexico or Canada, something with no history and with what appears to be a genuine DMV registration. I can offer you a sixteen-year-old Mercury Mountaineer with no GPS, with legitimate plates. If you email me photographs of yourselves and your associate in the Explorer, I can in three days send perfectly forged passports to any mail drop you wish."

"Not necessary," I said. "We won't be leaving the country." Then I realized my presumption and turned to Bridget. "We won't be leaving the country, will we?"

"We won't," Bridget agreed.

Erskine said, "The Mountaineer has a secret compartment for the transport of weapons and ammunition. If you want a backup arsenal, I can make you a package deal—the Mountaineer and guns."

"We have a lot of great guns," Wallace assured us.

Bridget put her hands together as you do when you're praying, and she nodded at Erskine. "Thank you so much, *padrino*. But the Mountaineer is all we need."

"Very well, then. Thirty-five thousand."

"Sold," I quickly declared.

"Forty thousand," he said.

"Wait a second. We had a deal at thirty-five."

Erskine smiled sadly at me and then with amusement at Bridget. "Mrs. Torgenwald, I recommend that you prevent your husband from playing poker."

"Forty thousand," Bridget agreed. "Give him twenty, darling, and I'll give him the other twenty."

"Please pay Wallace," Erskine said. "My nephew takes such delight in counting money."

Bridget and I got to our feet and together handed eight rolls of hundred-dollar bills to Wallace Beebs.

Remaining in his armchair, Erskine combed one hand through his salt-and-pepper hair, which was when for a moment it ceased being a hand and became an utterly alien appendage of six tentacles, each tipped with a wickedly sharp talon.

# 28

When we got up from our armchairs in the library, explosives didn't detonate under us. Neither did a score of poison-tipped four-inch-long spikes, driven by highly compressed air, pierce us from buttocks to brainpan. Neither did trapdoors open in the floor to dump the chairs and us into a pit seething with hungry crocodiles.

I didn't know if Bridget had seen what I'd seen—Erskine's hand briefly revealed as an arrangement of tentacles rather than fingers, the retractable talons deployed as if he would have liked to gut us with them. I was prepared to give her a pointed look, one that she might instantly interpret to mean: *Erskine is a Nihilim, a Screamer, a wormhead monster, I'm not kidding, I really mean this.* To my great frustration, my bride-to-be didn't look at me as we four moved out of the library, not when I cleared my throat meaningfully, not when I cleared it again at greater length, and not even when I pretended to stumble on the threshold between the library and the downstairs hall.

Earlier in the day, when we arrived in Peptoe, Bridget had worried that her ability to see through the Screamers' masquerades wasn't reliable. She'd said, *I have the disturbing feeling some of them are better shielded, better disguised, and I'm unaware of them.*

Now, as we set off for the only other building in the Republic of Beebs, she walked beside Erskine, out onto the porch and down the steps, engaged in some quiet conversation that I, in the company of the garrulous Wallace, could not quite hear. More than once, she put a hand on the Nihilim's shoulder, as if she had developed a degree of affection for him.

Saddle shoes clopping on the steps, my companion handed me a small pressurized can with a spray top. "This will help with your throat. It's the desert air that does it. This stuff has zinc plus emollient substances that really soothe inflammation." I assured him that I was fine, but he would not accept the little can when I tried to return it to him. "You think it's cleared up, the throat thing, but then it comes back. It's the desert air. I have to buy that stuff by the case."

The night was calm at ground level, but high-altitude wind had entirely stripped the mask of clouds off the face of the sky. The night was moonlit and moon shadowed.

As Wallace and I followed Erskine and Bridget toward the large single-story storage building, he said, "I buy books I can't read for a few reasons. For one thing, each copy I add to my collection is a copy that no one else can read. The fewer people reading books, the better off the world will be."

"I see your point," I said.

"For another thing, I like the homey look of a library, but I never want to risk polluting my mind with the thoughts of writers who disagree with me. You never know until you get into a book just what wrong thinking it might contain."

"Every book," I said, "is potentially a rattlesnake in your hands."

"That's an excellent analogy!" he exclaimed, and he clapped me on the back.

Erskine was a Nihilim whose real name was probably something like Cthulhu or Yog-Sothoth, but my best guess was that Wallace was nothing more than what he appeared to be: an ignorant, misanthropic, wardrobe-challenged psychopath whom the Nihilim could use to further the destruction of civilization; a useful idiot. Somehow he'd fallen under the insidious influence of the monster, had allowed himself to be convinced that he was related to it. He now filled the role of Czar Nicholas II to his so-called uncle's Rasputin, although in a venue less elegant than the palace in Saint Petersburg.

"Then," Beebs said, "I also have the books so that when the Day of Blood and Change arrives, I can celebrate by burning them."

"Won't that be a day?" I said. "The war of all against all."

"I can hardly wait," Beebs agreed.

"Well," I said, "I'm afraid we'll have to wait awhile yet. There are still too many people who don't understand why Utopia can grow only out of an ocean of blood."

"Too true," he said sadly. "So many people just don't get it. You're a truth teller, Bill Torgenwald. You're a wise young man."

He was talking about the kind of wisdom that is expressed in clichés, so I gave one to him. "We have to break a few eggs to make an omelet."

"We must break millions!" he agreed. "Millions and millions!"

The storage building had a steel frame and corrugated walls. Erskine instructed us to wait outside with his "nephew," while he went inside to fetch our purchase. He let himself in through a man-size entrance next to a big garage door.

Instead of turning to me, Bridget stretched her arms high and rolled her head as if working a stiffness out of her neck.

When I cleared my throat again, she didn't react to me, but Wallace Beebs said, "The spray will fix that in a jiffy. Just aim three squirts at the back of your throat. Give me the aerosol can, Bill, and I'll do it for you. What have you got to lose by trying it? Jeez, don't tell me you're some natural-remedy fanatic, you think everything can be cured with green tea. Gimme the can."

Even if Beebs wasn't a monster, but merely a bloody-minded psychopath, I didn't want the guy medicating me. Call me squeamish. To prevent his frustration with me escalating into suspicion, I opened my mouth and directed three squirts at my throat. The stuff tasted as vile as Satan's bathwater. I gagged on the second squirt and again on the third, which gave me the idea to gag a few more times to get Bridget's attention.

Just then the segmented door began to clatter upward in its tracks, and Bridget stopped rolling her head to focus intently on the imminent appearance of the Mercury Mountaineer.

In response to my strenuous gagging, Wallace Beebs seemed about to perform the Heimlich maneuver, so I stopped. "Hey, man, I'm sorry about that, but this stuff tastes as vile as . . ." Lest he might be an admirer of Satan, I edited my original simile to avoid causing offense. "As vile as possum piss. Not that I would know what possum piss tastes like. I'm only supposing it must be vile."

Puzzled by my reaction, Beebs said, "I've always thought the spray is kind of sour strawberry but minty," and I was then spared from further conversation by the arrival of the Mercury Mountaineer.

It was agreed that we would leave the key in the ignition of the Explorer. Later Wallace and Erskine would abandon the vehicle elsewhere in the county, far from their autonomous zone.

Bridget drove out of the Republic of Beebs, and I rode in the front passenger seat, where I said, "Did you realize, did you see, *Erskine is a Nihilim*."

"His masquerade is well maintained," she said. "I didn't see through it until he spouted that crap about what we love being defined by what we hate and how much we hate it."

"Oh," I said, somewhat deflated. "I didn't see him for what he was until we closed the deal and gave the money to Wallace. And then I only got a brief glimpse of his . . . of his hand-tentacle thing. I didn't know if you'd seen the truth of him. I was trying to get your attention and warn you."

"Yes, dear," she said. "I knew that you weren't just doing an imitation of a man choking on a fish bone."

"You kept touching Erskine. How could you know what he was and still touch him?"

"At first I wanted to distract him from your meaningful throat clearing. But each touch brought me a vision."

"You mean a presentiment?"

"No. Little visions, brief but frightfully vivid."

"Visions of what?"

"I'll tell you after we've loaded this baby."

On the blacktop lane, she turned right and drove past the Explorer, in which Sparky Rainking waited behind the wheel.

At a back-seat window, in the care of Panthea, Winston watched us drift toward a stop. He looked surprised that we'd survived. For an instant, as our stares locked, I saw myself through his eyes—saw the Mercury Mountaineer, my face pale in the light of the instrument panel—and I felt what he was feeling, the powerful delight and the love of an innocent canine heart. The connection lasted maybe two seconds, but the impact of it left me breathless for half a minute.

Bridget pulled onto the shoulder, stopped, and reversed until the liftgates of the vehicles were aligned.

When I could breathe, I said, "Something just happened. I'm developing your animal psychic-telepathic-whatever thing. I saw myself through Winston's eyes. I felt what he was feeling."

"I've never seen through an animal's eyes. You're ahead of me in that department, Quinn."

"What next?" I wondered.

"What indeed?"

In the light of the westering moon, the four of us quickly transferred our luggage from the Ford to the Mercury.

If as a child I ever imagined becoming a supernaturally gifted guardian of something or other, I'd never have thought that my powers would be so lame as they turned out to be, nor would I have imagined that I'd spend a significant part of my time dickering for used cars. If the idea was to keep me humble, so I wouldn't become arrogant like the Rishon of the first universe, it was working.

When we were all aboard our new wheels, with Bridget again in the driver's seat and Sparky in back with Panthea and the dog, I said, "Are we going to lay a trap for them? Are we going to take down the Nihilim, Erskine? What about Wallace? He's not a Nihilim. He's a dork, a pathetic feeb, but he's also a bad guy."

"We aren't taking down either of them. They'll be too wary. Anyway, we can't exterminate all the Nihilim in the world. We're only one of many teams. Isn't that right, Panthea?"

"So I believe," said Panthea Ching.

"Besides," Bridget said, "when I touched Erskine, I saw where we need to go, and we need to go there soon. Things are about to get wild and desperate."

Before I could ask what our destination might be, Sparky said, "What the hell happened in that stupid damn autonomous zone?"

By the time we explained, we had cruised several miles on the two-lane blacktop and then turned onto a gravel road, which was when I finally asked Bridget where we were going and what she'd seen in her series of quick visions occasioned by touching the Nihilim.

"Tonight, we're going to ground. Tomorrow . . ." She fell into silence, and in her profile I saw, for the first time, unalloyed fear. The happy warrior who found at least a thread of humor woven through every danger, every horror, could find nothing to make her smile at what waited for us tomorrow, could apparently not even bring herself to speak of our destination.

From the back seat, Panthea Ching said, "It's a weird place about six miles outside the town of Ajo."

Bridget looked at the rearview mirror. "You've seen it, too?"

"The moment you touched the Nihilim," Panthea said, "I received a vision of the place we must be tomorrow. He calls it 'the Oasis.' He says that the dark waters are holy, that they confer eternal life."

"He who?" I asked.

"He conceals his true name, calls himself 'the Light.' He calls his flock of followers his 'soul children.' But they're neither his flock nor his children in any sense. Some have succumbed to his propaganda, been brainwashed into a condition of pretend happiness. Others live in abject misery. In truth, they are his slaves.

This Erskine and Wallace you met, they regularly supply him with drugs—recreational drugs but also pharmaceuticals that he uses to control the soul children."

Sparky said, "Any guy who calls himself 'the Light,' somebody needs to switch him off."

"And the Oasis is no refuge, no haven," Panthea said. "Every day in that place is night. His darkness is a reduction of ordinary darkness, a bitter black syrup of hopelessness. Of all the things worth dying for, nothing is more worthy than dying to put an end to the Light and his Oasis. But . . ."

"But?" I asked.

Panthea said, "But I do not want to die."

After we rode in silence for a minute or so, I said, "Well, you know, maybe we can put an end to him and the Oasis without dying. Maybe we haven't been brought into the world and then been brought together only to die on our first mission."

"Yes," Panthea said, "isn't it pretty to think so?"

Bridget said nothing, nor did she glance at me. She stared straight ahead, following the gravel lane to a dirt track, the track to a paved road, seeking the place where we would go to ground for the night. The moon was high, yet the desert remained shrouded in gloom. In that wasteland, it seemed we might be traveling backward in time, searching for a lost Eden to which no paved or unpaved road would ever bring us.

## 29

In a solemn and weary silence, we passed under the interstate near where the San Pedro River, swollen with storm water, raced sullen and untamed and intractable toward Mexico. Putting distance between ourselves and Peptoe, leaving the ISA to search Graham and Gila Counties, we followed a state highway south toward the town of Tombstone in Cochise County, but then we took a second highway west toward Nogales and soon turned south onto a third. We continued to Sierra Vista, a small city on the eastern slopes of the Huachuca Mountains. Psychic magnetism drew us to a motel where four rooms were available and cash was acceptable. The license plate number of the Mountaineer was the only ID required. Shortly before midnight, we were ensconced in our rooms, having agreed to set out for the Oasis after breakfast.

This time, Winston chose to bunk with me, as though confirming that he was aware that a strange new connection had formed between us. I fell asleep with him lying beside me, his head resting on my chest.

In my nightmare, three Nihilim trapped me in a room and sought to devour me alive, requiring no condiments or beverages. When I woke, Winston's head was no longer on my chest, but he remained beside me, crying fearfully in a dream of his own, which might have been the same one from which I'd awakened. I smoothed one hand along his flank until gradually he quieted, and his breathing confirmed that his anxiety had abated.

I was reminded of Rafael, the golden retriever that had been the pride of the orphanage. Annie Piper, who enthralled us with both stories she'd written and stories she read by others, had been his primary caretaker, under the supervision of Sister Margaret. A girl named Keiko Ishiguro assisted in his care and took over when Annie went away to college. Keiko had been sweet and shy, a slip of a girl with large, beautiful ink-black eyes. When I was thirteen and Keiko was seventeen, Rafael had to be put to sleep because a fast-moving cancer ravaged him. Keiko was in tears for days and, according to her roommate, wept even in her sleep.

The death of Rafael moved me, too, not least of all because, when I was eleven and in deep depression over the murder of Litton Ormond, Rafael had often come to my room at night and slept by my side, though he had never done so before. If his presence did not soothe my anguish, I believe he did medicate my anxiety, because gradually I worried less that I, like Litton, would meet an early and senseless death.

Sister Theresa, psychologist and determined teacher, had said that dogs might be the only species on the planet, other than human beings, to mourn the loss of a loved one. Dogs had been known to grieve for months and even years, going so far as to journey on their own to a distant cemetery to lie on a master's grave. One could understand, then, that a dog might sense the grief of a boy who had lost his best friend.

Keiko had been gone from the orphanage for four years by the time I started working for *Arizona!* magazine. She'd moved to Austin, Texas, because she discovered a cousin, Ichiro Sugimura, resided there; he was her only living relative. Six months later, she sent the good sisters a letter announcing her impending marriage to a gentleman named Malik Maimon. I thought that there might be a good human-interest story in Rafael, the orphanage dog, so I tried to contact Keiko but failed to find her, though neither Ishiguro nor Maimon was such a common name that the search should have been difficult. Neither could I locate Ichiro Sugimura.

Considering how close we orphans were to one another, bonded by loss and by the uncertainty of our future, it seemed that we should remain part of one another's lives throughout our days on Earth, no matter how far we journeyed from Mater Misericordiæ. But time and desire—longing for what we have not and seeking for whom we might prefer to become—spirals nearly everyone away from even those they once loved. Only family has the power to keep people connected to a place and a heritage and the communal meaning of linked generations, though even many families are less tightly knit than needed to fill that role. And in my failure to find Keiko, I'd had to come to terms with the truth that a collection of orphans, brought together by necessity, was not the family that for so long I had wanted to believe that it was.

Now, while darkness still lay upon Sierra Vista, I showered and dressed. I clipped Winston's leash to his collar and took him for a walk as dawn broke. We found a park and stood for a while under a spreading oak, watching sunshine flood the San Pedro River valley and shadows slowly shrink eastward as the light came west.

When Winston and I returned to the motel, our companions were ready for the day. We gathered at a restaurant on the far side of the highway, where dogs were welcome on the patio. We drank mimosas with our food and took our time at breakfast.

Considering the evil that we'd been promised would confront us at the Oasis, Bridget and Panthea and I didn't want to go where we had to go, didn't want to be what we were born to be. We wanted to rebel against the mystery of our existence, refuse to act until all was explained. However, the master of that mystery, having endured two previous rebellions of historic nature and being averse to explaining His intentions other than through prophets sane and prophets mad, wasn't likely to take our little rebellion seriously enough to part the morning as if it were a curtain and welcome us backstage for a tour. Indeed, that didn't happen, and we hit the road.

The small town of Ajo—pronounced *Ah-joe*, but vulnerable to an embarrassing mispronunciation—is home to the copper-rich New Cornelia open pit mine. Two miles in diameter and over one thousand feet deep, the mine is a tourist attraction with a visitors' center and an observation area. Those who developed it and worked it deserve our gratitude, because without copper we'd lack many amenities of civilization, not least of all the ability to transmit electricity to light our homes, power our industry, and manufacture copper-infused underwear. Those travelers who enjoy the scenery and the unique architecture of the Southwest but who feel they must protest something in order to have a well-rounded vacation, railing against the mining industry at the site of an open pit is an opportunity for virtue signaling, although without much of an audience.

To fully grasp the weirdness of the Oasis, where the man who called himself "the Light" sat chanceled above those who adored him, and where he served as the warden to those he imprisoned, you must appreciate the circumscribed territory in which the town of Ajo is located. To the north lies a restricted area, the vast Barry

M. Goldwater Air Force Range. To the east, the Tohono O'odham Nation Indian Reservation allows neither bombing nor gunnery. To the south lies Organ Pipe Cactus National Monument, which doesn't actually produce music. To the west, the 860,000-acre Cabeza Prieta National Wildlife Refuge shelters desert bighorn sheep, pronghorn antelope, jackrabbits, pocket gophers, kangaroo rats, various lizards, and the ever-popular lesser long-nosed bat, which has a somewhat smaller schnoz than the long-nosed bat that, evidently, lives elsewhere.

Surrounded by a military installation, a tribal reservation, a national monument, and a wildlife refuge, the resultant irregularly shaped tract of unrestricted land measures about twenty miles north to south and fifteen miles east to west. Ajo sits in the center of the northwest quadrant of this jigsaw-puzzle piece of Pima County. Theoretically, therefore, Light's Oasis should have been no farther than perhaps eight miles from Ajo, but it proved to be much farther than that, inexplicably far.

Because Bridget didn't hurry toward the Oasis, because none of us urged her to drive faster, because we stopped at a convenience store on the outskirts of Tucson for candy bars and colas, and because we stopped again in the town of Sells for gasoline and sandwiches and a bathroom break, it was 2:53 p.m. when we reached the junction where State Route 86 met Route 85 at the miniscule, aptly named town of Why, ten miles south of Ajo.

We turned north on State Route 85. Four miles short of Ajo, Bridget slowed. She squinted into the sun-scorched land to the right and turned off the pavement onto a hardpan track, pulled forward by psychic magnetism. The way led—or seemed to lead—northeast, but the sameness of the landscape and a solar glare reflecting off every surface conspired to disorient us. Like cobras writhing to the music of a flute, heat snakes rose from sun-baked stone, so that what lay ahead of us appeared to be behind a transparent curtain that rippled as it was drawn aside, though it never fully opened.

Sparky was the first to suspect that somehow we were traversing the same few miles again and again, as if we had driven into a time loop, à la the movie *Groundhog Day*. "We're going nowhere but where we've already been. That rock formation, that cluster of cactuses, that pile of rubble that once might have been a mission church—damn if I haven't seen them all more than once before."

His declaration seemed to wake the rest of us from a trance, for now we noticed and confirmed what he had observed.

"According to the odometer," Bridget said, "we've gone eighteen miles from the highway." She checked her watch. "How'd that happen?"

"There!" Sparky said, pointing through the windshield. "That prairie falcon. At least twice before, I've seen it execute that same gyre, make that same dive for prey."

As the falcon soared off the land with whatever vole or lizard it had taken, I, too, remembered seeing it do that before. A fear of the unknown rose from under the primeval stratum of my mind, not unlike what the earliest humans might have felt when suddenly the day darkened with a solar eclipse.

Only then did I realize that the sun had seemed to move around us in curious ways that couldn't be explained by the turns in the hardpan track. I said, "If we've gone farther east than northeast, or farther north than east . . . then we should be either on Tohono O'odham land or on the bombing range. But there haven't been any warning signs."

Bridget brought the Mountaineer to a full stop.

No one bombed us. Neither did a hotel-casino beckon with neon brighter than the day. If we were anywhere, we were still in the approximately three-hundred-square-mile jigsaw piece where the good folks of Ajo lived and copper was mined.

In her soft voice marked by the calm confidence that ought to have been a synonym for *Ching*, our back-seat seer said, "The loop is the simple mojo of the Nihilim, the only sorcery they're capable of in their fallen condition. It's a deception of the eye and mind akin to their ability to masquerade as human. They wish to protect this place from those who aren't invited. People who come this way think they've driven a lot farther than they really have. Finding nothing of interest and fearing they might stray onto the bombing range, they turn back. For a time, the illusion foiled even us in spite of our gifts. But now that we've all seen through it, we can escape the loop. We've gone only a mile from the highway, not eighteen. And the Oasis waits a mile from here, a mile at most."

I said, "I wonder if . . . if they know now that we're coming?"

"Not likely."

"Not likely? Maybe but not likely? That's the best you've got, Panthea?"

"The spell of repetition put on this stretch of road is an automatic deceit requiring none of their attention, no maintenance. We are perhaps the first to succeed against it."

"Perhaps," I echoed. "Perhaps? But if anyone before us has succeeded, then they *don't* trust it entirely. They'll be wary." I put a hand to my chest. "I shouldn't have eaten that sandwich when we stopped in Sells. I've got big-time heartburn."

Although her own fear was evident, Bridget reached out and pinched my cheek and said, "Gonna be a piece of cake, boyfriend."

I said, "In every movie, at a moment like this, when someone says it's gonna be a piece of cake, it never is. That's always when the dying starts."

"This isn't a movie," she assured me, but there was an edge of fear in her voice that she could not hide. She drove onward toward Light's Oasis.

The inhospitable terrain rose gradually until we came to a crest and found before us a bowl in the land that was maybe a mile in diameter, like a crater where a large meteor or small asteroid slammed down millennia earlier, although it might have been a normal geological formation. I know nothing about geology except what I learned about Krypton, Superman's home planet, when I was thirteen. In Light's Oasis, the palm trees, shrubs, and flowers were so lush that the glen in which the Republic of Beebs did business seemed barren by comparison. Evidently a major aquifer lay under the place, and they tapped it with no concern about either conservation or the laws governing water use in this parched state.

The Oasis had other features not found in the Republic of Beebs, including a forty-foot-tall wicker man, a T. rex scaled twice the size of the real dinosaur and welded together from steel plates, and an Aztec temple.

Although the settlement below appeared to be deserted, Bridget quickly backed the Mountaineer down from the rim of the crater, if indeed it was a crater, until we were out of sight of anyone below, and she switched off the engine.

"Except for the vegetation," she said, "it seems like a version of the Burning Man gathering in Nevada—those strange constructions, those works of art if you want to call them that."

"It's a place of great evil," said Panthea Ching, "insanity and fierce oppression, slavery, murder. Rape that he calls liberation."

"If it's all that," I wondered, "then why does it fall to us to deal with it? Why aren't the authorities aware of what's going on here? Why haven't they shut it down?"

"Indifference. Corruption. Fear of being canceled by those who control the narrative. People high in government, industry, media—they come here now and then to enjoy all things that are elsewhere forbidden." Panthea got out of the Mountaineer and quietly closed her door.

The rest of us, including Winston, joined the seer where she stood in the ninety-degree heat, gazing toward the rim of the crater above us, toward the Oasis that remained out of sight, as though the air was rich with revelations that she seined from it in the manner of an angler scooping fish in her net. She looked otherworldly, as fragile as a fine porcelain figure yet as fierce as a heroine in a violent work of anime. The warm breeze ruffled her shaggy hair as though the Sonoran gods viewed her with affection. She seemed impervious to the heat; her face suffered no slightest sheen of perspiration, though the rest of us glistened and Winston sweated the only way he could, through dripping nose and lolling tongue.

Panthea said, "He's very rich and once renowned. He knows how power can be used, who can be bent by it, who can be broken, who will resist and how to overcome their resistance."

"Who is the bastard?" Sparky asked. "Don't tell me he's the Light. Who is he really?"

"I see . . . he once was . . . he is . . . Bodie Emmerich."

"I've heard that name," I said. "He was someone once. He was almost famous, I think."

"I'm enough older than you to remember," Panthea said. "In the early days of social media, Emmerich created one of the first dating sites, Heart4Heart."

"I think it's still the largest," Bridget said.

"He was among the first to realize the power of online retail, founding company after company, reaping fortune after fortune when he took them public, until he was worth billions."

"'Almost famous'?" Sparky said. "Guys like that, they're as famous as rap stars these days. How come not him?"

"He realized that what he called 'the lords of social media and the oligarchs of tech' were one day going to be household names as much as any movie star—and he didn't want that. He wanted privacy, anonymity as far as he could preserve it. He became so cautious so early that . . . I think very few photographs exist of him."

Bridget looked from Panthea to the rim of the crater above us. "What's he doing here? What is this place?"

"It started out to be his escape from a world that he had long found cold, from the masses that he thought were often irrational, envious, and regressive. He wanted to make a small world of his own, an oasis of reason that was at the same time a fantasyland filled with wonder. He imagined a commune of sorts, sustained by his wealth, where he could live with a select group of elites."

"God spare me from a place like that," Sparky said.

In the east, a prairie falcon glided in a gyre; whether it might be the same one we had seen before was impossible to say. Panthea's gaze had shifted from the crest of the slope to the bird. Her dark eyes were silvered by the reflection of a sky so pale blue it was almost white. If she saw the winged predator, she also saw something beyond it, saw into the past and into the heart of Bodie Emmerich, perceived what had been and what might have been.

Her voice softened almost to a whisper. "He was always a little misanthropic, though he didn't realize it. Most people frustrated and repulsed him, and on some deep level he repulsed himself. He meant to undertake a noble enterprise, create a retreat that was a fountain of intellectual stimulation but also a garden of earthly delights. However, those he brought into his inner circle were for the most part there because of his wealth, hangers-on and leeches whom he mistook for true friends—because he himself was incapable of genuine friendship. He didn't know himself at all, his deepest, truest desires. He thinks that intellectually and morally he has progressed beyond all the negative influences that shaped humanity's troubled past, thinks he's beyond error and excuse and superstition, when in fact he's the embodiment of humanity's darkest impulses."

Her stage whisper mesmerized me, so that I startled when she stopped talking. She pivoted away from us and went to the back of the Mercury Mountaineer.

When we joined her at the liftgate, she opened her ammunition case and took from it spare magazines for her gun and for mine.

"What are we walking into?" I asked, as I pocketed the spare.

"Nothing more than the very thing we were born to confront," Panthea said. She was carrying her pistol in her open purse, and she advised Bridget to do the same. "Quinn, Sparky, untuck your shirts and conceal your guns as best you can. If we encounter someone and we don't appear to be armed, there's at least a chance we can fake them out. Deceit is preferable to bullets."

"Last night," I reminded her, "when you spoke of this place, you said you didn't want to die here."

"I don't want it. But everyone dies somewhere. And we have only two choices."

I said, "We can go down there now or not go right away."

"That isn't the choice properly expressed," Panthea said. "We can go down there and put an end to him, free those he oppresses, before one more rape, before one more murder—or not go down there, and by not going become in time like the Nihilim."

Sparky spoke up to explain if not defend me. "The boy means that he thinks this situation should be analyzed, a plan developed, strategy and tactics."

Panthea was unmoved. "Our strategy is righteousness. Our tactics are surprise and relentless action."

Still explaining me, Sparky said, "The boy has matured a lot since he crashed in on us two days ago. But he's still an innocent soul. He doesn't quite realize how much he cherishes that innocence, how much he hopes to hold fast to it."

I was mortified to hear Sparky justify me to Panthea. I looked at Bridget and saw that she regarded me with an intensity that was humbling to behold, regarded me with love, I thought, but also with a keen eye of assessment.

"It's not that he's a coward," Sparky continued. "He isn't. He killed those two ISA agents who seemed certain to kill me and take Bridget only God knows where. But he killed them with a car, before he quite realized what was happening, killed one in self-defense and the other half by accident. If it comes to gunplay and worse—and it will, I speak from some experience—then he'll have to squeeze the trigger with cold intent. That'll be the end of whatever innocence he hoped not to forfeit, and he knows it."

To my surprise, he'd expressed what I felt but didn't know I felt, a sadness arising from the necessity of soon having to admit that I was fully of this beautiful but dark world no matter by what strange means I had been brought into it, that I was as vulnerable to corruption and as capable of evil as anyone. I, like everyone, would conduct my life on a high wire in the circus of this world, trying my best to retain at least a thin, bright filament of the incandescent innocence of childhood, always aware that I might not be the same person when I reached the far platform, and in fact might be someone I didn't like. The best friend I'd ever had, Litton Ormond, died while still an innocent, little if at all corrupted by any acts of his own. But even if I could have continued living for decades in my studio apartment, writing sweet human-interest stories for a regional magazine, eating at Beane's Diner, watching favorite movies again and again on my days off, taking my dry cleaning to Dirty Harry Clean Now, and yearning chastely for a romance with Sharona Shimski, philatelist and granddaughter of Julius, I couldn't hold fast to the virtues of childhood and remain a fair-hearted boy forever. Considering what I would have to do at the Oasis and in places like it yet unknown, if I were eventually to encounter Litton Ormond in a life beyond this one, he would never recognize me by my unstained soul. I would be profoundly stained. I might even have changed so much that I had become a stranger to him, which seemed to be a terrible thing.

Panthea poked my chest with a finger, as if aware that I needed to be refocused by an insistent prodding. "Does Frodo mean anything to you?"

"*The Lord of the Rings*. I loved those books."

"Of course you did. Was Frodo a hero?"

"Yes. A great one."

"After he carried the One Ring all the way from the Shire to the evil realm of Mordor, to the place where it could be destroyed, the ring corrupted him. He put it on."

"Only for a moment. He did nothing evil."

"Because Gollum bit Frodo's finger off to get the ring. Frodo would otherwise have succumbed to the lust for power."

"I'd like to think he wouldn't have."

"Of course you would like to think it. That's you. But Frodo lost his innocence and never was quite at home in the Shire again when he returned to it, never at home among the innocent hobbits."

"I never liked that part. I wish he could have been at home among them," I said.

"Of course you do. He was nonetheless a great hero. Had he not been, the hobbits would have perished, every one, and with them all others with any room for innocence in their hearts. Middle-earth would have been a place of endless horror. We're guardians. *Aluf shel halakha. Legis naturalis propugnator.* We are called upon to be scourges. We belong in that honorable and essential place between innocence and corruption, a place called *duty.* Either get with the program, Quinn—or your fate will be an early, meaningless death."

Wiping my face to slough from it sweat that was occasioned by more than the heat, blotting the hand on my shirt, I said, "You don't pull your punches, do you?"

She smiled. "What would be the point?"

"'Guardians.' You said it might be a quest, but now you call us 'guardians,' which sounds like . . . for life."

"I told you we might be in part on a quest to secure something, but at the moment I don't know what the object of the quest is. I know for sure that being guardians is our reason for being, and that will never change."

"Are we going into the Oasis to save someone?"

"You know as much as I do. Maybe someone waits to be saved. Maybe many someones. We'll know when magnetism has taken us to the task."

"Or," I pressed, "are we going down there to kill someone?"

"Emmerich won't peacefully abdicate. If he has a praetorian guard, perhaps we'll have to kill many to save a few. We will know when we know."

I wanted a clearer sense of our mission. However, I had been born into this world a mystery, and the clarity I wanted was not mine to demand. "All right. I'm with the program," I said at last.

How odd it seemed that making a mortal commitment of mind and heart and soul should be at one and the same time deeply satisfying and terrifying. Movies hadn't prepared me for that dichotomy. In fact, I was beginning to suspect that movies hadn't prepared me for much of anything.

Bridget came to me and put an arm around my waist and had the wisdom to know that nothing she might say was better than her touch. From his luggage, Sparky retrieved spare magazines for his and Bridget's weapons.

To Panthea, Bridget said, "There's a long slope to get down there, and no vegetation for cover until we reach the bottom."

"They won't see us. He sleeps by day and lives by night."

I didn't like what that might signify. I mean, Dracula slept by day and lived by night. I'm not saying that I believed in vampires. Or disbelieved in them. After the events of the last few days, I was willing to consider the existence of everything from werewolves to fairy godmothers.

"But the others," Sparky said. "How many others are in the Oasis?"

"I don't know. But they all live according to his rhythms. When he sleeps, they sleep. I believe . . . somehow they have no choice."

"Guards?"

"My sense is that guards are thought unnecessary. They believe they're safe behind their steel doors and electronic locks."

"Aren't they?" I asked.

"No," said Panthea Ching, and she started up the slope toward the rim of the crater and the Oasis beyond.

# BACK IN THE DAY

## THE INNOCENT BOY, THE EVIL FATHER, THE ANTS, THE FISH, THE BIRDS

A hard, steady, windless drizzle fell on Phoenix that morning. In the wing of the orphanage dedicated to schooling, in a classroom where I was expected to be learning English grammar, I heard the teacher only as a flat and distant droning, as though I must be in a parallel universe alone with my thoughts, her voice leaking through a rift in the barrier between worlds. The rain seemed not to be pure but as gray as the sky that dispensed it. Beyond the windows, the courtyard playground was now a cheerless realm, the swings and the other simple amusements transformed by the distorting skeins into a grim geometry that suggested devices designed to torment and restrain.

My mood was neither as solemn as the rain-drenched morning nor as light as in the days before the murder of Litton Ormond. In fact it was in flux between the pleasures of anticipation and a disquiet that arose from a better understanding of—and adjustment to—the world as it was shapen. My depression had in part lifted to the extent that I'd gotten out of bed without being coaxed to do so. I had eaten breakfast with an appetite that I'd recently lacked. I'd made my way to class not in a shuffling slouch, but rather as an eleven-year-old boy with a renewed, though tentative, sense that something was worth looking forward to in the day ahead.

At noon, I went not to the cafeteria but to Sister Theresa's office. Her door stood open, and she sat at her desk. Although she didn't look toward me, she must have seen me from the corner of her eye because she said, "Come in, Quinn."

Her habit looked whiter than usual on this gray day when she invited me to have a seat in the visitor's chair opposite her. "You're just in time for lunch."

On her desk were two plates with flatware, two napkins, and two glasses of cold milk. Lunch consisted of a large scoop of chicken salad on a bed of lettuce, sliced tomatoes, two hard-boiled eggs.

As I sat before my plate, on a pillow that lifted me to dining height, I said, "Our next lesson on fish isn't till three o'clock. How'd you know I'd come sooner?"

"You got out of bed without being wheedled and prodded. You ate a reassuringly hearty breakfast. You didn't shuffle to class like a zombie. I've got my spies, you know. And in spite of rumors to the contrary, I can put two and two together."

We ate in silence for a few minutes, and then I said, "If I was an ant or a bird or a fish in an orphanage, I'd expect to be there forever. I wouldn't know things could ever change."

"If there were orphanages for ants, birds, and fish," she said, "and if you were one of those things, what you just said would be true. You'd lack the imagination to envision new circumstances."

"Yeah, but it's more than that," I said. "I couldn't imagine a different place or life, and I couldn't, like, *do anything* to change anything."

"You are talking such good sense, Quinn, especially for someone who has put his poor teacher through ants, birds, and fish when ants should have made the case. How's the chicken salad?"

"Very good."

"There's a special dessert. But I don't mean to interrupt. I suspect that, as a repentant stubborn student, you have more to tell your patient teacher."

"If we were like ants or any other bug or animal, we'd be kind of like machines, programmed to do what we do and nothing else."

"And what would that be like, do you think?"

"It for sure wouldn't be fun."

"Why not?"

I paused to eat a hard-boiled egg. I didn't pop it in my mouth whole and moosh it up, as I might have done if I had been alone or with other kids. And I never for a moment considered mooshing it up in my mouth and *then* slamming my hands against my bulging cheeks and spewing egg debris all over the desk, which in those days could be funny in the right crowd. I cut the egg in four and used a fork and swallowed discreetly. Then I said, "It might be fun if we had small brains like birds and fish do. Their routines probably *are* fun for them. But our brains are too big for us to do the same thing every day, the same way, all the time. We'd go freaking nuts."

She blotted her mouth with a napkin, so I did, too, and she said, "What would be the point of making big-brain humans and then having all of them do the same thing as all the others?"

"Yeah, it wouldn't make sense. That's what I'm saying."

She smiled. "We need to have the ability—the right—to make our own choices, even though we make mistakes. We learn from our mistakes, or we should. Scientists learn from their mistakes, and that's how science advances. Trial and error. Without error, there would be no progress." We ate in silence for a few minutes, until she said, "Now we come to the hard part, huh?"

"Totally," I agreed.

"Tell me what you think the hard part is."

After I finished my chicken salad, I said, "If we can make choices, we can make either good ones or really bad ones."

"It's called 'free will,'" she said. "We can be kind to one another and love one another—or we can be cruel and do evil."

I didn't want to cry, and I didn't think I would, but then I thought of the evil that Litton's father committed, and tears came. They were quiet tears, but I couldn't stop them for a while.

Then I said, "So that's the deal, I guess, huh?"

"It's a package deal," she said. "Free will and freedom itself require the problem of evil. People who are truly grown up, not just in years but also in their minds and hearts, understand that freedom can't exist without the choice between right and wrong. To be free, we accept the problem of evil—and then resist it."

Resistance didn't seem enough to me. "Maybe someday aliens from another planet, like thousands of years more advanced than us, will show up, and they'll have figured out how to do everything right and how to stop people from ever making mistakes, doing the wrong thing, and then they can teach us."

"You better hope they don't show up, Quinn. Such a race would be a hive. A tiny ruling class, certain of its moral superiority, would have obliterated the free will of the drones, crushed those who resisted. They would have no patience to teach us. They would just destroy us." She smiled broadly. "Dessert?"

She'd bought the Italian equivalent of chocolate éclairs from Bellini's, the bakery and specialty store at the far end of the block from the orphanage. Anyone who had ever eaten one would know that these fantastic treats could have come from nowhere else.

After she put the plate in front of me, I stared at it for a long moment without picking up my fork.

Having returned to her chair, she said, "Something wrong?"

I met her eyes. "That's where it happened."

"Where Litton's father shot him. Where Michael Bellini then shot the father."

"Yeah. That's where."

She picked up her fork but didn't yet use it. "Bellini's has been in business sixty-one years, Quinn. They have made a lot of people happy. Three generations of the family have worked there. Should we tear the place down because of what happened on one day out of twenty-two thousand days? Should the Bellinis go out of the food business and start all over in another line of work?"

"No. But . . ."

She cut a piece of the éclair, though she didn't lift it to her mouth. "You know who in all the world has been the most hurt, the most saddened, by what happened that awful day? For all that you loved Litton, I'm not talking about you, dear Quinn. The Bellini family has been devastated, especially Michael, who saw Litton shot, who was forced to pull the trigger to save Sister Margaret from Corbett Ormond. They had to clean up the aftermath. They couldn't crawl into bed and surrender to depression. They had to go back to work the next day and every day after. Their store won't feel the same to them for a long, long time, if ever. Do you understand?"

"Maybe. I guess so."

"For weeks, months, there will be thoughtless customers who'll want to talk to them about it, as if that one horrible event is all that matters in sixty-one years of serving the public. The Bellinis are good people, and so they're haunted by this, by what they saw. And because it wasn't their fault, there is nothing whatsoever they can do to make amends. All they can do is go on, producing the best baked goods and selling the most wonderful specialties, hoping that the horrible images, the hideous memories, will one day fade. We mustn't make them close their store, must not tear it down, but instead give them all the support we can—and say a little prayer for them every day."

At last she conveyed the first bite of the treat to her mouth. She ate it with obvious pleasure.

She had taken a second bite by the time I ate my first, and she asked if it was good, and I said that it was delicious. I realized that her face and mine were wet with fresh tears, but we didn't stop smiling, and we kept eating until there was no more, because it was good, it was very good, *it was life*.

# PART 5
# THE WAY AND THE WAY NOT

## 30

Those of us who survived the Oasis and what came after it would later learn that Bodie Emmerich commissioned extensive geological surveys, mostly via satellite, in three states—Nevada, Arizona, and New Mexico—searching for a remote location with an aquifer suitable to his purposes. Ajo lies 140 air miles east of the mighty Colorado River, forty miles or so south of the less impressive Gila River, and over a hundred miles west of the Santa Cruz River, far from any apparent sources of water. The town of Sells, sixty-odd air miles from Ajo, has ample water, and tinier towns in the southwest reaches of Pima County get by with captured rain and deep wells. The geology underlying Emmerich's retreat was unique and strange to the area; it was as if, hundreds of thousands of years earlier, forces hostile to humankind even before we existed had worked diligently within the earth to prepare the site where, countless millennia later, a man of nearly infinite resources could build an elaborate temple to himself and devolve into his own perfectly evil god.

Relying on Panthea Ching's conviction that no one who lived in the Oasis would be awake in the afternoon, we descended from the rim to the floor of the crater and crossed a field of shattered stone that time had worn into smooth gravel.

The gardens covered perhaps two hundred acres at the heart of that massive bowl in the land. Wide pathways paved with limestone wound among hundreds of queen palms, majestic phoenix palms, flame trees and golden willows, dove trees and honey locust, Metrosideros and Australian umbrella trees, and others that I could not name—all of which had perhaps once been diligently maintained but were now overgrown and in a few cases diseased. Shrubs sprawled unattended. The flowers were withered in some beds but riotous in others.

The giant wicker man loomed in the middle of a grassy circle of several acres, which had not been mown in a long while. The figure wasn't crafted of wicker but of sturdy wood made to resemble wicker, and it bestrode the meadow like an evil Gulliver intent on crushing as many Lilliputians as possible. Along one of the paths, the twice-life-size Tyrannosaurus rex, welded together from steel plates and given an enduring polish, threatened us with teeth as big as sabers and fierce reflected sunshine that stung our eyes. The tiered Aztec temple—which the news media would eventually report was authentic in every detail—had been crafted of stone blocks quarried in central Mexico and decorated with disturbing pictographs in the Nahuatl language.

We didn't enter the temple. However, forensic pathologists who were later assigned to the case found that human blood saturated the porous stone altar. From the diaries of Bodie Emmerich, it became known that the temple wasn't constructed with religious intent; he had it built because he'd seen a photo of such a place and thought that it "looked cool." Years later, after sufficient psychedelics and other drugs, after self-worship "elevated his consciousness" and he had begun calling himself "the Light," he'd come to see that even among his spiritually awakened brothers and sisters who lived with him in the commune, there was now and then one who had sold his or her soul to "the dark side of Mother Nature, to the tormented half of that bipolar goddess who struggles against her own creations." Evidently, this dark aspect of Mother Nature, which he called "the Queen of the Void," lived within dead things, as well as in stone and all that was inanimate, and must be defeated if the planet was to be saved. As you might imagine, when followers of the Light were suspected of having sold their souls to the Queen of the Void, they were considered to be beyond hope, a threat to the world, and were conveyed to the Aztec altar before they might infect enlightened people with their dark faith. Emmerich's diaries noted nine such "existential excommunications," as though he understood what either of those words meant.

The Oasis was meant to be a playground for adults but also an open-air gallery for avant-garde artists working in unconventional mediums and genres, a place to spark the imagination at every turn and, as Emmerich put it, "stretch and enrich our hidebound minds with the revolutionary art of the new." Even I, still a callow youth at nineteen, knew that conflating newness and art would ensure the production of bad art, which indeed was everywhere in the Oasis. Those who create in protest against the history of art do not stand on the shoulders of giants, but on the treacherous ground of their own pretensions. The art in the Oasis tended to be immense, not because the subjects required it, rather because the egos of the artists demanded works of physical enormity. Here was a sixty-foot-long, twenty-five-foot-high Gillette razor blade presented on a block of Lucite, so it seemed to float in midair. And here stood a mixed-metal sculpture maybe fifty feet in diameter and nearly as high, so abstract that I couldn't decide whether it was meant to be a cancer-riddled colon or the scalp of a Medusa on which all the serpents were simultaneously trying to copulate with and devour one another. Nestled in a humongous ear was a giant mouth with a big eyeball clenched between its teeth; on the granite plinth that supported this grotesque work, the following words were engraved: I HEAR WHAT YOU'RE SAYING, AND I SEE THAT IT IS MEANINGLESS.

As we progressed through Emmerich's malignant wonderland in search of a front door, Winston grumbled at this and growled at that and lifted a leg to pee on the base of the ear-mouth-eye. Although he lacked language, he was a perceptive critic capable of expressing his judgment.

To the rest of us, the collection in this open-air gallery was increasingly disturbing for two reasons. If at first we found the more absurd works to be beguiling, our capacity for amusement faded the farther that we proceeded. Many of the artists appeared to have celebrated chaos and death. The wicker man reminded me of an old movie in which pagan villagers in modern England sacrificed a young woman by locking her in the chest cavity of such a giant construct and then setting it on fire. What was a wickedly gleaming, sixty-foot-long razor blade if not a tribute to a common instrument of suicide? Past a grove of graceful Metrosideros in early flower, we discovered a thirty-foot-tall sculpture of a sharp-faced cartoon rat that was definitely not Walt Disney's famous Mickey, though it was wearing the yellow shoes and red shorts in which the beloved mouse was always depicted. The rodent's teeth were bared in a sneer, and its red crystal eyes glittered. In its right hand was the naked body of a headless human infant on which the monster evidently feasted.

Equally disturbing was the thought of how much the Oasis had cost to construct, a sum surely in excess of a billion dollars. I estimated more than two billion, maybe three, depending on what awaited discovery. A man who would spend so lavishly on a fantasy retreat might have been a business genius, but even before he had squirreled away in this refuge from normality, he'd been wading in the shallows of insanity.

Eventually, psychic magnetism brought us to the front door that we had been seeking. By this time, we had intuited that most of the residence must be underground, a vast bunker insulated against the Sonoran heat. The door stood at the head of a wide ramp that led to a flying saucer that seemed to be of formed concrete skinned with slate-colored aluminum, serving as a reception hall. The earthbound alien craft was about thirty feet high at the center, maybe eighty or ninety feet in diameter, tapering to ten or twelve feet at the perimeter.

We would later learn that Emmerich hired a construction company that specialized in building top-secret military installations, and that everyone who worked on the Oasis had to sign a nondisclosure agreement with such fierce teeth that those who breached it would invite financial ruin. No one violated the NDA, perhaps not merely for fear of being impoverished by attack-dog attorneys. They also suspected that anyone who undertook such a project would be capable of retribution that bypassed courts in favor of specialists who could put you in a wheelchair for life, disfigure your wife, and mess with your children until they needed lifelong psychiatric care. Still more disquieting was the thought that some of the workers, tradespeople, and artisans who labored on the Oasis took pleasure in imagining to what libertine activities the place might be devoted on completion, and envied the dispensation from morality and even from the law that Emmerich's wealth might buy.

The immense flying-saucer entrance was styled neither like the sleek alien craft in the movies of the 1950s nor the extravaganza of light and glamour from *Close Encounters of the Third Kind*. It was more in line with the Gothic craft in Ridley Scott's *Alien*. Emmerich seemed to want to inspire wonder in his guests on their arrival, but also instill a sense of awe and a vague apprehension that would keep them slightly off balance for the duration of their visit, whether they were staying for a day, a week—or forever.

The eerie quiet of the Oasis unnerved me. Nothing moved but the leaves and fronds of the trees, stirred by a faint breeze, and the birds that flew among them. The warblers and swallows and phoebes that darted from shelter to shelter were songless in the heat. I had not given full credit to Panthea's assurance that everyone slept by day and lived by night, for that seemed impractical and suggested a regimentation that could not be imposed on an entire community, even if it was a congregation of true believers who had surrendered their free will to a guru who called himself the Light. Yet as we ascended the wide ramp to the flying-saucer entrance, no one challenged us. The Oasis seemed to be as devoid of other human life as any crater on the moon.

The ramp was skinned with slate aluminum, as if it were a part of the craft that had lowered hydraulically, and the dark metal door to the saucer was embossed with runes beyond our interpretation, set in a richly detailed architrave. The entrance offered no handle or keyhole.

"Does this maybe feel like a trap?" I wondered.

Bridget said, "My sense is . . . Emmerich feels no need for traps. He's lived by his own rules for so long, untouched and untouchable by any authority, never hearing the word *no* from anyone, that he feels invulnerable."

"Megalomaniacal," Panthea diagnosed. "His psychosis might be chemically induced, but he's psychotic nonetheless. He's not just your standard-issue cult con man who convinced a bunch of weak-minded followers that he has a direct line to God. He pretty much thinks he *is* a god, a god of sorts, immortal or destined to be. His PR became his dream of who he was, and his dream evolved into a toxic fantasy, and the fantasy became his truth. He's enchanted by all the lies that are his life."

"A freakin' bad dude," Sparky said succinctly.

Winston sniffed the ramp outside the rune-marked door. A low noise issued from his throat, the opposite of a purr.

"I don't need a key," Panthea said. "We are what we are, and we need to have faith in that." She placed one palm flat against the door and closed her eyes. Her brow furrowed. Her nostrils flared.

As though I might be developing a foreseeing talent of my own, the skin on my scalp seemed to crawl on the bone, and in spite of the desert heat, a chill as quick as a millipede climbed my spine.

With a pneumatic hiss, the door whisked aside. Beyond lay a realm of golden light.

## 31

It was a garage, just a garage, but a huge garage containing many millions of dollars' worth of vehicles displayed like items on a jeweler's velvet tray at Tiffany's. By also using it as a reception hall—a foyer—Emmerich no doubt meant to ensure that visitors would be abashed by the splendor of his wealth, reminded of the smallness of their achievements, and thus subtly prepared to be submissive. He was, after all, a man who knew the value of power and all the ways it could be employed to control others.

The width of the exterior ramp and the size of the pneumatic door ought to have been clues to the purpose of the faux flying saucer. However, we'd so primed ourselves for immersion in lunatic strangeness if not horror that we couldn't read the clues. Entering the garage, we held fast to the expectation of a loathsome surprise in spite of the surrounding, dazzling spectacle of automotive art.

In that six- or seven-thousand-square-foot circular chamber, cars were displayed in a double row around the perimeter. Each was revealed by ceiling-recessed projection lamps with apertures shaped to limit the light to the sensuous form of the vehicle, so that it seemed to float in a surrounding pool of shadow. Buicks, Cadillacs, and Fords from the 1930s and '40s. Bentleys and Rolls-Royces from the same period. Contemporary sports cars—Lamborghinis, Ferraris, Porsches. There were *two* McLaren Speedtails, a stunning vehicle with over one thousand horsepower, a top speed of 250 miles per hour, and a price tag well above two million dollars.

A few quick peeks into interiors revealed that, in the older cars, the keys were in the ignitions. Electronic keys for the new vehicles were in cup holders. No one seemed to fear that thieves could get in or get successfully away.

A fleet of four Mercedes Sprinter Cruisers, each seating eight or ten, seemed to indicate that there had been a time when followers of the Light ventured out in groups, surely for something more than pizza and bowling. It was difficult to imagine *what* such an outing might entail, other than perhaps the abduction of attractive candidates for brainwashing and induction into the dwindling ranks of the cult, for one unthinkable purpose or another. Our sense was that Emmerich and his apostles had in recent years turned inward until the residents of the Oasis were spiraling toward agoraphobia. The world now brought to them whatever they needed; therefore, they could reject the world with the smug presumption that they were superior to the unenlightened masses.

For all the flash and glamour of the car collection, the garage had the atmosphere of a graveyard in moonlight. My old fear of large parking structures returned. I wondered if evil presences watched us from inside and under the vehicles. This might have been caused by the room's techno-Gothic architecture: curiously ribbed walls, as if the metal was organic; a vaulted ceiling with thick tension struts like the spinal vertebrae of an ancient land leviathan.

At one end of the room, on a dais a foot higher than the rest of the floor, stood a Buick Super Woody Wagon, maybe vintage 1947. Although the Woody was a cool car, it was neither the most beautiful nor the most valuable conveyance in the building. We were drawn to it by the mystery of why it had been accorded the place of honor.

We circled the eggplant-purple Buick in puzzlement until Sparky suddenly dropped to his knees and looked under it and said, "The car is fixed solid to the dais. The dais isn't part of the floor, maybe a one-inch gap between them. What we're looking at here might be an elevator. The car is the cab. Hydraulics lower and raise the dais and with it the Buick."

Such a trick seemed in harmony with the playful nature with which Bodie Emmerich had begun the Oasis, long before he started calling himself the Light and came to believe he was a godling. *Get in the Woody, gang, and we'll take a ride downstairs.* It was more classic Disney design than the weird art that came later.

As cool as it might have been to ride the Buick Woody into the lower realms of the subterranean world that Emmerich had made for himself, none of us wanted to risk it. Once we were in the car, the doors would probably lock, and perhaps when we reached the level below, they would not open until someone vetted the passengers. As armed intruders, we would not be approved. With abrupt acceleration, we might then be dropped two floors farther, or four, or six, to a dungeon, or to an execution chamber where the car doors would then spring open and we would be ejected into a serpentarium of poisonous vipers, what started out as a Disney comedy like *Flubber* having turned into a scene more of a piece with *Indiana Jones and the Temple of Doom*.

The Brobdingnagian scale and pop grandeur of the Oasis were intimidating and inspired expectations of melodramatic events of catastrophic consequences. So I might have written if I had ever returned to *Arizona!* magazine.

Considering its impracticality, the Woodyvator most likely descended to a level originally intended, among other things, for the personal pleasure of Emmerich and the entertainment of important visitors. The need for a larger—and traditional—elevator suggested that the doors were incorporated in the ribbed walls. That one would be no safer than the Woody.

"Stairs," Bridget suggested, and we went looking for them under the assumption that they would be located somewhere along the round chamber's one long, shadow-draped wall. Winston padded quickly ahead of us and led us to a shaft recessed in the wall and fitted with a spiral staircase of stainless steel. We hesitated to descend until Bridget repeated what Panthea had said earlier—"We are what we are, and we need to have faith in that." As a call to war, it was not as bold as the taunt Frederick the Great used with his soldiers at Kolín—"Come on, you rascals, do you want to live forever?"—but it got us moving just the same.

A stairwell is one of the most dangerous places you can find yourself, other than between an ambitious politician and a camera. Once you commit to stairs, you can't get out between floors; you have nowhere to hide, and you can be riddled with gunfire from below or above, or from below *and* above. The stairs between the first and second levels of the Oasis were especially unnerving. Apparently to complete the illusion of a flying saucer filled with abducted automobiles, the round shaft through which the treads passed was lined with neon tubes programmed to send quick pulses of light from top to bottom, perhaps to suggest that, as per

*Star Trek*, we were being teleported from the ship to the surface of some alien planet. The effect was disorienting. By the time we reached the bottom and fled through a door into the end of a corridor, we were dizzy, disoriented, and easy targets for anyone waiting to gun us down.

The wide corridor was deserted, and here the extraterrestrial theme gave way to Art Deco. The limestone floor featured polished black-granite harlequin-pattern inlays along its flanks, and a pure- black baseboard. The walls were clad with limestone, and the stepped molding at the top was black granite. Along the entire length of the barrel vault, an artist of considerable talent had painted packs of running dogs, all lean and elegant borzoi, some black and others white, and naked men in racing chariots pulled by equally stylized black steeds.

The air was pleasantly cool and smelled faintly of garlic, basil, cinnamon, and spices that I could not identify.

The silence and stillness were alike to those at ground level, but we knew the facility had not been abandoned. In addition to Panthea's and Bridget's visions, we could all feel presences unseen, waiting perhaps beyond the next door, and Winston proceeded with his ears pricked and his nose twitching, as alert now as he had been when he'd served as an attack dog for a drug gang.

Without conferring, the four of us had come this far without drawing our guns, leaving them concealed as best we could. Step by step, however, I felt a greater need to have a weapon in my hand.

Sparky cracked a door on a pitch-black room. When he crossed the threshold, LEDs bloomed bright, activated by motion detectors. Beyond lay an institutional kitchen equipped as well as one in a large restaurant or a small hotel. Everything looked clean and functional.

No chef, no cooks, no bakers, no prep workers.

An exhalation of warm breath on the nape of my neck caused me to pivot with a start, but there was no one behind me.

We found storerooms with a variety of contents, food pantries, a room full of janitorial equipment, an expansive chamber containing the heating and cooling system, and two spacious elevators.

A prickling in the palms of my hands. I blotted the left on my shirt, blotted the right.

This level was larger than the ample square footage dedicated to the car collection on the ground floor. It was apparently also offset to some degree from that upper story, because we found no evidence of the shaft through which the Buick Woody was transported to a still lower stratum of the structure.

The two most interesting rooms were at the end of the corridor, the first on the left. A recess featured the marquee and box office to a home theater, a lavishly detailed Art Deco masterpiece with an Egyptian theme. Cast-bronze cobras for door handles. Two life-size figures of Tutankhamen covered in gold leaf seemed to welcome us to the cinema of Death. Stone columns incised with hieroglyphics. Cast-bronze bas-relief lobby-wall panels that depicted gods of ancient Egypt—Bast, Horus, Isis, Osiris, Amen-Ra. An impressive auditorium. Five rows of eight plush seats each, descending to a proscenium flanked by nine-foot-tall gold-leafed statues of Anubis, the god of tombs and weigher of the hearts of the dead, he in a human body with the head of a jackal, his eyes and fingernails of polished onyx in this depiction.

Throughout, the rich ruby-red carpet was patterned with stylized gold scorpions, their sharp-tipped tails raised.

The bright style and obsessive detail conveyed the playfulness with which Bodie Emmerich had begun construction of his retreat, while also revealing—these years later, in the light of subsequent events—that a morbid mysticism and a disturbing attraction to the power of dealing death had even then been sown in his subconscious. That fatal seed would eventually put down deep roots and produce poisonous foliage.

When we cautiously exited the theater, turning out the lights behind us, the continued silence and stillness had begun to chafe our nerves such that we might have welcomed a sudden showdown with the zombified followers of the Light, those whom Emmerich called his "soul children."

To our left, at the end of the corridor, an enclosed staircase led down to whatever lower levels might exist. Directly across from the theater, beyond a door that seemed out of place because it was so plain, the last space on this floor awaited exploration.

Bridget moved boldly toward it. Suddenly I felt as if I were in a dream, the highly decorated floor and walls and ceiling seemed to meet at wrong angles, and my head filled with ghost voices so faint that I could not make out their words, the voices of some legion beyond the door. I whispered a warning—*"Bridget, wait!"*—with the intention of taking for myself the consequences of being first to enter that room. She favored me with a look that said she neither doubted my chivalry nor would step aside like some demure maiden. Winston sniffed with great interest at the half-inch air space between the door and threshold. With the measured insouciance that made it possible for her to feed ice cream to a tiger without fear and breeze into a terrorists' bomb factory with the confidence that she could get out again alive, Bridget turned the knob.

The door was locked.

When Panthea touched Bridget, the lock was not engaged any longer, and the knob turned.

Soft amber lights shone at several points in the darkness, each producing a fraction of the brightness that a humble votive candle would provide, anointing the gloom with a strangely sacred quality, as if the steady flames were disembodied souls. Trusting her intuition, Bridget didn't enter fast and duck to the side, but stood exposed and fumbled for the wall switch and brought more light to the scene.

Twelve dead bodies, dressed identically in white, were laid out on catafalques, three rows with four in each row. As we all followed Bridget into this precise geometry of corpses, I smelled something foul and pungent. I refused at first to speculate on its source, for it seemed that speculation would lead inevitably to regurgitation.

A closer look revealed something worse than cadavers in a morgue, though it would prove to be the least of the horrors that the Oasis would soon reveal.

# 32

The rectangles on which the seven men and five women lay were not catafalques, after all. They were made of pressboard coated in white melamine for easy cleaning. Topped with three-inch vinyl air mattresses and vinyl pillows, the twelve slabs served as beds. Dreaming on in spite of the suddenly brighter light and uninvited visitors, the sleepers were not wound in shrouds; they wore identical white pajamas. Lying on their backs, nine of the twelve slept with their arms crossed on their chests, the position in which they'd evidently gone to sleep; as for the other three, their arms had slipped down to their sides, palms turned up like those of supplicants.

Beside each bed stood an oxygen tank, its air hose drooping into another device, a one-foot-square two-foot-high gray box. The readouts on these boxes were what had produced the twelve faint lights like spirits floating in the darkness when Bridget had first opened the door. The hose emerged from each box and trailed up to the sleeper, feeding a nasal cannula. As none of those on the beds appeared wasted by disease, I suspected that the gray-box device introduced a measured dose of sedative to the flow of oxygen, to ensure that each of these individuals would remain unconscious until someone came to turn the tanks off.

Again I heard ghostly voices, tormented people crying out from the bottom of an abyss. I wasn't able to discern words, but I could *feel* the anguish in their cries. If a nascent telepathic receptivity was aborning in me, then what I heard must have been the stifled unconscious pleas of these drugged sleepers.

Every one of the twelve who lay insensate in this dormitory was of Asian descent, in their thirties and forties. Beyond an archway lay what appeared to be a large communal bathroom.

Sparky said softly, "Emmerich would have done a lot of business with Asia before he retreated here. Maybe his companies still do."

Although it seemed that whispering was not necessary, Bridget whispered anyway. "But surely he wouldn't draw so many followers from halfway around the world. He doesn't advertise the cult."

With the certainty of a seer, Panthea said, "These aren't his acolytes. These are trained workers with special skills. They keep the mechanics of this facility functioning."

"But why would they need to sleep this way?" I asked. "They can't all be insomniacs."

"They're not *paid* workers," Panthea said. "Perhaps once there was a skilled staff, when the Oasis was a frolic. As it became a dark and then darker place, when Emmerich eased into depravity and powerful associates visited here for experiences that the infamous pedophile Jeffrey Epstein might have found alluring, staffing the operation would have become increasingly difficult. And now, getting skilled tradespeople and technicians to work in this slough of madness must be impossible. These people lying here are slaves. They can't be left awake when Emmerich and the others are sleeping. They might escape—or kill their masters. They're put to bed and awakened and overseen by the soul children or someone else."

Stepping to the nearest bed, she indicated a dog collar around the sleeper's throat. "They're all wearing one of these. It appears to be mostly copper mesh, with a small compartment that probably holds a disc battery, microwave receiver, and punishment mechanism. I'd guess that with a remote control, a painful shock can be delivered. Look closely at this man's throat. Scar tissue."

Sparky could not comprehend submission to such torture. "Why don't they strip off their collars?"

"They can't," Panthea said. "These probably aren't buckled on or held by a clasp. They're custom-fitted to each person and then fixed permanently with a crimping tool." She touched the face of the sleeper and closed her eyes and stood swaying for a long moment, as if she could turn the pages of his memory and read them. "If you try to cut the collar off yourself, you'll be severely punished. Succeed in taking it off, and you'll be caught before you can escape—and punished nearly to destruction."

The source of the foul and pungent smell that I had thought must be related to the presence of cadavers was now recognizable as the stink of urine and feces. Four or five of the sleepers, unable to rise to toilet in the long sleep of the day, soiled themselves and were lying now in their own waste, where they would remain until awakened and directed to clean up after themselves.

The cruelty of their enslavement, the regular humiliation they endured, brought hot tears to my eyes as nothing had done since the lunch I'd had in Sister Theresa's office, when we'd had pastry from Bellini's, more than seven years earlier.

If duty would require killing Emmerich and those who defended him, here was proof enough that the killing would be justified.

Looking around at the sleeping workers, Bridget said, "Sedated for long hours every day, enslaved, always under threat, the stress of living in this hellhole—they wear out fast, both mentally and physically. Habitual anesthesia is dangerous. There must be an ongoing need to replace them."

"In the making of his tens of billions," Panthea said, "Bodie Emmerich also made friends with the highest officials in governments worldwide, often with others as misanthropic and contemptuous of democracy as he is."

She didn't need to say more. We could figure it out. In any dictatorship where citizens are regarded as little more than chattel of the state, there would be leaders pleased to pad their pockets with millions from their friend Bodie in return for supplying him with the tradespeople and technicians he required. Bring them into the country on diplomatic flights where their names don't appear on the manifest. Convey them to the Oasis in vehicles bearing diplomatic plates. The saps aren't told to what fate they're being committed. What does it matter? Who are they anyway but beasts of the common herd, hapless plebes, bourgeois strivers who naively believe the platitudes of the ideology that claims to value them? Those above them in the political food chain, whether fascists or communists or high priests of a theocracy, deceive them and use them with no more compunction than they would feel after deceiving a hen to take her eggs or after using a hammer to drive a nail. To those who lack a conscience, there is no such thing as remorse.

I wanted to free the twelve sleepers, but we had neither the time nor the understanding of how to strip off their collars safely, nor a means of getting them out of here without raising an alarm. The alternative was to rescue them by killing those who used and brutalized them. *Murder* was an act of grave injustice, taking the life of an innocent or one whose crimes didn't warrant eradication. *Killing* was the righteous taking of a life, as a soldier acting according to the rules of war, as a policeman shooting an abusive husband who had slashed his wife and with the same blade threatened the child they conceived together, as a homeowner gunning down an armed intruder before he was gunned down himself. After what I'd seen here, I was ready to be a guardian. I still had no translation of *aluf shel halakha* or *Legis naturalis propugnator,* but in my heart the concept was complete and the limits of my license understood.

Without the need for discussion, Bridget and Sparky and Panthea and I—and Winston—arrived at the same conviction and the same intensity of desire for action. We didn't have to be clairvoyant to know worse horrors than the sleepers would be found in this oasis of narcissism and depravity, where all virtues were hated.

Throughout the room, automated oxygen-tank valves clicked off. *Click . . . click . . . click . . .* A sleeper groaned. They would wake, shower, dress, and begin a workday in perhaps half an hour.

The stairwell to the next, lower level awaited us.

## 33

As the day slowly waned, the night approached, and with each passing minute, the one who called himself the Light came nearer to awakening, to be followed by his soul children in all their terrible vacancy, who would then disconnect the workers from their tanks of fearful dreams and mock them in their soiled sleepwear. As darkness fell on the desert, life would return to this world below. It would not be life as we know it, but the life of a hive organized for the purpose of moral disorder and unaware of the contradiction.

The third floor, the second subterranean level, was the largest yet. Like the spokes of a wheel, five corridors branched off a large hub, and by the look of them—door after evenly spaced door, as in a hotel—these were bedrooms where the followers of the Light spent their days in sleep or other pursuits, waiting for their adored life guide to call the night a new day.

At the center of this level were three large rooms, one flowing graciously into the next, each an Art Deco masterpiece, sumptuously furnished, softly lit. You might even say the lighting was romantic, for it was cunningly layered and shaped to fold empurpled shadows and buttery incandescence into one another as if they were luxurious fabrics, and it revealed mysterious depths in the exotic woods that had a lustrous piano-quality finish. The artwork, surely commissioned for these rooms, was without exception sensuous, whether it offered visions of stylized flowers, ripe fruit, or naked human bodies; none of it was outright pornographic, but the intent was, with subtlety, to tease the libido, although also to provide such a high-class environment that even the most savage carnality, if indulged here, would seem sophisticated. I thought the furnishings, though the very essence of the 1930s and '40s, were in their arrangement and purpose reminiscent of drawings dating to ancient Rome, images of grand rooms where bacchanalian orgies were held, festivals of wine and flesh.

As I explored these spaces with my companions, I was reminded of Captain Nemo, the genius antagonist of *Twenty Thousand Leagues Under the Sea*, plying the oceans in his impossibly large, improbably Victorian electric submarine, the *Nautilus*, with its library of a thousand books and its museum of fabulous art treasures and its salon with divans and a pipe organ. Jules Verne had written of Captain Nemo that he was a "satanic judge, that veritable archangel of hatred." The word *megalomaniac* did not exist in 1870, when the novel was published; it wouldn't come into use for another two decades. If Nemo and Emmerich shared an unreasonable passion for ludicrously grand constructions, their motives weren't the same. Nemo was driven mad by loss and grief, by a sense of powerlessness that metastasized into a lust for vengeance and mass murder. Bodie Emmerich had lost nothing, grieved for no one, and had enjoyed great power from his midtwenties. However, he shared with Nemo a talent for hating and a lack of respect for the lives of others; and as Nemo's narcissism had condemned his crew to drown with him in the depths of the sea, so Emmerich had taken his followers into such depths of isolation that many of those who survived might never belong in the world again.

As we entered the third of the three rooms, we were met by the first conscious resident of the Oasis we'd seen. The encounter didn't unfold in any way that I would have imagined.

He appeared to be in his midthirties, tan and fit, his hair cropped on the sides but long on top, his smile generous, his teeth as white and even as memorial stones in a military graveyard. His eyes were as blue-green as tropical waters but as cold as an arctic current. He wore white sneakers but no socks, roomy pale-blue pants of wrinkled linen with a drawstring waist, and a white T-shirt that revealed biceps developed through much suffering with heavy weights.

"Hey, guys!" He sprang up from an armchair and tossed aside a magazine. "Welcome to the Oasis, where the only rule is there are no rules. The Light is the Way, and the Way is the one path, and the path goes anywhere you want it to go." He dropped to one knee and made a come-to-me gesture with one hand. "Hey, pooch, be a pal, gimme some fur." Winston was having none of it and stayed beside Bridget.

She said, "He's my therapy dog, trained to stay at my side so that I can deal with my anxiety."

As supple as a mime who had trained every joint and muscle in his body so he would be able to sway convincingly in a non-existent wind, the greeter swanned up to his full height. "Hey, that's cool, that's sweet, I'm down with that. A few other visitors have come with dogs. There are no rules about dogs, about anything. You can bring a dog for any reason, any reason at all if the Light invites you. In any case, whether you come here alone or in a group, with a dog or not, when you leave, your anima and animus will be perfectly aligned on both sides of your axis, perfectly aligned. I'm Soul Timothy, here to be sure you get everything you want. I didn't know we had guests. We don't get them as often as we used to. Hey, you know not to tell me your names, right? Make up a name or go without one, whatever works for you. If I don't know it, I can't remember it, and if I can't remember it, that's as good as if you were never here. Our real names are unknown to us anyway until we receive them on the day of the Singularity. Do you like your suites? The guest suites are fabulous, aren't they? Anything you want can be brought to your room, and you'll sleep well because the soundproofing is crazy. Somebody could be screaming in the suite next door, you'd never hear it. Now what can I get for you? What do you need, want, yearn for? What do the ignorant Moujiks deny you in the dying world outside?"

Soul Timothy was as eager to please as a puppy, a puppy on five milligrams of Benzedrine. I'd more or less expected Emmerich's soul children to be frail husks, pale denizens of their underworld, eyes glazed, as programmed as ants in a colony, though less industrious. Maybe most of them were like that. Maybe Tim was the social director on this earth-locked cruise ship, schooled to be enthusiastic while equating enthusiasm with verbosity.

Because Soul Timothy clearly focused his attention more on women than on men, Panthea saw an opportunity to gather information by playing the eager tourist fascinated by the minutiae of local customs. "This is our first invitation to the Oasis. Do all the others here—What do you call them?—do they sleep throughout the day as Bodie does?"

"They're my soul siblings," Tim said. "We're children of the Light by virtue of being enlightened by him. Because of him, we've found within ourselves the power we didn't know was there, the total freedom that was always ours but that the repressed and repressive Moujiks stifled in the dying world outside. We're born for the wild night, in need of no light but his, as we await the Singularity." He said all that with a solemn expression, with a rote delivery, as if reciting a portion of some catechism. Then he smiled broadly again and continued with his former emotional zeal. "Yes, we stay to our rooms during the day, resting for the rapture of the later hours. But we don't sleep throughout every moment of the sun's domination. We eat. We groom ourselves. We exercise, read what is approved to read, meditate, prepare ourselves to satisfy and be satisfied as our mood moves us. When visitors come, we're here for you. Every minute for you. Gee, guys, what's wrong with me, letting you stand there? Sit, sit, let's relax together. Since this is your first time—How exciting that must be!—you'll have a lot of questions. I'm your answer man on duty today. Sit, sit."

We settled on a sofa and armchairs, around a low sleek table that might have been by Ruhlmann, on which stood foot-tall Art Deco sculptures of exotic dancers that appeared to be by Chiparus.

The concealed Glock pressed uncomfortably against my right hip, but I was glad to have it. Tim's deference and fervent geniality were the cake-frosting-like gloss on a pile of guano; even if he might be sincere, beneath his pretty icing was a pile of shit.

Taking her cue from Panthea, Bridget leaned forward in her chair. With her eyes as wide as those of a child in a Keane painting, she asked, "Do your soul siblings sleep connected to oxygen tanks, like the Asians on the floor above?"

Tim looked surprised and hesitated before deciding to turn up the dial on his affability generator as well as accord us a greater measure of respect. "You're of that class of visitors to whom all doors are open. I'm sorry not to have realized this sooner. You've been modest in the presentation of yourselves. Rest assured, the desires that have brought you here will be fulfilled at least twice over, and the transcendence you seek will be yours." Those words seemed to have come from the ship's chaplain. The social director took control of the Tim entity again. "The twelve unfortunates you saw sleeping are typical Moujiks. They would oppress us if we didn't harness them to a better purpose and reeducate them." He smiled and shook his head and held his arms out and up in a palm-raised gesture of exasperation. "What else can be done with such sad people? But my soul siblings and I are all blithe spirits, freed from all chains of oppression and ignorance. We need no sedation to sleep, because we have no yearnings unfulfilled, no desires thwarted, no regrets. We live to *live!* To delight each other and ourselves. You'll see! You, too, will be exalted beyond your expectations, transformed by the gift of perfect freedom!"

If I'd been a regular seeker of the One True Snake Oil all my life, I would have been so taken with Tim's ecstatic endorsement of the Way that I might have bought a barrel of what he was selling. Instead, his rap increased my uneasiness, my sense that when the other shoe dropped, it would be a giant's boot.

Although Tim and his like weren't fitted with shock collars and daily sedated, they most likely had not arrived at their current condition exclusively by persuasion, indoctrination, and spiritual transcendence. According to Panthea, the odd couple at the Republic of Beebs supplied Emmerich not only with recreational drugs but also with pharmaceuticals that he used to control his soul children. If what our seer saw was correct, Tim and his grotesque family might unknowingly receive chemical programming through food and drink.

Panthea said, "The rooms in the five hallways on this level are occupied by your soul siblings. Is that right?"

"Yes. That's right. This is the communal level. This is where life is *lived!* Lived as it is nowhere else in the world of ignorance and oppression beyond these walls."

"How many soul siblings are there?"

He eased forward to the edge of his chair, smiling and nodding. He clasped his hands and shook them, smiling and nodding, as if to indicate that her question was precisely to the point and that his answer would please and perhaps even thrill her. "Currently, there are forty men and forty-eight women. All are *exciting* individuals."

I looked casually at my wristwatch. Sundown was still more than an hour away. Not until then would the soul children fly from their rooms like eighty-eight bats in a feeding frenzy.

Tim said, "We range in age from fifteen to fifty. The youngest look quite like children. You will be enchanted by them. The oldest can be a parental figure if that is wanted, a strict disciplinarian or not, and to a one they're of the most striking appearance. No seeker is ever accepted here just because he or she wants to follow the Way. We are *chosen by the Light*." Pride entered his voice. "We must have a look, a most special look." He sat back in the armchair, assuming a pose that allowed us to admire his physique, his face. "There is no ugliness in the Oasis. Ugliness is a consequence of the sick society of the Moujiks, from which we have divorced ourselves."

I wondered about the word *Moujiks*. I didn't seek a definition because that gap in our knowledge might disabuse him of the notion that we were friends of Bodie Emmerich and invited guests.

The availability of Tim and his soul siblings for whatever purpose we wished was implied in what he'd said, but Bridget boldly pressed the issue. "If I see those who interest me, how do I arrange for them to come to my suite?"

Tim slid forward to the edge of his seat again, a bright-faced hunk of burning love right out of the Elvis song, certain that she would include him in any arrangement that excited her. I wanted to pull my pistol and shoot him in the foot. I didn't. To this day, I remain impressed with my restraint.

He said, "You simply approach them and ask them. *No* is not in the language of the Way. You may follow the Way in your suite—or, if a larger scenario is envisioned, you may follow the Way here in these rooms, where many options can be available at the same time. It would be most exciting for us if you did that. It is an honor to follow the Way with the Light himself"—he touched two fingers to his forehead, his lips, and then his heart in what I suppose was some sign of reverence—"or with one of his esteemed visitors."

Sparky spoke up. Combining a scowl and a leer in an expression of subtle menace, looking less like a slimmed-down Santa Claus than like a degenerate whose presence at a grade-school playground would alarm any parent, he said, "Maybe somebody wants something rough. You mean every one of your soul siblings would be up for that?"

Tim clapped his hands as a child might clap when exclaiming *goody-goody*, and he once again sprang to his feet, as if he never got out of a chair other than by appearing to be propelled from it like a fighter pilot from an ejection seat. "Okay, yeah, many soul children may have a taste for what you suggest, but of course not all. It's not forbidden. It's a matter of desire, of interest. If the pleasure you wish isn't one my siblings wish to indulge, then you'll always be welcomed by the Special Selections. The Specials are reserved for the Light and his visitors. My soul siblings and I may not touch them. We aren't spiritually armored enough to play with their kind without being contaminated. We produce alpha waves in abundance. Those who are in the Special Selection emit only gamma rays, which is true of all their kind. They aren't and never can be of the Way. They're Moujiks, oppressed from birth and unable to rise above their prejudices. They take pride in their ignorance and enjoy their oppression. But they're ideal vessels for someone who has an interest in experiences of the sterner kind that you suggest. The Light himself and his spiritually pure visitors—you guys!—are impervious to the effects of gamma rays. Come along, come with me. We'll finish our little orientation with the Special Selection."

We followed him across the larger chamber to a corner bar with eight stools and a large TV screen, now blank. If you needed a break during an orgy, maybe you could come here and sit and have a drink and watch porn until you were revitalized to rejoin the debauchery behind you. Apparently, a deep dive into decadence involved periods of tedium and exhaustion.

Rather than sit on the stools and therefore turn our backs to the room, we stood, alert for arrivals.

Tim stepped behind the bar and took a Crestron control panel from its charging station. Whether the Oasis received a spectrum of programs by way of a satellite dish, I don't know, but

I doubt it. The soul children could best be controlled by keeping them away from those temptations of the world that were less urgently carnal than the lavish smorgasbord they could partake of here. Anyway, as good old Tim touched the Crestron screen, a closed-circuit menu appeared on the television. Among other options of local interest were THE LIGHT DEFINES TRUTH, THE LIGHT DEFINES LOVE, THE LATEST FROM THE LIGHT, and MEET THE NOVICES, from all of which we were spared when he opened instead SPECIAL SELECTIONS.

There was music that might have accompanied a BBC adaptation of a Jane Austen novel. The screen filled with a placeholder video loop of a field of wildflowers swaying sensuously in a soft breeze.

Soul Timothy conducted this tour rather like a museum docent leading us through a wing devoted to famous portraits. "Currently, as you will see, there are seven women and three men available as Special Selections. Visitors who are interested in the exercise of the freedoms of domination, who want to express their liberation to the fullest possible extent, tend to prefer Moujik women rather than Moujik men. Those of either sex that you'll see here greatly enjoy being subservient to whatever extent, to *any* extent, you wish to subject them. We'll start with the seven women. If any appeals to you, she is most likely available, as you are the only visitors at the moment, unless the Light has reserved her."

*Reserved her.* Like a table in a restaurant, a rental car at the airport.

Short of an extermination camp, I could imagine no place more disgusting than the Oasis, not merely because it was a cesspool of iniquity, not even primarily because of that. Even more repugnant was that Bodie Emmerich's "Way" had taken the human sex drive and separated it from all higher human feelings and noble aspirations, stripping romance out of it, romance and love and the creation of a true family and any meaningful connection of one heart with another. He had shown a bright genius for the construction of companies, and subsequently a sinister genius for the *de*construction of this most complex of human desires, reducing it to a crude animal compulsion. Even worse than that, there was a mechanical quality to all of this, as though he must be preparing his followers for the Singularity, the melding of human and machine. Thereafter, protracted orgasm might be achieved with no more effort than pushing a button on yourself where a navel had once been, a five-minute ecstasy that would not interfere with the individual's contribution to the GDP.

On the television, the face of the first woman in the Special Selections appeared. "We call her Acantha," said Tim. "Twenty-six. She meets all the criteria of an exciting partner, beautiful and ideally proportioned."

She was a lovely brunette who looked younger than twenty-six. Her eyes were wide, as if she was surprised to find herself before a camera for the purpose of being submitted for the approval of one kind of degenerate or another.

A second face appeared, that of a young blonde, and the docent guiding us through this museum of the lost said, "We call this one Bambi, because somehow she seems fawnlike. Isn't she adorable? Twenty-two, slender as a schoolgirl but ample where it matters."

A similarity between the first two was immediately apparent: Neither possessed a hard or vampish quality; both were graced by a tender innocence that made them seem heartbreakingly vulnerable. How satisfying it would be for a sadist to reduce such a fragile flower to a condition of terrified submission.

Face by face, my judgment of the Oasis became more fierce. It was not just a repugnant enterprise, but detestable, sickening, a slickly packaged libidinous Bedlam.

With the third face—"We call this one Camilla"—the Oasis qualified as an abomination that justified the killing of Bodie Emmerich as quickly as he could be found. "She's twenty-eight, but not at all long in the tooth," said Soul Timothy, whose soul had been purged from him long ago. "In fact, many think she's our most attractive Special. A work of art even if a Moujik. You might be interested in pursuing with her the intense pleasure that a recent visitor enjoyed—preparing her first with Rohypnol, so that she is profoundly unconscious throughout the affair, limp as the dead but warm, unaware of what unique desires are being fulfilled with her, leaving that knowledge only to the lucky one who feels unrestrained in the enjoyment of her."

The face before me was that of Annie Piper, the girl from Mater Misericordiæ who read stories to us when I was a child, stories by others but also stories she'd written. Annie, the primary caretaker of the orphanage dog, Rafael. Annie, whose soft voice was musical, enchanting. Annie, who had gone away to college on a scholarship and later disappeared without a trace. Her face was so fair and radiated such kindness that we younger foundlings were sure that angels must resemble her.

Nine years had passed since she left the orphanage, eight since she had disappeared, though on the TV screen she looked as if time had not touched her. However, her smile wasn't the Piper smile that I well remembered, not the inverted arc that was the curve of love itself, but stiff and formal, perhaps formed in answer to a threat. The misery in her eyes welled unmistakable, and about her hung an air of the sorrow of one whose soul is yet intact and who offers her suffering for the intention of others. Her chin was lifted in an expression of what I took to be defiance, what little contempt she could get away with in her current circumstances.

She had not willingly reduced herself to the status of a sex toy for the entertainment of those who felt their high self-regard was vindicated when they proved they could inflict humiliation and pain on others without consequence. She was not the type who would have left college to trail after an intellectually vapid guru who oozed perverse platitudes as if they were the wisdom of the ages distilled to inebriating truths. She had gone missing because she had been abducted. "Special Selections" identified those captives with whom visitors harboring extreme desires— and Emmerich no less—could satisfy their inner beast without any serious risk of criminal prosecution. But the term possessed a shadow meaning, suggesting that the women and men offered here hadn't come willingly to the Oasis, had instead been *selected*— identified, stalked, and uprooted from their lives—by agents of Emmerich who, like trained pigs on a truffle hunt, sought the most tender among the young and beautiful to serve them up for the delectation of those with enough power and wealth to convince themselves that they were the most sophisticated sophisticates in history.

I had not thought myself capable of an anger as sharp as the icy wrath that cut through me at the sight of Annie's face on that TV screen. Litton Ormond's death had little angered me because the depth and breadth of my depression had been a sodden blanket that smothered other emotions. Litton had been dead when I heard of the shooting at Bellini's, already beyond rescue. Annie was here, now, in need of being saved. Vindictive, violent emotion ripped through me, flensing away all caution. Anger became rage as Tim blathered on. Before I quite knew what was happening, I was beyond prudence and discretion, having rucked up my loose shirttail to draw the Glock from my holster. I pointed the gun at Soul Timothy.

"I know that woman. Her name's not Camilla. It's Annie Piper. She was a friend of mine. She's not a thing to be used. She's precious."

If Bridget or Panthea or Sparky was surprised, none of them showed it. We knew we were on a mission of meaning, and that it abruptly became personal only confirmed the feeling I had that our journey might prove to be a quest for some object of redemption.

"Take us to Bodie Emmerich," I demanded of Timothy, "or those Moujiks wearing shock collars will spend their evening cleaning your brains off the wall."

## 34

Psychic magnetism would have led us to Bodie Emmerich, per-haps so would have Winston, but probably neither would have been as swift a guide as Soul Timothy with a gun to his head.

In the tornado of my rage, I expected that my companions might disapprove of my rash action, but they all drew their weap-ons and none raised an objection. They were as incensed as I was. Besides, we shared the concern that, with the day soon to end, the task before us might be complicated by eighty-seven other soul children emerging from their rooms under the influence of whatever, alarmed into the defense of their hive and of the guru of the ephemeral and the excessive, who had spent billions crafting the place.

A button concealed in molding released an electronic lock, and a segment of the golden amboina-wood paneling in this third of three large communal chambers slid aside. A staircase led down to the lowest level of the building.

Responding to my question and to the insistent pressure of the Glock muzzle against his skull, Tim said, "Yeah, alone, he'll be alone with night not yet here. We gotta rebel against the circadian rhythm that says daylight is life and night is death or a preview of it. That's a construct of the evil side of bipolar Nature, the Queen of the Void. The Queen serves those corporate masters who want us to work our lives away according to their time clocks, and convert us from alpha emitters to gamma."

As we descended the stairs, I despaired that so many people, born with the knowledge of intuition and with the ability to reason, shaped their lives instead by sheer emotion. So many were swept away by boldfaced lies and swayed into currents of vicious fantasies, until they were so far from the shore of truth that they couldn't even see it. They were everywhere in our time, controlled by those who taught them to fear what didn't threaten them and receive with gladness those ideas and forces that would rob them of purpose, of meaning, of security—and sooner than later would take away their lives as well.

The stairs ended in a twenty-foot-diameter circular vestibule more lavishly appointed even than the spaces on the level above. The ceiling was leafed with gold and inlaid with what I took to be rows of real sapphires. Dimensional, layered crystal forms paneled the walls, and through them passed amber light from an unknown source, projecting prismatic patterns on us, so that we looked like puzzles assembled from sharp-edged geometric pieces.

We were meant to be awed, and we were not.

Soul Timothy said that the door to the left led to the rooms in which the Special Selections were, as he put it, "quartered," when he should have said *imprisoned*.

The door to Emmerich's apartment was on the right. Tim pleaded that the fingerprint scanner controlling the lock responded only to the hands of Emmerich or those of the two physicians who, at their election and in return for seven-figure fees, lived in the Oasis.

As she had done at the main entrance, Panthea placed one palm against that barrier, and by the power invested in her, she released the lock and swung the door open wide.

With a pistol pressed to his head, Tim hadn't shown any physical manifestation of fear. Now, when he crossed the threshold into the sanctum of the Light, he trembled visibly and paled beneath his tan. These were tremors born of the awe that the rest of us were expected to feel but didn't. When this soul child put two fingers to his forehead, lips, and heart, my contempt for him was softened by pity. His addiction to the Way was worse than dependence on any drug. He was surely lost forever, with no route back to a rational existence.

Inside the apartment, we were led toward our target by light music, voices, applause, a quick burst of laughter. A TV program.

The rooms were palatial in their appointments if not in their scale. But I was so exhausted by the extravagance of Emmerich's lifestyle that nothing interested me other than finding that emperor of darkness who called himself the Light.

Although he lived day for night, he wasn't at breakfast now that the declining sun would soon serve to mark his dawn. We located him in a neon-dazzled arcade with at least a dozen pinball machines as well as early stand-alone consoles like *Ms. Pac-Man* and *Galactic Invaders*. There was also a large TV on one wall and in front of it a podium. Emmerich stood at the podium, sidewise to us, barefoot and perhaps naked under a red-silk robe. He was facing the big screen, one hand hovering over a white button the size and shape of half an orange. He was watching what appeared to be a classic episode of *Jeopardy!* hosted by a fortysomething Alex Trebek.

As we entered the room, one of the contestants said, "I'll take 'Famous Littles' for a hundred," and Alex said, "In this 1986 movie, Steve Martin played a goofy dentist." Bodie Emmerich slammed his hand on the button, a buzzer sounded, and he all but shouted the correct response a second or two before the contestant on the program: "What is *Little Shop of Horrors?*"

The audience applauded, and I stood in the weird double grip of rage and incredulity, with my companions likewise halted by their disbelief. If I'd found Emmerich sprawled on the floor, playing with a puppy and cooing baby talk to it, I'd have thought, *Well, Hitler was an animal lover; even psychopaths melt over cute puppies.* Seeing this slave master, serial rapist, and probable murderer engaged with such delight in *Jeopardy!* suggested that the evil he committed was perpetrated with the frivolous intent of a dull boy who lacked the intelligence to grasp the consequences of his actions, a game-show savant whose extensive knowledge of trivia revealed a mind that was nothing but a warehouse of meaningless facts, where there was no capacity to know good from evil. Yet he was not stupid. Perhaps developmentally disabled in a moral sense. Or his conscience had been eaten away by the cancer of narcissism.

The contestant said, "Alex, I'll take 'Famous Littles' for two hundred," and Alex said, "Jodie Foster directed and starred in this 1991 film about a working-class mother struggling to keep custody of her gifted child." Emmerich smashed the palm of his right hand into the buzzer on the word "custody," and shouted, "What is *Little Man Tate?*" The contestant echoed him, and the audience applauded.

"Turn it off," Sparky demanded.

Emmerich showed no surprise when he used a Crestron control to mute the audio, although he didn't switch off the TV. He had known we were there from the moment we entered the arcade.

He turned to us. Fiftysomething. Lean, tan, well maintained. Only a few flecks of gray in his hair. Hands as long-fingered as those of a concert pianist, as powerful as those of a basketball star, the hands of a gentleman strangler. He was handsome in the sexless way that hosts of TV shows for children often are, his features soft at the edges. His expressive eyes were a warm golden brown, his stare direct. It was possible to believe that he was a man of the tenderest feelings—just as it was possible to believe that a hungry wolf in the wild is only a dog that will respond with a wave of the tail when offered a caring hand.

"Timothy," he said, "this will be resolved. You may go."

"No, he may not," I said.

"Go, child," Emmerich said. "I hold you blameless."

Gun or no gun, Tim meant to heed the instruction of his master. He turned away from me and started from the room, no doubt with the intention of alerting others that the Oasis had been breached.

I quickly stepped after him, reversing my grip on the Glock. Holding it by the barrel, I slammed the butt down hard on Timothy's head. All my anger was in that blow, and I hit the guy harder than maybe I intended, but I didn't care. He was down and out, and that's how I wanted him.

Bodie Emmerich remained at his personal game-show podium, his right hand resting on the frame of the Crestron panel. In addition to audio-video, climate, lighting, and other controls, that small screen might offer an icon that summoned help. I wondered if, when called, his misnamed children would come creeping in a silent horde or rush into the room like banshees shrieking a promise of imminent death.

If Emmerich knew that we looked upon him with abhorrence, he took no offense at our condemnation. He appeared to favor us with the loving patience that the Dalai Lama would extend to Buddhists who hadn't yet achieved *prajna*. But he was no bodhisattva. In his case, the loving patience was pure pretense. His smile was a cold, thin crescent moon. I didn't have to be psychic to know that he regarded us with amusement and contempt.

What I had done to Tim had no impact on Emmerich that I could discern, as though the soul child had meant less to him than a house pet, no more than an iRobot vacuum cleaner that I had disabled. His apathy revealed an absence of concern about those in his flock, but also a strange inability to assess the threat to himself in this situation.

As if speaking to errant children whom he could not bear to correct in other than the gentlest tone of voice, he said, "I see from your emanations that you are alphas, as are we all here. You need not resort to violence."

Sparky said, "That's reassuring, your majesty, but after a tour of your Playboy Mansion gulag, we still feel that a hand extended in friendship might be cut off at the wrist."

The words *your majesty* and the scorn with which they'd been spoken must have inflicted at least a small laceration on Emmerich's ego, considering that he considered himself a godling, above mere royalty. Yet he didn't react to the slight in any visible way. With papal beneficence, he said, "The Oasis is also the Temple of the Way. We gather in this sacred place because we believe two things about the desire for pleasure and possessions.

As to our pleasure, it is always an alpha's right to have whatever he or she wants, and one alpha will always agree to satisfy another. Among alphas, there is no competition, only a mutual seeking after the many pleasures that the body provides. Satisfaction is the source of peace."

His spiel was as puerile as that of any film producer flacking a movie crafted with the grandiose intention to change the world. I listened to it nonetheless. If I hadn't allowed him to drone awhile and cool my fury with his chilling nonsense, I might have shot him before he told me what I wanted to know.

Bridget, Panthea, and Sparky—and for sure Winston— evidently knew my trigger wire was dangerously taut, so they took their cue from me and indulged the Light.

"As to material possessions," Emmerich continued, "whatever an alpha wants is rightfully his or hers, to be taken not from other alphas, but from the masses of Moujiks by any means necessary. We revere Nature in her fertile goodness, for the ecstasy she allows. *They* revere her in her darker aspect as the Queen of the Void. We value life. *They* value death. I've taken fortunes from the Moujiks. You won't be taking from me, but from them, when I share with you what I wish. In recognition of your alpha boldness, I'll give you a few million dollars each. More important, I will welcome you into the Way and teach you how to use the internet and other tools to extract *your* fortunes from the Moujiks, so that each of you might build your own Oasis. I have been waiting for potentials as bold as you, that the Way might be evangelized across this troubled nation."

Emmerich's supreme confidence beggared belief. Four people and a formidable-looking dog had penetrated a front entrance that was as thick as a bank-vault door, bypassed his electronic locks, foiled his fingerprint scanners. We now stood with four weapons trained on him. Yet I had no doubt that his apparent calm was real. If he had founded his cult in the spirit of a con man, seeking an absolute power over others that money alone couldn't buy, he had nevertheless come to believe his own crazy rap. He thought he was immortal, that his words and carriage and demeanor and charisma wove together to form a body armor to ensure that no assault could even so much as abrade him.

I took a deep breath. "I'm interested in the people you call the Special Selections. Soul Timothy showed us photos. One was exceptional. He said her name is Camilla."

His pencil-line smile widened into a generous brushstroke. In his sun-bronzed face, his teeth appeared sufficiently irradiated to peg a Geiger counter at the high end of its scale. In part, Bodie Emmerich's delight might have arisen from the mistaken belief that we had recognized his invulnerability and had entered negotiations. But it was also the leer of a satyr, ravisher, rapist for whom the name Camilla conjured potent memories of the brutality with which he had treated her. His own words belied his pose as some New Age holy man when he said, "What you want to do with her is a confirmation of your alpha nature. If I had to encapsulate the fundamental meaning of the Way in a single word, it would be *Camilla*, for to do with her what you will is to do to all the Moujiks what must be done to make this a world of pleasure and peace."

"What's that word—'Moujiks'?"

"It's Russian for *peasants*."

"Why not just call them peasants?"

"Because 'Moujiks' is the better word. It means poor but not always in a financial sense. Moujiks may be rich or penniless or in between. They are peasants because they're ignorant and willfully so, grievously superstitious. The Moujiks are devoted to customs and traditions and stifling institutions and ways of thinking that they believe provide stability in their lives but that in fact only prevent them from being truly free."

For as long as I could tolerate, in order to be able to draw him out on the subject of Camilla, I needed to play to his absurd belief that he had, by his charisma, bespelled us into negotiations. I returned my Glock to its holster. Turning to my three companions, I said, "Hey, guys, we're all right. We're all of like minds here." I smiled at Emmerich. "Sorry about clubbing Tim. I wasn't sure how our unconventional entrance would ultimately be received. But you're a man I think we can do business with."

Bridget, Panthea, and Sparky might have been astonished by this development, but they did not object. They holstered their weapons. Their understanding was a testament to the supernatural connections that were, hour by hour, uniting the four of us in a cause.

To Emmerich, I said, "Camilla. So delicious. How on earth did you . . . acquire her?"

A narcissist absolutely convinced that he had transcended all human limitations, including mortality, Emmerich preened as if we were discussing nothing more dangerous to his future than collecting butterflies to pin to a specimen board. "I have field agents who're always scouting for a certain type, for women and men who combine beauty and innocence, who are intelligent but guileless. To qualify as a Special Selection, their elegance must make them appear to be delicate, even fragile, but they should in fact be mentally strong, so they can withstand being emotionally broken over and over again. Visitors who come here, people of accomplishment, wield great power in government, industry, media, and the arts—and yet can't risk fulfilling certain needs in the Moujik society. It is those like Camilla who draw them here. Because these elites find their desires fulfilled, their protection is extended to the Oasis, ensuring that we may forever operate as though we are an independent nation."

"Nihilim," I said.

He looked puzzled. "Excuse me?"

I struggled to keep my voice light, to seem merely curious rather than like an interrogator. "Your field agents, your scouts, those who find these Special Selections and present them to you—are they Nihilim?"

"I'm not familiar with that word."

"Well, I mean, do you know the true names of these scouts? Do you background them? How can you confidently vet someone to commit a kidnapping for you?"

He frowned. "They prove their worth and are rewarded. In some lines of work, you understand, résumés and letters of recommendation aren't in the interest of either employee or employer."

I smiled, nodded. "Yes, of course, snatching a delicious item like Camilla, leaving no slightest trail to be followed, making sure that those who cared about her are led only into blind alleys—that would require the scouts to have great skill in such matters. The trust between you and them would have to be mutual, beyond doubt. Listen, Mr. Emmerich, I want to be with Camilla."

Stepping away from the podium, as if prepared to lead us to her, he instead raised both hands with his palms toward me in a no-can-do gesture. "I'm sorry to say that's not possible. But we can review the others, any one of which will satisfy as surely as she would have done."

"But why not Camilla?"

He shrugged and shook his head. "It is the nature of desire that sometimes it becomes all consuming and all demanding and must be satisfied even at great cost. In Camilla's case, a recent visitor was required to compensate the Oasis in the amount of five hundred thousand dollars for his indulgence. A Moujik is only a Moujik, but one of them special enough for our Special Selections can't just be written off as if she were a sofa pillow stained by spilled wine."

I stood benumbed, unable to move, but I could think and feel. I felt too much, and all of it too sharply. My heart pumped more than blood through me, pumped a darkness that I'd never known before, not the sludge of depression, but the black fog of wrath. "She's dead?"

"The overly passionate visitor knew the cost before he did the deed. He didn't feel imposed upon. We are honored by the caliber of our visitors and never take advantage of them."

"Half a million dollars," I said. "That's what a life is worth here?"

"This one would have been worth more if she were twenty instead of twenty-eight, and if she hadn't been here six years already. Much good use was made of her, with less to come."

Emmerich's years in the Oasis, his long immersion in the Way, had left him so obtuse that when his moral sense evaporated, so did his survival instinct. Having never been punished for his heinous crimes, having redefined them as virtues, and having been rewarded—endlessly pleasured—for them, he was no longer capable of feeling guilt or of experiencing a fight-or-flight reaction.

"She was worth more, so much more," I said. "I would have done anything to keep her alive."

"Well," Emmerich said, "value is in the eye of the beholder. There are important visitors who will be very dissatisfied not to see her in the Selections henceforth. But the scouts are now busy searching. And in the end, as I said, even the most desirable Moujik is nothing more than a Moujik, after all. Another one who excites extreme desire will be found. More than one. A dozen. And then a choice will be made. Meanwhile, I assure you, others are available to bring you a satisfaction so intense, so complete, that it is beyond your wildest dreams."

I saw no point in telling him that he was evil or that the profundity of his evil had rendered him insane, as mad as any man who had ever lived. He believed that he had transcended humanity, and in that delusion, he was halfway to embracing solipsism, the weird conviction that only he was real, that all other people were figments of his imagination or eidolons that some higher power had projected into the Oasis to serve him as he wished. He could not be shamed or even humbled by words. The most vicious threats could not alarm him. A knife brandished at his throat would be nothing more to him than an opportunity to prove his invulnerability, for no mere instrument of metal could spill the blood of a godling.

I was a champion of the law (*aluf shel halakha*), a guardian of the natural law (*Legis naturalis propugnator*). I had never asked to fill the terrible role of a scourge. But I couldn't simply unpin a badge from my shirt and walk away, for it was pinned to my heart. With no concern that the sound would travel far in this solid and well-insulated structure, I shot Bodie Emmerich three times. The bullets did even to him what bullets do to anyone.

## 35

In the circular vestibule with the gold-leafed sapphire-inlaid ceiling and the cunning crystal walls, fractured light shaped us with prisms and graced our skin with rainbows.

Panthea bypassed the fingerprint scanner and put her hand flat on the door to the quarters where the Special Selections were kept. The electronic lock released and the door came open.

A corridor, less grand than those through which we'd made our way before, served twelve small suites, each with a stout door and an electronic lock. Here we discovered that Bridget and I could now fling them wide, as Panthea had done, with no need to say *open sesame*.

Our talents were maturing so that we might fulfill the task that had been set before us. I was excited but also apprehensive, because there would be no way back to the Quinn I had been when we fully became what we were becoming.

Now that Annie Piper was dead, there were six women and three men in these rooms. At first they came forth with trepidation, sure that they were being called to the suites of visitors whose desires might include inflicting humiliation or physical pain. On standby prior to the fall of night, they were disciplined to be ready to be used by visitors or Bodie Emmerich, perhaps by the merciless live-in physicians who practiced medicine in this place, and by others. They were all dressed demurely and in white, the better to project the purity and the innocence that especially inflamed those who traveled to this remote sink of corruption to abuse them.

As Emmerich had promised, they were preternaturally beautiful, though not in a bold, salacious sense. Ethereal. Elegant. None was unnaturally thin or frail, but each nonetheless seemed delicate, breakable. Their eyes were wells of sorrow, yet also bright with intelligence and challenge. When we threw open the doors to their rooms, they didn't immediately understand our intentions, could only assume that we meant to be their absolute masters. And yet they neither bowed their heads submissively nor gave us the satisfaction of evident fear, which would have been wanted by those they were accustomed to serving.

They appeared haunted, as well they might, but they were of the type who, across this troubled world and throughout time, had the character to endure, to survive the reeducation and hard-labor camps where so many others perished, and in time to stand before a court and testify against those who had enslaved and tortured them. They were of that character in spite of the beauty that could have eased them through the world, and they would have possessed it if they had not been beautiful. If we hadn't come along, Bodie Emmerich would eventually have learned, to his surprise, that one of these—whom he thought had been born to be emotionally broken again and again for the pleasure of others—would prove not to have been broken at all, and would have found the perfect moment to break *him* as thoroughly as I had done with three bullets.

As they were released from their cells one by one, they became quietly excited by the prospect of freedom. However, they were too smart and too battered by experience to let down their guard or even to share words of encouragement with one another. The Way had been a path of fire and broken glass for them, and they might expect the *way out* to be no less gruesome.

While we freed them and counseled them as to the manner and route by which we'd be leaving, I wondered how many Nihilim thrived in the Oasis, where they were, and when they might attack. If they did indeed sometimes eat human hearts for the taste and symbolism of that repast, they would seek a salad, an appetizer, an entrée, and a dessert from Sparky, Panthea, Bridget, and me.

I thought the only terrible surprise remaining would involve those Nihilim. Wrong. When Panthea opened the final suite in that corridor and freed the last woman, my heart felt painfully bitten when I recognized Keiko Ishiguro—that sweet, shy, slip of a girl with lustrous ink-black eyes—who had cared so tenderly for Rafael, the orphanage dog, after Annie Piper went away to college and to her abduction.

Later, I would learn that Keiko's cousin Ichiro Sugimura, her only living relative, had not been her relative at all or anything else he claimed to be. Soon after she moved to Austin and found a job there to be close to the only family she had, Ichiro introduced her to Malik Maimon, who courted her and proposed marriage. He was as much a fraud as Ichiro. Before the wedding could occur, Keiko awakened to find that she was locked in the Oasis. Thereafter she was schooled by Bodie Emmerich to satisfy his more extreme desires and subsequently those of the most eminent and depraved visitors.

When she saw me in that hallway, she came into my arms, and we hugged each other fiercely. With a sob of grief but allowing herself no tears, she said, "Annie," and I said, "Yes, I know."

She was no less astonished by the sight of me than I was to find her in that hateful place. I'd thought that Annie's subjugation to the predator Emmerich must be coincidence. But no. Two girls from Mater Misericordiæ condemned to this living hell couldn't merely be attributed to the Fates indulging in a sick and dirty joke. If human treachery wasn't to blame, then the Nihilim were. The orphanage that had been a haven for some had been a stalking ground for others.

From beyond the milling Specials, Bridget saw me holding Keiko. Although neither of us was gifted with telepathy, her shocked and compassionate expression told me that she knew the general shape of the extraordinary and dreadful discovery that had just been thrust on me and Keiko.

Emmerich's death didn't mean that our escape was a less urgent matter than if the creep had been alive. At any moment, the soul children would rise. Addicted to pleasure by habit and most likely also by drugs that Emmerich included in their diet, they would be greedy for all the sensation that they had to wait for nightfall to experience. Shattered by the discovery that their guru and sole means of support was dead, a lot of them—if not all—would seek the one pleasure still offered: vengeance.

Sparky, Panthea, and Winston led the freed prisoners out of that deepest level of the Oasis. They climbed the stairs toward the communal floor that included the orgy chambers and the private rooms in which residents of the hive even now prepared to swarm. Bridget and I followed.

In the gold-and-crystal vestibule, over the shuffling of feet, I heard a wretched sobbing issuing from the open door to Emmerich's apartment. Having found his master lying lifeless in red silk, Tim staggered forth. His brow and one cheek glistened with blood from the scalp wound that I had inflicted. His face, which he'd thought handsome, was wrenched now into an ugly expression that might have been part grief but that largely conveyed the shock and fear of catastrophic change. The billions of dollars that had been used to instill and feed Timothy's addiction and his years of idleness would now go to estate taxes and otherwise be locked away in trusts for the delectation of attorneys and to pay off the lawsuits that would make it into court in a decade or so. Convicted of whatever crimes he might have committed against the Specials, if in fact he ever participated in their abuse, he would find the accommodations of prison far less comfortable than those of the Oasis.

When Soul Timothy saw me, his face contracted with bitterness. His brow seemed to thicken as if he were undergoing a metamorphosis, and his eyes shrank in their sockets. The changes weren't physical, but the alchemy of fierce emotion. He bared his teeth and reached toward me as he approached.

Bridget leaned past me, her gun in a two-handed grip, and squeezed off two shots before I could bring my Glock to bear. She was Sparky Rainking's granddaughter in more than name. Timothy's shriek quieted when most of his throat dissolved. The sound of his body meeting the floor was as final as the thud of a coffin lid.

"You're something," I said.

"Yeah, well, I still owe you one for taking out the two thugs at the Sweetwater Flying F Ranch."

All of us hurried through the communal chambers, past entrances to the five hallways where the cultists had yet to fling open the doors to their rooms. Momentarily they would burst out, attired for easy disrobing, ready to feast and drink and have their rec drugs in a macabre celebration of their vacuity. This was Prince Prospero's castellated abbey in "The Masque of the Red Death," although the doomed partiers here were hiding out not from a plague but from the truth of themselves.

Quick then, up the Deco stairs to the first subterranean level that housed, among other things, the kitchen and the Egyptian-themed theater and the room where we left twelve Asian slaves in a drugged slumber.

Still no Nihilim. But for the sounds we made, quiet prevailed.

We brought our charges to the elevators we'd been reluctant to use earlier. The first cab connected this level to lower realms; the second went only up to the garage.

Sparky, Panthea, and Winston urged the nine Specials to join them in the second elevator cab, which was a squeeze. Bridget and I decided to resort to the spiral stairs in the blue-neon-lined shaft while the others ascended to the garage and boarded two Mercedes Sprinter Cruisers in the fleet of four, where the keys were waiting in the cup holders.

The getaway had gotten underway with admirable alacrity, and nothing could go wrong now except what always did in such a scene. Just when there seemed that nothing remained to this adventure other than roaring engines and spinning tires casting up clouds of dust and escapees cheering and the heroic rescuers being feted at some future function, *just then* would come the barrage of bullets or the ghost drone armed with Hellfire missiles, or an attack by denizens of the first universe with tentacles for fingers and talons that could gut a rock.

According to my watch, twilight was sifting down on the world above. If we were left with any grace at all, it would be a minute or two in duration.

As the lift doors slid shut, the door across the hall from the theater opened. A man stepped out of the room where the workers had earlier begun to wake from sedation. Bridget slipped her right hand—and gun—into her purse, and I held my Glock down and at my side, shielded from the stranger by my body.

Tall, slab shouldered, hawk faced, with a trimmed but dense black beard, this guy would have looked like serious trouble if he'd been wearing anything other than pale-green hospital scrubs with a stethoscope dangling around his neck. As a physician to Dionysius the Elder, medico at the Bacchanalia, dispenser of ecstasy in pill form, bone setter and abrasion patcher to the Special Selections, pulling down a million a year in addition to whatever orgy action appealed to him, he might have needed the man-of-medicine costume to maintain the authority of his position. Or maybe he was so seduced by what the Oasis had to offer that he required the scrubs and the stethoscope to remind himself who and what he was.

"Hey, Doc," Bridget called out as she moved boldly toward him. "I have this, like, thing in my hand that I don't know what it is. Kind of scares me, you know, so can you, like, take a look at it?"

We weren't dressed in the loungewear that Emmerich required of the soul children. The eminent visitors who came to strip off their sophistication and wallow for a while would be better dressed than we were, diamonded and Rolexed, Louis Vuittoned and Guccied. In our plebian ready-mades, we bewildered him. Like a goat in season, he gaped at Bridget after merely glancing at me. He was so certain that the Oasis remained an impenetrable refuge from all laws and social norms that he didn't suspect his situation until Bridget pulled the pistol from her purse and I showed him mine.

I didn't realize what I was going to say until I said it. Then the question seemed inevitable, considering his exalted position in this sinister pocket universe. "The Special Selection called Camilla—how did she die?"

"Oh, shit."

"Did you treat her?"

"Oh, fuck."

"Did you try to save her?"

"Listen, I couldn't."

"How did she die?" I asked again. It was less a question than a demand this time.

His eyes were the green of patinated copper. With the fingers of his right hand, he worked the shiny instruments at the end of the stethoscope as if they were prayer beads—the bell chest piece, the flat diaphragm chest piece, the corrugated diaphragm chest piece—beseeching the patron saint of corrupt physicians.

"Annie Piper," I said. "That was her real name. How did she die? *Tell me now.*"

From his perspective, the corridor must have gotten very dark, because his pupils were open wide. "The guy lost control. He beat her badly. She was . . . a mess."

"Who? Who did it?"

"I don't know."

I raised the Glock, let him look into that black Cyclopean eye.

He was shaking. "I really don't know. Some visitors are famous, their faces, but many I don't recognize. You wouldn't, either."

"What did you do with her?" I said, by which I meant to ask what had happened to her body.

His answer was that of a makeshift doctor, a *médecin Tant Pis*, who was no more guided by the Hippocratic oath than by the advice of a horoscope. "We had to put her down."

Bridget gasped, and only at her reaction did the physician seem to realize how callous his reply had been.

I said, "Then she was alive when you saw her?"

"Hardly."

"You didn't even try to save her? You *put her down* like a dog with terminal cancer?"

"Listen, believe me, you have to cut me some slack. I didn't want to do it. Emmerich made the decision. Talk to Emmerich. He made the decision. She was a mess. She would have been crippled, horribly scarred, maybe brain damaged. He said she wasn't usable anymore, she had nothing to contribute. Listen, all right, Emmerich is one sick sonofabitch, but he is who he is. He's got the power, and people who have the power get what they want. It's how the world works, that's the way. She was a mess, in agony. We don't have the facilities here to treat someone in her condition. Listen, listen, I couldn't let her suffer. I had to put . . . I had to end her suffering."

"Let me return the favor," I said, and shot him in the head.

The gunfire alarmed the occupants of the room out of which the doctor had stepped moments earlier. A carillon of anxious voices rang out in English and what might have been Korean.

I stepped around the dead physician, being careful about where I put my feet. He was a mess.

When Bridget and I entered the room where the twelve sleepers had been tethered to their oxygen tanks, the voices fell silent as one. The slab beds had been cleaned. The twelve had all showered. Instead of white sleepwear, they wore shapeless gray uniforms and gray caps, as though the human resources director of the Oasis had been inspired by that champion of workers, Chairman Mao, who had also interred millions of them. Twenty-four eyes fixed on our faces, then on our guns. Bridget pursed her weapon, and I holstered mine even though that allowed my shirt to obstruct it.

"Who speaks English?" I asked.

Twelve hands shot up, and one man stepped forward. "I am Mo Gong. We were brought here as skilled workers, but we have been treated like slaves."

"Understood. We're getting out of here. Come with us."

"Our collars," Mo Gong worried. "The pain nearly kills."

"We'll be out of range of the remotes that deliver the shocks before they try to use them. The collars can be taken off elsewhere. Let's go now. Quickly."

The elevator returned from the garage. As night settled on every town from Peptoe to Ajo to Flagstaff, eighty-seven cultists began to imitate life in the floors below. We dared not make two trips. Fourteen of us packed into the cab. We rode up to the garage in the silence of disbelief.

The big garage door stood open. The Specials had boarded two of the Mercedes Sprinter Cruisers. Panthea was behind the wheel of one vehicle. Sparky was in the driver's seat of the other, with Winston riding shotgun sans shotgun.

Bridget took command of the third Sprinter, and I settled in the fourth, and the gray-togged workers divided among the two.

Electronic key in the cup holder.

Engine roar.

Still no Nihilim.

We departed the flying saucer and rolled down the ramp as if motoring through a bizarre dream. The only proof of the sun was a thin line of blood-red light in the west. The moon hadn't yet risen.

The wicker man towered into the night, as did the steel T. rex. The eye-in-the-mouth-in-the-ear heard-said-saw. The Aztec temple offered a stone altar saturated with blood that would eventually be of interest to the gatherers of forensic evidence at the FBI.

We drove single file across the crater, if it was a crater, up the long-eroded wall, and down the slope to where we had left the Mercury Mountaineer that we had acquired in the Republic of Beebs the previous night.

From there, Keiko and another Special would drive the first two Mercedes Sprinters. Mo Gong and his crew would follow in Sprinters three and four. They would head north on State Route 85, then east on Interstate 10, all the way to Phoenix, which was about a two-and-a-half-hour trip. Once in the city, they would not risk taking their complaint to authorities, because virtually any police agency would be seeded with operatives from the federal Internal Security Agency. Conceivably, the ISA might be well aware that sympathetic patrons of theirs—government officials, media executives, titans of industry—had been to the Oasis to engage in atrocities. They might want to protect their own and deny Bodie Emmerich's victims the opportunity to name names. Therefore, the four Sprinters would be driven to the home of Mr.

Hector Luis Salcidero—my former boss, the publisher of *Arizona!* magazine—with a handwritten note from me. Hector was a good guy, one of the best. He had contacts. He would lead the accusers to one of the city's TV stations and get them breaking-news airtime to blow open the story in such a big way that it couldn't thereafter be squelched.

Driving the Mountaineer, Bridget would follow the same route, though our little squad had in mind a different destination and an even more urgent purpose.

We stood by the Mountaineer, watching the Sprinters follow their headlights into the desert dark, while we took a few minutes to discuss what we'd learned and to be sure we were agreed on the nature of the problem and the best solution.

Back at the Oasis, none of the cultists might yet have found Emmerich and Soul Timothy on the lowest level or the dead physician on the floor that included the kitchen. Soon, however, they would become aware of gaps in the functioning of the staff. Even the self-adoring and uncurious soul children ought to include at least one among them who would have the capacity to put down his wineglass, forgo whatever drugs were arranged like canapés on silver trays, ignore for ten minutes the insistent effect of Viagra, shift his attention from the multitude of crotches that attracted him, and have a look beyond the happening scene to eventually discover that their godling and sugar daddy had assumed room temperature. What would happen then I could not clearly imagine. If some despaired, would they pull a Jim Jones and swill poisoned Kool-Aid? Poisoned Dom Pérignon? A few perhaps, but not many. With so much expensive art—Tiffany lamps, original paintings by Tamara de Lempicka, works in silver by Jean Puiforcat—the temptation to loot the place and pack an antique car full of treasures would be great; and the soul children had been shapen never to resist temptation.

At first, a frenzy of violence seemed unlikely—until you considered they were schooled in bigotry and paranoia. Emmerich blamed all the ills of the world on ignorant, regressive Moujiks, peasant masses who insisted on the rightness of interdictions that limited the behavior and power of the enlightened. If the Light himself had been shot to death, who could the perpetrator be but a Moujik in their midst, masquerading as a soul child? A firestorm of suspicion could be ignited in mere minutes. Accusations and counteraccusations. Such a sexualized culture as theirs already valued sensation and emotion above reason, which could so easily lead to cruel and irrational actions; the fuse was lit.

As we watched the taillights of the Mercedes Sprinters dwindle in the dark, Sparky said, "Were there any Nihilim in that place? I thought it'd be a nest of wormheads, but we didn't find even one."

Panthea said, "Their mission is corruption and misery. The corruption of the Oasis and the cult members was complete. Emmerich and his savage sophisticates could visit misery on the Specials and the Asian workers as well as could the Nihilim. The beasts moved on from here some time ago."

The last red sunlight had bled away in the west, and the moon still lay abed in the east. Contrary to Hakeem Kaspar's promise, I didn't see any immense dark form, any alien craft without running lights, blotting out the stars. I never would.

However, I knew where one Nihilim had curled in the heart of an apple for a long time. In memory of Annie Piper and as justice for Keiko Ishiguro, we could go nowhere now but to Phoenix and find who at Mater Misericordiæ had been referring the fairest and gentlest among its girls for abduction and imprisonment at the Oasis. The same wicked person—or more likely a Nihilim in human masquerade—had ensured the murder of Litton Ormond by somehow locating his fugitive father, Corbett, and revealing to the murderer that his boy was sheltered under another name at the orphanage. I'd not had time to consider what lesser pains and sadnesses that same individual might have inflicted on the sisters and their charges, but I thought I knew in what identity the Nihilim had so successfully concealed itself for so many years.

## 36

In Phoenix, as in any large city, there would be numerous sources from which we could obtain yet another untraceable vehicle at an exorbitant price, but we didn't risk the Mercury Mountaineer by parking in front of the orphanage, where we were likely to be seen arriving or fleeing. The issue wasn't cost. We still possessed over a hundred forty thousand dollars in drug-gang money. Whenever we needed more, we had psychic magnetism to locate a Nottingham. Frankly, the problem was exhaustion—emotional more than mental exhaustion, mental more than physical, though we were also tired in muscle and bone. Being champions of the natural law was draining work. Plus we were hungry. By the time we completed our mission at Mater Misericordiæ, Hector Salcidero might already have escorted the Specials and the Asian workers to a TV studio and gotten them on air during the late news, after which my friends and I were likely to be public figures, known faces, once again hotly pursued by ISA agents with DNA on their minds. Thereafter, we would be well advised to get our meals only at the drive-up service windows of fast-food franchises, with baseball caps pulled low over our brows, and it would be more important than ever to be in a vehicle unknown to the authorities. Maybe in a couple of days, or even tomorrow, we could seek a replacement for our current wheels. As for undertaking that task tonight—forget about it.

After walking three blocks, we stood in front of that lovely Spanish Revival building in which I had spent most of my life. With four two-story wings encircling a courtyard playground, the school and orphanage occupied a third of a long block. In daylight, the plaster walls shone as white as the habits that the sisters wore, and the many planes of the roofs rolled away in rows of barrel tiles in countless shades of red and orange.

Now, at a few minutes past ten o'clock in the evening, the pitched roofs were black in the moonlight. The walls appeared to be pale gray in some places, vaguely blue in others. Mater Misericordiæ stood mostly dark at that hour. Except for a few of the older kids who might be bent to their studies and stressed about upcoming exams, everyone who lived there went to bed at 10:00 p.m. They rose promptly at six in the morning if not earlier, and made their way through each day by long-established routines, which children shorn of their parents found essential and comforting. Light glowed in the belfries of the bell towers that bracketed the front wing, frosted four curtained windows on the second floor, and spilled softly from a pair of bronze lanterns onto the stoop at the front entrance.

Winston proceeded to the steps and climbed to the broad stoop, where he turned to look back at us.

For a moment, I saw myself and my three companions through the dog's eyes. We stood on the sidewalk in the light from a streetlamp. This was not a highly trafficked avenue, especially at this hour. Behind us were the empty lanes of blacktop and a stillness of street trees in the warm air. Three- and four-story buildings on the far side of the block. Phoenix stepping steadily higher in tiers. The sounds of a vibrant metropolis were oddly subdued, and then they quieted away entirely. I heard nothing but the knocking of my heart and my suddenly quickening respiration, so that it seemed we were standing in a ghost city, the only people alive. A terrible foreboding overcame me.

I blinked away the dog's view of us. When I looked at Bridget and Panthea, I saw that they were assailed by a vision more intense than my presentiment of oncoming evil.

Sparky Rainking's mysterious career, prior to the day that Bridget had come into his care, had left him with the skills of a warrior but also honed his observational ability. Although he alone among us had no supernatural gifts, he understood that the three of us were in the grip of some shared dread. When he spoke, his voice broke the uncanny silence, bringing with it the sounds of the city, which was sweet music. "Hey, what's wrong? What is it?"

Bridget shuddered and hugged herself. "I saw . . . a dead city."

"I saw a dead *world*," Panthea said. "No human life from pole to pole. I don't know how or why or when, but it's coming if . . ."

"It's coming," Bridget agreed, "if we and others like us don't eradicate the Nihilim, every last one."

In an expression of canine impatience, the dog danced in place.

We went to him, gathering on the stoop, where the light of the lanterns was round about us.

The sisters employed a live-in property manager, Hilda Detrich, who shared an office with her daytime assistant, Rosa Jones, to the left of the foyer. At this hour, Hilda would be in her apartment on the ground floor and would respond to the rare visitor in the night. We had no intention of ringing the bell and involving her in this.

Panthea put one hand to the solid oak door. The lock released, we followed Winston into the foyer, and Sparky quietly closed the door behind us. On a sideboard, a small lamp with a tasseled shade served as a night-light.

I went into Hilda's office. Guided only by the ambient light of the streetlamps that penetrated the windows, I sat at Rosa's desk, one of two workstations in that spacious room.

The Panasonic phone featured a lighted display at the top of the slanted box, and along the left side, a lighted registry listed seven phone lines and sixteen intercom locations. Sister Agnes Mary, who served as Mother Superior, was at the top of the inter-com list. Not all the sisters could be summoned in their quarters, but the third on the list was Sister Theresa, the psychologist and counselor who'd taught me about ants, birds, and fish.

For many reasons, we didn't want to rouse the entire orphanage to the threat at hand, not least of all because, in a general chaos, our suspect might have a chance to flee or harm a few children in one last act of vicious violence. We needed to contain her for the interrogation and manage whatever reaction she might have.

The intercom operated on speakerphone mode, so I didn't need to lift the handset from the cradle. I pressed the button next to my therapist's name. An electronic tone would sound in her small room, perhaps loud enough to wake her if she was asleep. "Sister Theresa?"

She replied at once, sounding puzzled but not frightened by the double novelty of a man's voice in this female realm and a summons at this late hour. "Who's there?"

I kept my voice low. "I should have gotten the point with the ants, but I needed birds and fish."

"Quinn? Quinn Quicksilver?"

"Yes. I'm so sorry if I've alarmed you." I knew that I hadn't. Sister Theresa was not given to alarm. But I had been well trained in courtesy. "I urgently need to speak with you."

On the intercom registry on her phone, an indicator light would show the location from which I was calling. She matched my whisper. "You're in Hilda's office? Were we not properly locked for the night?"

"Secure as a bank," I assured her. "Can you meet me here?"

"Yes, of course."

"Please tell no one, and come quietly. I am in some trouble."

I disconnected, and turned on the desk lamp.

Preceded by Winston, Panthea and Bridget came in from the foyer and quickly lowered the shades at the two windows that provided a view of the street. Sparky followed, leaving the door ajar.

Not a minute later, we heard Sister Theresa in the foyer. These nuns wear simple white habits without starched wimples. Their heads are covered in part by a scarf that trails down their backs, though they call it a "veil." Evidently, Sister had not yet retired when I called her, for she entered dressed as she had been for the day.

She was no more alarmed to discover four people and a dog than she had been to hear me on the intercom. I'd forgotten how much she resembled the late Aretha Franklin. I remembered a spring talent show in which she had put the nervous student performers at ease by opening the show herself, singing with gusto a version of "Respect," the lyrics of which she'd revised to make it a song about the woeful fate that would befall students of Mater Misericordiæ who didn't do *exactly* what their teacher told them to do.

She came to me, and we hugged. When I introduced her to my companions, she shook hands all around and then she stooped to scratch Winston behind the ears. "What a handsome boy."

Sister and I sat in office chairs, facing each other. Bridget and Panthea stood by the filing cabinets. Sparky closed the door.

"You," Sister said, "are the last boy I'd ever expect to tell me he was in some trouble. I don't find the claim credible. What kind of trouble would that be?"

"I've news about Annie Piper."

Her made-for-smiles face formed instead a somber grimace. She knew that good news about Annie wouldn't have been delivered in this way. "That precious child."

"I am sorrier than I can express to tell you that when Annie went missing all those years ago, she was abducted and impressed into . . . sexual slavery. Recently, she was murdered by a man who horribly abused her."

Sister bit her lip, bowed her head, and made the sign of the cross. I was backlit by the desk lamp. She sat in faded shadow, but even in the faint light, her mahogany skin seemed to be polished like the face of a saint on one of the statues in the church. Unshed tears glimmered in her eyes. "Do the police have him, this monster? Has an arrest been made?"

"Not yet. And that's not all. It grieves me to tell you that Keiko Ishiguro was abducted by the same people."

Shock like fishhooks pulled her facial features into a mask of anguish. "Is she . . . ? No! She can't be, not Keiko, too."

"Keiko is alive, but she's suffered much. Her story will be in the news soon. And there's more."

Sister Theresa gripped the pectoral cross that she wore on a chain around her neck, pressed it tight in her right hand. "More? Please God not another of our girls."

I shook my head. "Litton Ormond."

Shock and grief made way for bewilderment. She regarded me as if I'd spoken gibberish. "Litton? Litton Ormond? What do you mean?"

"Someone—something—in Mater Misericordiæ serves as a scout for the sex traffickers who are responsible for Annie and Keiko. And that same individual almost surely told Corbett Ormond where his son had secretly been stashed away."

She blinked, blinked. Her lashes flicked away slivers of tears, and her eyes welled no more. Her face hardened in anger, as if grief were an insufficient response to the mounting horrors. "Quinn? How do you know these things?" She regarded each of my companions with sharper curiosity than before. "Who are your friends?"

If I began to talk about *aluf shel halakha* and babies born into this world without a father and with no DNA from their mothers, if I spoke of creatures from the first universe, I would lose her just when I needed her the most.

I said, "Trust me, Sister. All that will be made clear when we're able to sit here with Sister Margaret and question her."

"Sister Margaret? What would you need to question her about?"

"She's the obvious connection. She encouraged Annie in her writing and guided her to a particular college where she was provided with a scholarship perhaps funded by Bodie Emmerich."

"Who? Emmerich who? I've never heard of such a person."

"You will. Sister Margaret developed close relationships with both girls, the better to stay in touch with them after they left here and spot them for Emmerich when he needed new . . . talent. She chose Annie and Keiko to care for Rafael. She took Litton Ormond to Bellini's on the day his father was waiting there for him."

"Have you forgotten that she took other children as well? Not just Litton. Quinn, dear Quinn, this makes no sense."

"The other kids are lucky to be alive."

"No, no, no. Corbett was going to shoot Sister Margaret."

"I think she arranged with him to make a pretense of meaning to shoot her and then to relent and flee. Neither of them suspected Michael Bellini would pull a gun from under the checkout counter."

Sister Theresa shook her head. "Margaret is shy, quiet, the most devout among us. How can you know these things?" She looked again at my companions. "You can't know these things."

I reached out with both hands.

She hesitated to take them. "If this crazy thing were even half-possible, if there could be any truth in it, why aren't the police here to question her? Why you and your friends, not the police?"

Continuing to offer her my hands, I said, "If you'll just help us, you'll see. Everything will be clear. Dear Sister, when I was so depressed that I didn't want to live, you saved me from suicide."

She objected strenuously. "You never would've killed yourself!"

"Children do. More every year. These days, they're taught to fear the future for a hundred reasons, and they do. Back then, eight years ago, I considered it quite seriously, more than I ever let on to you. I was in an abyss of despair. You gave me hope. More than that, you taught me to be in awe of our free will, showed me that it's nothing less than a miracle. Please help me again. Please help me now. If I'm able to show *you* a miracle, at least something that seems like a miracle to me, will you help us?"

"Show me what? What will you show me?"

Intuiting my intention, Bridget said, "Are you sure you can do this, Quinn?"

I smiled at her and sounded more confident than I felt. "The talent matures, just as it does with you. Besides, what do we have to lose? We're coming to a rejection here." I leaned forward in my chair, beseeching the nun with both hands. "You have nothing to fear from me, Sister. You know that's true. I don't think you've ever feared anyone in your life, so it makes no sense that the first would be me. Just take my hands for a moment, and then help us if you feel you can. At the end of all this, we'll get éclairs from Bellini's—two each!—and never give a thought to the calories."

The bleak evils with which I'd charged Sister Margaret both offended and anguished Sister Theresa, but the reference to the éclairs, harking back to the day when she'd at last fished me from the dark sea of depression, spoke to her heart. Her clenched face softened, and after a hesitation she took my hands in hers.

Together, we saw ourselves through the eyes of Winston, and the tableau we formed together was more striking than I could have hoped for: the warm light from the desk lamp and the silty softness of the silken shadows, my dark clothes contrasting with her white habit, I the former student who had once bent forward to receive her wisdom, now she the student bent forward to learn something from me. Then Winston came closer, between us, and put his head on her lap. He looked up at her, and together Sister and I were gazing into her eyes from the dog's perspective. I could feel how the experience rocked her. For the first time in her life, she saw herself now as someone else saw her, in this case a loving dog. She peered deeper into her eyes than she could ever do when looking in a depthless mirror. As her irises widened and her pupils grew large, she might have felt as if she were staring into her own soul, into all the strangeness—the potential and the mystery—that is a human being.

If that was a little frightening, it was also exhilarating, and it was good.

## 37

Winston's new friend went alone to Sister Margaret's room to report that a stray dog had wandered into the building at some time during the day. She claimed to have corralled it in Hilda Detrich's office. As Sister Margaret had overseen student caretakers of the previous Mater Misericordiæ hound, the late and much-missed Rafael, she would of course tend to this one and select the children who would most benefit by having responsibility for the animal.

Sister Margaret had not yet retired for the night, and she returned with Sister Theresa in less than five minutes. Her red hair was flecked with gray, which it hadn't been in the days when Annie Piper, under her tutelage, learned to take proper care of a dog. Her freckles burned bright in her smooth pale skin, and she looked as fresh-faced and guileless as ever she had. She startled slightly upon discovering four people waiting with the foundling shepherd, but she played the shy and humble soul as she'd always done, meekly settling in one of the office chairs when told that I had a few questions for her.

Winston occupied the knee space under a desk to observe the proceedings from there, his ears pricked. Sister Margaret seemed to know at once that this was not about a stray dog, after all. She said nothing either about or to the shepherd.

I could see that Sister Theresa suffered regret at having so deceived the younger woman. She was, however, a psychologist as well as a nun; perhaps she'd begun to read some disturbing tell-tales in Sister Margaret's performance that she had never noticed before.

Sparky closed the door and stood in front of it, while Panthea went to stand with her back to one window, Bridget at the other. Sister Theresa took up a position by the filing cabinets.

This left most of the large office to me, and I intended to use it. Remaining on my feet, moving about not like a sharky prosecutor prowling in front of a witness stand, but rather imagining myself, at least for the first few exchanges, as being the still-tormented former student forever haunted by the loss of his friend.

"Sister Margaret, I'm sorry to trouble you at this hour. You must know I wouldn't do so if it wasn't absolutely necessary."

"It's no trouble at all." With a hint of an Irish brogue, her voice was like faraway music. Her hands rested in her lap, palms up. They began to curl into fists, but then she relaxed them once more.

"Sister Theresa has indulged me by bringing you here," I said. "She knows my torment. She saved my life back in the day, when the world seemed grossly misshapen to me and I wanted no place in it."

I watched her, and she waited without comment, as if a mutual silence in this situation was not peculiar.

"You know about that, Sister Margaret?"

"It was a time of great distress for all of us." She put her hands together as if remembering the concept of prayer.

I stopped pacing and sat on the edge of a desk. "Now those dark waters have pulled me under again. I'm lost, and I come to you."

Her mouth hardly moved as she spoke, the words issuing from her as if from a ventriloquist projecting her voice into a stage dummy. "I have no . . . no capacity."

"I'm sorry. I don't understand."

"I'm a simple person. Everyone knows that about me. I have many limitations. I have no capacity for anything but faith. Sister is the therapist, the better listener, with a kinder heart than mine."

I saw Sister Theresa's brow furrow as the younger nun spread the humility too thick.

After another silence that the interrogee did not interrupt, I said, "I'm sure you remember Annie Piper."

"Of course."

We shared another wordless moment. If she was only who and what she seemed to be, only human, then she was an odd duck.

She realized that she needed to offer more. "A tragedy. Annie is often on my mind."

"Yes, I imagine she is." What I told her next was true, as far as it went. "She's been found."

Sister Margaret glanced up and quickly returned her attention to her hands in their pale press of supplication.

"Sister, don't you wonder where she was found?"

She nodded. "I want to know, but I'm afraid to hear."

"Why would you be afraid?"

"After all these years . . ."

"Yes?"

"How could the news be good?"

"Now is when you need that capacity for faith. Annie has been kept at a remote location in Pima County, a place called the Oasis."

She met my eyes again.

"Keiko Ishiguro has also been kept there. To be used. To be raped and otherwise abused."

Sister Margaret covered her face with her hands.

When it seemed that she might remain in that posture for as long as allowed, I said, "We don't have hands so that we can hide from the ugliness of the world, Sister."

As she lowered the fingered veil, the look she gave me was fashioned poorly, too extreme in its representation of a shy and simple person. She was as blank faced and empty eyed as a simpleton, and she definitely was not that.

"Sister. *Legis naturalis propugnator.* What does it mean?"

Her pose of vacancy dissolved, her slack features grew taut, but she feigned bewilderment.

"*Aluf shel halakha.* What does it mean?" I asked.

She knew but would not say, as if the words were an incantation with which she would destroy herself.

I stepped in front of her and held out one hand.

She stared at it until she understood that I would not relent. Once again assuming the role of the demure and compliant servant of Truth, she did as I required and took my hand.

From his retreat under the desk, Winston was watching Sister Margaret. Now I viewed her—and she viewed herself—through the dog's eyes. Shocked, she tightened her grip on me, and she was so unsettled by this development that her power of masquerade faltered. Winston saw, I saw, Sister saw two of her fingers morph into

347

slender tentacles, and I *felt* one curl around my wrist—supple, slick, cold.

I recoiled, broke contact, involuntarily declaring, *"Nihilim!"*

That one word caused Sparky to take a step toward us, and it triggered a more spectacular—and unexpected—response from the thing that was pretending to be Sister Margaret. It ceased its impersonation. The penitent face of the *religieuse* collapsed into the greedy hookworm maw, as though it ate its own false countenance. Something pale and spiny whisked around and around deep within its toothless mouth, perhaps a sharp, rendering tongue. With a hiss, the creature shot up from the chair. The six members of each transformed hand seized the other office chair, hurled it. Sparky dodged, and we reached for our holstered pistols. The beast quickened into action, knocking Sparky aside. The old warrior's head caught the corner of the desk as he fell in thick spatters of blood. Stranger than all the devils of all our dreams seeking whom they may devour, the Nihilim tore open the door and disappeared into the foyer.

The creature must have taken intense pleasure in its deceit, living among the sisters as one of them, singling out some of their favorite children for death and suffering. I wondered who else—in addition to Annie, Keiko, Litton—might have been victims of the thing called Margaret. And who would be next?

Half of the sisters roomed on the ground floor, but all of the orphans and the rest of the nuns resided on the second level. The beast was strong, its talons sharp, its purpose bloody destruction. Free in the building, it would kill every child it came across, to declare that no heart was sacred and that violent death was the only reward for innocence.

I found myself in the foyer looking toward the open staircase that curved through shadows up to the second floor. The creature seemed to be making for them, but then pivoted to the right, into the main ground-floor hallway, and disappeared.

When I turned the corner, I saw the nun's habit that the Nihilim had torn off like thinnest paper and cast aside. Ahead on the left, a door was swinging shut of its own weight. I knew that beyond lay the stairs to the basement.

Pistol in hand, I stepped onto the landing. The Nihilim had gone down in darkness, evidently needing no light to see. I found the wall switch, and in the fall of light, the concrete stairs swelled up from the gloom.

I hesitated to follow my quarry. The orphans were forbidden to venture into that lower realm, though from time to time we went in little groups, more in a spirit of adventure than disobedience. A structure as large as Mater Misericordiæ had complex mechanical systems, and the world below was a maze of pipes and pumps and boilers, furnaces, chillers, and much arcane machinery that I couldn't name. There were uncountable places where the monster could lie in wait and spring upon me so abruptly that I might not have time to bring the pistol to bear.

Just then I experienced a Panthea moment, my gift maturing to include vivid clairvoyance. I saw the fiend retrieve a long-handled monkey wrench from behind a large holding tank full of super-heated water, where it had stashed the tool long ago. I saw it moving through a puzzlement of water lines and waste lines and electrical conduits, slouching past an array of breaker boxes. It stooped and applied the jaws of the wrench to a hexagonal coupling at a junction of pipes. Abruptly the vision fast-forwarded. A fierce blue-orange flash. Glass exploding out of the windows on the upper floors of the building. Fire churning through the hallways. The Nihilim intended to flood the basement with natural gas. The pleasure it would have taken in the slaughter of a few children was nothing compared to the joy it would take in roasting them all.

Pistol in a two-handed grip, I hurried down the stairs and located a pair of wall switches. The first lit the room around me, and the second activated a long string of pathway lights fixed to the ceiling beams.

Psychic magnetism. I focused on a mental image of the Nihilim and moved with caution, as quickly as I dared, under the string of lights, each about fifteen feet from the other, my shadow swelling and diminishing, swelling and diminishing.

The basement of the orphanage and school is like the thwarting maze of rooms that, in dreams of stalking Death, makes the sleeper's heart race toward rupture until he wakes sheathed in sweat, with a scream snared in his throat. At that moment, it seemed to have been constructed and equipped specifically to provide a Nihilim with infinite places of concealment. The path lights brightened only the center of each room, leaving shadows to crawl the farther reaches.

As I approached a doorway, a second moment of clairvoyance rocked me to a halt: a summer day, a patio splashed with sunshine, a wheelchair. I was in the chair, a paraplegic, my head tipped back as I watched birds wheeling across the sky. My left hand had been amputated, my right eye removed and sewn shut. My face was horribly disfigured.

Sometimes such visions are of what might happen, not of what will inevitably happen. So said Panthea. On the other hand, maybe both of these foreseeings would be fulfilled, the school blown to ruins in a gas blast and me—what was left of me—stitched together to pass my years imagining scenarios in which I hadn't screwed up.

When the vision passed and I could summon the courage, I went through the doorway low and fast, leading with the Glock. I moved sideways and put my back against the wall to the right of the door and scanned the room ahead. Nothing. Just the sound of water rushing through pipes and relays clicking and small motors purring and the *tick-tick-tick* of something.

I moved on, as champions of the natural law are expected to do even if they would rather not. Two chambers later, I was so deep in the bowels of the basement that the interior entrance I had used and the exterior entrance that lay ahead were equidistant. Which is when the lights went off.

My preternatural gift might be maturing, but my brain was stuck in late adolescence. In my rush to avert the destruction of Mater Misericordiæ, I had not been sufficiently clear of mind to foresee that my quarry, accustomed to being predator rather than prey, might blind me.

The path-light switch was rooms away. I had no idea where to find the one that would turn on other fluorescents or incandescents in this immediate space.

Disorientation doesn't take minutes to overcome a person in absolute darkness. It at once disables the gyroscope in your head, so the way before you seems to be the way behind; you soon perceive that the floor, which you know damn well is a concrete slab sunk firmly in the earth, is moving subtly underfoot, yawing like the deck of a ship.

Nihilim. Tentacled and taloned. Seer in the dark. Eater of hearts. It would be coming. *Was* coming.

I turned in place, the Glock thrust in front of me, cocking my head left and right and left, listening for a footstep, a rustle, an expelled breath. Bubbles of air rattled past in a water pipe. A pump shuddered to life. A valve opened with a thin screech. Still turning in place, I heard an exhalation but then realized that it was one of mine. I held my breath. Maybe I heard something other than the many ambient sounds of that space or maybe psychic magnetism told me *now*. I stopped turning and squeezed the trigger once, twice, three times.

Something metallic rang against the concrete floor, followed by a softer, heavier sound. I began to breathe again but didn't move. Listened. Waited.

After a minute or so, the path lights came on overhead. At my feet lay Sister Margaret, as naked as the day she'd been born. The Nihilim do not leave behind a monstrous corpse. They die as Rishon, preserving the secret of the first universe and the fact of their intrusion into this one.

I heard Bridget's voice in the distance, echoing softly through the maze: *"Quinn . . . Quinn . . . Quinn . . ."*

Such was my name, given to me by whom I do not know.

## 38

That night in the orphanage is now a year in the past, and Phoenix is not the ghost city that we glimpsed in a vision. Earth is not yet a tomb from pole to pole.

On even the most terrible occasions, good people find new strengths in themselves and rise to meet the ugliest of challenges. That is why I have hope that the worst things that we've foreseen can be forestalled or might never come to pass.

To Sister Theresa's way of thinking, she saw a demon in Hilda Detrich's office, and poor Sister Margaret was possessed by it. We shared with my therapist the origins of the Nihilim as we had been given to understand them, but she preferred her own explanation and taxonomy. Who knows if we might both be right?

Sister Margaret hadn't been human in spite of the appearance of her corpse, though the authorities would never be convinced of that. Even if some police and prosecutors might credit the idea of demonic possession, no exorcist ever dispossessed an unclean spirit with a handgun.

Consequently, the body had to be rolled in a tarp and conveyed up to the alleyway behind Mater Misericordiæ and loaded into the Mercury Mountaineer. Because the gunshots in the basement had not carried to the floor above, because even the late-studying students were in compliance with early-to-bed rules by eleven o'clock, and because the routines by which they lived comforted them through all awkward moments in the days ahead, the orphanage and school remained a happy place, and in fact happier than it had been in years.

We endured a long night that included a drive out of the city and the preparation of a grave in the desert. The long-promised storm of bugs and bats at last appeared, complicating the operation.

Sister Theresa needed to concoct a story to explain Margaret's sudden decision to leave that order of Poor Clares. Fortunately, her training as a psychologist served her in that task in a way that her formation as a nun could not have done. I sometimes wonder about the priest who heard her confession and what he made of it.

Sparky Rainking lost some blood from the cut in his brow before applied pressure reduced the flow. Prior to trekking to the desert for the interment of the Nihilim, we employed psychic magnetism to find a doctor who lived above his office, who was willing to close the wound and provide antibiotics for five thousand dollars cash. He was seventy-one, something of an alcoholic, a believer in a variety of conspiracy theories, and claimed to have seen UFOs on eighteen occasions, but he did good work.

The Oasis story broke worldwide, doubling the ratings of the cable networks that thrived on sensationalizing scandals that were already almost too sensational to be believed. Some of the depraved visitors to the Oasis were condemned and destroyed by the media, but others equally evil were vigorously defended against avalanches of evidence. As always in these strange times, justice was thwarted as often as it was dealt out, and some of the worst offenders were able to metamorphose into victims and then into martyrs; I suspect that in a few years, some will be seen as heroes.

Panthea, Bridget, Sparky, Winston, and I continue to be sought by the ISA. We live on the run, figuratively speaking. In fact, it's more like an amble, sometimes a fast walk, because we grow steadily more gifted. We use many names and alter our appearances in subtle but clever ways.

More useful than disguise, however, is a gift that three of us have developed and that we call identity projection. It's a trick similar to that of the Nihilim. If I want to be seen as fifty and pudgy and balding, I project that image, and thus I am perceived. Yesterday, Bridget was a witchy hag with a wart on her nose, and Panthea passed for a tattooed biker chick. This power can be also extended to our entourage, which of course consists only of Sparky and our canine companion. Winston can pass for any breed that we think him into being, but we've never made him pass for a cat.

I am not the easygoing Quinn Quicksilver who I used to be when I wrote for *Arizona!* magazine, had a fear of parking garages, and fantasized that my father might be a mob boss, my mother a former supermodel now disfigured and living with a sack over her head. I'm okay with not being him, because I wasn't in love with anyone then, and I am now. I didn't have a family then, and I have one now even if it is unconventional.

I didn't have a purpose then, either, except maybe to become a novelist. I'm pretty sure I wouldn't have enjoyed being a novelist. I used to think a novelist could change the world. Maybe some do, but maybe they as often affect it for the worse instead of for the better. They are human, after all.

Right now the world needs saving more than changing. And so we do our best, tracking down Nihilim and eliminating them when we can, a squad of vampire hunters without need of garlic or conventional wooden stakes.

In spite of Bridget and Panthea having foreseen tragedy, we have all thus far survived.

Perhaps the biggest difference between the former me and the new me is anger. It rarely troubled me in the old days. Now it can get its claws deep in me, and I must guard against righteous anger becoming something darker. I understand why the world is shapen as it is, that we should have free will and be more than ants, that we must know evil if we're also to know good. What leaves me sleepless some nights is the conviction that if there were no Nihilim, evil would flourish no less than it does now. Too many crave power over others, their minds autonomous zones where consideration of truths other than their own beliefs are not granted entry, and though few will ever have the wealth and power of Bodie Emmerich, they will make themselves insane in the pursuit of it. My anger must forever be a shield, not a weapon. Love is the only wooden stake that will change an evil heart; we must sharpen it and keep it ready in the name of those we've lost, like Litton Ormond and Annie Piper. Anger and the action it inspires must be reserved for those whose hearts will not relent from the idolatry of power. How strange is the world and all life in it. How strange am I. How much stranger still—mysterious, wonderful—that there is a world at all, or me, or you.

# ABOUT THE AUTHOR

Internationally bestselling author Dean Koontz was only a senior in college when he won an *Atlantic Monthly* fiction competition. He has never stopped writing since. Koontz is the author of seventy-nine *New York Times* bestsellers, fourteen of which rose to #1, including *One Door Away from Heaven, From the Corner of His Eye, Midnight, Cold Fire, The Bad Place, Hideaway, Dragon Tears, Intensity, Sole Survivor, The Husband, Odd Hours, Relentless, What the Night Knows,* and *77 Shadow Street*. He's been hailed by *Rolling Stone* as "America's most popular suspense novelist," and his books have been published in thirty-eight languages and have sold over five hundred million copies worldwide. Born and raised in Pennsylvania, he now lives in Southern California with his wife, Gerda, their golden retriever, Elsa, and the enduring spirits of their goldens Trixie and Anna. For more information, visit his website at www.deankoontz.com.